MW00564741

OF ONE TONGUE

Willow Dressel

First Edition Design Publishing

Of One Tongue
Copyright 2015 Willow Dressel

ISBN 978-1506-907-66-6 AMAZON
ISBN 978-1506-900-15-5 PRINT
ISBN 978-1506-900-16-2 EBOOK

LCCN 2015953583

December 2018

Published and Distributed by
First Edition Design Publishing, Inc.
P.O. Box 20217, Sarasota, FL 34276-3217
www.firsteditiondesignpublishing.com

ALL RiGHTS RESERVED. No part of this book publication may be reproduced, stored in a retrieval system, or transimitted in any form or by any means – electronical, photo-copy, recording, or any other – except brief quotation in reviews, without the prior permission of the author or publisher.

This is a work of fiction. Names, characters, businesses, places, events and incidents are either the products of the author's imagination or used in a fictitious manner. Any resemblance to actual persons, living or dead, or actual events is purely coincidental.

First editor - Jennifer Smetana
Cover graphics – Michael Smetana

Library of Congress Cataloging-in-Publication Data
Dressel, Willow
Of one tongue / written by Willow Dressel.
p. cm.
ISBN 978-1506-900-15-5 pbk, 978-1506-900-16-2 digital

1. Fiction / Historical. 2. Cultural Heritage. 3. Christian Historical.

031

Dedicated to my dear sister Jenny—
I love you motek!

Foreword

When first approached to write the forward for this book, my first thought was: "How can an entire historical fiction novel be written, based on the outline of history given to us in Genesis 11:1-9?"

I quickly found out as I started reading the novel that Willow Dressel has succeeded admirably in crafting a totally plausible story, incorporating the historical people from the first eleven chapters of Genesis, while faithfully adhering strictly to the biblical account.

This book is exceptionally interesting in how facets of daily life are fleshed out in a convincing manner, while the unpredictability of the plot tightly holds the reader's attention and makes it difficult to put the book down.

A very important facet of *Of One Tongue* is the weaving in of scientific subjects such as dinosaurs, the environmental and genetic components of the longevity of the patriarchs, real climate change, human migration, and early technology. Several appendices give succinct summaries of these subjects.

However the most important aspect of this book is its absolute fidelity in expounding spiritual truth as God has given it to us in His word the Bible. *Of One Tongue* is a marvelous vehicle to convey God's truth in a very entertaining and positive manner. The final appendix lays out God's plan for salvation. *Of One Tongue* deserves a wide readership and extensive dissemination to believers and non-believers alike.

Joseph Kezele, M. D.
President, Arizona Origin Science Association
Adjunct Professor of Biology, Arizona Christian University,
Logos Research Associate

Acknowledgements

Thank you first and foremost to our Lord and Savior Jesus who has been my constant Friend, Companion and Mentor throughout the adventure of writing this book. It was His leading that first peaked my interest in combining the facts of creation science into an entertaining novel and He has seen me through every step of the way.

A special big thanks goes to my sister Jenny Smetana who has been my first editor and creative writing encourager since the beginning. Your integrity, knowledge and faithfulness mean everything to me!

Thank you also to my writers group, especially author Sherry Rossman, who has given me unlimited encouragement, much needed advice, and her valuable time. Your friendship has been a blessing and a gift from God.

Special thanks to Dr. Kezele for his expertise in creation science, linguistics and ancient history.

Thank you Creation, Evolution and Science Ministries and especially to Russ Miller who took the time out of his incredibly busy schedule to review and endorse this novel. Thank you also to Arizona Origin Science Association, Inc., and Dr. Kevin Anderson of the Creation Research Society for their endorsements. And thank you Bodie Hodge, of Answers in Genesis for showing an interest in this novel and filling me with encouragement and historical facts.

Thank you to all my friends—most of all to Sherry, and my writers group and Holly, and Betty. And to my family—my kids Brian, Aaron, Amy and Joey, and especially to my nephews, Matt, TC, Michael, Ricky, Kevin, and my grand-nephews Kyan and Callum and to all who at one time or another reviewed portions of my book. Thanks a bunch to Father Pete Coletti for his expertise on spiritual matters. A special thank you to my husband, Greg, for his unending patience while I whittled away at this journey. And a big thanks to all my beta-readers and reviewers.

May the Lord bless you all!

Look for the exciting new video trailer for
Of One Tongue
Tower of Babel

on YouTube under Willow Dressel.
Scroll to the video that has the above title and dare
To journey into ancient Babel…

List of Characters

- **Abel** (Ā-bĕl)—Fictional character, male. Means breath. Teenager. Herds his father's cattle.
- **Adara** (Ă-ďară)—Fictional character, female. Means noble. Nabella's oldest sister. Barukh (Bă-ŕrŭkh)—Fictional character, male. Means blessed. Nabella's betrothed. Channah (Chă-nnăh)—Fictional character, female. Means favor or grace. Daughter of Shem and Machlah, wife of Eber, mother of Peleg.
- **Barukh** (Bă-ŕrŭkh)—Fictional character, male. Means blessed. Nabella's betrothed.
- **Channah** (Chă-nnăh)—Fictional character, female. Means favor or grace. Daughter of Shem and Machlah, wife of Eber, mother of Peleg
- **Cush** (Cŭsh)—Historical person, male. Means black or black countenance. Son of Ham, grandson of Noah.
- **Danya** (Dăń-ă)—Fictional character, female. Means she judged. Nabella's deceased mother. Jokaan's deceased wife.
- **Eber** (Ē-bĕr)—Historical person, male. Means enclave or Hebrew. Son-in-law to Shem, husband to Channah, father of Peleg.
- **Elah** (Ē-lăh)—Fictional character, female. Means terebinth tree. Sister to Nabella, wife of Jabari.
- **Gideon** (Gĭd-ēŏn)—Fictional character, male. Means hewer. Kfir and Barukh's father. Ham (Hăm)—Historical person, male. Means dark or black. Third son of Noah. Former World.
- **Ham** (Hăm)—Historical person, male. Means dark or black. Third son of Noah. Former World.
- **Jabari** (Jă-băŕ-ē)—Fictional character, male. Means courageous. Brother-in-law to Nabella. Best hunter and tracker.
- **Japheth** (Jă-pĕth)—Historical person, male. Means fair or light. Eldest son of Noah. From Former World.
- **Jokaan** (Jō-kăn)—Fictional character, male. Means he establishes. Adara, Elah, Nabella, Shoshana's father.
- **Kfir** (K-fīr)—Fictional character, male. Means young lion. Oldest son of Gideon, Barukh's older brother, neighbor of Jokaan and Nabella.

- **Machlah** (Măk-lă)—Historical person, female. Means my messenger or my angle. Wife of Shem. From the Old World, may not be the true name of Shem's wife.
- **Nabel** (Nā-bĕl)—Fictional character, male. Nabella's pseudo name when she posed as a boy.
- **Nabella** (Nă-bĕlă)—Fictional character, female. Means kind. Main character. Seventh daughter of Jokaan, twenty years old.
- **Nahni** (Nă-nē)—Fictional character, endearing term for grandmother.
- **Nimrod** (Nĭm-rŏd)—Historical person, male. Means rebellious. Grandson of Noah. Noah (Nōă)—Historical person, male. Means motion. Obeyed God's command to build an ark and take his family and two or seven of all the animals' kinds on it to endure the global flood.
- **Noah** (Nōă)—Historical person, male. Means motion. Obeyed God's command to build an ark and take his family and two or seven of all the animals' kinds on it to endure the global flood.
- **Peleg** (Pālĕg)—Historical person, male. Means earth is divided. Baby born at the time of the confusion of language.
- **Ra'anel** (Ră-ănĕĺ)—Fictional character, male. Means high, lofty, god. Head celestial advisor and an influential member of The City's government.
- **Semiramis** (Sĕmē-rămĭs)—Historical person, female. Means highest heaven. Wife of Nimrod.
- **Seth** (Sĕth)—Fictional character, male. Means appointed. Crippled boy that lives in the portion of the tent city bordering the Little Euphrates.
- **Shem** (Shĕm)—Historical person, male. Means dusky or brown. Second son of Noah. From Former World
- **Shoshana** (Sō-shăń-ă)—Fictional character, female. Means rose. Youngest sister of Nabella, seven years old.
- **Terach** (Tĕ-răk)—Fictional character, male. Means wanderer. Fourteen-year-old that Nimrod has taken under his wing.
- **Tomar** (Tō-măŕ)—Fictional character, male. Means tall. Brother-in-law to Nabella and is married to Adara.

One

"Zillah also had a son, Tubal-Cain, who forged all kinds of tools out of bronze and iron..."

Genesis 4:22 (NIV)

One Hundred And Six Years After The Global Flood
The Year 2241 BC
The Month of Second Beginnings

Nabella dared a glance through a hole in the stained tent wall and gripped clammy hands together. Two men locked eyes, a third towered over them. Her father, Jokaan, stood arms crossed over his brawny chest. She knew that stance…he had reached his limit.

"Oh Father, be careful," she whispered.

Her eyes darted to the thin man who confronted Jokaan. Pale eyes flashed at her father. She cringed from Ra'anel's glare, though it had nothing to do with her. A slight shift of her eyes and she took in the third man. Cush stared down at her father. A deep scowl tumbled across his rough features, and ebony skin stretched taut over his bulging muscles. One hand encircled the largest spear she had ever seen. She couldn't help but wonder if Ra'anel had brought him along only to intimidate.

Her lip curled. *Scum. Both of them scum.* Just the other day she had overheard her father speak with men he trusted. He had sought and received confirmation of his doubts about Ra'anel and Cush.

Her opinion matched theirs, scum. Worse than scum actually. Both were smart and educated, they were dangerous, for their ambitions seemed to outweigh their integrity.

All the more reason to secretly observe them despite Father's warning to stay out of men's business. The twenty-year-old tore her eyes from the hole and pressed an ear there instead. The muffled tones became clear.

"You think only of yourself. Perha-a-ps you should be less egotistical."

Nabella recognized Ra'anel's voice as it dribbled overt piety. The corners of her mouth tilted down. He sounded so, intellectual, but something still bothered her. *Father said Ra'anel possessed false humility, maybe that's it.*

"You're not welcome here if you choose to speak in such a manner," Jokaan's low voice stiffened.

"You *know* there are great benefits to living in The Cit—"

"Ra'anel, you have been pushing me to move into The City for twenty years. You know I will not disobey God."

"God, pah! He no longer rules like He used to. You know as well as I the benefits to living in The City. No more traveling to outposts endlessly carting your goods around. Just think. People would come to you, one central place that would benefit everyone, not just you.

"Let your workers live here in the orchards. Or your daughters' husbands and their families. But you move to The City and set up a permanent shop…" Ra'anel's voice droned on and on, then he paused. "Besides, you need a woman to care for you, Jokaan. It would be much easier to find another wife with all the people coming to you. You could devote time for, hmmm, courtship."

"No, Danya was the only one. And I already have eight daughters worrying over me," Jokaan growled.

"You could be a rich man."

"I already am a rich man."

"Hmmm, I suppose, for one who has no sons."

Nabella breathed in a small gasp the same time her fist landed on a hip. She could feel her father bristle, his anger radiating against the worn walls of the tent.

Ra'anel pressed. "Surely though, you would move to The City so you can be close to the new temple to worship your God."

"That tower's blasphemy! God did not ask for such a thing," Jokaan bellowed. "I'm this close to trading everything and moving far from here."

Nabella chanced another quick peek. Jokaan had thrust his hand in front of Ra'anel's nose, forefinger and thumb only a finger-width apart. Ra'anel stood his ground, eyes narrowed to slits. Cush stepped forward. Nabella jerked her ear back to the hole. Several strands of hair flew across her face, sticking to her lips. A shaky hand snatched the wisps away.

"That could prove to be very foolish." The threat could not be mistaken in Cush's deep timbre.

"In what way?" Jokaan challenged the warning. Nabella held her breath.

She shivered at the harsh laugh that erupted from Cush. "Do not be so offended, my friend. I only mean there are many dangerous animals out there. Nimrod has hunted most from around here, but you never know if one will show up in your orchards or by your house."

Jokaan's voice turned frigid, it reminded Nabella of the blast of bitter air before a storm. "I can handle anything that endangers my family. And God said to spread out. Even with the perils from living on the edge of the wilderness, or from people, I will *not* move to The City. Do not call me *friend,* and feel free to leave."

Footsteps stomped toward the tent. Nabella gasped, twisted away from the hole, tripping over her youngest sister. She grabbed the child's shoulders and yanked a foot from under small feet entangled with hers.

"Shoshana!"

Wide green eyes penetrated hers. "What'd they say, Bella?"

"Don't worry about it, Shoshana, and stop biting your lip. Hurry, we have to look busy before Fath—"

The tent flap flew to the side as Jokaan stepped through. Flushed face and deep brown eyes that glinted betrayed his anger. The man clenched his hands then pressed thin lips until they disappeared into a full beard.

"You!" He snatched Nabella's tunic dragging her to several large sacks. "Take food to your sisters, the two that are at the south end. "And you," He grabbed the smaller girl's arm shoving her toward a basket filled with figs, "prepare food for the workers here." He strode to the middle of the tent and rummaged through a bag that hung from the center pole. The girls scrambled to obey.

Nabella swung her loaded basket of bread, cheese and dried grapes onto her back then mouthed to Shoshana, "I'll tell you later." She ducked out of the tent and headed down the beaten path that extended into the grove.

"Nabella."

She turned at her father's call. In five strides he came abreast extending his hand. Her eyes flew wide when she saw her mother's old bronze dagger nestled in his palm. She raised eyes filled with unspoken questions.

"I know you overheard the conversation. I don't trust those men and they can't be very far. All your other sisters, save Shoshana, are married and under their husband's protection." Jokaan stared at the weapon, his mouth twisted into a sad smile. "It's not the same as a husband, but it will offer some protection."

Nabella's hands remained on the basket. "But Father, I have Barukh."

"He has not spoken to me yet. You are not betrothed nor under his protection. Take the knife, if only for a little while. And may this weapon serve you better than it did your mother."

Nabella lowered her eyes at the pained catch in her father's voice then took the proffered weapon and hefted it. It felt awkward, heavier and weighted differently than the food knives she used.

"No, like this." Jokaan turned the grip in her hand. "And if you must strike, do so like this." He lifted her hand and guided it in a narrow arc, then twisted it sideways. He sighed and turned to her, resolve etched deep in his eyes. "I will show you more when you return."

He took the dagger, returned it to the sheath, slid it beneath her sash then pushed the weapon snug against her body.

"In many ways you have almost been like a son to me. Your stubborn, strong willed, always-plowing-ahead-no-matter-what attitude is very boy-like. And I mean that as a compliment, for the most part." He gripped her shoulders and gave her a slight shake. "There were times when I have counted on you like a son. So now I ask, even with these men about, go to the end of the groves and report to me how many trees still need to be harvested. By the time you return, I'll be at the processing building so look for me there."

Nabella peered at her father, "Bu—"

Jokaan's palm flashed upright in front of her face, his lips pressed tight. With a quick shake of his head, he turned and strode away. Nabella's mind raced, but she gritted her teeth to stop the barrage of questions that threatened to spill. With furrowed brows she headed once more toward the orchard.

A slight breeze lifted damp tendrils from her forehead. She brushed the dagger with the tips of her fingers, scanning the trees ahead. Questions buzzed through her mind, and she fought the temptation to run to Jokaan. Would those men really hurt her? Were they still near? Nabella shook her head. *No, I will not let this bother me. Father must feel it's safe enough or he wouldn't let me go. What could possibly happen anyways? There are workers everywhere. And he's counting on me. Besides, if I were his son, I wouldn't be afraid at all.*

She slipped into the quiet of the wood. Each step pushed her worry farther behind. Nabella paused, closing her eyes she let out a long sigh. Then slowly drew in a deep breath, the rich smell of ripened olives satiating her. At last she opened her eyes. Sunbeams filtered between the petite leaves, surrounding her with a dappled radiance. She pivoted in place and the soft tilt at the corner of her mouth grew. *There is a peace here that I can't find anywhere else.* Nabella touched the grip of her mother's dagger, confidence rippling through her.

Branches murmured in the soft breeze. Somewhere in the near distance a bird trilled. A song thrush. The first she heard this autumn. *Winter's not far away.* Nabella started, then shook her head at her distraction. With light feet she hurried down the leaf-covered path, letting her eyes rove over the trees planted by her grandfather. Nabella knew at over fifty years old, the trees were in their prime. How she loved it when a portion of her large family camped every other year at the southern section of their olive orchards. The gathering always happened during the Month of Second Beginnings for the great harvests.

Feet skirted around small mounds of debris where earlier in the year the Euphrates River had spilled over its banks higher than Nabella could ever remember. She had heard that all the crops in the area hung heavy with fruit from the flooding and abundant seasonal rains. It certainly held true for her father's groves.

Rhythmic whacks caught her ear, and Nabella tilted her head in that direction. Friendly banter filtered through the trees. She hurried toward the sounds and could make out words long before she saw her extended family. She stooped under a low branch. Two of her older sisters, Adara and Elah, gathered olives off loosely woven linen. Jabari, Elah's husband, had situated himself in the tree above them. Nabella watched him use a thick stick with antlers attached at one end to comb branches in search of stubborn olives. At the same time, the smack of Tomar's long pole on the limbs pierced her ears. The two men created a rain of ripened fruit. By the looks of it, this year like every other year, the harvest would be enormous.

"Ah, there she is. We were just wondering if a lion ate you on the way."

Nabella furrowed her brows at Adara's husband. "Very funny, Tomar." Despite herself, she peered over her shoulder. Laughter erupted. Nabella slammed the basket to the ground with a thud. Eyes ablaze, fists flew to her hips. "Tomorrow you can bring your own food, Elah. I'll make sure there is enough bread left over from today for you."

"Oh come on, Nabella, we were just teasing." Her sister clicked her tongue. "You would really feed me moldy bread?"

In no mood to join in their jousting, Nabella ignored the comment. Without a word she tramped to the path.

"Don't go back without a full basket." Adara scolded.

"Just because you're the oldest, doesn't mean you get to push me around. I'm not going back yet. Father asked me to check to the end of the groves." Nabella darted away before she could be baited any further. She always seemed to end up the brunt of their jokes. Most of the time she didn't mind, but sometimes it got on her nerves. Like today.

Immersed in thought, Nabella studied her feet as they padded down the sun speckled path. It wasn't until she stepped from the shade of the wood into the bright afternoon light that she realized the groves had ended and the task Jokaan entrusted her with remained unfulfilled. Nabella sighed scanning the nearby branches that bowed under the weight of olives. Her lips tightened into a thin line. *I'll just have to check on the way back.*

She stood at the southern edge of the groves, trying to soothe her wounded pride. Her eyes roved from the wandering Euphrates River in the west, panned over the vast plain of Shinar and rested on the eastern mountains beyond. *A three day journey to those mountains. Maybe someday, but no—unless I can persuade Barukh to take me, it will never happen.* Again a fist came to her hip, *that means I'd have to talk him into marrying me first.* A thrill ran up her spine. *Oh how wonderful it would be to be married to Barukh.*

At the thought of Barukh, Nabella veered to her right and stepped back into the trees to cut through the southwest corner of the orchard toward the barley fields. She could get a better view of his father's vineyard from there. Perhaps Barukh would be there now harvesting grapes, maybe gazing in her direction. Even now she could see his deep blue eyes staring into hers. Her lips curved into a smile, and she felt heat rise at the thought of her intended. *Well, soon to be my intended.*

She trekked through rows of trees stopping at the western edge of the grove. The Euphrates caught her eye. The mellow autumn sun glinted off the river making it sparkle like the precious jewels that bedecked the celestial advisors. Nabella squinted. A faint shout floated on the gusting breeze. Her gaze shifted to the fields that stretched between the river and her father's groves. Men trudged alongside pairs of oxen that pulled seed plows through the rich soil. Three men worked each team, urging the oxen forward while women and children dotted the fields behind them. Their arms swung in a slow arc as they scattered barley seed across the freshly turned earth. Near the edge of the fields, more oxen stood harnessed to two wheeled carts. Nabella couldn't see the small kernels but knew children filled bags then raced to replace empty ones in the seeders' hands. From the looks of it, they had nearly finished planting that far end of the large field.

Nabella shook her head. It seemed like so much work compared to picking olives. She turned and stood on her toes. At the far northern edge of the barley fields she could just make out Gideon's vineyards.

The young woman tossed another glance at her neighbors then stepped into the barley field. Nabella clasped her *jupe*. Surely they wouldn't mind if she paid attention to step over the sprouting green shoots. She just wanted a better view of the vineyards. Nabella shaded her eyes. But even after several tentative steps onto the budding ground, she still couldn't see anyone at Gideon's place. With a sigh she gave up and turned back to the grove.

Nabella stopped in her tracks and gasped. A skinned and gutted animal hung from the corner tree. She relaxed, *a hunter must be going through the orchard.* She stepped closer, brows pulled down. Something seemed, wrong.

Ah-he that's odd, why isn't there any blood under the carcass? Nabella scanned the ground around the dead animal but still no blood or entrails. If someone had hunted this animal, the guts would have been dumped on the ground next to it. And the meat would have been stripped away. Nabella stepped closer. It wasn't even a game animal. She stared at the hind feet where it had been strung up. Paws, not hooves. And its head had been removed. Coldness crept from her stomach. Her feet shuffled backward. Something bumped the back of her head.

With a gasp Nabella spun around bumping into the animal's decapitated head. It swayed back and forth, drops of blood seeping from severed flesh. Empty sockets stared back where its eyes had been gouged out.

"Ahh." Her stomach clenched and wrung out the soft cry. Nabella's heart squeezed tight, and she reared back from the grisly sight. One hand flew to her throat as the other clasped and unclasped a fold in her tunic. She stumbled sideways to run around the head when dark loops caught her eye. Intestines hung from a branch to her right. She froze then forced herself to scan the other trees. The animal's innards had been strung in a semi-circle around the carcass. Blood splashed on the tree trunks still trickled down the bark.

Hairs prickled on the back of Nabella's neck. Her mind raced as she fought to keep her morning meal in her churning stomach. This must have just happened. Surely the carcass had not been there when she walked into the field. She froze in place, mind whirling. That meant whoever did this had to be close by. Her chest squeezed out shallow rapid breaths. She pressed her eyes shut for an instant then bound away like a frightened deer. *Faster*, she pushed, *faster*. Dagger completely forgotten with heart hammering, she charged through the grove.

"Tomar, Tomar!" She collapsed on the edge of the worn sheet.

The tall man paused in his work, dark brown eyes that peered around branches penetrated hers. "What's wrong?"

When she only gestured and looked back in the direction she came, he climbed from the tree and strode toward her. "Nabella, what's going on?"

Nabella stared at him, then pressed lips together as she tried to gather her thoughts.

Tomar grabbed her upper arms and hauled her to her feet. "Tell me! What is it?"

"There, there, is something wrong. At the end of the grove."

"What do you mean wrong?"

Nabella could only shake her head. Tomar's dark eyes glinted, and he shook her hard. "Tell me!"

"It, it just happened. When I was there, but I didn't know."

"You're not making any sense."

"It happened while I was there, but I didn't see them. They were there at the same time..." Nabella's eyes darted about as she clasped and unclasped her tunic.

Tomar glanced at Adara. He turned back to Nabella, concern etched on his face. She sucked in a deep breath and smoothed her tunic with a shaky hand. How could she explain what she saw? How could she explain the menacing feeling? She swallowed hard and tried to speak, but her tongue cleaved to the roof of her mouth. She would just have to show them. Nabella yanked free of Tomar's grip and stomped toward the end of the grove. She slowed long enough to make sure everyone followed.

"What did you see?" Adara panted as she caught up.

Nabella shuddered. "I, well, it was an animal, I think it was a ca—"

"Jabari, go back and get the poles." Tomar barked the order then continued, "was the animal frothing at the mouth, acting strange?"

"No—"

"Was there more than one?"

"No. Well, I don't think so."

"How big was it?"

"No, that's not it. Just listen. It was dead, but a person killed it because it was hung in a tree and skinned and, and its head was chopped off."

"Is that all, Nabella? It was just a hunter." Jabari's dark brows furrowed.

"No—there's something wrong about the whole thing."

Jabari's mouth tipped in a faint smile when he handed Tomar a pole. He turned to the others. "Everyone go back. I'll handle this with Nabella."

"No." She protested.

"Well, I want to see it now." Tomar brushed past Jabari, his muscular frame just a fingers length taller than the younger man's. Nabella looked at her sisters and their husbands. Her eyes sent a silent plea that beseeched them to understand.

"It's…evil," Nabella whispered.

"Evil?" Tomar laughed.

"Just wait till you see it." Nabella's voice shook, and she pushed ahead. Why didn't people ever take her seriously? Well, they would see soon enough.

They stepped through the last of the trees, and Nabella thrust her hand palm up in the direction of the carcass. Elah grabbed Adara and shrieked. Adara's hand flew to her mouth.

Jabari stopped dead in his tracks. "What in the worl—"

"Adara, Elah, stay put." Tomar's knuckles whitened as his hand clenched the wooden pole.

Nabella couldn't help herself. "I told you it's evil."

"Ah-he," Tomar muttered. "What do you make of this, Jabari?"

The best hunter in the family squatted, face pinched and stared at the ground. Jabari ignored the skinned animal and flies that now buzzed around the carcass. He leaned forward then gingerly tugged a leaf to the side. A small pool of blood. The solid man rose with slow deliberation then snapped a dead twig to the length of his arm. He circled the dead animal and one by one uncovered five more small pools of blood that had soaked into the soil. Jabari squatted, leaned forward, tilting his head near the ground. He sprang up and strode to the next tree at the edge of the grain field.

"Look," He swung the stick, eyes narrowed. "At the base of the trees." A small symbol had been carved on the trunk.

Tomar leaned closer, "That carving represents sacrifice. I saw one like it on Ra'anel's staff. He said it was a symbol for *his* gods, whatever that means."

"You mean the demons Father warned us about?" Elah whispered and glanced over her shoulder.

Nabella gasped. Her fingers wrapped around the grip of her mother's dagger. A tremble ran through her as her mind flew to capture details. Elah pressed into her and the three sisters bunched together.

"I know that wasn't here before." Nabella took a step back.

Jabari whirled the stick around his fingers as he strode forward then thrust it in the direction of a tree. "This one has a carving too."

Tomar's voice thundered, "Everyone spread out, look for more!"

Elah looped her arm through Adara's, and they crept up the edge of the grove. Adara's head, just a fist above Elah's, pressed against her younger sister's. Tomar and Jabari scanned trees in the opposite direction. Nabella felt as if her feet had grown roots. She couldn't decide who she'd be safer with. *Just go, Nabella!* She scolded herself and dashed to Tomar's side.

"There's two over here." Elah's voice shook.

"And three here." Jabari called in a tight voice.

"That makes six all together." Tomar rubbed his browned forehead. "The number of the serpent."

"And I bet…." Jabari moved back to the carcass and the others followed his lead. He poked the ground directly under the animal. "There is no blood here, and I'm right."

Tomar balled his fist. "It looks like a ritual of some sort was performed here."

Jabari ran a hand through his cropped, ebony hair and nodded. "Yes, someone drained and caught the blood. I bet if we go to the east end of the grove we'll find the same thing there."

Silent, Adara, Elah and Nabella stared at each other then hurried after the men. Jabari's prediction proved right, and Nabella's stomach once again churned as she stared at another sacrificial site.

Elah's shoulders drooped, and a shadow passed over her smooth olive complexion. "Poor creatures. What do you suppose they were?"

"Caracal cats. They're often used in pagan worship," Jabari ground a fist into the palm of his other hand.

"Ugh. Someone paid homage to a pagan god in our father's olive groves?" Indignation rose in Adara's voice.

"Worse than that. I think it's a curse." Tomar paced.

"I'll tell Father." Nabella spun on her heels but a strong hand clasped her upper arm.

"No." Tomar eyed the others. "We go back together."

"What do you mean?" Jabari demanded.

"We're calling it quits for today."

Jabari shook his head the corners of his mouth drawing down. "No we're not. There's far too much work still to be done."

Tomar hesitated and at last nodded in agreement. "Alright then, I'll return with Nabella. The rest of you stay here. I'll be back as soon as I can and be careful."

"Tomar, Father went back home." Nabella stared at the tall man.

"Then take a load of olives back when you go." Throwing them a stern glance, Adara headed toward the work site. She tossed her head and a long raven braid flew across her back.

Nabella followed behind the men straining to hear their quiet words. She pressed her lips tight. *I should be included in this.* When they reached the harvesting area, her steps dragged, and she hung back with Tomar and Jabari.

"Nabella, come help us."

With an impatient sigh Nabella obeyed. Filling baskets couldn't be more important than what Tomar and Jabari were planning.

The three women placed four, large, tightly woven baskets laden with olives into a handcart. Tomar slipped the broad leather strap around his shoulders then reached behind him for the handles of the cart. He leaned into the straps. With a creak the cart rolled forward then lurched to one side. The man strained, and his large hands tightened to steady the tumbrel.

"Watch out." Nabella and Elah called in unison then jumped to the side of the cart. The baskets shifted and settled. Jabari gripped the other end and helped to steady it. With a final shove he teased, "You're on your own now, Tomar."

The young woman lengthened her stride until she drew alongside Tomar. He grinned at her and grunted. "Adara would have me sleeping in the fields if I let that load dump."

Nabella studied Tomar, and her heart warmed towards the commanding, burly man. He could be such a pain at times, but then— *oh no, the food!*

She raced back to her bundle, broke off a chunk of bread and cheese, grabbed a handful of the dried figs then caught up with Tomar.

"Some food?" She offered.

Tomar chuckled then said, "Stick it in my mouth."

Even when Nabella helped push the cart, it took longer than expected to arrive at the processing buildings near their home. Tomar set the cart in front of several workers.

He glanced at Nabella. "My guess is Jokaan's in the handling area. Wait here." The man strode towards the low, baked brick building without waiting for a reply. Nabella hesitated then followed, trotting to keep up.

She blinked as she stepped into the dim, cool interior, nose crinkling at the overpowering odor of olive oil and human sweat. She followed Tomar as he headed for the storage area dug deep into the ground. When they neared the bottom of the ramp cooler air wafted around large vats of oil, the constant cool temperature keeping her father's goods fresh.

Nabella grabbed Tomar's hairy forearm. "There." She jutted her chin at a long line of men who maneuvered full clay vessels down a ramp on the opposite side of the room. Jokaan's face flushed red as he struggled with a vat tipped halfway off the ramp.

Tomar frowned down at her.

Nabella cocked her head. "See. You needed me."

Tomar shook his head. "Wait here and this time I mean it." He wove his way through the crowded room.

Nabella clapped her hands over her ears. The clamor of so many people shouting above the rumble of rolling vessels made her ears hurt. She stood on her tiptoes to watch her sister's husband. He dodged a man who spun an empty container toward an arched doorway and then disappeared from her sight. She paced stopping ever so often to scan the room. At last the men emerged from the crowd near the bottom of the ramp she stood on.

Nabella studied Jokaan's drawn brow and thin pressed lips and knew Tomar had already spoken of the foul deed. When her father neared, he glanced at Danya's dagger, and Nabella watched a flicker of relief pass over his face. He motioned for them to step outside.

"I want to see for myself, Tomar. Not that I don't believe you, but it would be better to report this as one who saw it firsthand."

"Before you do that let's check out the north orchard. Jabari thinks there might be more."

Jokaan nodded and ran a hand through dark russet, shoulder length hair. He brushed past Nabella, and jutted his chin toward three narrow tables. "You stay here and hel—"

"But Father I need to see too! I found the firs—"

"Nabella," Jokaan sighed and placed calloused hands on her shoulders, "Stay here on the grounds and help."

She tightened her jaw then followed a short distance behind the men. They passed by long tables set near the building where women and girls stood on both sides separating olives from leaves and twigs. Pausing at the end of one table she stared at her father straining her ears.

"First go see if the grandmothers need help preparing the evening meal," Jokaan called over his shoulder.

Nabella sighed. Her brows pulled down in a tight V. She didn't need to help with the meal, she needed to help the men. And besides she had a right to know; after all she made the discovery. An idea wormed its way through her thoughts, swirling faster and larger until a smile formed as she fingered the dagger.

She found both grandmothers, with dark, sweat-dampened hair, leaning over the *tannur* ovens. Three more women were finger deep in unleavened dough.

"Do you need another hand, Nahni? It looks like you already have several people helping you." Nabella bent and gave each grandmother a kiss on the top of their heads.

"We can always use another hand."

"All right, but first I have to run a quick errand. If Father asks, I'm still on the grounds." She lowered her eyes, *I'm not lying, I won't leave the orchard. Besides, if Father included me like the son he says I am, I wouldn't have to do this. And God knows that, so He must want me to go."*

Nabella walked to the front of the courtyard then strolled toward the groves. *Act normal, I'll hide when I get to the corner of the orchard then I'll be able to hear what Father plans to do, just act normal.* The temptation to look around was so strong she balled her fists to keep control. Once under the cover of the trees she ignored the dirt road weaving her way through the wood. Racing toward the northern edge of the orchard one hand gripping the dagger.

Two

The beast of the field shall honor me, the dragons (dinosaurs) *and the owls: because I give waters in the wilderness, and rivers in the desert, to give drink to my people, my chosen.* (Emphasis the authors)

Isaiah 43:20

And I hated Esau, and laid his mountains and his heritage waste for the dragons (dinosaurs) *of the wilderness.*

Malachi 1:3

Golden tanned skin grew taut against Barukh' s muscles as he helped toss off large nets extending over a long row of grapevines. He let his eyes travel over the last of the ripe clusters in his father's vineyard. Every now and then he shook his head. Even with the netting, birds still pecked the fruit. It amazed him just how much damage those small-winged creatures were capable of. But despite the birds' ravenous appetites, this season's bounty exceeded any other harvest he could remember.

Many families bargained for the grapes preferring to make their own wines, juice and raisins while others favored his family's finished products. His father, already pleased with the trades that had been going on since the Month of First Harvest, would be elated with this latest haul. Yes, this would be a good year.

Barukh paused midway in his inspection. The harvest had been decent last year too, and his father had paid him well as foreman. Barukh's well chiseled mouth skewed into a smirk. His brother, Kfir, had been a fool to give up his title, even if for only a few years while he explored the far regions with several others.

And Barukh had become all the richer.

His mind wandered to Nabella. He had been able to lay away a large dowry to give Jokaan. But that did not satisfy him. He wanted to brag to his friends of the enormous amount he planned to offer. This year would bring in much. He would let Jokaan set the price. If he had enough from last year, he would give that to Jokaan for a dowry *and* trade half of this year's profit for olive saplings. With the other half he would trade his father for grapevines and maybe have enough left over for that stallion he had his eye on. Then he and Nabella could start on a life of their own. Somewhere next to their parents' places—an arrangement that would satisfy both families.

"You two roll the net and the rest of you, let's start picking." Barukh wanted to finish the harvest by the end of the week. He'd have to drive the workers. But it would be worth it for then he'd have enough free time to speak with Jokaan.

By the time the sun became a glowing orange orb that lay on the horizon, the men began to grumble.

"Come on, a little more." Barukh pushed the men as he straightened his tall frame.

"You already said that. A while ago. Look even the sun is resting," A hired hand protested.

"Ah, leave him alone, he's in lo-o-ve."

Barukh turned in time to see Kfir stoop from under a row of vines. His older sibling's black, wavy hair had been slicked back and, as usual, pulled into a knot at the nape of his neck. It stayed, neatly tied by the ends of a wide, ever-present headband that covered half his forehead and the top of his ears.

Heat flushed Barukh face. "You might be my older brother but shut your mouth." With a wide grin he grasped Kfir's forearms. "When did you get back?"

"About a hand-span ago, I've been talking with Father," Kfir jabbed Barukh with his elbow. "Stud!"

His brother and the men laughed. Barukh snapped his mouth shut. He knew if he tried to defend himself the jabs would flow like the Euphrates at flood season.

"All right, all right, we'll go in *early.* Throw the net over the part we didn't pick. And make sure it's on tight." Barukh strode to the ox hitched to a cart and started it toward their house.

"Hey, where're you going?" Kfir scoffed.

"Back. You wanted to quit early, you can wrap it up." Barukh grinned and tapped the beast into a trot. The men shouted joking insults to his back. But he knew he had the better end and laughed at their dilemma.

All the way home thoughts of Nabella pushed their way to the front of his mind. By this time next year he would walk with her. Or return to a home where she prepared his dinner. And maybe, if the Lord blessed, even a son. But not a daughter. He knew his firstborn would be a boy. It had to be. Again, he felt heat rush up his neck. An awkward smile spread across his handsome features. He kept his eyes riveted on the ground while he strode alongside the full cart.

Voices penetrated Barukh's thoughts, his eyes widened when he scanned the processing and wine storage areas. Good, no one seemed to notice his mindlessness. Barukh straightened his shoulders and sucked in a deep breath. He prayed the red stain of heat had vanished from across his face.

At the sound of a deep voice his head snapped around. That had to be Cush. He knew no one else with such an immense tone. When Barukh rounded a tall, stone, winepress there stood Cush and Ra'anel with his father.

"Take care of this." Barukh thrust the ox's lead rope at a weary worker then strode to his father.

When Barukh caught Gideon's eye his father turned to the advisor. "Ra'anel, you remember my second eldest."

"Hmm…Barukh is it? I was just encouraging your father to establish a shop in The City. There're only a few empty rooms left for lucrative businesses."

"I was there just two weeks ago. There's more than a few empty rooms."

"There were, Gideon, but that was two weeks ago."

"A permanent shop *would* make everything easier." Gideon looked at his son.

Barukh's blond brows shot up. His father had always opposed the crowds that had campaigned for a city and the grand tower with a temple to worship in. Gideon and Jokaan had always been strong voices against this. Had his father's stand shifted?

"How many people live there now?" Gideon said.

"Several thousand at least." Cush interlaced fingers cracking massive knuckles while well-defined muscles rippled under his dark skin. "It is a grand sight indeed, all those people worshipping in one place."

"What does your grandfather think of all of this?" Gideon eyed the large man.

"Pah! Noah is getting cranky in his old age."

"Does he hear God's voice or have any visions from Him?"

"None."

Gideon's stout frame sagged. He looked disappointed, almost lost. Barukh ignored the confused look taking a step forward. "How much will a shop cost?"

"Five percent of your first crops."

"Ah-he, that's ten percent all together," Barukh watched Ra'anel stroke his long blond-white beard. "Doesn't the five percent we already give count for something?"

"Welll, that feeds the workers who are building The City. This additional five percent goes toward the maintenance and running of the place." Ra'anel pinned pale blue eyes on Gideon. "Anyway, you will save much more than that since the people will come to you, and you won't be wasting your time traveling. Your neighbor already sells large amounts of grain at his shop. You should see his profits. Perha-a-aps, your son would be willing to work the shop while you continue to run everything here?"

Barukh's eyes flew wide, move to The City? He had never considered it but that would be exciting.

Gideon laid a deep browned hand on his son's forearm. "We will discuss it."

Cush curled his right hand into a fist. "Discuss," he roared. "What's there to discuss? Come Ra'anel, we will give the choice spot to someone else."

Ra'anel drummed his fingers on his chin. "Perh-a-aps. Are you referring to the last space next to the Hall of Records?"

"That would be a good spot," Gideon hedged.

Ra'anel turned and murmured over his shoulder, "welll, don't wait too long."

Barukh shot a look at the first stars that already brightened the dusky sky. Protocol demanded he invite their guests to spend the night. Barukh glanced at Gideon's tumultuous face and swallowed. Though the thought of it at first rubbed the wrong way, but a shop in The City just might come out to their advantage. Barukh stepped in front of his father. "Thank you for coming. Please, spend the night, it's getting late."

Ra'anel and Cush glanced at each other. "Hmm, that would be. Nice." Ra'anel looked over his long thin nose at Barukh, "And beneficial."

"Yes." Barukh stepped toward the tent use to house travelers.

"One more question, Ra'anel," Gideon called after them. "Who are the maintenance people that get this five percent?"

"It goes to the scribes and celestial advisors, and those who work on the roads and other public places of course."

"Of which you are one," Gideon snorted.

"There are many of us. How can we study the stars by night and put disputes to rest by day, hmm? Then pray with people and keep all records unless we are given a share for our work? We would otherwise, starve."

Barukh quickened his step before his father could speak against the move. He stopped by the tent, opened the flap to reveal a lavish interior. "I'm sure you will find this comfortable. "We'll call when the evening meal is ready."

He didn't wait for an answer but instead spun on his heel to seek Gideon. He spotted his father by the corrals. "This could be good, Father."

"I don't know anymore. For such a long time Jokaan and I and others have spoken against this City. But so many have gone there. And it really doesn't seem to be bad, no harm has come to those who moved and their businesses are doing so well." Gideon rubbed the back of his neck.

Barukh thought about the turn in Gideon. "Father, you know I want to marry Nabella. I thought to acquire land between our two places to start a new vineyard and olive orchard. But I'd rather move to The City. It would be exciting. I'm sure Nabella would love it." *She better.*

Once more Gideon rubbed the back of his deeply tanned neck. "I know, son, I know."

***

Nabella pushed across a small wash that cut through a corner of the northeastern grove. Overgrown brush encroached upon the huge trees. A thorny bush snagged her jupe. She fought a rush of impatience and yanked at the material. *As soon as the harvest is over we need to clear this brush away again.* With a final jerk the cloth ripped free. Nabella inhaled a slow deep breath then tipped her head to look at the top of the olive trees, the height of five men at this older part of the grove. Not far ahead a large dead limb thrust its stark arm out into the blue sky. Jokaan had left the branch as a landmark for his children when they were young. Nabella smiled. She didn't cut through the grove at this angle very often. The big dead branch was a welcome sight.

Almost there. She didn't know which corner of the grove the men would go to first. It didn't matter, as long as she arrived at one spot first and hid. Then she'd be able to overhear their plans.

The drone of flies and the smell of blood reached Nabella before she spotted the carcass. She hesitated transfixed, then moved with measured steps toward the butchered animal. This one had been killed before the others. The blood looked dry and dark. Nabella waved flies away. Somewhere leaves stirred. She froze then relaxed. *It must be Father and Tomar.* More rustling, the snap of a twig. Then complete silence. *Why aren't they talking?* With hushed footsteps, Nabella backed behind a thick-leafed bush and craned to get a better look. Eyes widened when she realized the rustling came from something other than the men. Her skin tingled. A clammy hand clasped and unclasped her jupe.

Again a quiet rustle, this time closer. Nabella took a chance and leaned forward. She peered out from under the thick mass of leaves but could see nothing out of the ordinary.

Until it moved.

Dappled sunlight caught the side of the creature. It shifted, a gray and brown mottled side ripple as its muscles tensed. Her eyes squeezed shut then flew open at the slight crunch of a heavy footstep. Only a portion of the animal, a large one, became visible through the dense brush.

If only I could see what it is, I would know if it's a meat eater or not. Her hand crept toward the dagger. The creature shifted toward her. All at once Nabella felt trapped. If she stayed hunched under the bush, she could go in only one direction; the way she had entered. She drew in a quick breath. The animal froze.

Oh no, now it knows I'm here!

She pressed her lips together and waited, breath bated. The creature's sides moved in and out with rapid motions. Comprehension dawned with all its terror, the animal was sniffing the air. It could only mean one thing.

It had caught her scent.

The beast advanced several cubits, then stopped to sniff again. Nabella's eyes darted to and fro. She would have to veer left and run past the animal to reach the nearest tree. Nabella studied the path and the final jump to the lowest branch. Could she make it? Doubt slithered through her. The branch would be above her head. Without a sound Nabella clasped and unclasped her free hand. If she jumped high enough and scrambled up the tree she would be safe. But that meant she would have to pass within a hairsbreadth of the creature.

It took another step.

If she didn't do something soon, it would be too late. *If it's a meat eater I can throw my dagger and wound him, then I would have a chance.* Nabella drew the weapon. It slid against her sash with the smallest of whispers. The animal froze. She tensed her muscles.

Now!

Nabella sprang forward with a crash. She surged to her full height taking a quick look in the creature's direction. Her legs faltered and eyes flew wide. This was no deer that had come to nibble on the brush. Dark unblinking eyes set deep behind an elongated snout filled with jagged teeth stared at her. A straight, rigid neck held up the large head and widened into shoulders that supported short, powerful front legs, each ending with a massive protruding thumb claw. A small backward-pointed dermal ridge ran from the crest of its head down the length of its back turning into smaller bumps that extended out along the top of its long, thick tail. Its dimpled skin pulled taut over well-defined muscles of larger hind legs that ended in three enormous toes. Though it stood on all fours now, Nabella knew it could run fast as a cheetah on just its hind legs. Her stomach twisted.

An *azhdaha tanniyn*!

Except for flared nostrils the tanniyn stood immobile. Their eyes locked. The Azhdaha's muscles rippled then gathered ready to pounce. With a shout Nabella threw the dagger then watched mouth open as the knife spun in weak spirals through the air. The animal shifted its weight and flicked its head toward the passing weapon. It landed with a plop next to the beast's front foot. Hungry eyes rotated back towards her.

Horrified Nabella tore forward. Her feet felt like she moved through water, but she had never raced so fast in her life. Carefully planned steps forgotten, she bound for the tree. A loud guttural-hiss exploded behind her followed by the crash of breaking brush.

Is the branch close enough?

Nabella lunged for the limb. It seemed forever before her hands clamped onto the rough bark. The momentum propelled her upward, and her stomach landed against the branch. A grunt escaped. With a mighty heave she started to swing a leg over. At the same instant a yank on her jupe almost sent her tumbling backward.

Nabella collapsed onto the branch. She heard fabric rip and fiery pain burned the back of her right calf. Below Nabella the Azhdaha swept past, head twisted over its shoulder, fierce eyes locked on hers. She gave another heave, straddled the branch and jerked her legs to her body. Nabella thrust herself upright hugging the trunk for balance. Out of the corner of her eye she saw the animal spin and leap toward the branch she stood on.

A breathless squeal escaped as she grabbed at tree nubs and branches. Jagged pieces of bark bit into her palms. She scrambled upward, but her jupe snagged again. Nabella strained with all her strength, trapped halfway to the next branch. Legs and arms wrapped around the trunk, she peered over her shoulder and gasped. The tanniyn's huge thumb claw thrust through her jupe into the limb. It hung there by its front legs and stared with intense eyes. With a heave she tried to shimmy up the trunk. No good.

Her calf throbbed, and she could feel blood trickle down her leg. She let loose of one hand and wrenched the material in hopes it would rip, but to no avail. Her legs began to shake, then her arms, until her whole body trembled. *Didn't that tanniyn ever get tired hanging there? Oh Creator God, I'm not going to make it...*

Suddenly her jupe sprang loose. Nabella willed her weakened muscles to work. She clawed her way to a higher branch and once again hugged the trunk, gasping for air. Only then did she look down. The Azhdaha had tumbled to the ground. It scrambled to its feet and sprung for the branch. Once again it hung by its front legs while one back leg tore at the trunk in an attempt to maneuver itself onto the branch. Nabella clutched at her jupe. If the animal succeeded she would be within easy reach. She gathered her strength and climbed her way through branches until she perched high in the tree.

With back pressed against the rough bark Nabella straddled a limb. She ripped the torn piece off her jupe and wrapped it around her calf to staunch the dripping blood. Sweat trickled down her temple. With a quick swipe of her hand she wiped it away. She took stock of her situation as the tanniyn paced back and forth. The animal limped on its right hind leg. Nabella's eyes widened. *Ohh, it's wounded. That's why it couldn't get me. But why is it here, don't they fish at the river?* Then she remembered Jabari once told the workers Azhdahas would eat anything they could catch, even devouring dead animals. *That's why it's here, it came after the carcasses.*

The animal paced giving an occasional leap at the branch but seemed to have lost its drive. Nabella peered between the leaves. *It doesn't seem very big, only the size of a takhi. Didn't Jabari say they get to twenty-two cubits? So, this must be a young one.*

Abruptly the tanniyn backed away and crashed off in the opposite direction. *Why did it do that?* Nabella glanced around. Did she dare climb down or should she wait? If she waited too long it might come back.

Nabella heard Tomar's voice nearby. "Did you hear that?"

"We must have spooked some animal," Jokaan said.

Nabella caught a glimpse of the men and relief surged through her. The urge to climb from the tree and rush to them flew through her. But, she would be in *big* trouble. Hastily she tucked the loosed end of the jupe between her knees and pressed against the trunk.

"There it is. Same as the others," Tomar said.

"Looks like another caracal."

"I think Jabari is right. Someone *is* trying to curse you, Jokaan."

Nabella heard her father sigh. "I think I know who it is."

"Who?'

"I will not speak against another until I have proof."

Silence. Nabella craned her neck to get a better view.

"Do you want me to cut these carcasses down?" Tomar came into full view as he pushed his way through the brush and stood by the remains.

"No. Well, I don't know. What do you do in such a situation? I've never encountered something like this before."

Tomar turned, and Nabella saw him study her father. Her eyes flew wide. If Tomar happened to look up, he would surely see her.

"If we cut it down maybe it will break the curse," Tomar eyed the carcass.

"Or make it twice as bad." Jokaan rubbed his beard, and his voice became determined. "No, leave them. I will seek out Shem or Japheth first. Or if I can, speak with Noah himself. They're the only ones who would know what to do."

Nabella's heart leapt. The ancestors from before the great flood? Her father wanted to seek out these great men!

"I would like to go with you, if that is acceptable."

"You are the husband of my oldest daughter. I look to you as the son I never had, and I welcome you to travel with me."

"Thank you, Father. I best get back to the others. They will…"

Nabella strained to hear the rest of Tomar's words but the men were already too far into the grove. The sting of her father's words to Tomar as a son were dwarfed by the thought of the ancient ones. Her mind raced. She had glimpsed one of these ancients only a few times, the blond, fair-skinned Japheth. The man had a few creases around his eyes and across his forehead, and brow ridges that seemed to stick out, but otherwise he appeared no older than anyone else. It seemed unbelievable that he, and his brothers and their wives had all lived in the Old World over one hundred years ago. A world destroyed by water.

Once she even spotted Noah when he ducked into a tent to meet with Japheth and other men. She had caught a good look of Noah's face and besides the deep creases, what she remembered most had been how far his brow ridge jutted from his forehead. That and the strange white hairs mixed with the iron colored strands on his head. And even more were in his beard. She had been surprised at his height too, much shorter than Japheth.

Japheth used to hold formal teachings. When her father came home after a gathering he would tell his children about Japheth's experiences and of the wisdom he shared. She had always been awed by both the ancestor's knowledge, and her father's willingness to share with his children, his *girls*. It had been a long time since the ancestors had any teachings. But now her father wanted to seek them out.

Nabella's mind whirled. *Maybe I could…*a smile grew wide on her face then disappeared. She drew in a sharp breath. *The Azhdaha! Where is it? Should I warn*

Father? Oh but if I do, Father will have me under every man's watch. I'll never be able to get away to see the ancients.

Nabella waited only long enough to be sure the men wouldn't hear her clamber down the tree. With a loose grip on the last branch she finally let go and dropped to her feet. Full weight pressed on her wounded calf. Her hand flew to her mouth and pushed a balled fist against it to suppress a yelp. *This will be harder than I thought.* She winced, somehow she had to get to the house, bandage her wound and change, all without being detected.

But first, Nabella pushed thick-leafed brush aside until a gleam from the dagger caught her eye. With a quick scoop she gathered it and straightened. Eyes darted around for the Azhdaha, then came to rest on a thick stick. *Yes, that's perfect for a cane.* With a crack she snapped it over a rock then tested its height. A little short but it would do. She hop-skipped to the eastern edge of the orchard then down the road to home.

Nabella paused just inside the tree line. She watched workers move to the far side of the brick house Jokaan built many years ago for her mother. Not sure how long they would be out of sight she dropped the makeshift crutch and in a clumsy lope headed toward the house with gritted teeth. She aimed for the covered terrace, scurrying along its shadow, then slipped into a large storage room attached to the house. As far as Nabella knew her grandmothers would still be preparing the evening meal in the food courtyard on the far side of the house. All her sisters and their husbands would be in the orchard. She peeked through the open doorway into the inner courtyard. No one.

The window shutters to the eating room were wide open, the room vacant. *Good, all clear.* Nabella limped through the interior portico. Ten more steps and she collapsed into the sleeping quarters. She ignored the throb in her leg and reached for the one other garment she owned. It lay neatly folded on a stone bench that ran the length of the wall. She yanked the torn jupe from her body stuffing it between her low-slung pallet and the wool-filled mattress. Deft fingers fastened the clean jupe about her waist.

Once more Nabella hobbled across the central courtyard and out onto the terrace. She slipped into the semi-darkness of the large storage room blinking until her eyes adjusted. Slim fingers ran along the small stone jars that lined a shelf until she found the powdered olive leaf salve. Anyone living on an olive farm knew the astringent leaves helped heal wounds and prevent infection. Nabella shook her head. *Why didn't I get this on the way in?*

A low mutter of voices wafted through the opening. Three men, arms loaded with wood, rounded the corner of the house. Nabella pressed into the shadows and held her breath. Footsteps trudged past. She leaned over and peeked through a crack in the wall. They angled toward a small three-sided woodshed. A low sigh of relief escaped through her lips, followed by a groan. Her calf throbbed and blood oozed from the makeshift bandage. She made her way to the edge of the terrace and watched the men deposit their load then head to a group of workers gathered near the processing building. She knew her father would be in their midst to distribute the day's barley and oil rations in exchange for their labor. Something he did this time every day. *Good, no one will come this way.*

To be sure, Nabella scanned the grounds once more then limped to the well and drew water. With skilled fingers she rinsed and scrubbed the wrap and her wound, applied the olive leaf powder then re-bandaged it. Finally she rubbed the medicinal powder over the scrapes on her hands. *I need to help with the food or everyone will know I'm missing. If it's not too late already.*

Nabella dumped the dirty water and thrust everything back into its place. If she hurried the grandmothers would think little of her tardiness and if God was on her side, escape their interrogations altogether.

Walk slow, don't limp. Nabella clasped her jupe and meandered into the food preparation courtyard. Both grandmothers sat next to the tannur oven slapping dough to the hot inside walls.

Nabella gaped and blinked. There between them, sat Shoshana.

Her maternal grandmother smiled. "Good thing the meal wasn't left up to you two."

"I'm *sorry.* I wasn't gone all that long, was I?" Nabella's eyes remained riveted on her little sister as images of the Azhdaha raced through her mind.

"Yes you were. Where did you go?"

"Ah, Father said to let him know about the unpicked olives."

"You went all the way back to the tent?" Shoshana's wide eyes looked surprised.

"No, I ah, just had to tell Father."

"Well, that was a lot of jabbering. Quit wasting time and get over here. You can help with the bread." Her paternal grandmother pushed back a damp dark strand that had escaped from under her headscarf knotted at the nape of her neck.

Nabella glared at Shoshana. "When did you get here?"

Shoshana looked away, slight hands forming a bread patty.

"She *just* got here." Danya's mother elbowed Shoshana.

"Who came with you?" Nabella snapped.

Shoshana looked up, blinked and smiled. "No one."

Nabella looked away and swallowed. She twisted her head and stared in the direction of the northern grove. *Oh Shoshana, I'm going to kill you myself if that tanniyn doesn't.*

"Why didn't you stay at the tent?"

"I wanted to follow you."

"So nobody knows you left?"

Her sister looked down and kneaded the dough, a bony shoulder peeked through the neck opening of her tunic.

"Go tell Tomar you're here. Hurry, before he leaves. And don't *ever* do that again." The words hissed through clenched teeth.

A tongue clucked behind her. "Well, you don't have to be so snippy, girl. You used to run around by yourself when you were younger than her," Nahni piped in.

Nabella knew she'd been had, once again the brunt of everyone's misgivings. She eyed Shoshana and mouthed, "I'll get you later," then huffed to the well, splashed water on her face, and dried her hands on her jupe.

***

Seven days after Cush and Ra'anel had paid them a visit, Barukh finished the last section in the vineyard, and Gideon had agreed to accompany him for a call on Jokaan.

Barukh searched the olive groves when he and his father first left their vineyards and entered the northern orchard. His mind toiled, much depended on this marriage. He'd seen more beautiful woman, but Nabella would be useful. A union with her could prove to be most advantageous, and pleasurable.

"You are grinning like a mother holding a newborn baby. If you are not careful the sun will glint off your teeth and blind everyone we meet." Gideon laughed.

His father's tease broke into Barukh's thoughts. "Did Grandfather know you were going to ask him to have a marriage with Mother? Did he say no at first?"

"Yes, he knew. And he didn't say no, just put the date off for a while. He was firm about how I was to treat his daughter because he wanted your mother to have a husband that cared about her. He also wanted to know me before he gave her over to my protection."

His father laid a hand on Barukh's shoulder. "I was just as nervous as you."

Barukh shifted his eyes away. Was he nervous? Barukh frowned, *must be the pressure.* Everyone thought he was madly in love with Nabella. Wasn't he?

"I hope Jokaan doesn't put off the date, he's known me all my life."

"Yes, you have an advantage with Nabella living next to us."

Barukh scanned the grove again. "Where is she? I thought she knew I was coming. I don't even see any workers."

"Well, if you look closer, son, you'll notice the trees have no olives on them. So there won't be any workers here."

"Ah-he, you're right."

Gideon grinned, clasped hands behind his back and stared straight ahead. "You did good, son. Nabella is a fine girl, a little strong headed but properly raised. She will treat you well."

Surprised at the compliment, Barukh studied his father's stoic features. They rarely spoke of intimate things, conversations tended to center on vineyard business. Barukh clasped hands behind his back as well, relishing this time of camaraderie with no competition from Kfir now that he had returned. "Yes, Nabella's a fine woman."

"She will give me many grandsons."

Barukh felt heat rise in his face. "I hope so. She better. Even though she has only sisters."

"And we have only boys."

"So far."

They laughed and rounded the last curve in the lane that led to Jokaan's house. The bustle of the production site impressed both men. There had to be at least forty people that milled about and most of them were Jokaan's extended family. Out of Jokaan's eight girls, only four remained within his household, but all the husbands pitched in to help the patriarch this time of year.

Gideon paused to answer people's greeting. Barukh hung back, reluctant to be drawn into conversation. He crossed his arms to curb irritation at the trivial exchanges while his stomach ached from tension. He just wanted to get this over with. A young girl skipped up to him.

"Greetings, Shoshana," he managed a smile.

"Greetings, Barukh. What good news do you have for me?"

"Is this good enough news?" Barukh pulled a small jar of sweet grape juice from his pocket. "I brought this just for you."

Shoshana's face beamed as she took the offering. "I'll go get Nabella," she whirled around flitting toward the largest building.

"Wait," Gideon called. "Get your father too."

"Alright," she yelled over her shoulder. "But I'm getting Nabella first."

"Gideon, Barukh," Jabari strode toward them. With an embrace, he kissed each man on both cheeks. Barukh enjoyed Jabari's company most of the time, probably because they were close in age. Perhaps Jabari would teach him a few tracking skills once he became part of the family. Barukh wrinkled his brow. Well, maybe not. Especially if it involved scrounging around in the underbrush. Barukh turned his attention back to the men.

"Greetings. How does your family fare, Gideon?" Jokaan strode toward them.

"Very well and you?"

"We all fare well also. What good news do you bring?"

"A rich harvest this year."

"Yes, likewise. Please, come into my home." Jokaan turned toward the single-story dwelling and held a calloused hand out in welcome.

"Adara, find Nabella." Jokaan crossed the terrace and entered the brick building. "Sit. Sit. Please," he waved a hand toward the inlaid stone benches that hugged each wall of the large central room. Barukh crossed the burnt brick floor onto a large finely woven rug. Its deep plush enveloped his sandals with each step. Soft leather greeted his backside as he sank onto pads stuffed with wool. He leaned against the wall with a sigh as a light breeze brushed the window fabric against his shoulder. Matching textiles that hung by each opening were pulled aside to let light in. Grateful for the thick brick walls that kept a pleasant temperature within, Barukh dabbed at a drop of sweat that trickled from his forehead.

His well-set eyes roved about the room and landed on the entrance household altar. As usual no idol rested there. Fair brows crinkled for just an instant. Nowadays most dwellings entertained one or more deities. Barukh thought of both fathers and their strong belief in only the Creator God, a fact that had drawn the two families together. But he wondered on occasion, could that be right? Could they be too narrow-minded?

"I'm glad you came, Gideon. I've been meaning to stop by your place." Jokaan dropped onto the bench next to his friend, deep furrows lined his forehead.

"What's on your mind?" Gideon leaned forward.

Jokaan took a deep breath and scrubbed his face with a large hand. "Have you noticed anything strange at your place?"

"What do you mean, strange?"

"Well, out of sorts…"

"No. Everything's fine. Like I said, we had a great harvest this year. Why?"

"Last week, at each of the four corners of my orchard, we found a caracal sacrificed in ritual. Jabari and Tomar believe a curse has been placed upon my groves. Nothing like this has happened at your place?"

Barukh eyes widened, and he and Gideon exchanged a glance. "No," both said in unison.

Jokaan continued to explain what happened and just listening to the horrid details made Barukh's stomach churn. Jokaan's eyes glinted as he studied clenched hands pressed onto his knees. Barukh understood Jokaan's anger. He wouldn't want anything like that in their vineyards.

The young man flicked another drop of sweat. "Do you think it could have been Ra'anel or Cush? They were at our vineyards last week."

"Yes, they stopped here last week as well. But I have no proof, so I can't say one way or the other."

The men paused, each in their own thoughts.

"What are you going to do?" Gideon rubbed the back of his neck.

"I sent two men to find Shem or Japheth or even Noah, if he can be found."

"You wish to speak with the ancestors? Ah-he!" Barukh blurted.

Gideon's russet features pinched with concern. "It's probably the only way to figure this out. You were wise to go in that direction. This is very serious, my friend. What was their answer?"

"My men have yet to return. I expect at least one of them to come back sometime today."

Silence followed as each dwelled once again on their own thoughts. Finally, Barukh cleared his throat.

Gideon leaned back. "Jokaan, we also came here on serious business, though more pleasant. As I have already said we had a very abundant year."

Nabella's father nodded.

"My son has a proposal for you."

Jokaan's eye's shifted to Barukh. The young man felt like his stomach dropped through the floor. He swallowed then stood and opened his mouth but no sound came out. He started to pace then stopped. Was it rude to pace? It was important to stay on Jokaan's good side. He swallowed again. *Just say something...*

"Kuya Jokaan, son of E—," his voice squeaked. *Great, just great.* He cleared his throat and tried again. "Kuya Jokaan, son of Eber, I have gathered wine, vinegar, raisins, even olive trees for the past two years, and I have traded for much cloth, meat, seeds, goats, oxen, and a takhi. I even have several carts and pottery, lots of oil lamps that I thought you could use to trade with your oil, and, and, an—"

"Now why would you want to trade me oil lamps?" Jokaan's coy tone, Barukh knew, was meant to relax him, but he couldn't force himself to do so.

Barukh realized his whole body shook, "Kuya, may I have your permission to take your daughter, Nabella, as my wedded?"

Before Jokaan could answer, Adara's frantic voice clamored across the courtyard and shot into the reception room, "Nabella wai—"

"I will not. This has to be addressed and addressed now." Nabella swept into the room and froze. Jokaan and Gideon jumped to their feet.

Barukh stared, stunned. Olive oil greased one side of disheveled hair, plastering it to the side of her head. It clung thickly to one set of eyelashes, oozed down a cheek, then glop by glop dripped from her chin. Drenched, the side of her tunic stuck like glue to her every move.

Nabella's jaw dropped, and her eyes flew wide.

"Barukh!" She spun on her heel and dashed to the entranceway, face aflame. "Aaaderra!"

Three

As people moved eastward, they found a plain in Shinar and settled there. They said to each other, "Come, let's make bricks and bake them thoroughly." They used brick instead of stone, and tar for mortar. Then they said, "Come, let us build ourselves a city, with a tower that reaches to the heavens, so that we may make a name for ourselves; otherwise we will be scattered over the face of the whole earth."

Genesis 11:2-4 (NIV)

Cush stood, feet splayed on the topmost terrace of the brick tower. He watched people below travel the length of its precipitous steps. Behind him, warmth from the autumn sun radiated off sandstone temple walls. *This must be the largest thing man ever built.* Yes, Cush was sure of it. Ham had never spoken of anything so immensely constructed in the Old World. His father surely would have told him if it were so. Cush nodded. Yes, Ham would like the tower. He ventured this even rivaled the ark. And *that* had been an incredible feat of labor and skill.

Cush didn't know the whereabouts of his father, or even if Ham remained alive. But he knew Ham would approve of this tower even though it had taken fifteen years to build. He sneered at the thought. Had it been his way, the tower would have taken half the time to complete. But those who studied the stars insisted the populace needed to live close by. So, construction of living quarters and commerce buildings had commenced the same time as the tower. Cush gave his head a slight shake and studied the bustling crowds beneath him. Had it already been twenty years since that first council? Since the community's family leaders had been called together to discuss a permanent settlement? The man crossed arms over his massive chest. Yes. It had been.

He remembered it like yesterday. Of course, there had been those opposed to building a city. They insisted that systematic colonization of the world, each with its own local government, would honor God's command to fill the whole earth. Cush's fists tightened at the thought. Rebels!

Wide nostrils flared with a deep breath, and he forced himself to relax. First, as it turned out, most had felt an establishment of a strong central civilization to be best. His back straightened. They *wanted* a self-sufficient society. Then, they said, everyone could spread out and make other cities. Cush grunted, *yes and under our control.*

Second, the discovery of *chemar*—asphalt—had swung the decision in favor of a centralized government. Shepherds that migrated along the valley between the Euphrates and Tigris Rivers had stumbled upon abundant pits of the tarry material. Cush remembered when he thought the black slime useless. It was Nimrod who realized its value.

Up until then most people dwelled in tents. With mud for mortar, only sheepfolds and storage sheds were constructed with fire-baked bricks. Frequent ground quakes made the block structures unsafe to live in. The dried mud cracked and bricks fell. With the use of chemar, asphalt, in all but the most severe quakes the blocks stayed in place. Cush gave a grudging nod. He had to admit Nimrod's suggestion to make an industry out of brick construction, chemar gathering and timber production was brilliant. It required many people to labor as one, to be supported by others, and this could only work with a centralized society.

Third, the decision to build a city centered on religion, was brilliant. Cush and his relatives had persuaded many family leaders that those who studied the stars were vital to the government. The leaders realized when a government embraced a strong spiritual aspect the multitude would finally be motivated to overcome their knowledge, and fear, that God had indeed commanded them to fill the whole earth. A soft snort escaped. Gullible fools.

He paced a few steps; the gentle breeze it created felt cool upon his face. Sure, discussions of the issues and alternatives continued for several years. But finally a formal decision had been made. "Let us go," the people cried, "And build a city and a tower, whose top may reach to the heavens. And let us make a name for ourselves!" Cush couldn't have been more pleased. The fact remained, the majority of people had been afraid to scatter abroad.

Cush and the other leaders who wanted a central position really didn't do anything; they just let the people stew on their fears. He smirked. The masses had decided for themselves to stay together. Influential family leaders, of whom the man belonged, were selected to run the organization. Ra'anel had insisted a tariff be placed on the people to give five percent of all their labors to the government. Cush wholeheartedly agreed. The government now controlled resources and occupations, doling out necessities to those who worked for their fledgling regime.

But there remained a small minority who spoke strongly against settling in one place. Like Jokaan. Cush's upper lip curled at the thought of the man. The olive picker had always been a thorn in his foot. Jokaan and his allies continued to argue people needed to spread out, colonize the entire earth and develop resources in a manner that would glorify God. Sometimes they even swayed a few government leaders with their exciting talk to explore unknown regions.

But the celestial advisors were able to sway the tide again. Cush could still hear part of Ra'anel's magnanimous speech;

"A time shall come later for exploration. Now is the time for unity. We must appease God, hmm? The lofty grandeur of the tower will symbolize the might and majesty of the Creator God of heaven. It shall be constructed with a great temple at its apex. At this central altar all men can come to offer their sacrifices and worship God. No longer shall we be scattered, giving puny thanksgiving on our own. Now we can worship together."

Once the tower had been built the people admired its beauty and sacred purpose. Cush had been pleased when they reasoned the tower would satisfy God and more than compensate for defying His commandment. After all, they did not think God wanted them to get lost.

"Quite a sight, hmmm?" The advisor drummed his fingers against his jaw.

Cush jerked and stared at Ra'anel. His stomach tightened. He could not help but wonder, was the head celestial advisor friend or foe, or a little of both?

"Yes." Cush narrowed dark eyes and perused The City. The carefully planned settlement had been constructed for permanence. Everything contributed to the optimum efficiency of the entire complex. Even the citadels were strategically located. One at the main northern gate where the river flowed through the center of The City and another where the river exited the fortress walls to the south. Satisfaction settled over Cush as he surveyed its orderliness. He felt the tension ease.

"Nimrod finished the bridge yesterday." Cush gave a sideways glance at Ra'anel. "Only two years to complete. I tell you, there is no stopping that young man."

"He is rather, hmmm, ambitious isn't he?" Ra'anel's tone gritted on Cush's nerves.

"He is rather indestructible."

"He may be, he may be," Ra'anel stroked his thin beard.

Cush focused his eyes once more on the people below. Already in the early morning a thin line of citizens tramped up the stairs, their long shadows gliding in front of them. As of late, the celestial advisors did not allow the commoners into the temple. Instead, the people left their offerings on the topmost eastern terrace. The side of Cush's lip curled upward. So much for a place where all people can worship together.

He spun on his heel and entered the temple. A chill surrounded him, permeating him, and not just because of the cooler air inside. It was more the chill of an unseen presence. Cush had felt it before. He squeezed his right fist in an attempt to stifle the sensation.

He forced his attention to several advisors balancing on ladders. Thick eyebrows shot up when he realized they were painting the walls of the temple. Cush felt a rush of heat and tried to control the rising anger. "What are they doing? This wasn't discussed at the council meeting."

"It did not need to be discussed, these paintings are essential."

"Essential? They're just representations of men, birds, tanniyns and creeping things."

"We felt these additional aids to worship were, beneficial."

Cush's laugh held a sardonic ring, and he made a wide sweep with his arm. "What? You already have the *mazzoroth*, the twelve star assemblages, that tells of creation emblazoned on the ceiling. Isn't that ornate enough?"

"Well...these new paintings have more to them than you know. They contain actual, hmmm, spiritual entities. That is why the commoners had to be restricted."

The edges of Cush's mouth creased downward. *What was the man saying?*

"For example, the stars of the virgin," Ra'anel's tone oozed. He strolled under the depiction of the star assemblage and swung his arm along it. "Is to remind us of a supernatural Seed, but I believe she is more than that. She is an actual queen of heaven. And the lion assemblage is a great spiritual King of the heavens."

The hairs on Cush's arms prickled. Could it actually be true? As if Ra'anel could read his mind the celestial advisor twisted his head, pale blue eyes bore through Cush.

"There are specific angels, Cush. And they have their own stars. These beings, are concerned with every aspect of our lives and the processes of this world. They can move from the heavens to here. And here, we are making a place for them. When we pay reverence to these, we worship the Creator God."

"How can worshipping something else be worshipping the Creator?" Sarcasm ran through Cush's voice.

"Because when we do, God, through these spirits and their stars and animals, responds by giving us protection. And provisions. You do realized, they guide us in our lives, hmmm?" Ra'anel spread both arms and turned in a slow circle, "As is evident."

Cush riveted dark eyes on Ra'anel. "I don't think God needs these spirits to respond to us. He spoke directly to my grandfather in no uncertain terms."

"Hmmm, and if I recall correctly, it was Noah who cursed Canaan, when he had done no wrong."

Cush ground his teeth and turned his back on Ra'anel. He remembered all too well his father's gloating when Ham had found Noah drunk and unclothed; a characteristic very unlike the highly honored patriarch. Ham had rushed home rejoicing in his father's weakness. He had gathered his sons and traveled to Shem and Japheth's dwellings. There he proceeded, uninhibited, to express his long-hidden resentment of his father's authority and moral righteousness. Cush had felt at that time justice had been done for he knew just how hard his grandfather had been on their father.

Cush's younger brother Canaan had joined with Ham's delight when they retold the story of Noah's condition. But much to his dismay, neither of Cush's uncles spoke against Noah. Instead, Shem had glared at Ham and said, "Shame. Shame on you." Then he and Japheth immediately left. Cush found out later his uncles walked backward into the tent and covered Noah without even a single glance at him.

Then Cush discovered his grandfather had cursed Canaan. "He will be a servant of servants to the generations of his brothers." He had felt the hairs on the back of his neck rise the more he listened. Somehow he had heard the ring of prophesy and knew it to be true. The words still echoed in Cush's mind.

He knew God did not need other spirits to be praised in order to be worshipped. God was more powerful than that. But what of the sense he encountered when he first entered the temple? Could there really be something to these spirits? *Probably, but I doubt they're of God.*

Feet splayed, Cush crossed his arms. "You play with fire, Ra'anel."

"No. I have been given a great power. And I intend to use it."

The big man snorted, "But you still have to live off the people's offerings and sacrifices?"

"You do the same, Cush."

"I serve the people. I *work* as part of the council that decides disputes, building projects, governing sanctio—"

"I know, I know. The list goes on." Ra'anel held up his hand. "But mind you, the spiritual realm is just as, if not more, important. By devoting our lives to the study and interpretation of these celestial beings, we are able to guide the people in their dedications and sacrifices. And how to order their lives so they will not offend these beings."

"So you intend to fill the heads of the stubborn few who refuse to come to The City with worship of other beings? Do you really think their awareness of Creator God will go away?"

"Yes, and their concern to obey Him as well."

Cush's eyes drifted to the open entrance as he mulled over Ra'anel's words. He had long since stopped worshipping the Creator God. And nothing bad had happened. Yet. Were his thoughts wicked like the people of the Old World? The ones who drowned? Would God's patience run out again? Was God still even around?

Cush mused more to himself than to Ra'anel. "You know, I think God made the Flood happen and then left us to ourselves. No one has heard Him in over a hundred years."

Ra'anel lifted both hands high. "Indeed. And we are doing just fine without Him, let these beings worship Him for us."

Cush looked at the paintings, the creatures to be worshiped. Some were formidable to be sure. Powerful lions, wolves and tanniyns, snakes and bears. He remembered the chill that had encircled him. Perhaps Ra'anel was right. These animal spirits might possess something mystical, powerful. Maybe one of those could replace where God used to stand. A wall of stone crept around his heart and Cush's fist tightened.

Four

And the whole earth was of one language, and of one speech.

Genesis 11:1(KJV)

Nabella bolted from the reception area, tears stinging her eyes. She barely felt the lingering ache in her calf from the Azhdaha's claw. She wanted to kill her sister. How dare her! *How could she let me go to Barukh when I look like, like a slimy fish?*

"Adara!" Nabella burst into the kitchen courtyard in time to see her sister suppress a smile.

"How could you?" She stomped a foot.

The humor disappeared from Adara's dark, honey-colored face. "I tried to stop you. But you are so pigheaded, you wouldn't listen to me."

Nabella stood speechless. The truth stung.

"Here, come to the well and I'll scrub your hair."

Adara removed a small, baked-clay cylinder from a shelf. "Oh…the soap is almost gone, but I think there is enough left to get rid of your mess. Go get a comb while I get water."

Nabella glanced into the eating room. Good, no one lingered there. She dashed inside and grabbed a comb off the bench in her room. When she returned she saw Adara had gathered two water jugs from the fire.

Her sister took the seven-pronged comb and placed it next to the cylinder. She motioned for Nabella to remove her tunic then held up a woolen wrap.

Nabella grabbed an edge of the cloth and wiped the oil from her skin then secured it around her shoulders. Adara pulled Nabella's head down, released the two thin braids on either side of her head then poured half a pot over her hair.

"Hey, that's hot…"

"Oh hush, you'll be fine." Adara's sturdy fingers scrubbed soap through the oily mess. "You know, when you are married you'll have to stop this impulsive behavior-"

"But the boys were wasting oil!"

"Nabella. That was none of your business."

"They were fooling around. You know Father thinks I'm like a son. I went over there to tell them to get back to work."

"I know Father thinks that. But you have to stop desiring to be his son. You're one of his daughters and that should be enough. None of this would have happened if you had let a man reprimand the boys. You *have* to stop getting involved in men's business."

"It's not fair that men get to do whatever they want and we don't. I'm just as good at telling other people what to do as a man. Besides men get to go wherever they want, when they want. And what do we get to do? Stay home and obey. A lot of fun that is." Nabella mumbled.

"We do get to go places and it's an honor to run a household. You must understand this before you get married." Adara sighed, grabbed a scrap of wool cloth then rubbed Nabella's deep sable hair with furious strokes.

Nabella moaned. "How will I face him?"

Adara stopped, picked up the comb carved from horn and looked Nabella in the eyes. "With confidence, dignity and, beauty."

"Beauty? I'm not beautiful like you, or like Shoshana's going to be. My nose is too big and my hair too thin and I'm too tall." She stared down at her sister, glanced sideways and lowered her voice. Then leaned forward a hand on her chest. "And, and I have nothing here."

"Nonsense. You do have a little and don't worry, in time you'll get more. Barukh is taller than you so don't worry about that part either. But if you think you need help with the rest, then we will flatter him with your eyes, cheeks and lips."

"What do you mean?"

Adara sighed. "It was going to be a wedding present but under the circumstances…"

Her sister's *jupe* swished as she hurried around the corner only to return with several tiny clay pots. "It's something I made."

Nabella looked at the minute jars full of rosy creams. "What are they?"

"Have you ever noticed that sometimes I have flushed cheeks and bright lips?"

"Yes, isn't that because you're warm?"

"Well, sometimes but other times I put this on to make it look that way. Tomar likes it and so will Barukh. And this," Adara placed a small pot that contained something black and hard on a stone in the tanner oven coals, "is for your eyes."

"Where did you get these?"

"Well," Adara leaned closed and whispered, "it's a secret handed down from the Old World."

"Who? Who told you?"

"I told you, it's a secret."

"Why is it a secret?"

"It's not for men to know."

"Then tell me."

Adara's well-shaped lips parted wide and then she laughed. "Alright. I learned it from Channah—"

"Eber's wife?"

"Yes. It was a wedding present ten years ago. She learned the formula from Salah's wife, who learned it from Madai's wife, who learned it from Magog's wife, who learned it from Japheth's wife, who brought the formula from the Old World."

"Ah-he, Adara, that's amazing. I wonder who in the Old World knew of these, treasures for making women pretty."

"I don't know, but Channah whispered it came all the way from first-mother Eve."

Nabella let out a low ah-he. "Do you think first-father Adam thought Eve was pretty?"

Adara chuckled and finished untangling Nabella's hair. "I don't know that either. And I don't really know if this knowledge came from Eve."

Adara studied Nabella's light olive skin then reached for a jar on the far end. "This one will work better for you since your skin is lighter than mine."

With deft hands Adara rubbed the cream over Nabella's cheeks, then reached for a smaller jar. She dipped her finger into the stiff pomade and with practiced dabs painted Nabella's lips. Adara removed the pot that contained charcoal mixed with beeswax and lard from the cooking coals. She took a thin brush made from a few strands of camel's hair and dipped it into the mixture.

"Now close your eyes and hold very still. This might hurt just a little because the wax is too warm, but I don't want to keep the men waiting any longer."

With great care Adara lined Nabella's eyes then fanned her face to hurry the drying process.

"There, now open your eyes."

"It feels kind of funny."

"Wait until you see the results."

Nabella started to jump, but when her leg protested, she slowed and shifted most of her weight to the other foot. She glanced at her sister. Adara stretched for something on the upper shelf, not seeming to notice.

"Wait, put this on first," she insisted holding out a garment.

"Oh, but that's your good tunic, Adara, the one you wore at your marriage."

"I know, and I haven't even worn it since I washed it last. When you ran by covered in oil I brought it just so you could impress Barukh. So here and don't mess it up. Go on, hurry, I still need to put your hair up and the men are waiting."

Adara unfastened the wrap and held it around Nabella while she slipped into the finely embroidered tunic. When Adara finished her hair, Nabella stood over a shallow basin of water. The reflection that gazed back did not look familiar. With hair up and color on her face, she almost looked—

Nabella tore her eyes away from the basin and stared, mouth open, at Adara. "You made me look, pretty."

Adara put her arm around Nabella's waist and gave her a hug. "*Motek shele*, you are beautiful, here *and* here." Adara's soft black eyes smiled as she touched Nabella's cheek then her chest. "Now, go back in there with confidence and humility. Don't be embarrassed."

Nabella nodded. She felt an overwhelming love for the sister who took care of her since their mother died. She opened her mouth, ready to tell her about the Azhdaha, then clamped it shut. They just had such a good time together she didn't want to spoil things now.

"What would we do without you? Tomar is such a treasure to move you and the children back here after Mother died."

Adara winked and smiled. "You're welcome, now go." she gave Nabella a shove. "And don't run."

***

After Nabella left, Barukh glanced at both fathers, out the window, at his feet, then back at the men. Jokaan motioned for him to be seated. Barukh studied his fingernails picking at a speck of dirt. At last Jokaan straightened and asked with a strained laugh if the young man still wanted to marry his daughter.

Barukh could only nod with mouth open wide and stare through the empty entranceway. What in the world was Nabella doing, bursting into men's conversation like that? She knew better.

After a few uncomfortable mumbles and cleared throats, Jokaan and Gideon exchanged news of their farms' progress. Barukh squirmed. Should he announce they would come back later? What if Jokaan says Nabella's not ready for a marriage? *I know he'll agree to it, but he might make me wait a year, or two, or three.*

Barukh angled his head at a slight noise. He sprang at the sight of Nabella at the entrance. His mouth dropped open and before he could catch himself, whispered, "Ah-he."

Could this be the same person? He had never seen Nabella look so, so refined. Barukh realized his mouth gaped open and snapped it shut. Nabella smiled, and he let out a long breath. *She really looks pretty.* A gloating grin spread across his face. Just wait until Kfir sees her like this. *And to think I will inherit a part of this vast business as well.*

Her voice sang out, "You called, Father?"

"Yes I did. Barukh has asked my permission to make you his wife. He has offered a large dowry. It's mine and Gideon's decision the two of you would have a good marriage. You and," Jokaan turned to Gideon's son. "Barukh have my blessing."

***

Nabella remembered Adara's reaction when, so many years ago, Jokaan had given her sister and Tomar his blessing. Though she wanted to run and throw her arms around her father's neck, smother him with kisses and say thank you a hundred times, instead she copied Adara's lead. With a deep bow of her head, Nabella took Jokaan's hand and kissed it.

"Thank you, Father," she beamed.

Jokaan kissed her forehead then gave her hand to Barukh. The touch of his large, warm fingers encircling hers stole her breath. *He's so handsome. And I love the way he cropped his beard short like Kfir's.* Her eyes lingered on blond wavy hair that she knew Barukh had brushed away from his face with great care. Nabella blinked back the sudden threat of grateful tears. *What does he see in me?* Gradually she brought her gaze to his. The world slowed. The hum of their father's voices droned on in the background. Nabella's blood pounded through her veins and time stood still.

Barukh pulled her close. She caught his sweet, masculine scent and became hopelessly lost in deep blue eyes and a stunning smile.

"Harrumph."

Nabella blinked. Where did that annoying noise come from? It sounded like someone cleared their throat. Wait, someone *did* clear their throat. The world rushed back and Nabella felt heat rise in her cheeks. Gideon grinned and held out his arms.

"Welcome to the family." He embraced her and kissed each cheek. Out the corner of her eye she saw Jokaan grasp Barukh's forearms. Laughter bubbled past her smile. One glance at Barukh and she just *knew* he felt the same. He fixed his eyes on her, and she felt heat rise once more. *Oh no, I hope my cheeks aren't flaming with the red cream.* She took a deep breath but failed to stop the warm rush.

"When should we set the date?" Her father's sounded, almost as if…as if he were proud of her.

It felt good to stand next to Barukh. She glanced at him, and he squeezed her hand.

"The sooner the better." Barukh grinned smugly. But Gideon held up his hand and motioned for Jokaan to make the decision.

"We will set a proper time." Jokaan's voice became firm. "Ten months from today."

"Oh, Father, that's wonderful." Nabella knew the proper time could take up to three years. Her father had picked the shortest time possible. She could contain herself no longer and raced to him throwing her arms around his neck. Jokaan patted her shoulder awkwardly then pulled her arms from around him. Nabella backed to Barukh and once again grabbed his hand.

"Yes. Thank you, *Kuya* Jokaan." Barukh gave a bow of respect to Jokaan.

"Well, I think we can give these two the rest of the afternoon off. They have much to discuss. Gideon, you are welcome to come with me or just relax here, but I must go, I have much to do."

***

The following day news came of Shem's whereabouts.

"Nabella, pack enough food for five days," Jokaan instructed. "For both Tomar and myself."

"Yes, Father." *And enough for me too.* "When do you plan to leave?"

Jokaan gazed into the distance murmuring, "Today, just as soon as I can."

Her father left the storage room and Nabella stared after him clasping her jupe. She racked her mind. *There must be a way I can go with them, I need an excuse...*a smile spread across her face. Nabella filled a sack with flat bread, hummus and lentils. In another she deposited nuts, chickpeas and dried berries. Last, she laid a small jar of olive oil on top of the food. Finished with the men's journey sacks she filled one for herself, then hid it amongst the bags of lentils and chickpeas. The men's sacks slung over her shoulder she hurried to the outer courtyard to draw water into wineskins.

Nabella lifted her head at the dull plod of hooves. Jokaan walked across the small meadow toward her, an old mare eyeballing Nabella followed. She passed them the food sacks while the mare snorted.

"Thank you, we'll be back soon with answers." Tomar took the packages securing them to a pack saddle already loaded with blanket rolls. Then handed Tomar the wineskins.

Nabella gave a wry smile and glanced at her father. "See why it would be good to have several riding takhis, Father? You're going a long way."

"No for the last time, Nabella. Tạkhis aren't as strong as oxen and eat a lot more." Jokaan smacked the animal with the palm of his hand as Tomar clucked his tongue and tugged on the lead rope.

She placed a hand on her hip and watched them go down the lane. Nabella knew her father was right. Takhis could be unpredictable and surly, hence the name, spirit horse. They were not reliable for work on an olive orchard. But she knew he hung on to this last old mare because it had been his father's favorite. Even so, it didn't stop her from trying to convince him otherwise. *Well, at least it'll be easy for me to keep up. And soon I'll be married to Barukh and he has takhis.* With one last glance over her shoulder, Nabella slipped into the storeroom to retrieved her sack.

"Where are you going?" A little voice sounded behind her.

Nabella's heart skipped a beat as she whirled around. Shoshana looked up at her with big, round eyes.

Nabella gritted her teeth. "I must see Barukh. There's still so much to plan for our marriage." The lie slid off her tongue.

Shoshana gnawed her lower lip then said, "You shouldn't go when Father is gone."

"That's the best time, then Father won't miss me."

"Does Father know you are going?"

"Father gave me the day off yesterday." Nabella's voice became stern. "And this time, do not follow me."

"Why?"

"For one, Father did not give you the day off. And two..." Nabella thought of the creature that came to the groves. She had not told anyone for fear of being questioned. But she had to make sure Shoshana did not wander away by herself.

"Listen, I..." briefly Nabella thought about another lie. Just a small one. It wouldn't hurt, would it? And it just might save Shoshana's life. "Yesterday when I was with Barukh, I saw a big ferocious Azhdaha."

Shoshana's eyes flew wide, and she gasped, "A tanniyn?"

Nabella hung her head for just an instant. Had she pushed it too far?

"Did you tell Father?"

"No, only I saw it, and Barukh kept making fun of me. So I didn't want to." Nabella glanced away. Another lie.

"Bella, you shouldn't go out there alone!"

"I'll be fine. Look, Father gave me mother's dagger. If I get into trouble, I can use it. I know how, Father showed me."

Shoshana's eyes grew wider. Little fingers brushed the dagger. "Will you teach me someday?"

"I will, motek, but for now stick around here where the men can protect you, all right?"

Shoshana nodded. Nabella's shoulders relaxed, and she kissed her sister's forehead.

Good. She won't disobey now.

A twinge of guilt niggled through Nabella as she headed through the entranceway. She lifted her chin, shrugged the feeling aside and strode across the clearing. That little exchange should have given the men enough time to get ahead. She scanned the grounds for Jabari and found him by the olive presses.

"Jabari, I'm going to Barukh's. I'll be back in a few days."

"Does Jokaan know?"

"He gave me the day off yesterday," she said with forced gaiety over her shoulder then strode down the lane in the direction of Barukh's place.

"Be careful," he called after her.

She waved and looked toward the house. Shoshana stood there, her lower lip clamped between her teeth. As she turned and waved, another stab of guilt tightened her chest. Was this worth it? What she was doing? She had just lied and deceived the ones she loved. And that disrespected her father. At the edge of the trees she paused and looked back at her home. Nothing seemed out of place. The processing of olives lumbered along without Jokaan and Tomar. Or her.

Oh, but to be able to hear and see Shem. God would understand her disobedience. After all, she only wanted to gain a closer knowledge of Him through Shem. Nabella grinned. *Yes, God would understand. He may even approve!*

Worry set aside, she moved into the trees. But with each step another concern crept in. The Azhdaha. Without thinking her hand crept to the dagger. Nabella's gaze swept left and right, then behind. After several paces she realized even in the trees she had a good view around her. Her hand slipped off the dagger, and her stride quickened. Only where the brush invaded the far northern corner of the grove had her sight been so obscured. And the grasses on the plain of Shinar were just waist high, not enough to hide the Azhdaha.

Nabella made her way through the trees until she reached the path that meandered through the middle of the grove. No sign of the men. Alright, they must have gone the other way. She made her way to the eastern edge of the orchard and paused by the last row of trees. Her eyes darted about for any more sacrificed caracals. Nothing unusual. Nabella let out a slow breath, unaware she had been holding it then let her gaze sweep over the grassland.

Palm, wild pear trees and tall bushes lay scattered along washes that cut into the flat, grass-covered plain. Her eyes followed the course of the drainages lined by the lush, taller grasses and weeds. Though she could not see them she knew shallow puddles pooled there, evidence of recent rains.

Close by cattle munched on wild grasses. Nabella's eyes lingered on a large herd of camels. They nibbled the reddish brown autumn leaves of terebinth trees and wild berries, their keepers nearby, whips in hand. A little farther out goitered gazelles drifted along while they fed on rich grasslands. And was she mistaken, or did a cheetah lie atop a distant mound? The gazelles did not seem edgy even though they glanced in its direction every now and then. She wasn't worried about the cheetah, they never hunted people. In the far distance she could barely make out shepherds moving around with their herds of sheep.

And there, coming out of a low dip near the camel herds, two men leading a takhi with packs traveled eastward. Nabella smiled to herself. She stayed within the boundaries of the trees and headed northward. When the cattle were between her and Jokaan, she headed east across the plain of Shinar. As Nabella neared the cattle they began drifting away from her. How splendid. She could just move with them keeping the animals between her and the men. That way she could hide behind them.

The warm afternoon sun beat on her head. She paused to get her bearings then wiped the sweat beaded across her forehead and the bridge of her nose. How she preferred to walk through her father's cool orchards. She had never ventured so far out onto the plains. The farthest she had ever been was to The City, and that had been with her father, Tomar, and Adara.

Stories she heard about the plains crept unbidden into her thoughts. Someone once mentioned the great maned lions dwelled here. And hadn't she heard that camels attacked without warning? Nabella glanced around again. The camels were far away, and she could see no other threats. The only thing near her was a man on a takhi traveling in her direction. Nabella straightened her back. She caught a glimpse of her father far ahead. *I can do this, I'm alright.* But it wouldn't hurt to get a little closer. She increased her speed. Mooing their protest every now and then, the cattle trotted in front of her.

"Hey you! What're ya doin?"

Nabella jerked. She swung her gaze around and saw the man on the takhi was no man at all but a boy of fourteen or fifteen. A frown soured his face and his reddened skin crinkled spattered freckles as he scrunched his light brows.

"What do you mean?"

"Why are you runnin' the meat off of my father's cows?"

Nabella glanced at the cattle then the boy. "What? I haven't touched the cows."

"You keep pushin' them in front of you. They should be hangin' about, eatin' grass and chewin' their cuds. But no. Here comes a girl, and she keeps chasin' 'em and chasin' 'em. Dun you know? They wunt gain any weight that way. My father can't trade skinny cows for very much." He jabbed a hand in the air with the last word.

Nabella glanced at the cattle. They had settled heads down in the grass. "Oh. I'm sorry. Greetings?"

"Greetings. Do you bring any good news?" The boy relaxed as his herd went back to grazing, and they exchanged the customary welcome.

"What are you doin' out here by yourself anyway? I never saw a girl travel by herself before. You're jus askin' for trouble."

Nabella wasn't sure if she liked this boy or not. Would he make her go back or tell on her? She straightened her shoulders. "I am going…"

The boy waited. She looked toward her father again. Did she have to tell yet another lie? No. She probably would never see this boy again. Nabella lifted her chin and took a deep breath. "I'm going to see Shem."

"Shem? From the ol' world?"

"Yes."

Loud laughter spilled out as he rocked back and forth holding his stomach.

"Stop it." She stomped her foot. "What's so funny anyways?"

"Jus how far you think you'll get? A girl, travelin' alone? The first man you come across will send you right back home."

Nabella clutched a fold in her jupe. "Well then, I'll just avoid men."

"Fat cow chance of that. Look around. People can see you from a long way off. 'Sides, you'll never get to see Shem. Everyone wants to see him. They would never let a girl go by herself to see any of the ancient ones."

The boy spoke the truth. Why hadn't she thought of these things earlier? Her foot tapped the ground. Somehow she had to think of something. Squinting, she looked around; her eyes finally came to rest on the boy. "I'll trade you."

"For what? What do you have?"

Nabella shrugged her journey sack off and set it on the ground. "Five days worth of food. Good food. Bread, hummus, honey, lentils, nuts, olive oi—"

"Olive oil! You must come from the groves." The boy waved his hand back the way she had come.

"There's also ground pistachio butter, dried fish seasoned in rosemary, salt, pepper …"

The boy dismounted and peered into her sack. He licked his lips then looked at her with narrowed eyes. "What do you want?"

"Your hat and your clothes."

"What?"

"You heard me, all this for your hat and your tunic and pants."

"You just want my clothes?"

"And your silence."

"You want to dress like me?"

Nabella propped her hands on her hips. "No, I just want to look like a boy. And you're going to help me."

Five

Nimrod: he began to be a mighty one in the earth.

Genesis 10:8b

Ra'anel ambled along the main thoroughfare of The City. Euphoria lingered from worshiping the animal deities earlier this morning. He had beseeched the gods to intercede on his behalf while laying out sacrifice after sacrifice brought in by the people. His fingers twitched at the thought and a familiar power surged through him. Ra'anel clasped his hands behind his back, best to contain himself amongst the commoners.

The deities' powers would help him convince Jokaan and Gideon to obtain shops. If he could persuade these two, the rest of that tiny faction would collapse. There would be no more threat. Ever. All the people of the world would be under his...well, they would be under the control of the upper echelon of government. Ra'anel knew the truth. He would not want to challenge Cush, nor Nimrod for that matter.

The head celestial advisor strolled to the bridge, halting midway across. Icy blue eyes peered over the edge. The moving water mesmerized him. Some people still launched boats to haul their goods from one bank to the other. Ra'anel sniffed and peered down the length of the bridge. Intelligent people used this over-the-water roadway. He had to admit even he was surprised at how well then oxen pulling carts took to the bridge.

Nimrod had forced his takhi across the first time. He whipped the steed unmercifully until it crashed across in a barely contained frenzy. The young man had laughed when he reached the other side and drove his stallion across again and again. *Those dumb animals must see the hoof prints. That's why they are going across so easily.*

The thin man turned toward the business section celestial robes flowing behind him. The beautiful Hall of Records, near its final stages of completion, caught his eye. Ra'anel nodded approval; it already contained important records inscribed on tablets, cones and parchments.

He perused the streets that surrounded the two-story building. From his vantage point he could see the business section had increased. Even the marketplace where vendors set their carts full of seasonal foods bustled.

A rumble in his stomach sent Ra'anel in the direction of a baker's cart. Vendors turned away when he neared. His upper lip curled but he quickly pulled it under control. He knew why these people turned from him. They didn't want to give him the food tariff. The vendors treated him like he stole their goods. Fools! Didn't they realize that because of him they had such lucrative businesses? They could be scattered by now, left to scrape a living off the land and be devoured by wild beasts if it weren't for him. They should thank him, no, bow down to him and... *Well look who's here.*

Gideon ambled around a cart full of melons. Ra'anel threw a glance skyward. The spirits must have guided the farmer here. Hunger forgotten, the head advisor suppressed a smile extending his stride to catch the man.

"Gideon. What good news do you bring that you returned so soon, hmm?" Ra'anel smothered a snicker when Gideon started at the sound of his voice. The man eyeballed Ra'anel. The advisor tried to straighten his back but the permanent hunch prevented it. *What is Gideon thinking, why does he stare at me?*

At last Gideon spoke. "Greetings, Ra'anel. I have good news. I have been thinking. I would like to look at some of the shops you spoke of. If they are in the right spot, I might consider bringing my business here."

Ra'anel recognized the carefully constructed words and saw right through them. Gideon wanted a shop. *Ahh, the gods are with me. I'll be able to ask a high bargain.* "That is good news. Come, there are still several available that you may be interested in." Ra'anel took him to the less desirable areas first and named his charge. Gideon's russet features creased, and he shook his head in displeasure.

"Think about it. These buildings are cool year round, just like your wine cellars. You can store grapes here for several weeks before they go bad. And your wine would last here quite well, hmmm?" Ra'anel let his words sink in. "Supplying the temple with wine and grapes is but a small price. And I know you have wine you still need to trade out before it goes bad. By giving it to the temple, you will have lost nothing, yet gained a permanent place here."

Ra'anel studied Gideon. He knew the man to be shrewd but nevertheless still a simple farmer. He brushed past the man. *Now I can draw him in.* He led Gideon to the main street just down from the Hall of Records.

"As you can see this is our best location. There are several people considering this site already."

"Who?"

"A tanner, a weaver, and a scribe. But I would prefer you moved in here. The wine industry is well, more prestigious, shall we say?"

"Prestigious?"

"The tanner would have this whole area smelling like dead animals. How much better, sweet grapes?"

"What do you want for it?"

The barter went on for a while until Gideon made his final move. Surprised the man had the nerve to bargain so low, Ra'anel realized he could squeeze the farmer no more. The celestial advisor agreed knowing in the end he would have the better deal. With a kiss on each cheek Gideon placed a small satchel of salt into Ra'anel's hand to seal the agreement.

The advisor turned on his heel and slipped the satchel into a fold of his robe. Ra'anel sneered. He had them. With Gideon anchored in The City, Jokaan would be close behind.

The celestial advisor strode past the Hall of Records. He swiveled his head at the sound of pounding feet. Cush charged down the twelve terraced steps heading in the opposite direction.

"Cush!"

The man halted, his dark face souring as he turned. Ra'anel's eyes narrowed. Why did he put up with this man's insolence? *Because he could do away with me without flinching a muscle.* Cush continued to march forward and the advisor scurried to catch up. He tried to lengthen his stride to match the larger man's, but even so Cush had to slow down. Ra'anel watched the scowl deepen across the man's face. The advisor tried to stifle his irritation. *Another mark against me.*

"I have good news, but if you are too busy to listen, I will inform the other council members first."

Cush's arrogant laugh ended in a snort. "Do you think that would bother me? Go ahead."

Ra'anel had a mind to do just that but changed it when he eyed the man. He wanted to be on Cush's best side.

"I have just struck a bargain with Gideon. He now has a shop here." Ra'anel gloated as he dangled the bag of salt. It had been a personal victory for him. Cush slowed his pace and glanced sideways at Ra'anel.

"What made him change his mind?"

"Hmm, several things." Ra'anel intended his pious tone to put Cush in his place. "His competitors already have two shops here. He was losing business."

"And…"

"And his son is soon to wed. He wants a secure future and, of course, I prayed to the gods this very morning that he would change his mind."

Cush ignored Ra'anel's jab rubbing his hands together. "Jokaan is next."

"Precisely." Ra'anel couldn't help but wonder at the venom in Cush's voice.

***

Cush sprinted up the steep temple steps two at a time. With a final grunt he crested the top terrace gasping for air. *I'm getting out of shape.* If he didn't watch it he'd start to whine and complain like Ra'anel. *Still, I'm not as young as I used to be.* Cush pushed the thought away and peered at the paintings of animal deities. It made sense they were gods. Maybe not all-powerful like the Creator God, but he couldn't deny these supernatural beings had an influence in his life. He could *feel* their presence.

Heavy footsteps echoed in the temple. Cush spun around surprised the man had been so close behind him. Nimrod strode forward, a thick leather shield hung snug against his broad chest and back. A long dagger swung at his side and tapped in rhythm to each step. A youth clad in similar breastplate paused outside the entrance, javelin pack strapped to his back. Two men with large, bronze-tipped spears brought up the rear. Cush felt his chest tighten. Nimrod had changed. The man, along with his followers, presented a strong presence. The way he carried himself reeked of over confidence. Cush fought to keep his face expressionless. *He's not even out of breath.* "Greetings, Nimrod. What good news do you bring?"

The man stood silent.

"You have no need of such measures in The City, Nimrod." Cush jutted his chin toward the men. "No one will attack you here. The wildest beast within these walls is your stallion."

Nimrod stared until Cush looked away. He gritted his teeth. Despite Nimrod's young age the man unnerved him.

"I never know when and where I will be called," Nimrod's voice, clipped and hard, echoed throughout the entrance way. "I only came into The City this morning."

"Did you slay the maned lions bothering the shepherds to the north? That's where you went, right?"

"The great male's hide is now at the tanner's. It will make a grand rug for the palace."

"Not a scratch, I see."

Nimrod looked at him like he had lost his mind. "Why would there be? Lions are no challenge. I'm about to hunt an enormous *kabiyr* tanniyn in the eastern mountains."

"Past the Tigris River?"

"Yes."

"Why do you go so far?" Cush sighed.

"If I don't, they will come here. Once I cleared out this area, it made room for others to move in."

Cush rubbed his temples and nodded.

"Why did you call me here?"

The dark man could not detect any emotion is Nimrod's voice.

"Do you see these new paintings? Ra'anel claims they are spirits of gods."

"They are." Nimrod's tone remained flat, uninviting.

Cush shook his head. "You think they're real then?"

"They are."

"Well, I concede there must be some power emanating from them. Gideon now has a shop in town."

Nimrod crossed leather wrapped forearms over his chest, feet splayed. His lip curled upward. "Jokaan is the last. I will pay him a visit."

"No. *I* will do that. You can come with me if you want, but I'll do the talking."

Nimrod laughed, black eyes hollow. "You do that and if he doesn't change his mind, then I will pay him a visit."

Cush's voice hardened. "Don't be another Cain, Nimrod. It would be foolish to slay him or any of his family."

In an instant hardness replaced the flat look in Nimrod's eyes. "Do you think of me as a fool? Is that it... *Cush*?"

The dark man inhaled and clenched his hands. The insult slapped him across the face. At last he shook his head, he did not want to challenge the man. At least not here, not yet. "A fool? No. Just unpredictable."

"I'll take that as a compliment."

Cush paced then turned to Nimrod. "Jokaan is not the last. There are still the patriarchs."

"Let their God deal with them. I say make them move away, then see just how long they last."

"You would do this even to Noah?"

"Noah can move here, have a comfortable life. If he wants to be a stubborn old fool, that's on his head."

"He's your great grandfather." The big man felt a rush of uneasiness. Such total disregard for any who had come from the Old World just might wake up the Creator God. Or bring His wrath.

As if Nimrod could read his mind he mocked. "Let his God speak again, if He can. Even Noah doesn't hear from Him."

"You and Ra'anel both play with fire."

"When have you known me to get burned?" Nimrod stared at Cush with dark eyes.

"I haven't, Nimrod, but that doesn't mean your time isn't coming. This blatant disregard for the ancients just might make it come sooner."

Nimrod snorted. "I have a tanniyn to kill." He strode from the room, the boy and men on his heels.

Cush watched the man march down the long staircase. A ripple of voices rose from the people below. He strained to catch their words. Praises for Nimrod's hunting skills drifted up to the terrace. A sudden chill crept through Cush, and he rubbed a hand across his brow.

Nimrod is turning into a dangerous man.

Six

Also for Adam and his wife the Lord God made tunics of skin, and clothed them.
Genesis 3:21 (NIV)

"Turn around," Nabella commanded. She took the dagger and sliced a wide swath from her jupe. With a grin she tossed it at the boy so he could fashion a wrap for himself.

"Here, hold the reins."

Nabella took the ropes and turned away.

"And don't peek." He walked to the other side of his takhi.

She squatted to get out of the boy's view and surveyed the olive groves. How inviting they looked.

Thwack!

The boy's tunic and pants hit her head, his hat flopped to the ground next to her.

"Don't turn around." Nabella yanked her tunic off and unwrapped the remainder of the jupe. His pants hung loose around her waist. A small gasp escaped when she wriggled the tunic over her head. Whew they smelled! She wrinkled her nose and held her breath.

Nabella gritted her teeth, secured her sash around the tunic then slipped the dagger in its place.

She placed her discarded tunic on the remnant of her jupe then tied the four corners into a bundle.

"How do I look?" Nabella stuffed the last of her fine, mid-back length hair under the boy's hat.

"Well, the sash looks kind of girly bu—"

"How would you wear it?"

"Take the sash off."

He went to his takhi and cut a length of rope then hung it low around her hips. With a skilled twist, he attached the dagger's sheath and stepped back.

"That's better. Pull the end of the tunic out of the rope, make it look baggy."

Nabella did as she had been told. "Do I look like a boy?"

"Sort of."

"What's wrong now?"

"You're too clean."

"What?"

"Look at my clothes. Do they look clean?"

"No, and they smell too."

The boy looked down crimson creeping up his cheeks, a near match to the color of his hair. "I didn't mean..."

"It's alright," He mumbled, "Jus stop by the next wash and rub some dirt or mud on your face and hands."

"Good idea, thanks."

"Sure, bye. Thanks for the food." He snatched the reins from Nabella's hand and jumped onto the takhi.

Nabella turned and took a few steps in the direction she saw the tiny figures of Jokaan and Tomar.

"Stop!"

The boy's voice rattled her."What now?"

"A boy doesn't walk like *that.*"

Nabella gritted her teeth. With a hand on her hip, she made a slow deliberate turn. "Just how does a boy walk?"

"Well, not like that." He hopped off the takhi. "And boys don't do this." He shifted his weight and put a hand on his hip.

Nabella giggled. "I guess not."

"A boy walks straight. See, like this."

At last she strode around with the boy's approval.

"Yes. You might make it. Jus keep practicin'."

Nabella smiled. "Thank you."

He grinned and once again swung onto the takhi's back. "Hey are you gonna come back this way?"

"Yes. Well, I think so."

"If you do, tell me what happened."

"I will. Are you going to be right here?"

"Well, I figure you'll be back this way in about a week. Yes, I'll be back by here then. I don go any farther then where I can't see the tower."

Nabella glanced toward The City then lifted her hand in farewell. She took a few concentrated steps on her new walk then stopped.

"Hey, you!"

"Name's Abel."

"Oh. Mine's Nabella. Listen. I saw, that is, there's an Azhdaha hanging around here somewhere."

"An Azhdaha here? I thought they hung out by the river."

"Well, this one has a wounded back leg. It's not very old and only about as big as a takhi. I think it's finding dead things to eat."

Abel nodded. "Come to think of it, the cows were really restless two nights ago."

Nabella swallowed and without thinking glanced at the orchard.

"Is that where you saw it?"

She shuddered at the memory and nodded. When Nabella turned back to Abel, his eyes scrutinized her. With a determined lift of her chin, she straightened tense shoulders.

"Just be careful."

Abel nodded once, "Likewise."

Nabella skirted around Abel's cows and headed out. At the first puddle she splattered muddy water on her face and dug hands into the soft ooze. She splashed some of the mud off her hands and arms then examined herself with satisfaction.

"I'm a boy," she murmured. Nabella studied the way she had come. The olive groves looked like a miniature line of trees, and Abel and his cows the size of small birds. She twisted around and could just make out her father and Tomar. *I better move closer, I don't want to lose sight of them.* She broke into a trot. *Is this how a boy jogs? I better not run when people are around.*

Nabella closed the distance and saw Jokaan and Tomar stop by a shepherd. She slowed heading toward the nearest tree-lined wash. Jokaan turned, waving a hand back the way he had come, and looked straight at her. Nabella held in a gasp. Instinct cried to fling herself into the grass, but she willed every muscle to remain still.

Walk like a boy, she commanded herself. Her father's gaze shifted forward without a second glance. Nabella forced herself to amble to the small stretch of wood. By the time she slipped under its canopy, her legs wobbled like a newborn calf. She sank to her knees hugging the trunk of the nearest tree. She could just see her father's head and shoulders above the grasslands. From the way his hands moved she knew he engaged in deep conversation.

It worked, her disguise had worked! Nabella heaved a sigh of relief. The corners of her mouth tugged upward as she settled onto the ground. The disguise and her ploy had fooled her father, if only from a distance. Still, what a good idea it had been. Confidence surged through her. She pulled herself to her feet and leaned against the tree, one foot on the trunk. Like a boy. Jokaan and Tomar turned from the shepherd and headed east once again.

The soft tinkle of a brook lured her in its direction. Nabella knelt, and submerged her face into the cool water then sucked in great gulps. She lifted her head, water dripped from her chin. With a swipe of the back of her hand, she wiped her mouth, just like a boy. Her stomach growled, and she glanced round. A wild grapevine meandered over the nearest bush. A quick glance at Jokaan and she gathered bunches of grapes, both dried and fresh then stuffed them into the makeshift sack. She swung it onto her back and tramped out of the wood. A tinge of sadness, or was it guilt, grabbed her heart. The grapes reminded her of Barukh. That's where she told everyone she would be. *Will he be mad at me?*

"Oh, Barukh, please don't be," she whispered.

With a sigh, Nabella trekked through the grass stuffing a handful of grapes into her mouth. Another glance ahead brought her to a standstill. No Jokaan or Tomar. She took several hesitant steps, her eyes darted in all directions. They had to be near. She squelched the urge to run and instead studied the horizon. Nothing. Her eyes rested on the shepherd. Perhaps he gave her father different directions. She would have to confront him.

Nabella's heart sank when she realized a man, not a boy, walked among the sheep. A very grungy man. Could she do this? Would her disguise be good enough? Well, if not, maybe this man would help her like Abel had. She concentrated on her movements. *I'm a boy, I'm a boy* Nabella repeated with each step. She lengthened her stride and paced toward the man.

He turned, and she almost halted mid-stride. Matted brown hair with eyes that matched glared at her.

"What do you want, boy?"

Nabella sank back on her heel. No formal greeting? She did not like this. *Act like a boy, act like a boy.* She cleared her throat and tried to lower her voice. "I have a message for the two men who just passed by. Which way did they go?"

"Information, everybody wants information! Well, it's going to cost you, just like it did them. What do you have in that pack?"

"Grapes, Kuya, you can have some if you want."

The man studied Nabella, one eye narrowing. "What else do you have in there?"

Nabella tried to think of what Abel would say. "Nothin'."

The man crossed his arms over his chest. What would Abel do now? Abel seemed brave, so she must be too. She took a step forward and tried her best to glare at the man.

"Look, do you want the grapes or not. I can find the men myself, it just would be easier if you told me."

The man raised an eyebrow. "Well, you don't have to get all huffy."

"I'm not. You're just mean, that's all." Nabella resisted the urge to place her hands on her hips and instead balled her fists the way she had seen her father do.

The shepherd looked her up and down. His eyes lingered an instant on her dagger.

A cold knot grew hard in her stomach. She shook her head. "Never mind. I'll find them myself."

"Ah-he. What's wrong with you? I know I'm a grouch after being out here alone for so long but what's your problem?"

With deliberate motions, Nabella crossed her arms over her chest in imitation of the man. He broke out in harsh laughter. "Go find them yourself. I don't need your grapes."

Nabella gritted her teeth and spun on her heel. She would just continue east unti—

A rough hand gripped her upper arm. Her feet flew out and she landed hard on her front. Broken stalks of grass poked into her mouth and nose. His foot pressed against her neck and she felt him pull at the pack. Nabella tried to turn, but he leaned more weight onto his foot and pinned her. A jagged rock jammed into her cheek. The crispness of crushed grass blades and dirt mingled with the foul stench of his body. Nabella arched her back when he tugged once more on her bundle. Her fingers clamped around the grip of the dagger. The man cursed, and she heard him draw his knife. Her breath came in ragged lungfuls.

"Grapes, nothing but grapes! And a girl's tunic?"

The shepherd shoved her over with his foot. Nabella lunged and remembered her father's instructions to slice upward. Her stomach churned when the blade dragged through the man's leg. He grunted and cussed. Grapes spewed everywhere. She rolled and sprung to her feet. But not before a solid kick caught her in the shoulder and staggered her backward. It almost dislodged her dagger. With a shock she realized the kick had been meant to do just that.

I am no match for this man. He weighs at least twice as much as me. Run! Nabella, vow to not run in front of anyone forgotten, snatched her sack and spun around. She didn't have to look to know he pursued her. Heavy breaths gave him away. She heard him lunge, and she darted to one side. An oath erupted. From the corner of her eye she saw the man charge past. Nabella darted in another direction flying across the ground, around a boulder and through the edge of his flock.

"Yah!" She waved her arms scattering the sheep.

Another oath. She heard him slow.

"Thanks for the grapes," his sneering laugh followed her. "And you run like a girl!"

"Like that's really going to bother me," she panted, slowing to a jog. For a while Nabella gave an occasional glance back. But the man remained with his sheep and on occasion brought his hand to his mouth. Nabella scowled, *there go my grapes.*

Her hand made its way to a hip. Nabella jerked her hand away and stomped for the nearest tree line. Once there, she sank to the ground. Her whole body shook. Eyes riveted on the blood covered dagger, she noticed for the first time red stains that colored her hand. With a gasp, she dropped the blade and rubbed her hand in the dirt. She spit and rubbed until most of the blood had come off. The dagger would have to wait for water, she had no more spit left. Legs drawn tight, she hunched over and blood rushed hot and furious to her head. Nabella's temples pounded. That horrible, ugly man had stolen her food. And would have probably killed her too, just for her knife. She saw how he had looked at her mother's dagger. Her dagger. And it had just saved her life. *Oh Father, this dagger has already fared me better than it did Mother.*

Nabella drew in a ragged breath fighting tears. She had to pull herself together. A glance at the sky impelled her to place a fist at arm's length, little finger and thumb spread as far as they would go. Nabella adjusted her thumb over the sun and projected its course to the western horizon. *Oh no! The sun sets in half a hand-span and I've only traveled a half day's journey.* She jerked the corners of the makeshift bundle back together, thankful the tunic had not fallen out.

Nabella scrambled to her feet, the vast emptiness of the grasslands stared back at her. A stab of pressure wrapped around her head like a tight band. Where could her father and Tomar be? She had imagined a fireless camp close to his, so close she could hear the men when they spoke. If anything happened, Jokaan would be right there. Granted, her disguise would be discovered, but at least she would be alive.

Again Nabella scanned the plain that stretched in front of her. In the far distance a thick line of wood extended across the length of the eastern horizon.

That has to be the Little Euphrates. If it is, and this far away from the great Euphrates, I must be way to the south of The City. I know the two rivers come together north of The City walls so I better angle this way. Nabella skirted a pile of dung and turned until the late sun caressed her back and left shoulder. The bundle bumped against the opposite shoulder, a light thump that kept rhythm with her stride.

Old, shallow river basins dotted the terrain. Nabella clutched at her pants and stood on her toes. Maybe her father had made a camp in one of these. That would explain why she couldn't see them.

The question was, should she take the risk and try to find her father or go back to the relative safety of the little grove. After a slight hesitation Nabella gave a determined nod. Better to be near Jokaan and Tomar.

Her shadow stretched out long in front of her by the time she reached the third shallow dip. She lay on the grass and wiggled her way to the edge. Only thick clumps of grass waved their heads at her. Nabella's heart sank. She clambered down then up the opposite side just in time to watch the sun's crest sink below the horizon. Not too far ahead, the low basin meandered, cutting off any view of what it contained.

Again, Nabella wondered should she go back to the trees? She hated to backtrack so far, it would only put her closer to that awful shepherd. What if her father decided to hurry? Would she ever be able to catch up?

A takhi whinnied. Nabella caught her breath. Could that be the old mare? It sounded pretty far off. Had they traveled that far already? She stood on the edge of the shallow wash looking around. Nothing offered assurance. *Well, I don't know whose takhi whinnied, but it's better than this.*

A loud growl rumbled from her stomach. She shrugged the bundle off her shoulder and groped through the material. Nothing. Not even a lone raisin. Nabella's shoulders sagged, and she plodded in the direction of the takhi. But the threat of impending darkness pushed her into a good clip along top of the basin. A long, shrill whinny floated across the basin up ahead. She scrambled down the small slope and with each cautious step peered around every bend. Twilight closed in, yet Nabella still didn't smell smoke or hear voices. Should she call out?

Suddenly a hoof clipped a rock. A jubilant grin broke across Nabella's face. She found them! *All right, stop. I'm not going to risk my cover now.*

She worked her way up the slope, each step placed with silent care. At the top she wriggled amongst the grass worming forward, thankful for the noisy takhi. Then she peered into the dip.

Disappointment sank deep. Below, a group of eight wild takhis had gathered around the small mud hole to settle in for the night. Several stood already sleeping, heads hung low, stiff manes standing straight up with white muzzles a cubic from the ground. A tawny foal nuzzled its mother' white underside. Another dun female and her youngster lay next to each other. One stood ankle deep in the water drinking, black legs with banding just above the knees dripping wet. Some had a small ring of white around their almond-shaped eyes while in others the darker tans of their necks and large heads came right up to their black eyes. But all had a black strip down their back going from their coal colored manes to their ebony tails. Nabella's head dropped until her forehead rested on her hands. Tears threatened to spill.

What do I do now? Nabella began to elbow her way back. The takhi in the water hole lifted its head and stared in her direction, water dripping from its muzzle, black nostrils flaring. She froze. It stared for a long time. At last, the stallion turned and sloshed from the puddle. With one last glance in her direction, it settled next to the mother and foal.

With silent stealth Nabella elbowed her way back and rolled over. The air had cooled and caressed her with the relief of night. Stars twinkled in the darkened eastern sky. She twisted her head. Muted streaks of orange and red painted the western horizon. With a sigh, she realized the takhis offered some protection. If nothing else they would warn her if danger approached.

Careful to not make noise she removed her sack and pulled out the tunic. She slid the hat off and placed the tunic inside for a makeshift pillow. With the remains of the jupe spread near to pull over when the temperature dropped, she forced herself to relax. All seemed quiet except for the takhis' little shuffles and snorts that floated across the night air. Nabella yawned and a sense of peace settled over her. Fingers reached for her jupe and caught on the rip inflicted by the Azhdaha. Her hand froze and eyes flew wide. The Azhdaha! What if it followed her here? Nabella jerked her head up, eyes darting into the dusk.

After a few sharp breaths she forced her hands to unclench and inhaled deeply. Heavy, steady breathing drifted from the herd. The tension drained from her muscles, yes the takhis would alert her of any trouble. And she now had experience with the dagger. When she encountered the Azhdaha she barely had a clue how to use the weapon. Since then Jokaan taught her good techniques, and she had practiced. Her hand tightened around the dagger hilt. She'd already put it to good use. But could she do so against a large and strong predator?

I need to think of something else like, Barukh. Nabella sniffed. Maybe she should have asked him to come with her. No. He would never have agreed. Betrothed, they could not travel together without a chaperone. But if she had approached him with her disguise, they wouldn't be traveling as a man and a woman. Except she didn't have that idea until she met Abel. What would

Barukh think of her now? She felt heat rise to her cheeks. She would embarrass him. *Alright, Nabella, this is the last of your crazy schemes. After this is over, I must learn to settle down and become a good wife.*

Relief washed over her at the decision. But a small part of her cried no—don't snuff me out yet, or ever.

Seven

Thou shalt tread upon the lion and adder: the young lion and the dragon (dinosaur) shalt thou trample under feet. (Emphasis the author's.)

Psalm 91:13

Cush's eyes riveted on the man bent over the fresh tracks. Nimrod leaned this way and that to get a better angle from the early morning shadows. He motioned for the fourteen-year-old to come close and pointed to the ground. It seemed Nimrod allowed this youth to be near him more and more. Maybe he reminded Nimrod of his deceased son, so Cush could understand why the youngster came along. But why had Nimrod insisted Cush come?

"I have never seen tracks this big before," the man had exclaimed, eyes agleam.

Cush originally intended to refuse for he had other plans that day, including a most important visit to Jokaan. But in afterthought he decided it wise to put that off for a day or two. It would not do to offend Nimrod, and Cush feared his refusal would do so. Better to stay on the man's good side for Nimrod now took a group of his most trusted men with him everywhere he went. And it seemed the number of his followers grew day by day. On this foray alone, he had six plus the youth, and several more waited at the head of the canyon with the oxen and wagons.

Cush had not hunted for the last twenty years and could feel it in every muscle. While he had been busy with construction of The City, Nimrod endeavored to make a name for himself. Oh yes, the dark man was well aware of what the people had begun to call Nimrod: the mighty hunter. He felt a surge of envy course through his veins. There had been a time when Nimrod looked up to him. But now, he did not even acknowledge what they had shared in the past.

Cush had been surprised when Nimrod invited him to come along on such a monumental hunt. And this time he really didn't have an excuse to back out. Both the tower and the bridge were finished, and many buildings had been constructed. He suspected there would always be houses and businesses in construction, at least as long as the people multiplied. Cush gave a soft snort. The masses seemed to have no problem with that command of God's.

Nimrod shifted his weight fastening raven black eyes on him. Cush blinked. Had he heard him snort? Impossible! It had barely been more than an exhaled breath. In one lithe motion Nimrod straightened and pointed up the gully. With swift and silent movements he strode forward. Cush admired the man's hunting abilities. A fair huntsman himself at one time, he realized he could not match Nimrod. That man took it to the extreme, as if he had an unquenchable thirst to pit himself against the most dangerous and largest of predators.

But the people loved it. Whenever an outpost, or farmer, or herdsmen had trouble it was inevitable they called for Nimrod. On many occasions Cush had witnessed Nimrod prepare to respond. The man devoured the attention. And he and his band of loyal cohorts were always well received, treated with respect, far above what the average visitor could expect. It bordered on worship.

With a slight shake of his head Cush glanced at the tracks and made his way up the gully. The tracks *were* huge. And not of an animal he recognized either. Instinct drove a hand to tighten around his spear. He felt cold sweat bead across his forehead.

And this is the other reason I quit hunting. He highly preferred not to dangle his life in front of some unknown, fierce creature. He shouldn't feel envy toward Nimrod at all, the man deserved every bit of respect and lavishness the people gave him.

Cush flexed his arm and chest muscles then paced himself behind Nimrod. By far the oldest in the hunting party, he was still in his prime. Yet the younger generations seemed to treat him like an elder. He clenched his teeth. Maybe it didn't have anything to do with his age. It could be they acted with reserve because of his work, and his position in the government. But somehow it felt different. More like an outcast. Pushed away from Nimrod's inner circle.

Well, so be it. Cush wasn't sure he wanted to be a part of that anyway. But this, this hunt, could turn into something big. Maybe the people would associate his name with Nimrod's growing force if the hunt went well. With a quick glance at Nimrod, the big man forced himself to pay attention.

Nimrod paused and sniffed the air. A slight breeze stirred and Cush watched it push aside the man's wavy black hair. Thick neck and shoulder muscles bulged. He had stripped to the waist and commanded the boy to do the same. At Cush's silent question Nimrod had grunted a reply. Less for the tanniyn to grab.

Nimrod pointed his bronze-tipped spear to the other side of the gully and jutted his chin at two men. They responded at once and melted into the thick brush. In one breath it seemed like they had never been. He had to admit, Nimrod's men were well trained.

The gully narrowed and the sides inclined into a harsh slant. A small trickle of water meandered along the bottom. Nimrod made a slight gesture with his head and two more men came close. Several quick hand signals were exchanged and the men began to climb up the steep slope on the near side of the gully. Once again they disappeared after a few strides. Cush strained his ears, yet could not detect anything out of the ordinary. He watched his every step so he would make no noise.

Nimrod pushed forward. When next Cush glanced up he saw him a good distance ahead. The dark man lengthened his stride. Too late he felt a twig under his sandal just before his full weight pressed on it. If he tried to shift his weight now he would crash through the underbrush in an attempt to regain his balance. There was nothing he could do.

Snap!

A quail squawked to his right then flew away. Cush swore a silent oath. His eyes snapped to Nimrod. The man glared and held his hand out, fingertips up. Everyone froze in place. Though his muscles remained tense, Cush forced his mind to relax in hopes it would sharpen his rusty senses.

After a while he heard murmured chirps and caught glimpses of the remnant covey of quail that zigzagged up the slope. Little feet blurred with their swift retreat. A half a hand-span passed. Still Nimrod waited. Cush refused to twitch a muscle, he would not make the first move. A fly buzzed and landed on the corner of his eye. He blinked. It flew away and came back seeking dissolved salts. An intense itch prickled his skin where it landed. Cush squeezed his eyes shut to chase it away. The fly returned. Again and again he battled with the fly but the deeper battle came from within. It took everything in him to keep from swatting the bothersome bug. Cush flicked his eyes toward Nimrod in desperate hope the man would soon move on.

They were gone. Cush cursed under his breath and squashed the fly. All right, he would just have to steal forward as fast as his tarnished skills would allow. A little slower pace would ensure the integrity of the hunting party. He wasn't all that keen to run into this beast anyway. It didn't bother him in the least to be the last one. Cush advanced, flicking his eyes between the tracks on the ground and ahead for Nimrod.

The trickle of water had become a small creek by the time he came to a place where the vegetation narrowed. Cush turned sideways to slide through the branches. He lifted his foot, but a hard hand seized him by the shoulder. His gaze snapped to the right. Nimrod stood a half body length from him. Only the youth remained by his side. The last two men must have already been dismissed. Cush narrowed his eyes. How had Nimrod melted into the brush like that? And the youth, he moved with such skill too.

Nimrod leaned close, his voice a bare whisper, "It rests in that cave."

The big man followed Nimrod's gaze. The gully had come to an end and through the leaves he could just make out a darkened hollow halfway up the slope. A small waterfall cascaded next to the cave. He studied the tanniyn's shelter for any sign it resided there now.

Nimrod gestured for him and the boy to wait then slipped into the thick brush. Cush saw him once, twice then no more. He tried to search the man out, but Nimrod had vanished. *Wait, didn't that branch just move by the cave?* The youth lean forward. Sure enough, Nimrod appeared then melted into the cave. Ten breaths later he reappeared.

With a tap the youth gestured to let him by. Jaw clenched and eyes narrowed the boy moved with the stealth of a caracal and soon disappeared. Cush gritted his teeth. What now? Should he follow? He stared at the cave. No, he preferred to wait right here.

There! The boy scrambled up the last bit to the cave without rolling a single stone from its place. Nimrod grabbed the youth's arm and yanked him up onto the shelf. Nimrod signaled with his hands then the two faded into the dark opening. *He's taking the boy into the kabyir's lair? Fool!* Did Nimrod do that to ensure his own safety?

A great roar cut into Cush's morbid thoughts. He fully expected to see Nimrod come out alone. The dark man's stomach muscles tightened, and his jaw clenched again.

A flash of movement appeared at the mouth of the cave then just as quickly receded. Suddenly the empty-handed youth burst through the opening and dove to the side into brush that grew along the edge of the shelf. A breath later Nimrod leapt from the cave, rolled to the side, and bound to his feet. Furious roars and thrashes spewed from within the tanniyn's lair. Cush jerked his spear arm into a throw position.

One of Nimrod's men appeared above the cave tossing his leader two more spears. He snatched them midair with one hand. Abruptly the tanniyn staggered from the cave. Cush stared in horror and amazement. It had to be the largest animal he ever laid eyes on. The tanniyn swung its thick heavy head to and fro. Again and again it snapped bone-crushing jaws roaring in pain and furry. His mouth dropped open. He blinked to make sure he saw correctly. Each eye had been impaled with a spear.

The creature managed to stay on its two enormous hind legs, balanced by a thick hulking tail, while it tried to grab at the embedded spears. Its front legs were so short they couldn't even reach its mouth let alone its eyes; tiny, two fingered hands useless. This had to be the most grotesque creature he had ever seen.

All at once the mighty hunter sprang forward and thrust two spears into the animal's chest. The tanniyn gave another great roar and blindly charged forward. Cush's eyes flew wide, and he drew in a sharp breath. After the thrusts, Nimrod ran between the animal's hind legs barely dodging its massive thrashing tail. The men rushed in. They slashed and jabbed at the tanniyn's hind legs attempting to hamstring the great animal.

The creature plowed ahead for a few blind steps then lost its balance. It toppled forward, its body landing on the slope below the shelf. The monster rolled faster and faster down the incline. Too late, Cush realized its force would carry it right on top of him. He tore to the side of the gully throwing a desperate glance over his shoulder. Its enormous head crash toward him.

With a yelp, he bound to the side but lost his foothold and slammed to his knees. His heart surged and throat tightened. He pushed his legs. It felt like they moved through mud. At last one foot landed flat and he gave a mighty heave. The crash of the tanniyn hovered above him and with a final thud the beast rolled to a stop. Cush twisted but the heavy weight slammed him onto his back. Its massive head crushed into the ground. Wild-eyed, the big man yanked at his legs trapped under the animal's shoulder.

Whack!

The ferocious kabiyr's jaw hit Cush's body. It swung its head away as it thrashed. Winded, Cush managed to yank his dagger free. Then the head, almost the size of his own body, bore down on him once again. He sliced at the flesh. But his blade could not penetrate the tough skin. Massive teeth gnashed less than a cubit from him.

"Nimrod!" He bellowed wrenching and twisting in a desperate move to free his legs. At the same time he hacked at the animal's neck to no avail.

Suddenly Nimrod appeared on top of the tanniyn's neck, long dagger raised. He plunged again and again into the creature's throat. The beast roared and writhed.

Abruptly pain ripped through Cush's side. He swore. The monster's enormous hind claw slashed through his muscles.

In the same instant blood from the tanniyn's neck spurted like the waterfall. It gushed over and pooled around him. He gasped for air as the stream of warm liquid engulfed him. Cush shoved against the flow straining to move out of its torrent. Ducking his head into the small space under his raised arm he gasped for air. Then a torrent of liquid caught in his throat. *I'm going to drown!* Coughing, black dots floated before his eyes.

All at once the flow parted around his head, and he felt hands grab his shirt. In a dull stupor he realized someone's body blocked the waterfall of blood. Between wrenching coughs he sucked in a great lungful of air.

At last a deep gurgled groan erupted from the tanniyn. It gave one more trembling convulsion and arched its back. Suddenly Cush's legs were free. He yanked them to his body and rolled to the side. Then staggering upright he latched onto the man who had helped him. Cush jerked when he realized by the small frame, it was the youth. The two slipped their way through slimy red pools making their way from the bloody tanniyn.

Once they reached dry ground Cush stumbled a few more steps, collapsed dragging the young man with him. He lay back, sucked in great jagged breaths then coughed out the last remnants of the animal's blood. A glance at the beast satisfied his fear; it lay dead. He could hear the youth's heavy breaths next to him and turned. Covered from head to foot in blood he made a dreadful sight. Cush glanced at his own body and realized he looked the same.

His lip twitched and a small chuckle escaped. His shoulders shook when he tried to hold back the pent up emotions. At last he gave up, threw his head back and exploded into a full-bodied, hearty laugh. Next to him light laughter burst from the youth. Cush sat and held his stomach, tears pouring from his eyes. He wasn't sure if they were from laughing or crying. And he didn't care. He was alive.

Cush slapped the youth on the back. "Let's find that spring and get this tanniyn's blood off of us." The boy nodded and the two headed up the gully on an upper path which led directly to a small shelf that protruded under the cascading water. Cush glanced at the small pool two cubits below. Too small, better to go under the falls. With a nod he let the youth go first and heard him suck in his breath.

He chuckled then said, "Cold?"

"Y-yes."

Cush stood as far from the frigid stream as he could and helped the youth scrub his hair. He watched the blood rinse from his own arms and hands. It *was* cold. The boy scrambled to the side, and shook water from his dark hair. Cush leaned forward and stuck his head under the water. Determined not to show his discomfort, he gritted his teeth. When he stepped into the frigid water all the way, he couldn't help but let a grunt escape as it ran over the wound in his side. As the beast's blood washed away, he saw his own blood seep from the gash.

"You're hurt!"

"It clawed me with its back foot just before you came."

"Then I wish I had been there sooner so I could have taken the blow for you."

The big man started. "Why would you want to do that? You don't even know me."

"To save you the pain, Rayis."

Cush felt an unfamiliar rush of warmth run through him.

"Besides," the youth continued, "I'm younger. Nimrod always tells me I heal faster because I'm younger."

Cush wasn't sure if he should be offended or not. He decided the boy had spoken in innocence and scrubbed the last of the blood off in silence. He came from under the waterfall and looked the youth in the eyes. "Did Nimrod also tell you to go into the tanniyn's lair?"

"No, Rayis. When he first told us his plan, I volunteered to go with him. So did some of the other men but Nimrod chose me. He said it would be good for me to come with him. Then I could prove myself."

Cush studied the sturdy youth before him. He could see by the youngster's eager face, he spoke the truth. "What's your name?"

"Terach."

"Well, Terach, I think you have proven yourself. You don't need to go on any more of Nimrod's rash schemes. He is very powerful. Not that you won't be likewise someday, but you are still growing right now. Let him take the risks, wait until you are a man."

"I'm almost a man."

Cush covered the youth's shoulder with his large hand and they began the trek back to the dead monster. "Yes you are, but you still have some growing to do. You don't want to end your life before it's even begun."

"I won't, Rayis. Nimrod teaches me a lot of things."

"Be careful of some of the things he teaches. I don't always agree with his line of thinking."

Terach stiffened under his hand. "Not that he doesn't have a lot to offer…just don't give up thinking for yourself."

The youth relaxed. "I won't."

"What do your parents think of you apprenticing under Nimrod?"

A slight hesitation, then, "They're dead, Rayis."

"No older siblings or someone to take care of you?"

"One brother."

Was that a sour note in Terach's voice?

"What does he say about your endeavors?"

"Oh, he's fine with it, maybe even glad."

Cush sensed the youth's discomfort and let his hand slip off Terach's shoulder. "Let's see what Nimrod wants with this great tanniyn. And thank you, Terach, for saving my life."

Eight

And Adah bare Jabal: he was the father of such as dwell in tents, and of such as have cattle.

Genesis 4:20 (KJV)

The warmth on Nabella's face felt good, soft and comforting. She blinked and turned her head toward the heat. *Ahhh, the sun.* She stretched and a hard lump pressed against her thigh. Nabella shifted, sat up then ran her hand down her thigh and fingered the dagger. Why did she wear her dagger to bed? Why did she lay on the ground outside? She kneaded her temple to rub the fog from her mind. With a rush memories filled her—following her father, Abel, the horrible man, then her camp with the takhis.

And the sun had ready climbed one hand-span over the horizon. Oh no, her father would be long gone. She rolled to her knees, threw the tunic onto the middle of her torn jupe, snatched the corners and tied them together then jammed her hair under the hat. This time Nabella didn't care if the takhis spooked, and she bound to her feet.

"Ouch," Nabella gritted her teeth. She'd forgotten her calf still ached in the mornings from the old Azhdaha wound. Teeth still clamped tight, she ignored the stiff muscle and limped to the edge of the basin.

But the little herd had already meandered away. A flash of heat coursed through her. How dare those takhis just up and leave! What were they thinking? Nabella stared at the empty mud hole then burst into laughter. What was *she* thinking. She scrambled down the bank and took off her sandals. A gasp escaped when her feet sunk into the cold mud. She waded to the middle, scooped a handful of the semi clear liquid and drank deeply. She brought a final scoop to her face with the intent to wash off the grime then remembered her disguise. A boy, a dirty boy. She let the water slip through her fingers and stared longingly at the pond. Her eyes roved back to her hands. Dried blood still lingered on one wrist.

Her stomach roiled. She scrubbed at the stain until it disappeared then straightened and pulled the dagger out of its sheath. Nabella lowered it into the pond and rubbed the knife, mindful of the sharp edges, until the water became crimson. With a twist, Nabella dunked it a final time where the water had not been tainted. It was one thing to cut an animal that would provide meat, and quite another to cut a man for protection. Nabella shivered despite the warmth of the morning sun on her back.

"Well, if I can't be clean at least you can." She spoke to the dagger with affection. For the first time Nabella understood why men were so possessive of their weapons. Sometimes even giving them names. *Should I give you a name?*

A grumble in her stomach reminded her of more vital things. She waded to the bank, tied her sandals back on wet feet and scurried to the top of the basin. There she paused long enough to scan the horizon. Perhaps a few grapevines or sumac bushes would be nearby. Instead in the distance sheep dotted the landscape. Her lip curled. With eyes narrowed she tried to pick out the shepherd. A hand clenched and unclenched the dagger. Nabella tore her eyes away and forced a deep breath to calm down. She searched the edge of the plain to the east. There they were. The wild takhis grazed peacefully and far beyond them a herd of giant fallow deer, huge antler racks sticking up from the grass even when the deer had their heads down to graze. But no sign of…

Wait, Nabella shaded her eyes. There to the north next to the line of trees it looked like two people. She squinted. Nabella examined the horizon again but saw nothing else that could resemble her father's small party. She broke into a jog. One of the wild takhis whinnied and she glanced in their direction. The entire herd had fixed their gaze upon her. Nabella smiled then lifted her hand in farewell. Several animals turned and trotted a few paces away then stopped and stared at her again. Another snorted. Nabella laughed. Even though they had abandoned her she felt linked to them.

They were still in sight when a deep grumble in her belly reminded her of the lost grapes. It felt like her stomach had shrunk three sizes since she ate last. A thick grove of trees loomed ahead and to her right. Nabella studied the men while she jogged. They seemed to hold the same direction and she had already shortened the distance. Even if she lost sight of them she could pick up their trail. All she needed to do was head northeast. With one more glance she veered toward the small forest. Surely one of the trees would be an almond, or pistachio, or even a fig. Nabella's mouth watered at the thought.

Halfway to the wood she slowed to a walk. Her stamina had ebbed after her forced fast yesterday and the excitement of the day before. She caught her breath then alternated between a jog and a walk. A half of a hand-span later she arrived at the edge of the grove. Nabella stopped, hand on her dagger and peered into the trees to listen. Satisfied of no immediate danger, she slipped through the curtain of trees into the cool dampness. The shaded wood still held the chill of autumn in the early morning air. Nabella shivered and rubbed her bare arms. The dank smell of decomposed leaves rose when she stumbled over a rotten branch.

Nabella drew a deep breath through flared nostrils and turned in place. What a delightful little wood! It seemed like she had stepped into a golden room. The yellow and green leaves allowed just enough light to give the illusion of dappled amber. Splashes of orange completed the decoration. How beautiful. Nabella stole forward, eyes darting around. Her lips curved upward then formed an O. Ahead a yellow beam of sunlight cut through green and brown shadows. A strange light danced on the bottom of the leaves. Hunger forgotten she tiptoed toward the odd light. A huge tree had been uprooted and left a hole in the ground now filled with emerald-blue water. With silent feet she padded to the edge of the small pond and wandered around a worn path to giant roots that towered over her head. Sun rays streamed through a gap in the canopy above made by the fallen giant. Its roots curved outward from the partially hollowed trunk to form a small cave. Autumn butterflies danced on summer's last flowers that edged the white sand of the pool.

Nabella sank to the ground. Her smile widened and shiny eyes drifted from the butterflies to the sparkle of clear water then back to the miniature fluttering creatures. She heard a gentle trickle and noticed for the first time a tiny artesian well bubbling on the far side of the dead tree. Chirps and twitters announced a flock of warblers as they descended on the spot. They clung to several low branches and dipped their tiny beaks into the cool liquid. A soft rustle on the opposite bank pulled her eyes in that direction. Nabella froze. One half of a low bush swayed in the quiet air. Her hand slid to the dagger.

Abruptly an animal stepped from the brush. A timid visaya deer's nose twitched then stilled, and she lowered her delicate head to the water's still edge. Nabella drew in a quiet breath smiling at the dainty animal's soft slurping.

"You're so beautiful." Nabella hadn't intended to speak aloud. Even so, it was no more than the sound of a breath. But the deer knew. Her head snapped up and with a stomp of a fragile foot she bounded into the wood. After one leap Nabella lost sight of her. The animal's spotted coat blended in perfect patterns with the dappled forest light. Mesmerized, Nabella sat motionless soaking it in. *I can believe there is a God here.*

All at once she leapt to her feet. The flock of warblers scattered with chirps of protest. *God, Shem, the curse!* She dashed around the enchanted pool charging down the trail. Nabella slowed at the sight of a sumac bush, fruit still clinging to its branches. Deft fingers plucked several handfuls of the small red berries and stuffed them into her makeshift journey sack. Around a small bend she found wild grapes, the fruit already half turned to raisins. The first handful of the semi-tart fruit went straight to Nabella's mouth except for one cluster, the rest went into the sack. She hefted the bundle, it would do for now.

When Nabella made her way to the edge of the wood, cluster of grapes in hand, she didn't even bother to look for her father but jogged in the direction she last saw him. Several times she stopped to take a cluster of grapes from her pack. Each time she studied the terrain ahead, it had changed. Where wild grasses once grew, now a vast field of belly-high flax pushed their green shoots skyward. As Nabella moved to the edge the field to follow its contour she couldn't help but wonder if the curse on the olive groves had been an attempt to force them into The City. She pressed her lips tight at the thought. *How dare they—just wait till I get to Shem!*

A man on a takhi crisscrossed his way through the crop. Farther along four workers leading oxen walked along the edge of the field. A large deer bolted from the field in front of the takhi. His mount reared and tried to buck but the rider pushed the animal into a charge. Too far away to see the man's javelin, Nabella knew what happened when the deer faltered and dropped to the ground. She watched the worker jump from his takhi and run toward the animal.

She couldn't help but think of the peaceful little doe at the emerald pond. Shifting her head toward the small forest she whispered, "Stay safe in the wood, little one."

Nabella jogged paralleling the field. She hoped her movements would, at least at a distance, look like a boy. Her eyes strayed back to the man who killed the deer. She could see him field dress the animal and knew he would take the meat home for many meals to come.

An idea popped into her head, and she veered toward the man. Slowing to a walk when she neared and concentrated on looking like a boy. From a distance, the plan to trade grapes and sumac for a cut of meat seemed great. But when she drew closer, doubts filled her mind. The man glanced over his shoulder at her then went back and continued to cut the meat. What if he turned out to be like the shepherd? Her feet dragged. A quick check of the other field workers revealed they took no interest in her. Nabella relaxed a little. At least they wouldn't swarm her.

The man stood, stretched his back then stepped to the far side of the dead animal kneeling to face her. She halted a few paces in front of him. Nabella tried to deepen her voice without making it sound unnatural. "Greetings."

He paused and leaned an elbow on his knee. Both hands were covered in blood past his wrists. "What good news do you bring and what can I do for you, boy?"

Nabella swung the pack off her back and untied it. "My family fares well and the harvest has been good. I have grapes and sumac for a piece of meat, if you're willing to trade."

The man studied her, and she could see his face soften. *I guess I look as hungry as I feel.* He pulled himself to his feet, moved to her display, and squatted.

"Yum, wild grapes. I like their tartness. My wife makes a good jam with them. Go cut yourself a piece of meat."

Nabella strode to the deer and knelt by the animal's hindquarters then sliced a chunk from where the man had left off butchering. When she returned to her sack she saw the man had taken only one small cluster. Her smile faded. Surely he would be mad at her greed. Quickly she stooped, snatched two more clusters, and offered them to him. She hoped he would see that as an even trade.

The man studied her proffered hand with a thoughtful look. He held up a finger then went to the deer, rummaged through his stack of cut meat, pulling out the liver. Nabella's eyes flew wide. Liver was a prized cut of meat. She watched while he sliced a thick piece then walked back to her. He reached for the clusters then slapped the liver in her empty hand.

"There. We're even."

She felt tears well up in her eyes at his kindness. Nabella ducked her head and gritted her teeth then shoved the meat in her wrap. When she looked up, her eyes were clear and she gave a deep nod to seal the bargain.

"Where are you headed?"

"My father and, brother are ahead of me. I bring a message to them."

"Leading and ancient mare?"

"Yes."

"They camped back there last night. You're not too far behind them. If you hurry you should catch them by nightfall."

"Thank you, Kuya. Did you speak to them?"

"No, just saw them traveling north along the edge of the field this morning."

Turning Nabella lifted a hand. The man responded in kind. Heartened, she swung into a boyish jog, or at least she hoped it looked boyish, then continued along the edge of the field, her faith in mankind restored.

The field stretched a long way, but to the North scattered trees abounded. Small, dingy, structures dotted spaces between and under the trees. *Those must be tents.* Beyond that, she could just make out the top of the massive tower in The City.

Encouraged, Nabella broke into a ground-eating trot. Two hand-spans later she traveled across a small dry wash. She looked at the thickets and a grin crept across her face. Nabella scrounged around gathering enough dry sticks to make a small fire. Except she had no coals, or a fire starter. What a waste of time that was, to gather all those sticks. No! She would take them with her. When she camped near her father tonight, she would sneak in to his campfire after he and Tomar fell asleep and get a coal. Then she could make a fire and cook the meat. She smiled at her cleverness bundling the sticks to the top of her pack. But the heaviness of the extra weight bit into her shoulder. Oh well, it would be worth it, who knows where she would camp tonight. If she wound up on the plain again, there might not be any firewood.

Once again she lengthened her steps and at last spied the men in the distance. Moisture pricked the corners of her eyes. By the time the sun had almost reached its zenith, she began to slow. If she kept to this fast walk she would be close enough by nightfall.

Nabella breathed a sigh of relief then tried to swallow. Her tongue cleaved to the roof of her mouth like flatbread in a tannur oven. She had not come across water since the beautiful emerald pool. And she had neglected to drink there.

When the sun perched directly overhead, Nabella knew she would have to head for the Little Euphrates. *Well, I'll just have to jog again.* Nabella angled toward the river. *Father's flasks must be full, otherwise he would be heading to the river too.* A glance at her father brought a pang of longing as once again the distance increased between them.

Nabella slid down the river bank, plunged her face into the water, and sucked in great mouthfuls. Surely even a boy would do that. The temptation to scrub her face surged, but she let it go. Nabella climbed the bank and looked across the expanse of the grain field. Ahead lay scattered trees, tents, and even a few brick buildings. Her father and Tomar journeyed in that direction. She had no choice but to parallel their course staying next to the waterway since the river would cut across their path anyway.

The strip of field between her and the men narrowed the closer she came to the tents. A hand-span later Jokaan and Tomar entered the mass of tents that stretched between the Southeast wall of The City and the Little Euphrates. Nabella caught her breath. *Oh no, I'm going to lose them.* Her steps quickened until she saw people crowd around her father and Tomar. A smile spread across her face as she slowed. This would be easy, the horde of people would lead her right to the men.

A quarter of a hand-span later she arrived at the outskirts of the tent city. The field had petered down to nothing on this side of the bank. Nabella paused, took a handful of sumac berries from her sack then inspected the layout before her. A well-worn dirt trail curved from the river into the tented area. She headed up the path.

"Greetings."

Nabella started. Off to the side, a boy of eleven or twelve perched on a mat tucked under the low branches of a sycamore tree. His legs, thin and twisted, lay at an odd angle in front of him. She had never seen legs so deformed and could only stand and stare.

"Don't worry, your legs can't get sick like mine. I was born this way."

Heat rose to Nabella's cheeks, and she lowered her eyes. Here she traveled on a grand journey to see ancestor Shem, and this boy couldn't even go down to the river.

"What are you eating?"

"Ah, greetings. Sumac berries." Nabella stared at the river, she just couldn't bring herself to finish the customary greeting. What good news could he have?

"They look good."

"Here," she walked over and gave the boy the rest of her handful. Nabella bent her aching legs and eased next to the boy.

"You come from far away?" The boy's dark, slanted eyes studied her with curiosity.

"Over a half day's journey."

"What's it like that far away?"

"Well, my father has a great big grove of olive trees and we live close to the Euphrates Riv—

"The big river?"

"Yes."

"I heard it's twice as big as this one."

Nabella studied the Little Euphrates. "More like four times as big. And in the rainy season it gets even bigger than that, maybe ten times as wide."

"Ah-he," the boy's face shone. "I bet it would be fun to ride on a boat there!"

"Well, I guess, except the water's very rough and swift."

"But a strong man could row a boat through it, right?"

"I suppose so."

Both remained silent for a while then a corner of her mouth tugged upward. "Hey listen, where could I get some coals? I have meat, but I need to cook it. I'll share it with you if you help me."

"Mother!" The boy bellowed.

Nabella jerked and bound to her feet.

"No, no, don't go," he reached up, grabbed her wrist, and tugged for Nabella to sit. "My mother will bring you some coals."

A slight woman with beautiful, straight black hair came from the nearest tent. "What is it?"

"My friend—"

"Ah, Nabel."

"My friend Nabel would like some coals to cook his meat."

Nabella cleared her throat. "Greetings, I wouldn't impose on you, I have firewood." The woman stood, hands on hips, her slanted eyes roving over Nabella.

She finally spoke. "How fresh is the meat?"

"I traded for it just two hand-spans ago, cut it right out of a fresh killed deer."

"How did you get a fresh killed deer?" Her almond shaped eyes squinted until they looked closed.

"I didn't kill it. A field worker did. I saw him do it too. So I traded wild grapes for some meat. And I'm willing to trade some of the meat for hot embers."

The woman looked Nabella up and down then finally held out her hand. "Give it to me, young man. I'll cook it for you."

Nabella started to protest, but the woman cut her off. "Just give it to me before I change my mind."

Nabella swung off her bundle, untied it, and unrolled the meat and liver from the edge of her jupe. The woman stooped to retrieve them, her long hair touching the ground. "Liver." She took it, sniffed, and nodded approval. With one more glance at Nabella she turned and entered her tent.

"Nabel!"

Nabella realized the boy had already called her several times.

"Tell me more of where you come from."

Nabella spoke of her father's olive business. For an instant she wondered if she should tell him of the Azhdaha. But it might frighten him and that would call attention to herself. Anyway, she reasoned, with its injury the tanniyn would never make it this far. Nabella finished with vague details of the pagan sacrifices. "And that's why I'm here. I need to get a message to my father." She looked away and pressed her lips tight. *Just this one lie then that's it.*

"There were two strangers leading an old mare that came through here about a hand-span ago. Big men with dark hair and beards."

"That sounds like them."

The boy leaned forward, a smile played across his face. "I asked Mother to take me to where they had stopped so I could listen to them. I love to listen to stories. And since they were strangers I was sure they would have some good ones."

"What did they talk about?"

"They talked about their search to find ancestor Shem. That's so exciting! I hope you get to see him too."

"Did anyone know where Shem is? Did they tell my father?"

"Yes. Do you want to know where?"

Nabella eyes flew wide. "Yees!"

"I overheard the elders say Shem is at an outpost by East Lake."

"I didn't know there was an outpost by it."

"Well, I think they just moved there."

"Why would people want to stay that far away?" Nabella moved her hand to a hip,

raising her brows.

"They're not staying there forever, silly. They just went to harvest cedar trees."

At last it made sense.

"You sure are strange. You act like a girl. Do all the boys act like that where you're from?"

Nabella sighed. *What would a boy do now?*

"You know what I think? I think you're a girl dressed like a boy." Nabella peeked at him then looked away. Was it that obvious? The boy had only to tell one person and her cover would be blown. "Please, please…"

"Don't worry, I won't tell anyone. But why? Why do you want to look like a boy?"

"Well, I don't nec—"

"Shh, wait. Here comes Mother."

Nabella glanced over her shoulder and saw the petite woman balancing a tray of meat and bread. The aroma of the still sizzling venison made her mouth water. She didn't mean to be rude, but she couldn't take her eyes off the food.

The woman set the tray between the two of them then turned to leave.

"Mother, stay and eat with us."

"Yes. Thank you for cooking this, please have some."

The boy's mother shook her head. "You are of age now, my son. It is only proper that you are served first. You boys enjoy."

Biting her lower lip, Nabella glanced at Seth. He had clamped a hand over his mouth and as soon as the woman went back to the tent they burst into laughter. At last the boy managed to stop. "Well, you fooled my mother. She thinks you're a boy."

No longer able to resist, Nabella grabbed a piece of liver and bit off an oversized chunk. The woman had seasoned it with salt, onion, and a spice she didn't know. It tasted so delicious. Juice dribbled down the corner of her mouth, but Nabella didn't care. She groaned with delight.

"When did you last eat, Nabel? Or whatever your name is?"

"Except for berries. Almost two days ago." She mumbled around a mouthful of food, a piece of meat in one hand and a chunk of flat bread in the other.

"Well, you eat like a boy."

Nabella smiled and wiped her mouth with the back of her hand.

"All right, now you're looking like a boy." He grinned then picked at his piece of liver. Nabella frowned. "You need to eat, you're too skinny."

"I know, Mother always says the same thing. But I haven't walked for two days like you so I'm not that hungry."

Nabella nodded, cramming another morsel into her mouth.

Full at last she leaned back on the ground with a great sigh, hands folded beneath her head. She must have eaten half the liver. Nabella rolled to her knees, pulled her dagger from its sheath then cut off a large chunk of meat. She laid it and the rest of the liver, next to the boy's unfinished meal. "For your mother. And tell her she's a good cook." With a smile she wrapped the remainder in the cleanest edge of her jupe and tied the whole thing back into a bundle. It felt good to help Seth and his mother. *This will just have to last until I get back home.*

"I better get going. I have to catch up with my father before nightfall. How far is it to East Lake?"

"I heard that you can walk there in four hand-spans if you hurry. Well, maybe five. Just cross the river and head to the northeast. You'll run right into it."

Nabella slung the pack over her shoulders, "Thank you—"

"Seth."

"Thank you, Seth. Thanks for everything."

"You're welcome, Nabel, and good journey to you."

Nabella hesitated, ready to give Seth her name but decided against it. Instead she cleared her throat, not quite sure what to say.

Seth filled the awkward silence. "Let me know what Shem says, all right?"

"I will." Nabella smiled then headed for the river.

Nine

Pairs of clean and unclean animals, of birds and of all creatures that move along the ground, male and female, came to Noah and entered the ark, as God had commanded Noah.

Genesis 7:8-9 (NIV)

Every part of Cush's body ached. He couldn't remember the last time he pushed himself this much. Mounds of the great animal's meat that he helped Nimrod and some of the men carve lay piled around him. The rest had returned to the base camp for the ox drawn wagons.

The better part of the day had passed when the butchering finally was completed. It surprised Cush how little fat had been on the tanniyn. Even so, a pile of raw lard stood half the height of Cush and only a single heap of unusable parts remained.

But the most prized pieces, at least according to Nimrod, were the tanniyn's head and hind feet. Cush stared at the enormous and formidable trophies. No doubt they would cause a tremendous stir among the people. Cush snorted, just what Nimrod intended.

The dark man clenched his teeth, a battle rising within between disdain for Nimrod's arrogance and admiration since he most likely had saved his life.

Nimrod's men turned to one another and retold their part in the demise of the tanniyn. Still covered in blood they slapped their leader on the back. The mighty hunter remained silent only on occasion laughing the compliments off.

Cush shook his head, he couldn't figure the man out. Someone broke out a wineskin. When it reached Nimrod he approached Cush, downed a swallow, then offered it to him.

Cush hid his surprise by tipping his head and drinking deeply. Wine sloshed down his chin and neck. He looked at the low orange orb resting on the horizon and slid an arm across his mouth.

"We spend the night here?"

Nimrod nodded. "Yes, and we will drink to our victory. No one was injured except for you."

Cush fingered the slash on his side. He could still hear the monster gnashing its teeth. He glanced at his wound to cover a shudder. Dried blood crusted the makeshift wrap. Then he shrugged his good shoulder. "It's only a scratch." Cush took another swig and tossed the wineskin to Nimrod.

"You are still alive. It is a good day." Nimrod gulped the liquid and pursed his lips after he swallowed.

Cush inclined his head. "Since that kabiyr didn't bite me in half or claw my guts out, I should say so."

"Not to mention almost being crushed under its body then drown in its blood."

Cush studied Nimrod. He didn't know the man had witnessed his entire struggle. Dark eyes stared unblinking back at him. It might have been the wine on an empty stomach but all at once the whole situation struck him as humorous. He threw back his head bellowing a great laugh. Nimrod joined him. Astonished, Cush twisted his head and glanced at the younger man. Glee danced in Nimrod's eyes. Cush shook his head in amazement and allowed himself to laugh freely.

The smell of sizzling steaks pushed through Cush's thoughts, and his eyes drifted to the fire. Flames sputtered as juice dripped off the abundant portions. He stomach cramped at the tantalizing aroma yet he refused to make the first move.

"Come." Nimrod jerked his head in their direction.

At the fire he held out the wine flask, "Eat, drink, laugh. The wagons arrive."

Cush started, glanced at Nimrod then down the gully. He couldn't see anything. Then, the unmistakable sound of a distant curse announced the return of the party. Before long, six men appeared around the fire, each with a pack on their back.

"Two men are with the oxen, *Rayis*. We brought four wagons but couldn't get any farther up the gully." The man sounded tired.

"An' we brough' wine and bread!" Another shouted, painfully obvious he had sampled the wine.

Nimrod stared at him, eyes narrowed.

The smile fled the man's face and he straightened. "My Rayis!"

Nimrod turned dark eyes on the men. In the twilight, they seemed hollow, even unnatural. Cush drew back a step.

"You," Nimrod nodded at Cush, "Make sure there is enough meat roasted for everyone. And you," Nimrod jutted his chin at another. "You and Terach go to the oxen and build a circle of fires around them. We will roast the rest of the meat there. Everyone else, move the meat to the oxen."

A few of the men dared to grumble. "What about the wine?"

"And bread?"

Nimrod turned malevolent eyes in their direction. "Then stay. After Cush leaves with the meat, you will be drunk here alone to deal with the night predators. Soon your bones will be next to the tanniyn's."

The men split without a single word. Someone tossed an empty sack at Cush's feet. He strode to the spit and checked the meat. Several pieces could already be removed from the makeshift rack. With deft twists of his wrist he sliced off sections that were ready, dumping them into the sack. A quick flick of his dagger, and he jabbed a small portion with the end of his knife. He held the steaming chunk and inhaled the aroma. He couldn't wait any longer. Cush curled back his lips biting off a section then sucked in several breath to cool the morsel. When he ground it between his teeth, hot juices covered his tongue. It tasted as good as it smelled, a touch gamey, and a bit sweet, just like tanniyn. *I'm going to thoroughly enjoy eating this monster! And glad I'm doing the eating.*

Soon the sack bulged with cooked meat. Cush slung it over his shoulder and grabbed a thick branch from the fire pit for a torch. Rather pleased he had been spared the burden to trudge back and forth with the raw meat, Cush made his way to the lower party more by sound than by sight. He strode into the ring of firelight and dislodged the sack. "Meat!"

Men shoved their way forward. Cush stepped back, looking for a sack of bread.

"You know when to show up, Cush, just when the last of the meat is in the wagon."

"He did wait 'til all the work was done."

"Did you see how he stepped away from the meat? He's been there eating away while we labored!" Another bantered.

"I bet there was twice as much meat when he started cooking."

Cush laughed, yellowed teeth showing against dark skin. He tore a chunk of flatbread and walked toward the men. With the exception of Nimrod, Cush stood taller than most. He shoved his way to the front of the pack with ease. With one hand he grabbed a hunk of meat, tucked the bread into his tunic then snatched a wineskin from the nearest man and held it high.

"To being so close to the jaws of death and walk away," he boasted.

"To slaying the tanniyn," another shouted.

"To getting away with only a scratch on my side," Cush continued.

"Death to the monster!" Someone yelled.

"To Nimrod who rode the thrashing beast and sliced its throat." Cush turned to Nimrod just in time to see his dark countenance become stoic. Though the wine had already gotten to Cush's head, he realized enough to back down. After all, he stood in the company of Nimrod's loyalist men.

"To all the warriors who risked their lives and won."

Shouts rose. "Death to the tanniyn, death to the tanniyn!"

Laughter and drunken boasts continued. Cush sank to the ground a short ways from the group. He devoured his meat then dripped wine over the bread and shoved large pieces past his teeth. He felt the burgundy liquid dribble out the corner of his mouth and wiped it away with the back of his hand. Nimrod stared at him from across the fire. The heat waves gave an unnatural aura to the man's outline. Cush sighed. The earlier camaraderie with Nimrod had evaporated.

Cush took a big swig and emptied the wineskin. He lay back with an arm under his head. The stars moved in a slow swirl. The man knew the effect of strong drink for he had been inebriated many a time under the night sky. He sighed again.

Would it always be like this between him and Nimrod?

***

"Hey!"

The voice broke into the edges of a dreamless sleep. Pain stabbed Cush's side.

"Ah-he, wake up."

Again pain ripped through him. He sucked in a sharp breath and moved his hand to the throb. A foot nudged him. With tiger-strike speed he clutched the ankle and sat up.

"Do that again and you'll be missing a foot," he growled.

"It's your turn to guard."

Cush pushed himself to his feet. He could hear snarls and yips in the gully. "Wolves?"

"Ah-huh. They found the scrap pile."

"Didn't take them long."

"Just keep the fires going. Nimrod thinks that'll be enough, and they'll stay away since they have plenty to eat up there." The man jutted his chin in the direction of the kill.

Cush made his way to the closest fire. His eyes meandered over the six pits positioned in a circle around the meat-laden wagons and the unleashed oxen. Firelight danced across the animals. Most of the livestock lay asleep with legs tucked under them or chewed their cud. Only two stood, ears pricked toward the sound of the wolves.

I wonder if that's instinct for them. According to Cush's father oxen were one of the domesticated animals on the ark. God allowed seven of each domesticated kind and fowl of the air, and two of all the wild animals aboard. But why would these domesticated oxen have an instinct to take guard?

Cush added more wood to the fire pit and watched another man do the same across the circle from him. And, why would man have the instinct to stand guard? Cush shook his head. His mind felt sluggish from the wine. He didn't want to dwell on such deep thoughts right now. But when he stared at the oxen and heard a wolf howl memories of long ago flooded back of asking Shem what brought the wild animals to the ark.

"Out of all the animals in the Former World as God created them, He gave only two of each animal kind, one male and one female, an instinct that urged the animals to travel many days-journeys."

"But Uncle Shem, how did God make it so they moved to the ark?"

"Instinct gave the animals a sense to identify and move from impending danger. Almost like they sensed something bad was going to happen."

"But how did the animals know to go to the ark?" Cush had persisted.

"If you were in a riverbed and you knew a flood was coming, where would you go?"

"Up the side until I was at the top of the cliff."

"Well, God gave two of each animal kind the same type of instinct to migrate away from an approaching flood. By instinct these animals came to the ark where they must have felt a sense of safety. And that, young Cush, is why the animals of today know to migrate to better places and have the instinct to know and avoid bad situations like erupting mountains and flooding rivers. This gift is passed down to each generation of animals from the original two all the way to those that boarded the ark and still to this day."

Cush stretched. The man on guard came around and stood next to him.

"Glad we had the last watch. Everyone else had to cook the tanniyn." He nodded to the wagons.

Cush stared at the mounds of meat. "I guess it had to be cooked, or it would've spoiled by the time we got back."

"Guess so." The other man shrugged and wandered away to the other fires. Cush threw several pieces of wood on the low blaze in the nearest pit and watched sparks spiral upward, then let his eyes drift to the stars. He turned northward and read the time from the celestial assemblages. His forehead creased as his brows pushed upward. From the position of the stars, the eastern horizon would soon turn grey.

Cush stared towards the east, thoughts returning to his uncle's answer. What Shem had said did make sense. He could understand how this instinct to migrate or know of impending danger would be passed from generation to generation. Many a time he had snuck up on a deer only to have it sense danger and flee. But what about in the Old World? How many animals had this instinct there? He remembered his grandfather told him they ate no meat in the Old World. Cush could still hear Noah's vibrant voice. *"The differences are great between the Former World and this one, my grandson."*

For once his Uncles Shem and Japheth and his father all agreed. So why would animals have this instinct in the Old World? Or maybe they didn't and God just gave it to the creatures that came to the ark. And the animals had it ever since.

Suddenly Cush felt a strong urge that his grandfather was right. Maybe the time had come to seek his Uncle Shem. It had been many, many years since he had spoken to the man. Ever since Shem and Cush's father had become estranged. Cush shook his head. It had been a long time since he thought of Ham. He wondered what his father did nowadays. *Is he even still alive?*

And what would Shem do if he suddenly showed up? At the thought, Cush crossed his arms over his chest. Would Shem criticize him for his father's actions, or that he had stayed away for so long? Cush snorted. No. He knew without a doubt Shem would criticize him for his part, a big part, in construction of The City. Shem and Noah were the ones so adamant that people spread throughout the world.

Maybe, just maybe, he could get Shem to come to The City to see the monster they had just slain. *Yes, that's it.* A smile began to stretch the corners of Cush's mouth. Surely once Shem saw the head and hind claws of the tanniyn he would finally understand that it would be better to stay in a walled city than to have the people wander in small groups all over the world. Certainly once Shem saw Nimrod's prize he would recognize that the people would be annihilated by such beasts if they spread out.

Then good graces could be restored between the brothers. And maybe even with his grandfather. And he, Cush, would be the one to accomplish this.

***

Barukh stared at Shoshana. Obviously the little girl believed Nabella came here to be with him. And had been here for the last several days. What to do now? If he told the truth he would dishonor Nabella. And that would reflect back onto him. If he lied, well, he didn't even want to think in that direction. Abruptly a thought occurred to him.

"What are you doing here by yourself, Shoshana?"

"I came to find Bella." Round emerald eyes stared at him.

"Does your father know you are here?"

"Nooo..."

"Does Tomar know you're here?"

"Nooo..."

"Does Adara know you're here?"

"Nooo..."

Impatience crept into his voice. "Does anyone know you're here?"

Shoshana shook her head biting her lower lip.

"Did Nabella tell you she was coming here?"

"Ah huh." Shoshana stepped on a large flat rock.

Just what I thought. Now I have two problems. "I'll be right back. Stay here."

"Can I help?" Shoshana hopped down from the rock.

"No. I'm getting a takhi and taking you home."

"On the takhi?"

"Yes."

Shoshana dashed to his side.

"No, no, no. You stay right there on the rock."

"Ahhh." Shoshana's whole upper body sagged until her hands hung by her knees, bottom lip protruding as she stared with big pleading eyes.

"Go. Now. Or we'll walk."

Shoshana straightened and bound to the rock.

"Stay there, and stay out of trouble until I come for you with the takhi." He turned and strode away. But after only two paces, she called after him.

"Here?"

She had one foot on the stone and one foot on the ground. Barukh clenched a fist and growled, "There are small wolves all around the rock. You're only safe on the rock. If you step down, they'll bite your toes off."

Shoshana gasped yanking her foot to the rock. Barukh turned with a sneer. That should keep her for a while. He had seen Kfir use it on their youngest brother, and it worked. Once. He caught the takhi from the corral throwing a saddle on it. Astride, he looked for his father. He found the older man at the end of the long rows of drying racks.

"Father, I'm going to Nabella's."

Gideon straightened. "Do you plan to return today?"

"I'm not sure. Maybe tomorrow or the next."

"Is something wrong?"

"No, I just need to speak with Nabella and Jokaan."

Barukh could tell by the look in Gideon's eyes he had fooled no one. Without a word, he turned the takhi and trotted away. He wanted to gallop but knew that would really trigger alarm and Gideon would likely send Kfir after him. Something he wanted to avoid.

Shoshana remained perched right where he had left her. She squatted on the rock swatting the ground with a stick. When she heard him she stood, branch still in her hand.

"Drop the stick and grab my hand." Shoshana obeyed, and he flung the child behind him. "Now hang on to my waist and don't let go."

Not sure how well the girl could stay on a takhi, he started at a fast walk. His brows came together at the thought of Nabella. If she wasn't here like Shoshana thought then where could she be? Should he ask around her household or would that get her into trouble? If he showed up at her place would *that* get her in trouble? And what if she really were in trouble?

"I had to get down once." Shoshana said.

"What?"

"I had to get down once. To get a stick."

Barukh tried to force his mind to the present so he could listen to the girl. "Why did you need a stick?" His tone came out crisper than he intended.

"I had to have a long dagger to kill the little wolves."

"Little wolves?"

"Yes, the ones that were biting my toes."

"Ah, good thinking."

"Then you're not mad at me for getting down?"

"No, but I'm mad that you came all this way by yourself."

"I'm sorry." Remorse filled her voice.

"Shoshana, promise me you will never, and I mean never, go off by yourself again. There is an Azhdaha somewhere about. Kfir and Father found its tracks at the south end of our fields. That's the end toward your place."

"I know, Bella told me about it awhile ago."

"Nabella?"

"Yes. She saw it. She said you knew about it, she told you—"

"When?" Barukh gritted his teeth. He didn't like the way things were shaping up.

"A long time ago. That's why I knew it was safe to come here."

"How long ago was it, think."

"It was past last week."

"Two weeks ago?"

"I guess."

"Shoshana, that's not very long ago."

"Yes it is!" The child's insistent voice held such innocence. Barukh tightened his hands on the reins.

They rode in silence for a while, then his voice became stern. "Just promise me you won't wander off."

"Alright, I promise."

"Good. Now hang on, we're going to gallop!"

Ten

This is the account of Shem's family line. Two years after the flood, when Shem was 100 years old, he became the father of Arphaxhad.

Genesis 11:10

Nabella stared at the fields across the river. Was this really a good idea? To go straight to East Lake outpost rather than follow her father? It would avoid unwanted attention if she stayed out of this tent town that surrounded the walled City.

At last Nabella stripped off her sack and sandals and held them high over her head. The deepest part of the water came to her ribs, and she let out a sigh of relief when the river once again retreated to her knees. She wiggled a foot forward to feel for solid footing. Seth shouted words of advice giving her encouragement. The crossing had been easier than she thought. *Almost there.* Nabella moved her foot, and it plunged into a low dip. She careened forward like a turtle's head emerging from its shell then wobbled, twisted and landed on her back. But somehow she managed to keep her arms out of the water, sandals and pack dry.

Behind her peals of laughter erupted. Jaw clenched, Nabella swung the bag to the hand with the sandals. She pushed herself out of the trough one-handed, scrambling to her feet then trudged up the bank. With a disgusted thump she dropped to the ground and tied on her sandals. *So much for trying to keep my head above water.* Nabella turned and waved to Seth then headed into the field.

Water ran down her pant legs puddling in her sandals as she slogged along. The same thing had happened earlier in the day when she left the wild takhi watering hole. The damp leather had stretched them, causing the sandals to slip which had chaffed her feet all day.

Nabella started off again glancing at her feet when the pain grew. She blinked at the sight of blood, her feet didn't feel that bad! Stripping off her sandals she tried going barefoot. But that didn't work either. The plowed dirt clods had hardened since the last rain and bit into her soles. Frustrated she plopped to the ground yanking the bundle off. Nabella ripped two long strips from the remnant of her jupe, then wound one around each foot. Once her sandals were back on, she laced them tight. If the leather wouldn't loosen she'd be fine.

She took a few tentative steps then went faster. It was working, and since she gave Seth's mother the firewood the sack didn't poke into her back or weigh her down. *I can do this.* Nabella shaded her eyes trying to see her father. Was he ahead now, or still caught up in the tent city?

While she walked, Nabella twisted in place and projected the sun's course to the western horizon. "Oh no!" Only three hand-spans left until dark. She pushed into a jog, her wet shirt and pants plastered against her sending shivers through her body. But by the time she reached the edge of the field, the damp clothes felt good against the autumn sun's warm rays.

Nabella slowed to a walk, and her eyes roved all around the horizon for any sign of her father and Tomar. She knew from here it had to be less than a half day's journey to East Lake and the temporary outpost. But this part of the vast plain had taller grass and low rolling knolls blocking her view. At the top of a mound she glanced once more at the sun then fixed her eyes on a thick patch of distant trees. *That must be the lake. I bet they set up their tents there.* Her eyes flicked to the west. She could always use the tower as a landmark. As long as she kept that in view, she would not get lost. Nabella clutched and unclutched her tunic. *I have to get to Shem, I don't want to move to The City!*

Every time Nabella topped out on a small slope, she glanced around to reorient herself and search for Jokaan. When she spotted several herds of sheep she angled herself to avoid them altogether. Her shadow had grown long when at last she drew close enough to see tents grouped in a long stand of trees. The line of trees meandered northeast as far as she could see. Nabella paused on a tall knoll and thought she could see deep blue through the tree branches. *The trees must line the lake.* She inhaled a sharp breath then broke into a huge smile at the thought of a body of water so large. What a treat it would be to see such a sight.

Cool air settled around her as the sun sunk below the western horizon. Nabella picked up her pace. She still had a little less than a quarter of a days-journey to go. *Well, maybe it's better this way, I can sneak in when it's dark and listen for talk of strangers. Then I'll know if Father and Tomar got there.*

But when Nabella finally reached the outer edge of the tents, she sank to the ground. Her feet throbbed and belly rumbled. She hadn't even the energy to get food out of the pack. Enthusiasm to see the great lake had dwindled with the last of her strength. That would have to wait until morning.

At last she shrugged the bundle off, gathered it in her arms, then leaned her forehead on it. Somewhere in the back of her mind she thought to move into the midst of the tents where it would be safer.

Nabella sat straight with a gasp. She hadn't intended to fall asleep. How much time had passed? Firelight still glowed inside most of the tents and a swift glance at the sky showed a tiny sliver of rosy light clung low to the western horizon. Nabella relaxed; she had only dozed for a little while.

Then she heard it. A rustle off to her right. Is that what woke her? There, again, closer this time. Nabella didn't wait. With a giant leap she bound to her feet, dashing between the first two tents and hugged the nearest tree. Nabella swung to its back side and peered around the trunk. Tall grasses shimmered faintly in the dim light. She waited, but the creature did not move toward the tents. Nabella let out her breath. Hopefully whatever it was would stay there.

Now, if only she could find out if her father and Tomar were here.

She tiptoed farther into the array of tents pausing by the nearest one. Mumbled voices leaked through. She squatted to keep a low profile then pressed an ear to the thick material.

"You will have to hunt soon, we're almost out of meat." A woman's voice sounded tired.

"See if you can trade for meat," a male voice answered. "If I can rest my back another day or two…"

A sad laugh then, "Bargain with what?"

"Maybe you could weave your pretty pattern and use that."

"Yes maybe," Nabella heard a thud and a shuffle then the woman's excited voice. "Here are a few pieces I've already started!"

"That's good because when the baby comes you won't have much time."

Nabella backed away from the tent. She felt uncomfortable eavesdropping when the conversation turned personal. They didn't mention any strangers. *I would think they'd say so when their talk turned to trade.*

Nabella slipped to another tent. This time she didn't have to press her ear to the side. A man's deep timbre carried to her with ease. She waited while he went on and on about his crops and his animals. The whole time his children interrupted and cried, and his wife scolded. Yet no mention of visitors. Nabella shook her head and made her way to the far side of the outpost. She listened here and there, but no one said a thing about strangers.

That could only mean one thing. *I beat them here.* Nabella smiled. This could work to her advantage. She would wake early, hide in the outskirts then follow her father and Tomar in. After a final perusal of the area, Nabella made her way to the edge of the tents where she first entered.

A few lengths inside the perimeter she found a small open patch where a mid-sized tree spread its branches. She pulled a chunk of meat, a cluster of grapes, and her old tunic from the sack then hung it along with its remains of her precious food high on a branch. With a groan she leaned against the trunk. Every muscle protested when she stretched. The scar on her calf pulled and throbbed as she massaged the muscles. With a weary bite of venison, she ignored her feet. She didn't even want to look, let alone try to take care of them. A heavy sigh escaped, she swallowed the last piece of her meal and tucked her hat into the tunic for the night's pillow. Then she curled against the tree's base, her back pressed to its trunk.

Loud chirps woke Nabella. Grey light infiltrated through a thick fog. She groaned and huddled her face against the tree trunk. Sleep had come in fitful pieces. Nabella shivered. The cold, autumn night air had chilled her through and through. She was grumpy, damp, tired, cold, wanted a blanket and to sleep, but those birds! They carried on with their squawks and at full volume too. She sat drawing a deep breath sure if she hollered at them, then she glanced around.

Oh, the outpost, the lake. Nabella let the air out in a slow sigh, peering into the tree canopy. Though she couldn't see the small feathered creatures her irritation washed away. *Thanks, I'd have overslept without you!* With a soft moan, she pushed upright, gathering her sack from the branches. Nabella took a step, gasped then pressed her lips tight to silence a groan. Fresh blood oozed from a raw blister on her foot where the wrap had slipped away. Without the herbs to treat her wounds, Nabella didn't know what to do. So she did the next best thing, ignored the pain and pushed on.

Nabella jammed her hat on making her way past the mist-shrouded tents to a cluster of shadowy shrubs in a low dip. There she relieved herself and thought about the plan to wait for her father. It still seemed like the only thing to do. She trudged to the top of a grass-covered incline, faced west then sank to the dew covered ground. Nabella inspected the area. It did give her a good vantage point and once the mist lifted, she should be able to see well enough through the tall stalks that hid her. She pulled a few handfuls of the stiff shafts closer. With the fog it would work, at least from a distance. Father and Tomar would never know she was here.

Now for more important matters. Food! Nabella opened her sack spreading the small array of provisions in front of her. She tore a chunk of flat bread, slapped a piece of venison on top then piled it with raisins and sumac berries. She couldn't remember when anything looked so good. Mouth watering, she took a small bite. Eyes closed a groan escaped as the delicious tastes melted in her mouth.

Nabella twisted to watch a glow rise in the mist as the sunlight filtered through the trees. She lingered listening to the birds chirp in the thick fog. Glimmering glimpses of light caught her eye. Could that be the lake? Nabella watched the thinning fog drift between the tents. Already the higher areas were clear.

Whole meal devoured she licked each sticky finger. Nabella scanned the land in front of her and froze. Only cubits away, Jokaan and Tomar trudged in her direction, lead rope taut against the tired steps of the ancient mare. With a finger still in her mouth, her eyes flew wide. When they drew abreast, Tomar glanced in her direction. She wanted to duck but knew that would attract attention. There was nothing she could do. He gave her a tired half grin and a nod. She sat, finger still in her mouth, and managed a weak nod in return. Quick shallow breaths burst past her fingers as she watched the two men disappear between the tents.

Abruptly the village exploded with life.

"Somebody's here, strangers are here!" The yell of a small boy sounded from behind the dwellings.

"Strangers!" The hint of fear rang in a woman's call, but a male's voice sounded confident.

"Visitors!"

Nabella craned her neck to see. Children skipped behind the two men, shouting questions all at once. Adults spoke from behind raised hands as they emerged from their tents to stare. At last a large man strode to Jokaan.

With a start, Nabella swept her belongings into the bundle and slung it over a shoulder. She wiped her hand on the shirt then followed at a distance close enough to hear.

"Hey who are you?" A boy her height shouldered Nabella.

"I'm, ah, Adara's cousin. Come to visit." Nabella picked the most common name she could think in hopes somewhere here resided an Adara. Her hand tightened around her journey sack rope, and she held her breath. Another lie. Why didn't she say sister? No one would have known the difference, and she wouldn't have lied.

"Oh. Did you come with the strangers? Do you know who they are?"

Nabella's eyes darted around, and she tried to think. She wanted to avoid any more fibs. "Nooo, I didn't come with them. Do you know who they are?"

"No. I wonder what they want."

"Ahhh, where's Adara's tent?"

The boy waved a hand past Jokaan. "She's the last tent before the lake, that way."

"Thanks." Nabella ambled in the direction he indicated. She realized she had the good fortune to journey in the same direction her father traveled. A quick glance around and her confidence grew. No one paid her any mind. Nabella relaxed and made her way, keeping several dwellings and trees between herself and Jokaan. A grin broke across her face. Since most everyone crowded around her father, Tomar, and the man who first greeted them, it was easy to do.

But the grin faded when Nabella realized she had been so caught up in her conversation, in her lies, that she missed what the man had said to her father. From now on, she would have to pay better attention. She worked her way past several tents peering around an edge.

Jokaan had stopped the mare, facing the man. Ah-he, now she had gone too far to hear. Nabella wove closer. But before she could get near, the big man faced the crowd and clapped his hands.

"Everyone go! Their dealings are not with us. They have come to see Arphaxad. Go back to your lives, there's still much timber to cut and harvest. When these men finish with their business they'll spend the night here and share news from where they came." The man turned and grinned at Jokaan with his last statement.

Nabella knew her father had been ensnared. To refuse would be an insult. With a respectful nod Jokaan spoke a few quiet words before continuing his trek. The man shooed the children away from the visitors then headed back the way he had come. The last of the fog had lifted, and Nabella squinted against the brilliant sunlight then slipped through the myriad of tents. She angled away from her father as she traveled in the same direction.

Soon the dwellings thinned and beyond them stood a great blue body of water. She stopped and stared, mouth shaped in a silent O. This had to be the most beautiful thing she ever saw. Even the emerald pool couldn't match this. As if in a trance she wandered past the last tents to trees that bordered the lake. A well-worn path led to the water's edge, curving to follow the contour of the lake. Several boats moored to makeshift log ramps bobbed to the rhythm of the lake's ripples. Nabella glanced up and down the shoreline. More ramps with water-crafts lined the shore while other boats moored to trees dotted the bank. Men balanced on the cut logs and prepared their boats for the day's excursion. Vessels glided to deeper areas, v-shaped ripples spreading out behind them. Fishermen shouted, and nets arced over the water. Nabella stood transfixed at the wondrous sight before her. At the sharp ring of distant axes biting into wood, she jumped. Nabella glanced over her shoulder. *Father*!

She dashed up the path toward the tents and slid to a stop within the cover of trees. Scanning the area she saw Jokaan and Tomar were nowhere in sight. Her shoulders drooped. *I've already lost them and the sun isn't even two hand-spans above the horizon!*

A takhi whinnied off to the side. Nabella peered in that direction. There, tied to a tree by the last tent, was her grandfather's mare. Adara's tent? *Great. Just great.* After all that happened in her travels it figured her father wound up at the exact same place she had set up for cover. It would seem Arphaxad and Adara were married. *Well, I guess it's still alright to go there, especially if that boy tells everyone I came to see Adara.* Nabella shook her head placing a hand on her hip. Eyes flew wide then she jerked it into a clenched fist.

In four quick strides she reached the nearest tree and leaned against the large pine. The tent sat fifty cubits away in a small meadow. Its opening faced the path behind her and a stack of firewood lay on the lake side of the dwelling. Grandfather's takhi, tethered to a post, stood in the shade of the tent on the side opposite the firewood, black tail swooshing at the few late season flies. Somehow she had to sneak there and not look like she was, well, sneaking.

First she would have to hide her sack. It was a dead giveaway she didn't live here. Eyes searched branches and trunks and soon found a hollow in a tree stump. She stuffed her sack in it covering it with a few dead sticks.

Nabella cut across the meadow back to the lake strolling along its shore then headed toward the stack of firewood by the tent. She sank to the ground next to the pile of logs, worming her way around it. The mare gave a soft snort on the far side as she crept to the wall of the tent and put her ear to the material.

"… yes, Kuya. Thank you." Nabella recognized her father's voice.

"Adara, please fix us a warm drink." Another man's quiet voice spoke.

That must be Arphaxhad. No one else would address his wife that way. She heard several shuffles then the slap of the tent flap as it opened. Nabella gasped. A warm drink meant a fire, which meant firewood. She scrambled on hands and knees to the back of the tent. The mare peered around the edge and snorted again. Without thinking she brought a finger to her lips. The old takhi flicked its ears. It must have recognized her scent for she settled, ears pricked forward.

When the scrape and clunk of wood being removed ended, Nabella peeked around the corner. Adara in a long, deep blue jupe and brown tunic, straightened. A single long braid swayed in rhythm to the swoosh of her jupe as she carried an armload of wood toward the front of the tent. Nabella twisted and pressed her ear against the fabric once again. She strained to hear Arphaxad's quiet voice.

"I am glad your travels went well."

"Thank you. Yes, we're grateful the journey has been uneventful."

Nabella stopped just short of a loud snort. Easy for Father to say.

"I am sorry you came all this way and cannot meet with Shem. Perhaps there is something I can help you with?"

Nabella's jaw dropped. Not see Shem? What did he mean?

"I had hoped to speak with someone from the Old World, would it be possible to see Japheth?"

"I am afraid I do not know where Japheth is."

Silence. A deep sigh.

"I know I am not of the Old World but maybe I can help. It seems to me you are here on grave matters."

Nabella could picture her father nodding. When he spoke he related all that happened in his groves. After Jokaan finished, a long stretch of silence followed.

"I can see why you desire knowledge from the Old World. You do need to speak to Shem, and he needs to hear of this as well. I shall try to find a way. Adara, send for one of the great grandsons, I don't care which one as long as they move rapidly."

A slight shuffle then, "Yes, Arphaxad. Do you need anything before I go?"

"I will be fine, motek shele. My new friends can help should I need anything."

Once again Nabella heard the flap smack the side of the tent then soft footsteps receded as Adara headed toward the outpost.

"Take your takhi to the lake and water her. Then go to the center of the village. We have erected a tent for travelers and their animals. You may wait there for any news."

"Thank you, Rayis. I'll be there." Jokaan's voice sounded weary.

"Thank you." Tomar's gruff voice echoed Jokaan's fatigue.

She listened to her father and Tomar withdraw in the direction of the mare then scrambled around to the firewood. Their low voices murmured as they untied the animal. Nabella timed the hoof beats, and when she thought they were going to come abreast retreated again to the back of the tent. Once there she peeked around the corner watching the men head toward the water.

Finished at the lake Jokaan headed back to Arphaxad's dwelling. Nabella squirmed backward, pressed herself flat along the bottom of the tent, praying the grass would cover her. Jokaan's voice drifted through the solid, tightly-woven material.

"Do you want us to wait for Adara?"

"No. I have something to attend to, I will be fine. Wait at the log shelter for word."

When the footsteps of man and beast faded, Arphaxad spoke. "You can come out now."

Nabella gasped. *Is he talking to me?*

"Come on, girl; do not be deceiving with me."

Nabella's mouth dropped open. *How does he know I'm a girl!*

"Come, come into my tent."

What could she do? He already knew she was there. She sighed, pushed herself up then hesitated by the entrance.

"Come on," he urged again. "Come all the way in and sit down."

Nabella obeyed. Arphaxad sat cross-legged on a rug woven with intricate patterns, his back against a wooden rest. Shoulder-length black hair lay neatly tucked behind rather large ears. Nabella's eyes lingered on a small scar that extended a fingernail length from under the right side of his long black beard. She stood at a loss of what to do while the man stared at a wooden cup in his hand. He swirled the liquid in a slow rhythm.

"Sit right here in front of me," he gestured with his other hand. "And greetings."

Nabella drifted forward then knelt before the man. Still he swirled the liquid. Why didn't he look at her? She laced and unlaced her fingers.

"Are you going to tell me what you are doing sneaking around outside my dwelling?"

Nabella's mouth dropped open. How did he know that? "Are, you one of those seers? Those people who know everything?"

Arphaxad chuckled then paused. "Well?"

Nabella took a deep breath. "Promise not to tell my father?"

"Your father is Jokaan, or Tomar?"

"Jokaan."

"I cannot give you my word on that." Arphaxad took a swallow of his drink. "I can however, promise I will tell him you are here if you do not disclose to me your actions."

Nabella hung her head. "All right. But promise you won't think badly of me."

The man positioned his cup with great care on the ground.

"Lean close, girl. I won't hurt you."

"Ah! *How* do you know I'm a girl?" She bent toward him.

For the first time Arphaxad turned his face to her. Clear brown eyes seemed to look right past her. He reached up with both hands, placed them on her face, and gentle fingers touched her features. When they reached her hat, he began to grin. With a yank he pulled it off and felt her mid-back-length hair. He patted her shoulders and arms down to her waist and laughed out right when he felt the dagger.

"You're, well, I mean, you're blind." That would explain why he looked past her.

"Yes."

Compassion filled Nabella.

Arphaxad felt for his drink. "Tell me why you are dressed like a boy."

"But how do you know I'm a girl?"

"I cannot see, so when I picture a person it is from their voice and their actions that I hear. I am not thrown off by their looks. For one, your voice is too high for someone of your weight and height. And boys don't gasp." He took a sip from the cup.

"Oh." Nabella's heart sank. She had failed to fool a blind person, what about all the others?

"Now tell me why you are here."

Before she knew it the trials she had encountered poured out along with her intent. The only thing she left out was her bout with the shepherd.

"And the scratch on your face?"

Nabella fingered the scabs on her cheek. "I, fell."

Arphaxad said nothing then fumbled for her hand and wrapped his large fingers around her wrist. "You were attacked, weren't you?"

Nabella looked down. She began to shake. Her free hand clasped and unclasped the bottom edge of her tunic.

He let go. "Tell me."

"Yes. But that man didn't know I was a girl. He wanted my dagger. I had to cut him to get away." Nabella's voice trembled.

"The Lord spared you." Arphaxad sighed. "I understand why you would want to see my father but to trav—"

"Shem is your father!" Nabella gasped.

"There you go gasping again. Yes. I am his firstborn."

Nabella blew out her breath and clasped her arms to her chest. "You were here before all of us."

Arphaxad nodded and turned his head to the side. "It is truly amazing how many children have been born over the last one hundred and six years."

"So, do you know everybody?"

A slight chuckle then, "Did I know you? There are too many now to even know all the names, let alone who they are and who they're related to."

"Did you spend a lot of time with Noah?"

"I spent a lot of time with both my grandfather and grandmother. Very wonderful people. Caring and thoughtful, full of unbelievable knowledge. Their word is as good as gold. I miss them both."

"So they died?"

"No. Only my father knows their whereabouts and my father avoids people nowadays."

"But why?"

"He fears God."

Nabella felt the hairs prickle on her arms. "Why?"

Arphaxad fixed a vacant stare upon her. "For each person's disobedience there are consequences. God sees all, knows all. He counts all the hairs on everyone's head, even yours. That is how powerful He is. And He will do whatever is necessary to bring the true relationship between Himself and man back into order."

"But what have we done that's so bad?"

"Individually I do not know. But as a people, many have lied and some taken advantage of others. And we have not kept His command to fill the earth."

Eleven

And the Lord said, Behold, the people is one, and they have all one language.
Genesis 11:6a (KJV)

The takhi galloped a short distance before Barukh had to rein it to a trot. Shoshana kept slipping from side to side and even when he'd reach behind to shove her upright she'd slide to the other side.

Barukh's patience snapped. "Stay in the middle."

"I'm trying!" She squeaked.

The fear in her voice made him slow his mount to a walk. He had been willing to shove her from side to side until she got the hang of it, but if she was that scared she would never get her balance. Barukh gritted his teeth and tried to sound patient. "You all right?"

"I am now."

"Shoshana, is everyone at the tent or the house?"

"The house."

They walked, trotted until Shoshana protested then walked the rest of the way. Shoshana happily chattered away answering most of her own questions. Barukh endured the child. He normally didn't mind her, but right now he just wanted to gallop to Jokaan's, toss Shoshana from the takhi, and take off after Nabella. But he had no idea where his betrothed might be. He would have to get information first. When they finally rode into the front of Jokaan's place, Barukh spotted Adara and urged the takhi into a jog.

"Greetings, Barukh."

"I brought your wayward sister home."

Adara frowned at Shoshana then helped her from his mount. "What do you mean, wayward?"

Barukh glanced at Shoshana. "Do you want to tell her or do you want me to."

Shoshana hung her head and mumbled, "I went to find Bella."

"What do you mean?"

"Shoshana thought Nabella was at my place."

"What!" Adara placed a hand on her hip glaring at her youngest sister. "You went all the way to Barukh's alone?"

Shoshana imitated Adara and put a hand on her hip. "I-"

"Ah, I don't mean to interrupt, but I would like to speak with Jokaan. Where can I find him?"

Adara tore her eyes from Shoshana. "He isn't here."

"Ah-he! Then where is he?"

"He and Tomar went to speak with Shem."

"Shem! How long ago did they leave?" Barukh swallowed his irritation. Without a doubt he knew where Nabella went.

"Two days ago. They should be returning in another two or three days. If you would like some food and drink, someone will be in the house to help you." She eyeballed Shoshana, "I have things to attend to, I'm sorry Barukh,"

"No, thank you. Do you know exactly where your father went?"

"Tomar told me they had a lead and went to the portion of the tent city that edges the Little Euphrates. That's all I know."

"Good enough, Ha-yah!" He turned his takhi and raced down the lane then out to the edge of the orchard. When he scanned the vast plain of Shinar to the east he felt the hair on the back of his neck rise and reined his takhi in. His mind raced. She could be anywhere. She could be hurt and lay dying somewhere. Or maybe she had been dragged into some animal's lair. That better not be the case, at least not until he married her. Barukh's lips pressed into a thin line.

He would go straight to the tent city. It's what Jokaan would do and if Nabella followed he might just catch her. When he arrived he would ask around. If no one saw her, then he would zigzag back and ask whoever he ran into of her whereabouts.

He pointed the takhi's nose to the grassland. At first his mount hesitated, the vast ocean of grass unfamiliar. But it soon realized the pleasure of traveling through grass and Barukh now fought with the animal while it grabbed mouthfuls of succulent greens.

"Ah-he, you're just going to have to jog the whole way if you're not going to cooperate." Barukh pulled the reins kicking its sides. With a shake of its head, the steed settled into the pace. Barukh studied the landscape. Sheep, cattle, and wild aurochs dotted the plain. Antelope bound toward the horizon. Small groups of animals he didn't recognize grazed farther out. Most paid no attention to him except to drift away.

He had been worried about Nabella. But with each step of the takhi's monotonous pace he began to think how this situation would affect him. A frown tugged at the corners of his mouth. What in the world could Nabella be thinking to take off by herself? It would be just like her to want to see Shem, and they both knew Jokaan would not permit her to go along. But to disobey her father—inexcusable. It would reflect poorly on the family, and him. And if something happened to her, how would he make his alliance with Jokaan?

As darkness drew near Barukh's takhi plodded toward the first few dwellings of the tent city that lined the Little Euphrates. He had stewed over Nabella's actions most of the day. Anger seeped through the very core of his being. *Just wait until I get my hands on her. She will not be so insolent with me!* He glanced at the tents with their glow of oil lamps or fires and knew he had to calm down. It would be necessary to present himself respectable and collected.

With a groan Barukh dismounted. He had never ridden so long. Bent legs protested when he tried to straighten and another groan escaped when he hobbled toward the river. The animal smelled water and nudged him. Barukh pushed sore limbs to a fast walk. His takhi wadded ankle deep into the slow moving water slurping with each gulp. While he waited, Barukh took the opportunity to study the settlement.

As far as he could see, a vast array of tents and trees stretched to the north and west. Beyond that, the immense tower from The City raised skyward, the lighted temple and steps appeared unnatural but exciting. Barukh turned his eyes to the waning light. His emotions seemed as varied as the sunset's colors. Bright red for annoyance, deep blue fear for Nabella, yellow hope that she would accept his move to The City, orange uncertainty. Inky black the anger he held for her inconsideration.

Barukh sighed. His takhi lifted its head. Water trickled from its muzzle while it stared at the bank. The man's eyes followed his takhi's gaze to a boy resting under a nearby bush. The boy smiled and waved. Barukh narrowed his eyes. *Well, I might as well start my questions with him.* When he neared he realized with a start the boy's legs were crippled. Had he been sitting there the whole time? *And I never noticed? Ah-he.* Impatient with his lack of observation he ignored the formal greeting.

"Have you been here the whole time?"

"Greetings and yes, I like your takhi."

Barukh scowled. He didn't want to get drawn into a long conversation. "I do too."

"If I had a takhi, or even an ox, I could get around."

"You'd still have to have help getting up and down."

"I know. But I could get around better."

"I bet you could. Listen," Barukh paused scratching his stubble. "I'm looking for someone."

"I know."

"How do you know?"

"She was here."

"When? How is she? How long ago?"

The boy looked down, suppressing a laugh. Anger rushed through Barukh again. Why did the boy try to hide a laugh? Was something wrong with the way he looked? Barukh glanced at his body.

"I knew someone would come looking for her."

Barukh blew out his breath, "How did you know?"

"Because she's nice. Someone that nice always has people that love them enough to look for them. Do you love her?"

"She's my betrothed."

The boy's eyes widened. "She's old enough?"

"Of course." Barukh glared, indignant. What did this boy think of him? Or had Nabella said something about him?

"Well, she looked different, really young. Maybe because she was by herself."

"When did you last see her?"

"Yesterday."

Barukh sighed. If Nabella made it this far unharmed, she most likely had already arrived at Shem's.

"Do you know where she went?" Barukh could not be sure in the twilight, but did the boy frown?

"There were two other strangers here. She was following them."

Barukh's eyes narrowed again. Why did the boy evade him?

"And where were they going?"

"You'll have to ask Melek. The strangers spoke with him and left."

Barukh knew the boy chose to remain quiet about something, and he also suspected no more information would be volunteered.

"Where will I find this Melek?" The question rolled into an exasperated growl.

Undaunted the boy twisted and gestured at the tent city. "Go that way and the first tent you run into that has corrals is his."

Barukh nodded and pushed past the boy. He passed tent after glowing tent. The smell of cooked food that lingered on the still air made his stomach grumble. And he was thirsty. Why didn't he get a drink from the river too? Barukh limped down the well-worn path muttering to himself. His legs would never be the same.

Lost in his thoughts he jerked at the stomp of a takhi. Three pairs of eyes stared at him from a wooden railed pen. A yell filtered through a worn tent set just past the corral. The flap burst open and a small, lithe man stepped through the corral poles to quiet the animals.

"Greetings, ah, Melek?" Barukh moved within a few cubits of the enclosure.

"That is I, and how do you come by my name?"

"The crippled boy by the creek."

"Ah yes, Seth."

"I didn't catch his name."

"He is our official greeter for those who enter our portion of the tent city. And greetings. What good news do you bring?"

Barukh gritted his teeth and finished the formal greetings. *Good, now that we have that out of the way.*

"And what can I do for you…"

"Barukh. My name's Barukh. I'm trying to find the two men who came through here yesterday with an old takhi."

"Oh yes, I spoke with them. But first let me help you with your animal. You will go no farther tonight. You can stay here and leave first thing in the morning."

Barukh's shoulders sagged. He didn't realize just how tired and hungry he felt until now. He accepted Melek's hospitality without hesitation. After a modest meal Melek and his wife spread blankets over a pile of pine boughs. Barukh lay his aching body down. He closed his eyes and the last thoughts he had hung on Nabella. First he prayed for her safety and for this insane trip to end quickly. And second, he planned to give her the tongue-lashing of her life.

***

Cush watched the first light begin to brighten the light grey of dawn then rose from the fire pit. But the men who had drunk and made merry the night before snored soundly. He treaded silently to Nimrod peering down at him. Nimrod lay face up, eyes wide and unblinking. Had he slept at all? Cush shook his head. The man was an enigma. The big man shifted to move away, but Nimrod's quiet voice stopped him.

"What are your intentions?"

Cush fixed his eyes on Nimrod then squatted. "I thought we'd be on our way by now. It'll be slow going with the oxen."

"I don't plan to be back by tonight."

"What?"

"Give the men a break, Cush. They won't be ready to go for two hand-spans or more."

Cush pressed his lips into a thin line then stood.

"What aren't you saying?" Nimrod said.

For an instant, Cush thought Nimrod referred to his disapproval of the men's laziness. Then comprehension dawned. Nimrod somehow knew his thoughts. "I'm going to get Shem and bring him to see this monster."

Nimrod snorted softly. "He won't come."

"If I go now and get him, he could see it before we get to The City."

Nimrod said nothing for such a long time Cush figured he had been dismissed. He spun on his heel only to be stopped once again.

"Take my takhi."

The two men locked eyes in the vague light. Cush nodded then strode toward his blankets. He just did not understand that man anymore. All too happy to accept the animal he lengthened his stride before Nimrod could change his mind. With only a whisper of noise now and again, Cush shuffled around camp. When he had collected a small pack of food and a wineskin of watered down wine, he saddled Nimrod's takhi. Cush glanced toward Nimrod. He hadn't moved. *Did he ever blink?*

Cush knew Shem's oldest son stayed close to his grown children so would be with the temporary outpost at East Lake. And if anyone would know his uncle's whereabouts, it would be Arphaxad. Cush pointed the takhi towards the big lake.

In previous years his attempt to get his cousin, nephews and others in the family to move into The City had failed. He turned his eyes toward the west. *Maybe I can get some of them to come back with me. It would do them good to see the tanniyn as well.* Really they only duped themselves. All those people were hypocrites. They didn't want to move into the walled city, because it would go against God's command. Yet they moved only short distances away, stayed for a while then came back to The City to bargain their goods. Content to fish, harvest timber, gather chemar or anything else that they could trade for fulfilled their needs. If he could convince them of their folly, he felt sure they would move their business into The City permanently. Once they realized they were still in disobedience to God, why would they want to roam about and set up unprotected transitory outposts? God's wrath could still find them there.

Cush set the animal into a ground-eating lope. From his vantage point in the foothills, he could see the mighty Tigris River and the big lake below him to the west. The huge shadow of the mountains behind him stretched across the river and the plain, to where he guessed the Euphrates meandered. Though small, he could still see the beautiful tower and the two and three-story buildings that rose above the stone walls. Pride surged through Cush at the sight of the last twenty years' accomplishment. He watched the early morning sunlight bathe the top of the tower. They had built the temple out of sandstone, and now it shone, vivid and domineering. Cush longed to get back to his City. He imagined the place as it awoke and began to bustle. How could Shem and Noah, and even Japheth, think The City a bad thing? Cush pressed his lips together. *They're wrong, that's all there's to it.*

He studied East Lake with its surrounding mature cedars. A spot to the north lay bare from the felled trees and to the west young cedars dotted a large area where several years ago a harvest had been gathered. Cush shifted his gaze to the mass of broad-leafed trees that dotted the tent outpost, extending around the east side of the large lake. He could even see a few dull specks of tents in between the trees. Cush urged his takhi faster. He would need to push the animal to its limits in order arrive at East Lake outpost by mid-morning.

Twelve

Now the earth was corrupt in God's sight and was full of violence. God saw how corrupt the earth had become, for all the people on earth had corrupted their ways. So God said to Noah, "I am going to put an end to all people, for the earth is filled with violence because of them. I am surely going to destroy both them and the earth. So make yourself an ark of cypress wood; make rooms in it and coat it with pitch inside and out.

Genesis 6:11-14

Nabella swallowed. Even though she knew the actions of the Old World people had caused The Flood, she never thought of God being personally displeased with each individual who sinned. And that this compiled result brought on God's wrath and The Flood.

"Is God always so vengeful?" She whispered.

"God is not vengeful, He is a God of justice, mercy and love and gives us chance after chance. He did so in the Old World too, right up until He closed the door of the ark."

Nabella swallowed again clasping and unclasping her hands upon her knees. Look at all the ways she had disobeyed her father, and therefore God, just in the last few days. Had she run out of chances? She let out a long breath. "I'm in trouble."

Arphaxad laughed. "Aren't we all?"

"No, I'm serious. I deceived my family, disguised myself, and lied to people along the way. And I eavesdropped on you. I can't imagine God being very happy with me right now."

A small bleat came from outside the tent. Arphaxad sighed, pursed his lips and let out a low windy whistle. At a sound by the tent flap, Nabella twisted in her spot just in time to see a small lamb push its way in.

Arphaxad clucked his tongue. The little animal bleated again then trotted to the man bumping its head against his hand. With a chuckle Arphaxad wrapped a hand under the lamb's belly, pulling it unto his lap. "I see my great grandson has forgotten you again, little one," he murmured. A gentle hand stroked the soft fleece.

Nabella blinked. An animal inside the tent? Father would never have heard of it. "Why do you let the lamb inside?"

The man lifted his head in her direction. "He was injured at a very young age and we took care of him here. Now he thinks this is his home." The older man paused, "And yes, I believe you are correct, God is not pleased with you."

"I don't know what to do. I would have to sacrifice animal after animal because I can't stop my wrongdoing! I don't like that, I need someone to help me."

Arphaxhad's hand stilled on the lamb, lifeless eyes staring at the small creature. He carefully set it on its feet then let a hand trail over the animal's white head. "It would be wonderful if someday someone could take away our sins. But it's not me."

Nabella's heart sank. Still, she leaned forward straining to hear his last words.

"If that's possible we must wait for God's timing." He cleared his throat then faced Nabella. "So, what can you do now to make things right?"

Nabella hung her head and mumbled, "Go home."

"You're headed in the right direction. But there is a flaw."

"I shouldn't go home?" Hope spiked her voice several pitches higher.

"I did not say that. Look closer, there is a flaw in your thinking."

"That I really, really want to see Shem?"

"There is no wrong in wanting to see my father."

Nabella scrunched her face in an attempt to will the answer to come forth. None came. "I don't know what you're trying to tell me."

"Obedience is better than sacrifice, and sacrifice is better than disobedience."

It finally sunk in. Arphaxad would have her go home without even the chance to see Shem. "You mean I came all this way for nothing?"

"Not for nothing, and there is still a flaw. Something you have to remedy before you go home."

"Please don't make me go home without seeing Shem. I'm so close!"

"There is one way that would still make things right."

Nabella hunched over. She knew the answer but didn't want to say it. For if she spoke it then she would have to do it. And she didn't want to. She scooted back and straightened her dagger. *Think Nabella, think. There must be another way.* Tentative fingers reached for her hat then wrapped and unwrapped around its rim. Finally she put it on, tucking her hair beneath the brim, glad for once the strands were thin. The chin strap dangled against her throat. Bit by bit she tightened then knotted the strap under her jaw. At last she let out a long breath.

"I have to go to my father."

Arphaxad nodded. "Yes. And he just might let you go with him to find Shem."

"No he won't. He would see that as a reward and, believe me, he will want to punish me—"

Suddenly pounding hooves slid to a stop in front of the tent. Then a takhi's frantic snort. The tent flap ripped open and a large dark figure ducked into the shaded interior. When the man straightened Nabella gasped. Cush! *Ah-he! Stop gasping.* She balled her fists.

"Where is your father?" He glared at the blind man.

"Greetings to you too, Cush."

"I don't have time for small talk, Arphaxad. Where is he?"

Nabella drew her knees to her chest and tried to become invisible.

"I am not sure."

"You lie, cousin!" Bitterness edged Cush's voice. He lunged forward grabbing Arphaxad by his shirt front and dragged him to his feet. A plaintive bleat escaped from the lamb. Cush's huge foot snapped against the little animal's side and sent it across the dirt floor. It rolled then scampered from the tent with a loud cry. "Tell me where Shem is!"

"Hey!" Nabella bound to her feet and grabbed Cush's massive fist. Both of her hands did not fit around his one.

Cush shoved Nabella to the ground and stepped on her chest. His eyes spewed forth barely contained fury. A deep snarl rumbled from his throat. "Stay there if you know what's good for you, boy."

Nabella stared back, eyes narrowed.

Arphaxad turned his head in her direction. "Remain where you are. My cousin and I have had this feud for the past ninety years." His vacant eyes turned in the direction of his cousin. "Let go, Cush, or are you going to fight a blind man?"

Cush loosened his grip, and his foot shifted. Nabella rolled behind Arphaxad as Cush shoved the man. He stumbled back and she threw up hands to steady the man. With wobbly legs Nabella scrambled to her feet.

"You're no better than the rest. You think you are so high and mighty, but you lied right to my face." Cush's cheeks flooded deep crimson a vein bulging on his neck. He crossed his arms over his chest. "Are you going to tell me?"

"Why would I? You're acting like a raging bull!"

Cush's dark face stormed.

Nabella's throat squeezed tight. She had disliked Cush before but now, fear settled like a heavy wet blanket its weight engulfing.

Suddenly the dark man's hand shot out, wrapped around Nabella's shirtfront yanking her to his side. "You better tell me where Shem is. If you lead me wrong, well, no telling when your great grandson or whoever he is will make it back to you."

"Cush, look, you don't want to do this, believe me."

"Tell me or I swear the boy gets hurt." The threat hung heavy between the men.

"Don—" Pain exploded against her cheek and tongue. Cush's hand had lashed out so fast she didn't see it coming. She tasted blood, but her only thought was her hat. It stayed firm, held in place by the strap. Fists balled as she spat blood into the fire. Like a boy.

Arphaxad managed to step forward and grab Cush with one hand, holding Nabella's arm firm with the other. "Let him go."

"Don't tell me what to do, cousin!" Cush tore Arphaxad's hand off his shirt and thrust him to the ground. The blind man landed with a grunt. At once he came to his knees and crawled, one hand in front of him.

Cush backed to the opening pushing Nabella through then stooped, half in half out the entrance.

"Where?"

"It's not worth it, Cush."

The large man cursed squeezing Nabella's arm until it hurt.

"Ouch!" Nabella punched him with her free hand then grunted. The man did not even flinch. What was he made of? Rock?

"Where! Or do you want him to come back blind?"

Nabella's eyes flew wide, and she struggled in earnest.

"No wait!" Arphaxad held an arm in front of him, "Try the caves in the cliffs directly east of here, on the other side of the Tigris."

"He better be there."

"That is where I knew him to be last, at least a year ago."

"Like I said, he better be there." Cush snarled over his shoulder. Hands flew as he whipped a leather cord around Nabella's hands and pulled tight. In one bound he mounted his takhi jerking her behind him. "You better stay on or it's going to hurt when you land."

"Cuuush!"

Arphaxad's jagged shout carried over the pounding of the takhi's hooves.

***

Barukh trotted his takhi into the meadow. A man stood outside his tent arms raised muttering to himself, or was that a prayer? Either way it seemed odd. He stared at the strange man from atop his mount. Barukh called, "Are you Arphaxad?"

The man stared straight up continuing to mutter. Barukh glanced around.

"Greetings," he called in the direction of the tent, but no one answered. He glanced once more at the muttering man, dismounted then lead his mount to the side of the tent. A pile of fly-swarming dung welcomed him as he tethered his takhi to a post. The trampled ground looked fresh to his untrained eyes. He stooped and took a closer look. Yes, there were both takhi and man-sized tracks, and they were fresh. But over there deeper markings abounded. Deeper takhi tracks were on top of the other imprints as if this steed carried a heavy load.

This Arphaxad is popular.

Barukh stood to one side and cleared his throat. The man still ignored him. Barukh scrubbed his dark blond stubble. "Ah-hum."

The odd man continued in his own world. At last Barukh lost his patience. He stomped his way to the front of the man, placing one hand on a hip.

"Look, all I need is some information then I'll leave you alone. I'm trying to find two men who are looking for Shem."

Still no response.

"And I'm looking for a girl who is following them."

The man let his arms drop and turned his head. Unseeing eyes stared past. Barukh started then waved a hand in front of the man's face. *He's blind.*

"Are *you* Arphaxad?"

"What do you want with the girl?"

"You're blind! Ah, never mind. She's my betrothed and I've come to take her home."

"Did she leave you?"

"Yes, I mean no! I didn't even know she was gone until her little sister came looking for her." Barukh grimaced. Why did he just disclose his personal life to this stranger?

The man finally gave a curt nod as if he had come to a decision. "Follow the tracks who carries a heavy load," Arphaxad pointed, and Barukh wondered how he knew where they were. "Cush has her."

"Cush?" Barukh's brows raised in disbelief.

"He came here less than half a hand-span ago. I'm afraid my cousin has a grudge against me and took the boy with him."

"The boy?" Barukh threw his hands into the air. "Ah-he!" *What is going on?*

"Your betrothed is disguised like a boy." Arphaxad's dry tone lay flat.

Barukh's mouth dropped open. He could only utter an astounded. "Ah…ah."

"Go after them, man! Cush can be cruel and vindictive especially to get at me."

"Where did they go?"

Arphaxad told him finishing with, "Cush will be looking for caves. It would be wise to keep her disguise, who knows what he would do if he discovers she is a girl."

"Yes," Barukh swallowed hard and glanced at the tracks. *And who knows what he would do to me.* "Ah. Do you think I should get Jokaan and Tomar?"

Though the man was blind the disgusted look on his face could not be mistaken. "Their takhi is old and weary. Now go!" Arphaxad fumbled for Barukh's chest and gave him a shove.

Barukh walked to his takhi stiff-legged in a trance. He would have to get Nabella from Cush? How was he supposed to do that? Maybe he should get Jokaan and Tomar. Arphaxad would never know. He mounted with the intent but realized they would just ask him to ride ahead and get her. For the first time he could remember, he cursed.

Barukh swung his takhi around heading for the cliffs, one eye on the takhi tracks. He set his mount to a slow lope eyeing the tracks. Cush had circled the lake on the south side and crossed the Tigris not far downstream. Barukh turned his takhi to the river. He kicked the steed and leaned forward, but it laid ears back sidestepping. Again and again he urged the takhi forward, but the animal balked each time. Barukh muttered under his breath. He pressed his lips together and glanced up and down the river in vain hope to spare his clothes from a soaking. But he could see no other way. At last he dismounted and marched into the water. With a snort the takhi pricked its ears and followed. Barukh glared at his mount. He would find a more suitable mount when this mess came to an end.

The water, swift and deep, carried them far downstream before his miserable takhi dragged them both out of the water. Once they climbed onto the bank, Barukh fought the urge to wring his clothes dry. Instead he opted to look for Cush's tracks. The large damp spot thirty cubits upstream was a dead giveaway. He managed to follow the galloping tracks with ease for some time. Then, despite the wide swath that cut towards the cliffs, he somehow lost the tracks. Barukh stopped and backtracked until he saw where they veered from a straight course toward several canyons. The tracks headed northeast. Barukh pulled up and scanned the terrain in front of him. Sumac and berry bushes, cedars, and tall seasonal plants made it impossible to see very far. *What are you doing, Cush?* Barukh hesitated. Should he follow the tracks or go straight to the cliffs in hopes of running into them? What if Cush discovered Nabella was a girl? Barukh's stomach lurched. *I guess I better follow the tracks.*

From what he could tell, Cush headed northeast along the front of the cliffs. The brush and rock became thicker and before long he could not find the trail despite his best efforts. Barukh dismounted to take a closer look. If Jabari were here, he would know which way to go. Barukh's eyes narrowed, jaw jutting forward. Without thinking, a hand went to his hip. Stubborn visage set in and he searched in earnest. He went back and forth and back again several times. But in a short while the ground became so churned even Jabari could not have found Cush's tracks. With a sigh Barukh gave up and angled toward the canyons and cliffs.

On either side jagged crags raised their stony arms skyward. The takhi slowed and picked its way through rocks and fallen debris. Barukh loosened the reins and twisted in the saddle. There, between breaks in the vegetation a few caves blackened the canyon walls. He would just start with the first one and work his way up the canyon.

Barukh tethered his takhi to a low branch. He scrambled up the incline and paused by the mouth of the cave.

"Greetings," his voice echoed in the empty cavity. No sign of Shem. Barukh didn't bother to get his takhi; instead he climbed over the rocky path to another cave fifty cubits away.

"Anyone here?" The darkness swallowed his voice. Yet there seemed to be a faint light toward the back. Barukh tried to squint through the shadowy blackness. Maybe someone lived back there and couldn't hear him. His tongue cleaved to the roof of his mouth at the thought of entering the vast unknown before him. *But if Nabella*, Barukh gritted his teeth and crept in. Dank air closed around him. Somewhere up ahead the rush of running water echoed. When he could no longer see his feet he groped for the damp wall. Slime oozed around his fingers. He yanked his hand away. *Yuck, just great.* Now what was he supposed to do with his gunk-covered hand? He held it in front of him and crept forward. Dangling roots warned him when the cave ceiling dropped low, and he ducked under their spidery fingers.

At last he realized the light came from a crack in the cave ceiling. Narrow shafts of sunlight streamed onto the surface of a small pool. Barukh stopped near its edge and stared. Water cascaded down the back wall into the reserve. Sunlight danced across the water then reflected onto the walls. A colorful prism shimmered in the mist. Why didn't Shem live here? This would be the perfect cave. It had water. He shook his head. Barukh knelt to wash his hand then froze. Tracks. Big strange tracks. With deep claw marks. He scrambled upright and took a step back. Shallow breaths escaped in small blasts. Wild-eyed he scanned the cave then spun around scurrying toward the entrance.

Thud!

Pain exploded in his head and light burst in front of his eyes. The sunlight at the opening of the cave shrank smaller and smaller to the size of a lentil. Thin roots caressed Barukh's face as he sank to the ground. Then blackness closed in around him.

A moan woke him up. There it was again. Barukh's eyes flittered open. Why was he lying on the ground with his face in the dirt? And why is the light so far away? *Where am I, oooh, the cave.* He groaned and pushed himself to his knees. Barukh heard another moan but from a distance. He gasped then realized the sound was an echo of his own voice. A laugh almost escaped out loud, but his head hurt too much. Barukh raised his hand to his head and felt a sticky bump. A grunt escaped when he pulled a hand out of his thick blond hair and saw blood in the dim light. How long had he been out? Barukh shoved himself upright, lurching toward the opening. This time he held his hand in front of his head as he ducked under the low spot of the cave ceiling.

A sigh of relief escaped when Barukh stumbled from the cave and realized the sun had hardly moved. So he hadn't been out very long after all. He looked back into the entrance. Images of large strange footprints, with claws, poured through his mind. Barukh jumped and bolted to his takhi. Hands shook while he untied the animal then he noticed the takhi. It stood eyes half closed, a wisp of grass hung from its mouth. Barukh leaned his throbbing head against the saddle.

"Get a grip on yourself, man!" Barukh drew in a shaky breath. *There's no wild tanniyn here now. It's facing Cush that has me all unnerved.*

He detested this running around. He just wanted to be back at his house, working in his new vineyards, and sipping wine in the evening. Let Nimrod be out here in this part of the country, this wilderness. He was the one who liked to hunt the wild beasts, like the owner of those footprints. Barukh shuddered and mounted. *Just move on, the sooner you find Nabella the sooner you can go home.*

***

Nabella eyed the ground as it flew by. Two things stopped her from throwing herself off the takhi. First, even if she landed unscathed Cush would just run her down. And second, would the chin strap keep her hat in place when she hit the ground? Her long hair would be a dead giveaway of her identity. The last thought propelled her to stay seated behind the man. She gripped his tunic tight between her tethered hands. Her riding skills were limited, though she was gaining experience rapidly. But when Cush reined to a sudden stop her face smashed into his back.

"So which one of the great, great grandsons are you?" Cush let his takhi pick its way through a jumble of fallen boulders.

"I don't know."

"Well, who's your father?"

Nabella pressed lips together. She refused to lie to the big man. He wasn't worth it.

Cush laughed harshly. "I won't hold you for a bargain from your father if that's what you're worried about. I have no gripe with him."

Yes you do, you tried to bully him into moving to The City! If you found out who I really am you would *hold me for a bargain.*

Cush let out a growl at her refusal to speak. "Forget it."

The silence thickened. Neither spoke until they entered a side canyon rich with colorful autumn leaves and berries. Cush reined in, grabbed her arm then dropped her to the ground. Nabella grunted as she fell on her backside. *My hat!* Her hands gripped the brim and yanked it down securely. She rolled over scrambling to her feet. The man had already tethered his takhi and with long strides stomped toward her.

"See that cave?" He jutted his chin to a dark crevice above their heads. "Go and tell me if anyone's in there or if it looks like someone's ever lived there."

Nabella stared at the cave. It would be a hard climb with hands tied. She glanced at Cush and knew he would strike her if she refused. With a deep breath she shifted her eyes to the cliff wall scouting for the best route. Nabella clambered over rocks and skirted a few boulders. She grabbed onto roots and branches and anything else that offered a good hold. A rock protruded out of the soil, and she reached to grab it. A jagged edge of the stone ripped half of her fingernail off.

"Ouch." She shook her hand and stuck her finger in her mouth.

"What are you doing? Get going."

"I am." Nabella felt the heat of anger rise up her neck. *What would a boy do, what would a boy do?* She pulled herself upright and glared at the man. But he stood still, cold eyes locked on hers. Without a sound Nabella turned and scrambled the rest of the way to the cave.

"Greetings?"

No answer. She tiptoed into the darkness and paused. No one had been here, but Cush couldn't see her where she stood. One glance around told her no jagged stones lay about. She tried to gnaw on the leather straps but when that didn't work, pulled at the knots. A strip loosened, but she couldn't flip it over her fists.

"Anything?" Cush's voice came to her faint from outside the cave.

Nabella clucked her tongue. Maybe if she had more time, but she didn't want to arouse his suspicion. She spun on her heel and marched to the opening. "No."

With each step she sought solid ground, working her way back to Cush. He already sat on his takhi and when she neared, snagged her arm swinging her behind him. Cush continued deeper and deeper into the canyon. Under different circumstances she would have enjoyed the ride.

They passed several openings in the side of the cliff wall and as the takhi clip-clopped beneath them Nabella wondered why Cush didn't stop. Then the man halted and swung her down.

"Those two caves," he pointed to larger ones. Nabella wrinkled her nose when Cush lifted his arm. *Phew!* All too happy to obey, she slid off the takhi pulling in a deep breath of the tangy aroma of the early fall season. But again no one had been in the either of the rock shelters. She zigzagged her way back to him mounting from the uphill side of the takhi.

The canyon walls closed around them the farther they moved into the chasm. Nabella craned her neck to stare at the steep walls in hopes of finding another cave. *What will Cush do if we don't find Shem?* She didn't want to think about her captor's temper. Cush's muttering broke through her thoughts. She peered around the man's upper arm. Huge boulders and dirt lay strewn across the path forcing them to hug the opposite cannon wall. Once they rounded the jagged pieces sheered from the cliffs above, Cush yanked his steed to a stop. He cursed. "This is the end of the canyon."

He reined his mount in a tight circle. Nabella grabbed his tunic so she wouldn't fall off. When she scooted to right herself she saw a cave high on the far wall.

"What about that one?"

Cush glanced over his shoulder at the back of the canyon. "Where?"

"On the other side."

He snapped his head around.

"Higher."

Nabella gritted her teeth at his sarcastic laugh. "You really want to climb that high? Well go to it."

The big man urged his mount as close as possible then let Nabella slide off. She leaned into the takhi to catch her balance then turned and hauled herself onto a boulder. Her tethered hands once again grabbed at anything that would help. Halfway up she wondered why she ever opened her mouth. Yet only once did she stop to catch her breath and knot the leather ties of her hat tighter. Panting, Nabella straightened and fixed her eyes on Cush. He stared back, arms crossed. She got the message and after a few more deep breaths scrambled upward.

Just below the opening she stopped. *Well, I think at least here you'd be out of the reach of most animals.* She eyed the shelf above and decided the only way to get there would be to climb the old oak in front of her.

It proved difficult only because her hands were tied. At last she scooted out on an upper limb. She leaned forward and gripped a smaller branch above her head. Nabella swung her legs to the front, arched her back then landed with a grunt on the flat rock protruding from the mouth of the cave. When her legs collapsed she fell to her knees. She gasped. A woman squatted over dried berries, the spear in her hand pointed at Nabella. Quickly Nabella brought a finger to her lips then motioned with her arms for the woman to stay low and move back into the cave. The woman studied her, brows pinched together. Her eyes lingered on the straps that held Nabella's hands together. At last she nodded and crawled backward.

Nabella pushed herself up and looked over the edge. Cush stood, arms still crossed. She would have to make this quick. Nabella strode into the cave. This must be where Shem and his wife lived.

Nabella came to the woman and grasped her hands. "Greetings don't be afraid. Cush has captured me and is forcing me to look in all the caves for Shem. He is angry with Arphaxad for some reason."

The slim woman's shoulders slumped. "Arphaxad," she whispered. "They have been angry with each other for many years. Why does Cush want to see Shem?"

"I have no idea. You'll be safe. I'll tell him no one is here. Don't come out for a while in case he turns back or looks around."

"Do not lie on my account, child."

Nabella grimaced. The intend to lie slipped off of her tongue so easy she hadn't even realized it would be lying.

"But you can tell him that Shem is not here."

Nabella's eyes brightened.

The woman studied Nabella's hands. "Now. What can I do for you, child? He is holding you against your will?"

"Yes but it's," Nabella paused. "It's complicated. You are Shem's wife?"

The woman nodded persisting in gentle tones, "What can I do for you?"

"I would love to talk with you and Shem. Is that alright?"

The woman smiled clasping her hand over Nabella's. "Yes, and thank you for keeping our home a secret."

Nabella's eyes shone. "Thank you…"

"Machlah."

"Thank you, Machlah, I'll try to return under better conditions. I need to go so Cush doesn't get suspicious." Nabella marched from the cave, grasped a branch, and swung onto the tree. She maneuvered her way down the limbs. Though her heart pounded from the discovery, Nabella forced herself to move slowly and deliberately. She refused to look at Cush until she neared the bottom.

"Well?"

"Shem's not here either."

Cush swore and stomped in a circle. "Hurry up and get down here."

"I'm trying," she scowled at the man taking her time. After all she didn't want to fall and injure herself or loosen her hat. Nor did she look forward to riding behind the angry, smelly man.

"Come on, what's your problem?"

"I'm coming. This isn't the easiest to do with my hands tied."

Cush strode the rest of the distance to her snatching the loose ends of the straps. Nabella assumed he meant to steady her. Instead he lifted her with one hand and while she dangled carried her to his mount. Without a break in his momentum he let go of her straps, leapt to the takhi's back then held out his arm. She inhaled a deep breath, took a flying leap, swung from his arm and landed behind him.

"Ha-yah!"

They headed out the canyon, and Nabella closed her eyes. Weary beyond what she ever thought possible she tried to ignore the pain in her knees. And the hunger that pinched her stomach. How long would they do this? Would Cush really make her do all the work while he sat around with the takhi? *Yes, he would.*

The canyon widened. A rock crashed from the side of the cliff. Nabella jerked. The takhi snorted, tossing its head. Cush reined in studying the terrain.

"What is it?"

"Shhh," he glanced at his takhi. It stood quiet, weary under the weight of two people. With another glance at the cliffside Cush gave a shake of his head. "I don't know. Not a meat eater or this takhi wouldn't be standing still."

The takhi whinnied. Another whinny sounded from behind the fallen jumble of boulders. A takhi and rider rounded the debris. Nabella's eyes flew wide. *Barukh? What in the world is he doing here?* Suddenly she knew and cringed. He had come to rescue her.

Barukh yanked the reins hard. The animal's mouth flew open as it tucked its chin, dancing backward. He eased up on the reins, and his mount stopped with a snort shaking its head.

The men stared at each other. At last Barukh looked past Cush to Nabella. His head jerked back, and his eyes flew wide. A scowl followed. Nabella ducked her head behind Cush.

"What do you want, son of Gideon?" Cush finally demanded.

"Ah," Barukh looked around then scratched his forehead. "Well..."

Before Barukh could continue Cush kicked his takhi. "Get out of my way," he growled as his mound jumped forward. Barukh's steed swung its rump to the side and sidled from the advancing Cush.

"Ahhh no, wait." Barukh gave a great amount of attention to his sidestepping mount.

Why doesn't he just demand me from Cush? Her captor's takhi made another leap forward, and she clutched the back of the man's tunic. Nabella's eyes darted to the rocky ground. Should she jump? Maybe Barukh could gallop past her and swing her onto his takhi. But one glance at her betrothed and she dismissed the idea. Barukh kept his eyes riveted to his mount and besides, Cush would just catch her. And she couldn't take a chance her hair would fall from under the hat. Cush pushed his takhi abreast of the young man, and Nabella caught Barukh's eye. *Do something!* For an instant she let go to show him her tethered hands.

Barukh's face clouded. "Let her—him go."

With a laugh Cush brushed past Barukh then gave the man a shove with his sandal. The younger man grunted when he hit the ground.

"Barukh," Nabella gasped.

All at once a large takhi and its rider sailed over the last edge of jumbled debris blocking Cush's path.

Thirteen

I am going to bring floodwaters on the earth to destroy all life under the heavens, every creature that has the breath of life in it. Everything on earth will perish. But I will establish my covenant with you, and you will enter the ark—you and your sons and your wife and your sons' wives with you.

Genesis 6:17-18

"I thought you might need some help brother," Kfir grinned. "Greetings, Cush. And ah, Nabel?"

Nabella's mouth dropped open. Kfir had come to help rescue her too? Stunned she could only stare as the man turned his gaze to Cush, his features hardening.

"Do as my brother says."

Cush's muscles tense. "Right now this boy means more to me than he does to you, so back off!" He kicked his takhi, and Nabella almost tumbled to the ground when the animal leapt forward. Kfir charged Cush launching himself at the man. Cush lurched sideways when Kfir's chest rammed into the big man's shoulder, his arm wrapping around Cush's neck. Both men toppled to the ground. The animal bolted. Nabella, knocked sideways, clung to the saddle, one leg over the takhi's rump, the other flopping loose. Her muscles strained as she tried to hang on. As each hoof pounded her body jarred against the stiff leather, but she managed to dangle for a few strides. Cush's mount took a turn in the path, and her fingers tore loose. Nabella flew into the air. Her hat flopped over her eyes. She rolled and pushed herself up. With a quick shove Nabella pushed her hair back under the hat staggering toward the men.

The flash of Cush's dagger gripped tight in his hand sped through the air toward Kfir's chest. She dropped to her knees, tethered hands covering her mouth. "No!"

Kfir twisted kicking Cush's forearm. The knife sliced past Kfir. Nabella tore her eyes from the struggle and glanced at Barukh. He had dismounted and busied himself tethering his takhi.

"Barukh, go!" Nabella screamed.

Barukh turned, face pale. He slung the reins over a low limb then loped in the direction of the fighting men. He grabbed a branch swinging it at the big man. The stick broke across Cush's back and he turned. With a slow fiery gaze upon the offender he leapt to his feet.

Barukh stumbled backward holding his hands in the air. "Look, all we want is the g-boy. No trouble."

"I told you I need him right now. You can have him back in a few days."

Kfir thrust his feet under him and launched onto Cush's back. In one motion he wrapped his forearm against the large man's throat and wrapped his legs around Cush's waist. He grabbed his own wrist with his other hand. Kfir's muscles bulged as his grasp tightened into a chokehold. Cush lurched backward and with his free hand tried to break Kfir's hold. A wild swing brought his dagger in an arch at the young man's arm. Kfir jerked a leg upward to deflect the blade the same instant the stub of Barukh's branch bounced off the dark man's chest. Cush grunted when Kfir's heel dug into his stomach and swung the dagger at his attacker's head. The younger man twisted to the side, and Cush nicked his own ear. A string of strangled curses escaped. The large man swung his body around, but Kfir hung on.

Kfir shoved a knee in the small of Cush's back. Veins bulged on Kfir's neck as he pulled with all his might against Cush's throat. The dark skin of Cush's face turned deep purple. He stabbed blindly with the dagger and blood spurted from Kfir's arm.

Horrified she scrambled to her feet. "Barukh, *do* something!"

Barukh, face twisted in fear, darted in. Cush's foot shot out, slammed into Barukh's stomach knocking him to the ground.

With a yelp Barukh clutched his elbow.

Nabella stared at Barukh then forced her eyes to the two grappling men. Cush fell back crushing Kfir beneath his massive frame. Kfir grunted, his grip loosening. Cush sucked in air and spun around. Kfir twisted, but the large man's knee ground into his chest. Cush drew his hand back, flipping the dagger blade down, and smirked.

Nabella screamed.

She dashed at Cush then gripped his arm, but he flicked her to the side like a discarded olive pit.

"Nabella, run!" Kfir managed to get out.

"No," she panted. "Cush, stop!" Again Nabella flung herself at the formidable man. From the corner of her eye she saw a massive sandaled-foot kick Cush. He landed on his side and rolled several lengths dragging Nabella with him. A spear sliced through the air into the side of his shirt, pinning him to the ground.

Nabella sprung to her feet. The tallest man she'd ever seen strode toward them. He ducked under a tree branch that hung at least five cubits from the ground. Bronze skin contrasted sharply with dark blue eyes that creased at their corners. He glared at Cush, nostrils flaring. Too stunned to move Nabella could only gawk. Vaguely she realized Kfir had placed himself between her and the two men.

Cush grabbed the spear and yanked, but it had lodged tight into the ground. He re-clamped his hands, face grimacing as he tried again.

"Enough, Cush!" Authority rang in the giant's voice and he raised another spear, "Or this one will pierce your skin."

Cush stopped and cursed again, hands still on the shaft, eyes narrowed to slits.

"What is the meaning of this? You were taught better." The giant man boomed, unperturbed by Cush's temper.

Before Cush could answer a clatter of hooves echoed against the canyon walls and a whinny rang out. Two men rounded the fallen debris, one led a tired takhi, the other Cush's takhi. Nabella sucked in a breath as her eyes flew wide. She ducked her head.

Father.

The giant glared in their direction bellowing, "What now!" He gestured toward the newcomers. "You two, over here, now!"

Nabella peeked from under her hat. Both men moved near the man.

"I want an explanation from everyone. Starting with," his spear tip lowered to Cush's chest, "You."

Cush's lip curled. "I came to take you to see the monster Nimrod and I killed yesterday."

"Why the captive?"

"To make Arphaxad tell me where you were. To get through to you!"

The giant inhale through his nose, face stoic. "You two obviously came as a rescue," he glared at Kfir then Barukh who cradled his arm. "So why are you two here?" He jutted his chin at Jokaan and Tomar.

"We came to find Shem. It is a grave matter that we seek him," Jokaan spoke with a curious glance at Cush, Nabella, and his two neighbors.

"The matter is so pressing Arphaxad told us where to find him," Tomar added.

The giant's eyes narrowed. He gave a curt nod and turned to confront Nabella.

"And you. How did you get into all this mess?"

"I, ah, was with Arphaxad when Cush came," Nabella glanced at her father. His eyes bore through her. Her head drooped, and she stared at her worn sandals and bandaged feet. She started to clasp her clammy hands together, but the tethers prevented it. A heavy pit grew in her stomach.

The man turned his attention back to Cush. "Go and do not come to me again until you make things right with Arphaxad." One handed, he yanked the spear from the ground. Immediately Cush sprang to his feet, arms stretching toward the man, hands splayed open.

"You have to come see this monster, Shem."

Nabella's eyebrows shot up. Shem? This giant was Shem? She dared to raise her head and stare at the man. When her eyes finally reached the waves of his dark hair Nabella realized he wouldn't even fit through the doorways of their house without ducking. His frame, though muscular, tended toward the lean side. He reminded her of the tall strong cedars that grew throughout the foothills and mountains.

Cush took a step grabbing Shem's sinewy forearm. "It took eight of the best fighting men to bring it down. And there are many more of these creatures. Huge tanniyns, meat eaters that can sever a man in half in one bite. Shem, we can't split up and roam this earth. We'd all be annihilated by such beasts. You have to understand, you have to come see for yoursel—"

"Enough! I have seen this creature. You think I knew not of what took place just a few canyons from here? With all the noise you made? I have been living next to this animal for five seasons now. We had a pair of these creatures on the ark, and I was the one who took care of them. This was just a juvenile compared to the massive adults that roamed the Former World. I know every single kind of creature that lives out there. And it doesn't matter, Cush. God gave us dominion over the animals. He gave us the order to multiply and *fill the earth*. He would not do that if we were to perish because of these animals. Your lack of trust in the Lord has greatly increased over the years."

Cush snorted. "What do you expect? God demands impossible things. Have you even heard from Him lately? Has Grandfather?"

Shem looked away drawing a deep breath. "Not since we build the altar and gave thanks for a new beginning. My father does not need to hear from God. *I* do not need to hear from Him, I know His presence. We trust in Him. And God gives us what seems like impossible tasks so we will depend on Him, to see and know His mighty strength. To increase our faith. Of which you obviously lack. Go now, you have my answer. And do not foul yourself more by harming the innocent."

Cush stared at him eyes narrowed, fists clenched. He turned, pausing by Jokaan and hissed, "You, I will speak with later." He yanked the reins of his takhi out of Tomar's hand and in one fluid motion jumped on its back.

"Ha-yah," Cush slapped the animal's neck with his reins, disappearing within a few strides. The rattle of hoof beats rang down the ravine.

Shem turned to Jokaan. "If Arphaxad sent you, it must be important. Come. Come to my humble dwelling." He stared at Barukh and Kfir. "You two take the girl and go home."

"The girl?" Jokaan said in a sharp voice.

Heat rush through Nabella's face. She looked down staring at her grungy disguise. Suddenly Father strode to her and snatched the hat off. Ratty, dirty hair tumbled past her shoulders.

"Nabella!" Jokaan's voice quivered, shock and anger unmistakable. "What are you doing?"

Nabella's heart contracted and lungs slowly squeezed out the last of her air—the last breath she would ever breathe if it were up to her. It felt like the time when she turned five and nearly drowned in a large basin of water. She couldn't even claim it to be something heroic like rescuing Shoshana from the Euphrates—that had been Adara, or worse like the time when she knocked over a vat of oil, and it knocked over another vat, then another and another, ten in all and she tried to clean it up, but the men in the processing building wouldn't let her, they just told her to get her father when all she wanted was to run into the groves where she wished the trees would scoop her up so she could hide in their leaves, but she had to tell her father.

And she had to tell the giant.

"You do know her then?" Shem nodded at Nabella.

"Yes. She…was my daughter."

"And these two?"

Nabella tucked her chin and peeked at her father as he tried to regain control. What did he mean *was* his daughter? An icy finger of terror wrapped around her spine as the reality of what she had done began to sink in.

"Forgive me." Her father's voice shook again. "This is Barukh and Kfir. My neighbors."

Nabella winced trying to clasp her hands again. She squeezed her eyes shut to keep tears from spilling but to no avail. She blinked several times, then glanced at Shem. He studied the two men, stared at her then turned to Jokaan.

"Come with me, all of you."

Kfir turned to Nabella, grabbed her dagger then sliced the tethers around her wrists. Without a word he flipped the weapon handing it to her grip first. She looked into his eyes and saw pain. And knew it didn't come from the wound in his arm. A tear slipped from one eye as she reached for the knife. Kfir winced then set his jaw tearing his gaze away.

Nabella slipped the dagger back into place rubbing her raw wrists. She stole a glance at Barukh. The scowl on his face discouraged any thought of communication. One hand held his elbow, and he gestured with his chin for her to follow the men. Shoulders slumped she obeyed.

Shem led them on a different trail than the one Nabella had used, and they entered the cave along an easy path from above. Machlah met them at a small corral at the side of the cave. Nabella stood unsure what to do while the men removed saddles and let the animals into the pen. Shem crossed to his wife.

"Arphaxad sent Jokaan and Tomar. Barukh and Kfir came to rescue Nabella, whom you have already met."

Machlah's face relaxed and she smiled at Nabella. "Yes we have." She padded to the young woman putting an arm around her. "Shem, may I get her cleaned up?"

"Yes, but first there a few wounds that need tended to." He glanced at Barukh and added, "minor wounds. Can you see to them?" He shifted his gaze to the men. "Come with me." Shem rubbed a hand through his dark beard and fixed an eye on Nabella. "Obey everything she says."

Nabella's stomach quivered. Misery that welled up in her eyes threatened to flow again. She nodded.

He turned to Machlah once more. "And when you get a chance will you prepare some food?"

Machlah smiled, nodded then led the young woman to the back of the cave. Nabella glanced behind her. The men disappeared from her view. Their voices drifted in and she guessed they sat near the opening in the shade of the cliff.

Shem's wife poured water from a jar into a large wooden basin then reached for lye soap and an old woolen cloth from a protruding rock. "You may freshen up with these while I see what I can do for the men."

Machlah padded to the other side of the cave, picked up a basket, filled it with herbs and small clay jars then headed for the entrance. Nabella turned and stared at the surface of the still water. Could that reflection really be her? Dirt had smeared and crusted on every part of her face. Her fine hair pressed flat against her head, matted and dull. Here and there small bits of twigs and leaves stuck out of the mess. Her two thin braids had pulled loose in the back and hung limp on either side of her head. Nabella clutched at her shirt with one hand. *Oh what have I done?* With trembling fingers she plucked at the debris.

She started when Machlah appeared at her side with a large piece of material. Without a word the woman measured a length against Nabella's waist, cut it to size with a small knife, then gauged another piece for a tunic.

"Oh, Machlah." Nabella burst into tears when she realized what the woman planned to do. "You don't need to do this. I'm not worthy."

"Shush now. You are a child of God. Of course you are worthy."

"But look what I've done."

"Dry your tears, child. You have made a mistake."

Nabella sucked in a shaky breath.

"There. Now bathe yourself. You will feel much better." She held up a large rectangular piece of fabric. "You can use this to dry yourself and as a wrap when you are finished. Then come help me with your new clothes."

Numbness washed over Nabella as mental and physical exhaustion enveloped her. She willed herself to follow Machlah's instructions, remembering her agreement with Shem. *But Father*, a small moan escaped. Nabella clutched her bosom. The tears she had held at bay broke loose flowing uninhibited down her cheeks. She had no one to blame but herself. She pulled Abel's thirst over her head and slipped out of the baggy pants. With heavy breaths she splashed the water onto her face and arms then rubbed until her skin tingled. Jaw set she patted her skinned knees, scratched legs, and raw feet. At last she wrapped the piece of cloth around her body. She loosened the tangled braid, lowered her head then pushed her hair into the bowl.

Gentle hands touched her own moving them aside. Nabella turned her head and from the corner of her eye saw Machlah. The woman poured a bit of liquid from a vial into the water then massaged the matted strands. The heady smell of summer flowers encircled Nabella. Closing her eyes she let the older woman tend to her. At last Machlah lifted Nabella's head from the bowl and twisted her hair into a strip of cloth.

Nabella gazed at her. "Oh Machlah, my father…"

"Shhh. Everything is in the Lord's hands. Come, child."

She lifted the edge of the wrap above her sore knees and followed the woman. After Machlah removed one of the burning oil lamps she settled by the cave wall leaning against it. Nabella sank down beside her. Machlah was right, she did feel better. With deft strokes Machlah combed Nabella's hair straight and braided it. Then she handed Nabella a small roll of woolen thread and moved the lamp closer.

"If you hem the bottom of this piece I will work on the tunic. Then I will show you how to wrap the cloth into a full jupe like mine."

Nabella's fingers trailed along the material. "This is such fine cloth. You must've made it yourself. How can I ever repay you?"

Nabella studied the older women's face. The area around her slender eyebrows stuck out like Noah's only not as much. Fine creases fanned out from the corners of her eyes. Deeper ones accented her jowl lines. The woman's long straight hair fell across her shoulders and cascaded onto the ground around her. The few grey streaks reminded Nabella of a waterfall in the moonlight.

Machlah glanced at her, a shy smile transformed her face into gentle beauty. "I did not make this. It is from the Former World."

Nabella's brow gathered together, her fingers stilled. "No, I cannot take this."

Machlah chuckled then said. "I have more."

"But it's from the Old World, from before, The Flood." Her voice reverent as her fingers stroked the fine material. She bit her lip, eyes moistening. Nabella had never seen or touched, let alone owned, anything from the Old World.

"Things were so easy to get there, like this metal needle." Machlah handed her the needle, thread dangling from the eye. Nabella took the sliver of metal, turned it between her fingers staring in awe. Finally she stabbed it through the material.

"It goes through so easy, not like the bone needles at home. How clever!"

"Yes. We had so much and in great abundance. Here we, meaning mankind, have not yet gotten the metal industry going yet."

"Industry?"

"Yes. An industry is when many different things must be done to get the final result. In the metal industry, first the exact rocks must be found. Rocks that have the metal in it. Then the rocks are mined—"

"Mined? What's that?"

"The rocks often are part of a cliff. So they have to be chipped from there, then crushed to small pieces. That would be mining. After that, the pieces that contain iron, copper or tin ore, are separated then melted down to take impurities out. Once this is done, the metal is left. Then you have to re-melt the metal to form it into whatever you want. All of that put together, Nabella, is the metal industry."

"It sounds like so much more work than growing olives."

"It is much more work. And very hot work. Two of Shem's brothers work at smelting the metal and forging them into objects. I'm afraid sewing needles are far down on the list. Weapons and big tools like axes and plows will be made first." Machlah paused then held up her needle. "These two are the last I have. Many I have broken over the last one hundred and six years and I have given so many away to my family."

Nabella rubbed the needle studying Machlah. She thought she detected a wistful note in older woman's voice. "What was it like in the Old World?"

"Oh, very different. So many people, so much commerce. You could go anywhere to get anything you wanted. I miss the food most." Her gentle laugh made the corner of Nabella's mouth tweak upward. Then Machlah looked down, and her face saddened. "But there was so much crime, so mu—"

"Cr. Crime?"

"Yes. Crime."

Machlah looked at Nabella. "Crime is when someone does something against someone else. If something that is not yours is taken without permission, or if someone injures another on purpose. Or even if they take someone against their will. That is crime."

"Like Cush did to me. Oh, Machlah, did I do that by dressing like a boy?"

"That gets a little more difficult. Why did you dress like a boy?"

"I wanted to see Shem and I knew if anyone saw a girl they would send me home. I wanted to hear what he had to say to my father. I wanted to hear wisdom from the Old World, and I knew Father would not tell me everything when he got back."

"Your intent was harmless. Just curiosity. But in the Former World people would sometimes dress like the opposite sex to commit a crime or for sexual pleasure."

"A crime or for sexual pleasure?" Not only did the new word feel odd on her tongue, but what did crime have to do with sexual pleasure?

"Yes." Machlah shuddered and paused in her work. "Nabella, this will be hard to understand but many men had sexual relations with other men, and woman did the same. Sometimes one partner would dress like the opposite sex and would parade themselves around. This is not what God intended for sexual relations. God designed us male and female so we would have that pleasure within our marriages of one man with one woman. By this sacred union children are brought into the world. And through the love of nurturing parents they become adults strong in the Lord. Men and women who cleave together within their marriage become one. But the old serpent found a way to distort that too." She ended in a whisper.

Nabella swallowed hard. Could that be true? It must be for Machlah said so, and she had lived there to see it. Nabella shook her head to push the ugly thought from her mind. "I knew there was a lot of evil in the Old World and that's why God sent the flood. So those are some of the evil, the crimes?"

"Yes. And it breaks my heart to see people doing evil again." Machlah reached over and fingered the red marks around Nabella's wrists.

"I'm fine." Nabella tugged her hands away flicking her eyes at Machlah. The older woman looked so sad. Nabella pushed her own concerns aside. She wanted to cheer Machlah up, but how? A small thought almost like a whisper wafted through her. Nabella's heart stirred. *The ark, talk about the ark.* She hesitated until her heart fluttered again. "What was is like on the ark with all those animals? I would have loved it."

A smile returned to Machlah's lips and she patted Nabella's leg. "Well, motek, it would have been nice to have you there. It was a lot of hard work. I think God planned it that way though, to keep us busy. And it was frightening as well. Especially when the ark first began to float. I lost count of how many days of rain it took before it broke free of land. Then one afternoon everything started to creak and the boat lurched, and we could feel it moving. Oh Nabella, I thought the whole thing was going to fall apart it moaned and groaned so much. The thundering had been so great outside, I was frightened anyway and that made it worse. I left my duties and ran to find Shem. I knew he was upset too. His face had turned so pale."

Machlah's hands were busy the whole time she spoke but now she paused. "Then Noah called us all together. He said, 'Notice the animals, do any of them appear frightened?' I looked around and none of them did. So we prayed and finally my heart could feel God once more." Joy radiated across Machlah's face.

"Did you ever se—"

"Machlah." Shem appeared at the cave entrance, his back toward them. "We are famished."

"My apologies, husband." She sprang to her feet. "Here, this is finished, put it on and come help." Nabella took an instant to admire the beautiful stitching in the tunic then pulled it over her head. She wrapped the jupe around her waist the best she could and draped the damp wrap over a protruding rock then joined Machlah.

The older woman pushed a few small earthen jars aside then paused. She threw a quick look at Nabella a chuckle escaping.

"Let me fix your jupe." She rearranged the cloth and tied the upper end at Nabella's waist. Machlah gave a critical once-over, nodded her head then strode to a wooden chest.

"Here," she handed Nabella three platters then reached for a basket of greens and a clay jar containing nuts. "And here is olive oil, salt and pepper. Mix that with the greens then sprinkle lots of nuts on top. Oh, and see those two jars? One has olives and the other raisins. Add those as well."

Nabella did as she was told then watched Machlah prepare a platter of cool meats and another of flat bread. Oh, the sight of all the food. Mouth watering her stomach rumbled. Nabella tried not to stare at the supper before them.

"We will eat after the men." Machlah smiled as she handed her the plate of greens to take out. Nabella's eyes widened when she saw how low the sun hung in the sky. No wonder her stomach complained.

The men sat, backs to the entrance deep in conversation. Suddenly Nabella felt shy. She lingered at the mouth of the cave then slipped behind Machlah. She watched fascinated while Machlah gracefully padded behind the men to set the platters of food before them then turned to Nabella nodding encouragement. Nabella stepped forward doing her best to imitate the older woman.

Shem dipped his head, a hand lingering on Machlah's arm when she placed the last platter on the ground in front of him. They exchanged a quick glance before Machlah straightened. She moved toward the cave entrance, Nabella following behind. The women waited in silence while the men ate. As Shem chewed on a handful of raisins Nabella let her eyes slide to Machlah's profile then back to her husband. He had heavier brow ridges too, just a bit bigger than Machlah's. *Does that happen to everyone when they get really old?*

"I agree. It does appear you have been targeted since none of this has happened with their father's vineyards." Shem swallowed his first mouthful then nodded at Barukh and Kfir. "Have any other neighbors had this attack?"

Tomar leaned forward. "I looked at the croplands next to us and saw no sign of pagan dealings. But my brother by marriage has seen the signs and footprints of an Azhdaha hanging around. Could it be possible the two are connected?"

Shem chewed another mouthful before he answered. "Possibly, but is it likely? I do not know. The animal may have wandered into the area or Nimrod may have placed the animal there. I also know Cush, Nimrod, Ra'anel, and many others all want each family to be connected to The City so everyone will be under their rule."

"It's not what God wants." Jokaan voice crackled with anger.

Shem eyed Jokaan and rolled onto an elbow. "That is correct. But to what lengths will those who rule go? It is pos—"

Barukh interrupted, "I think it was Cush. I think he brought the Azhdaha and Ra'anel did the sacrifices. After all they were in the area when it happened." Barukh shoved meat into his mouth while he spoke. Nabella watched from the corner of her eye while Kfir discreetly kicked his brother and motioned to his mouth.

Shem ignored the insult and instead examined the bread and meat in his hand. "It is not Cush's style. And Ra'anel is much more clever than that."

"But how is the curse to be broken?" Jokaan sounded weary and for the first time Nabella noticed age in her father.

Shem pushed to a sitting position and gestured for Machlah to take the platters away. She moved quietly among the men gathering the dishes. As she passed Nabella she nodded for her to remove the plate with the last of the greens then disappeared into the cave. Reluctant, Nabella moved like a bear after hibernation. This is what she wanted to hear. This is why she came all this way and went through all the trouble. She picked up the platter then took one step away from the men.

She glanced over her shoulder watching Shem lean forward. "God knows what is happening, Jokaan. And who is doing it. If He chooses to reveal the culprit to us then so be it. And to break the curse you must fast and pray. Call on the power of the Creator. Go to each site, build an altar to God and pray for..."

"Nabella." The young woman felt gentle arms around her shoulders and looked into Machlah's understanding eyes.

"I know it is intriguing to listen to the men," she continued while guiding Nabella into the cave. "But it is not our place. Especially when it comes to spiritual warfare."

Nabella jerked, and her eyes flew wide. She'd never heard that before. Machlah smiled patting her cheek. "Here, let us eat then you can help me clean these few dishes."

They sat near the small open hearth at the center of the cave. Machlah stirred the embers then added wisps of dried grass and small sticks. "It becomes quite chilly in here once the sun goes down."

Nabella waited until Machlah handed her a platter of food. One bite and Nabella knew not only was Machlah a wonderful person but an amazing cook also.

Shem's wife chewed a morsel, her eyes focused on something unseen. "You have no idea what you are up against. The powers of darkness are strong and can overthrow those who are not secure in God. And, Nabella, how do you think the serpent determines your weak areas? What makes a person weak?"

"I, don't know."

"Take some time to think about it."

Nabella chewed a handful of nuts. Her thoughts turned over the events of the last few days. What *did* make a person weak? The women finished their food and cleaned the dishes in silence. She knew Machlah meant a spiritual weakness and concentrated on that. When she thought she had the answer Nabella turned to ask Machlah, but the woman had headed for the entrance. She looked around for something else to do and added a branch to the small fire. Machlah's quiet call drifted from outside.

"We are to gather fodder for the animals. Everyone will spend the dark time here."

Head down Nabella scurried past the men. From the corner of her eye she saw Barukh cradling his arm. For an instant she hoped he would look at her, but instead he turned his head. Nabella clutched her jupe pulling it above her raw knees then lengthened her stride to match Machlah's.

The older woman led the way through the long shadows to the rim of the canyon. They picked their way around a few large rocks and stepped up onto a flat meadow above the chasm. Nabella stood transfixed by the sight. The tall grass rippled in the slight breeze and small purple and yellow flowers dotted the edge of the meadow bobbing their heads. At the far end of the field deer stopped grazing to stare in their direction. Above, pink clouds soaked in the brilliant hues of the vivid orange ball. Her eyes lingered on the lower distant mountains whose tops poured out orange and yellow streaks of melted rock. She sucked her breath in.

"Oh, how beautiful. And the fire! I hardly get to see it flowing from those mountains. My father's orchard lies too low. And The City blocks the view."

Machlah drew in a deep breath as she glanced at the fiery mounds and the meadow then nodded. Peace settled over her face. She unsheathed her knife to cut handfuls of the tall grass. Nabella followed her actions.

"Is it because you don't follow God? Would that make you weak?"

"Certainly when a person does not follow God your strength is lessened, and you become more vulnerable. Now, what are some ways people do not follow God?" Her hands never rested while she spoke.

"Well, all the things you told about the people in the Old World."

"Make it more personal."

Nabella felt heat rush to her face, and her stomach twisted tight. "By disobeying my father."

Machlah nodded. "Have you asked for your father's and God's forgiveness?"

"I haven't had a chance to ask my father…"

"And God?"

The gentle prompt undid Nabella. She dropped to her knees bowing her head. How did she get herself into such a mess? "Because I was selfish," she whispered to herself. Deep sobs surfaced from the depth of her heart. Machlah knelt beside her laying a hand on Nabella's arm. The young woman did not notice the soft touch. She rocked back and forth, arms pressed to her bosom. At last Nabella prayed. When no more words came she lowered her head to her lap utterly spent. A quiet voice spoke next to her.

"Creator God," Machlah prayed. "We come before You and ask that Your mercy be poured out upon us…"

Nabella listened in awe at the depth and sincerity of Machlah's appeal. These were not merely words but rather a deep communion with the Creator. Nabella sat upright, brows raised and eyes wide that this woman whom she had only just met had such concern for her soul. Hope began to seep into her heart.

When she finished Nabella leaned over and wrapped her arms around the woman's neck. "I can see why God chose you to come from the Old World and teach us the right way."

Machlah sighed. "If only people would listen."

"I'll listen, Machlah, and do better. I promise."

"I know you will. Now come we have much more fodder to gather." Machlah stood and sliced through the grasses. "Ask for God's help. Our fight is not against each other but against the evil principalities. Evil can only be conquered through our Lord God. We are no match for the serpent on our own. Always remember that even innocent Eve who walked with God was fooled by the evil one. When we think we can handle things ourselves, watch out. That is exactly where the serpent wants us. So you see, as much as you would have liked to have listened to the men, it was not your place. Not because you are a woman, but because you were not ready to join in that spiritual battle. Remember, Nabella, God will always guide. You need only to listen and obey. He *always* gives warning when we are not on the right path, His path."

Nabella sighed and clutched her jupe. "How will I know?"

"Keep your heart fixed on God, child then you will know. He will give you a sign, an *oth*."

Nabella nodded, hope flamed inside her. "Oh, Machlah I'll miss you!"

"And I you." Machlah chuckled then added, "It is good not to be caught in all the turmoil below in The City, but it is lonely for me up here. I forgot how much I miss the company of other women."

"Maybe I can come back sometime."

"Yes, but the right way, Nabella, with a chaperone."

"Yes." Nabella cast her eyes down, deflated. She had no idea what punishment lay in store for her. But she knew one thing for sure: Her father would not agree to come back with her any time soon. And neither would Barukh.

"Come, we have gathered enough. The dark time settles and we must get back."

Both women tied huge bundles to their backs and carried overstuffed armfuls back to the cave. Nabella and Machlah crawled into the pen and divided the fodder between the animals. Then the older woman moved to the back of the cave motioning for Nabella to help her collect blankets and dried grass for bedding.

The men had moved inside and reclined around the fire, still deep in discussion. The urge to overhear their conversation no longer pulled at Nabella. Both women padded quietly behind the men constructing the makeshift pallets. Then she followed Machlah to a rear niche in the cave.

Nabella lay a blanket over more dried grass for herself. Machlah moved to her own pallet, "I am exhausted and morning comes very early around here." She covered a yawn with her hand. "I will need your help to serve the men in the morning."

Nabella lay on a blanket between Machlah and the side of the cave. She turned so she could see the men. Barukh had his back to her. Jokaan and Tomar sat sideways, Kfir and Shem faced her.

Nabella sighed and before she knew it one tear then another and another rolled over her nose. These were the people she loved and she had caused them pain and anger. *Oh please Father, look at me. Am I no longer special to you? The daughter who is like a son?*

As Jokaan spoke and sipped wine, a jolt ran through her when she realized he purposely avoided eye contact. Nabella brushed the tears away. Briefly Kfir lifted his cup and when the mug almost covered his face he met her gaze and gave a quick wink. When he lowered his hand he looked away leaning toward Shem to speak. The acknowledgement had been so fleeting, did she imagine it? The man twisted his head again. And when he did, Kfir caught her eye. He held her gaze for the briefest instant and the shadow of a smile played across his face. Then he shifted to listen to the rest of the men.

She closed her eyes. *Thank You, Creator God, oh thank You. You knew I needed that, and You came to my rescue.* Nabella drew a shaky breath and her lips moved in silent prayer. A gentle embrace wrapped around her raw and worn spirit.

Fourteen

He was a mighty hunter before the Lord: wherefore it is said, Even as Nimrod the mighty hunter before the Lord.

Genesis 10:9

The next morning Cush found the hunting party with ease. They had not gone far. Shouts echoed along the canyon walls as loaded wagons creaked over rocky ground. Nimrod led the way, bare to the waist. His shoulders and back, browned almost to the color of Cush's skin bulged while he gripped the reins of the six oxen team. Cush eased the takhi alongside the wagon. Nimrod threw him a glance, and Cush clenched his jaw. The younger man's smirk said it all. Nimrod had known from the beginning Shem wouldn't come.

Cush's eyes narrowed to thin slits. He threw his shoulders back and sat rigid in the saddle. Not only did Shem's refusal humiliate him in front of Jokaan and Tomar, but also now with Nimrod. Why did those two want to find Shem? What could be so important that Arphaxad sent them? He would find out, later.

Right now he planned to wipe the sneer off Nimrod's face. He would make the hunting party's entrance into The City the most impressive ever.

"I need another takhi."

Nimrod turned black eyes upon him.

"I intend to go to The City and prepare for your arrival. It must be done with a flair that these men don't know how to do."

Nimrod rotated his head forward. At last he nodded. "Take Terach's. Tell the boy to join me here."

The acid that churned through Cush's stomach settled. He gave a curt nod then reined his tired mount in. When the wagon had nearly passed he jumped to the ground tethering the takhi to the back. He spun on his heels and marched down the line of cumbersome wagons to find the youth.

"Leave your takhi and go to Nimrod." The command rose with a growl from the back of Cush's throat.

Terach dismounted without a word and handed the reins to older man. The youth sprinted for Nimrod's wagon. What kind of future lay in store for Terach with a mentor like Nimrod? Cush shook his head. *Not my problem.*

He mounted, kicked the takhi into a run and headed for his beloved City. Once the takhi broke loose of the canyon he could see the walled-in buildings on the plain of Shinar. The temple gleamed in the mid-morning sun, it's holy walls beckoning. The whole place emanated safety and comfort. It looked so inviting. *Why did Jokaan and Gideon refuse to be a part of this?* His lip curled, they were such fools.

Cush's face stormed. He wanted to do something, anything, to wipe out the memory of what just happened with Shem. He pushed the takhi until it's nostrils flared and it's sides glistened with sweat and foam. Every time the animal slowed, Cush lashed the reins across its neck and dug in his heels. He purged his anger onto the takhi spurring it on. As the sun tipped below the horizon Cush galloped full speed toward The City's eastern gate.

"Open the gate! It's Cush, open the gate." His bellow carried to the top of the citadel.

The gates were pulled much too slow for his frantic steed. Cush reined in while a crack opened in the heavy doors. He yanked on the reins, and the animal reared. Yes, he would enter in style even though the animal was about to drop from exhaustion. The takhi's hoofs thudded on packed dirt as he flew through the entrance. When he reached the main road where baked brick stones had been laid, the dull thuds turned to a sharp clatter. From the corner of his eyes Cush saw people run to their windows and turn in the streets.

"Out of the way. Get out of my way," he shouted over and over. People that lingered leapt to the side.

"It's Cush," he heard again and again as he sped by. His teeth flashed in a grin at the power he felt when people called out his name.

He yanked his steed to a stop at the celestial palace, his home for the last ten years. Shared with Nimrod, his wife, the celestial advisors, and even family leaders who stayed in one of the spare rooms when they visited The City, at times irked him. But he learned early on how to evade them when necessary.

Cush dismounted and led the takhi, head drooping low, around the side of the building. He shouted for a stable hand and when a boy dashed across the courtyard, thrust the reins at the youth. Without a word he stalked through a back courtyard taking the broad steps two at a time. When Cush passed through the entranceway he pressed his head against one of the large sculpted idols that lined each side of the hall. The stone felt cool against his forehead, and he began to pray against Shem, Arphaxad, and Jokaan—those he now considered enemies. In the past he had disagreed with Nimrod on this point. Cush had thought no one his enemy, only that people were ignorant. Until today. *Nimrod was right, we do have enemies.* His stomach unclenched and muscles relaxed when he pushed away from the carving. Gratitude washed through him, and he dropped to his knees bowing low. At last he stood. A grumble from his stomach broke his reverence.

Cush strode to the storage room scrounging for food and a wineskin. How he looked forward to a full stomach, a long draught of wine and his own bed. Nimrod would not be near The City until late tomorrow. Tomorrow, it would come soon enough, and he could figure out how to make things grand then.

***

"Cush."

The man cracked an eye open. Light pierced through and a stab of pain seared through his head. He threw an arm over his eyes.

"This better be good."

"Ah, there's a boy here. He wants to see you."

"Tell him to go away."

"He said to tell you Nimrod sent him."

Cush bolted upright then cringed. He held his head between huge hands and moaned.

"Give me a little then send him in."

The celestial advisor left, and Cush pushed himself upright. After two wobbly steps he leaned against the wall. A curse tried to escape, but his tongue clung to the roof of his mouth. When the room stopped spinning he staggered to a basin of water. submerging his face, he drank deeply then straightened and shook his head. Not a good idea. He moaned, grabbing the edge of the table. When the room steadied once again, he snatched a piece of woven cloth drying his face. Cush turned and trudged to the entrance of his room.

Terach waited outside. Cush glanced out the nearest window and swore. He had intended to get up at daybreak. But from the looks of the bright sunlight it was well past mid-morning. He cursed again.

"When will he arrive?"

"By late afternoon."

"Terach, how many of Nimrod's men are still in The City? Ones who can be trusted."

The youth gave him a funny look. "A lot."

Cush ground his teeth then stopped. It only made the headache worse. "Go round up ten of the best and bring them here."

Terach nodded without a word and turned on his heels. Cush watched the youth leave then went to find Ra'anel. He didn't have to go far. Cush burst into the advisor's chambers and found the man sound asleep.

"Ra'anel. Wake up."

The man's snoring faltered as he smacked his lips.

"Ra'anel," Cush gave the man a shove.

"What, what, what."

Cush couldn't tell if Ra'anel muttered in his sleep or was awake.

"Ra'anel!" The big man slapped callused hands together under the celestial advisor's nose.

"Hmmm, what, what?" Ra'anel bolted upright and looked around the room. "You? What do you want. I have been up all night reading the stars. Well, tell me then go away. And go bathe, you smell like an animal."

"Get up." Cush ignored Ra'anel, "Nimrod is on his way to The City with the great head of a monster. A celebration is in order for his mighty victory."

"Is that all you wanted to tell me? You can't handle it yourself?"

Heat rushed to Cush's face. He grabbed the advisor's upper arm dragging him out of bed. With his face only a finger's width from Ra'anel's, Cush spoke through clenched teeth. "*You will* make a grand welcome with all the celestial advisors and family leaders present. And make it special. Come up with something to honor him. And do it fast. He will be here in less than six hand-spans."

"B-but, Cus—"

"Shut up and do as I say. If you don't. Nimrod will know it is you who has failed, not I."

"Nimrod is just one man."

"One man who is admired by almost all the people. The mighty one, they call him. Or have you forgotten? He is not one to fool around with. And he is expecting something grand." Cush let go shoving the smaller man.

Ra'anel brushed his fingers across the front of his shirt as if he removed moldy bread crumbs. "Very well."

The big man strode to the entrance and paused. "And Ra'anel, the people might just be right. You should have seen him slay this tanniyn. Nimrod attacked it like he knew he wouldn't die. Wait until you see its head."

Cush didn't wait for an answer. Instead he headed to the central baths near the expansive inner courtyard. There he drew water and dumped it into a large stone basin. If he was going to present himself to Nimrod's men with authority, he better look the part. These men were used to Nimrod who always seemed to look his best. He didn't wait to heat the water. He had to hurry, Terach could return with the men anytime.

Cush stepped into the cold water gritting his teeth. The cool autumn air added to his misery. He grabbed the lye soap and scrubbed. When he got to his side he ground his teeth again and rubbed the reddened scratch. A growl escaped when he examined it. The monster had gotten him good, from his ribs all the way to the top of his thigh. This scar would be one to brag about. He dunked his head to rinse his hair, and his brows shot up in surprise when the water turned pink. The monster's blood. Cush immersed his head again, scrubbing. Droplets of water sprayed from thick, kinky curls when he flung his head back. He hated to admit it, but Ra'anel was right. He did need a bath.

Cush stepped out of the washbasin, wrapped a cloth around his waist and stomped toward his chamber. He would catch a tongue-lashing, because he left the dirty water but he had more important things to attend right now. Inside his room he grabbed a four-prong ivory comb and began to pick out his hair then stared at the reflection in his water bowl. He didn't have time for this. He pulled on his spare tunic and pants then wrapped a turban around his head. With a small one-sided blade he trimmed his beard and shaved his neck.

"Cush."

He started then strode from his room. Terach waited for him in the hall with ten formidable men. Cush wrapped his hand around the grip of his dagger sheathed at his waist. He strode in front of the men and held the gaze of each while he inspected them. Finally the big man nodded.

"The four of you," Cush thrust his chin toward the men at the end of the line, "Ride in all directions and summon the most important family leaders. Bring extra takhis to get them back here in three hand-spans. And make sure Jokaan comes." Cush turned. "You four, go through The City and tell everyone they are to line up along the promenade twi hand-spans after noon meal. When you're done, round up as many people as you can to help cut palm and willow branches. Lay the fronds on the promenade near the northern citadel and as people arrive, give them the branches. When Nimrod is near make a final ride through The City and the tents to announce his arrival. Make sure the people know it's expected that everyone comes. It should be easy to convince them, they will not want to miss this event." Cush paused narrowing his eyes at the last two.

"You and you, gather material to build a platform in front of the tower. I don't care where you get it. Tell the people it's for a festival, and they need to cooperate. Make it strong enough and big enough to hold the head of a huge tanniyn along with the celestial advisors and twenty family leaders. I don't care if you need to get help just get it done." Cush saw the men glance at each other. His jaw muscles clenched as irritation flared.

"Terach," he snapped the boy's name out. "Go to Nimrod. Take a cart filled with palm fronds and streamers to decorate the wagon that carries the tanniyn. Bring poles to hold that great head and its claws. And see if there's anything else he needs. Now leave." Cush did not wait for questions or answers; instead he spun on his heel and strode towards Ra'anel's quarters.

The man better not still be asleep. The celestial advisor stood by a tall narrow window, a foul look on his face.

Cush crossed arms over his brawny chest. "Everything's in order on my end. The people will be lined up long before Nimrod arrives. A stage is being built for you and the others. Just get the rest of the advisors, in full dress, to the promenade before Nimrod enters the citadel. It'll be a sight to see. And he intends to hand out the tanniyn's meat to the people."

The celestial advisor sputtered, "Meat for the people? Are you mad? Do you wish to invoke the wrath of the gods? It is the gods who deserve the meat, not those, those commoners."

"Do you wish a riot on your hands?" Cush glared. "When Nimrod brings *wagon loads* of the beast's meat those *commoners* will want to eat it."

Ra'anel paced, and Cush ground his teeth. "I don't have time for this. Find a way to appease the gods and the people both. And make sure your advisors bring their staffs with those fancy carvings on them."

Ra'anel stepped onto a bench, drew up his tall thin frame the best he could then looked down his nose at Cush. His face, pinched and drawn, crinkled sallow white skin.

"*I* know what to do, Cush. I am no imbecile. Just have that platform ready." He grabbed flowing robes and, with a flounce, hopped off the bench. He swished the robes with pompous authority as he marched away.

Staring after the celestial advisor, Cush's whole body tensed. At last he rubbed his temples heading for the stairs. The throbbing had doubled from the rush of anger. He really did not like that man.

By the time the hunting party neared the northern citadel curious people lined the promenade, fronds in hand. More greenery covered the road, and the platform held important members of the community. Cush sat atop his mount a smirk playing across his face. His intuition proved correct; the commoners were excited to see what Nimrod brought back. If he understood the people this well, he could control them just as easily.

With a great groan the gates crept forward. Four men balanced what had to be the monster's head on top of long poles mounted in the lurching wagon. A tarp had been thrown over the prize. He guessed at the proper time the covering would be removed with flair. Cush nodded his head. *Good touch, Terach.*

Men pushed at the brass bars of the gate until they swung wide. The dark man leaned into the saddle. His takhi obeyed moving in front of Nimrod's wagon. Tight grip on the reins, Cush squeezed his legs until the takhi, neck arched and stiff mane curved, pranced in place. The corner of Cush's mouth curved upward when he saw the people pushing to the front, craning their necks. He glanced around, the crowd must number in the thousands. People hung out of second-story windows and packed rooftops. *They're in for a surprise.* He trotted his mount forward, pride doubling with each step.

Suddenly the volume of voices rose to such a din that for an instant Cush wanted to cover his ears. Screams and shouts came from all around. He didn't need to look to know the cover had been torn from the grotesque animal. People flowed onto the promenade. Cush struggled to push them back so the wagons could move forward.

"Move back, let them through," Cush shouted with little result. Finally he kicked his takhi into the crowd. A path cleared as people fell under the hooves of the cavorting steed. He heard a cheer go up and twisted in his saddle in time to see pieces of meat being flung into the crowd. Cush chuckled. This would be a day remembered.

When the wagon came abreast the makeshift platform, Nimrod vaulted onto it while the celestial advisors pounded their staffs in unison shouting, "The mighty hunter is here; the mighty hunter is here!"

People nearby picked up the call and chanted along. Cush caught Nimrod's eye and the two men exchanged a nod. This is what it was all about. Cush's chest swelled while his steed pranced in place.

"Build a stand to hold this beast," Nimrod commanded his men. Then he turned to the crowds.

"Behold the monster. This tanniyn will no longer harm anyone. And the walls of our great City will keep others like it away, even if they dare to get this close. And we can see all that comes near from our grand tower. A tower built to worship god, whose top will reach the heavens. We can continue to construct our buildings higher and higher. Three and four layers tall. There is enough room for everyone. No one need remain outside the safety of the walls of our City."

Again cheers and shouts of agreement went up.

"We will make a great name for ourselves," Nimrod continued. "Feel safe, people. Tonight, celebrate with wine and tanniyn meat. Let this creature's head be a reminder of the protection this great City offers. How much better to live here than to be scattered abroad." Nimrod held his sword high in one hand and a spear high in the other. Cheer after cheer rang through the air.

Cush sidled his prancing takhi close to the platform and jumped off. He strode to the middle crossing decorated arms over his chest, feet splayed. He perused the crowd, and his head spun with vanity as he drank in the shouts. One by one the advisors left, then the family leaders, each with sacks of meat and wineskins. Cush caught Nimrod's eye, black and emotionless. The younger man gave an almost imperceptible nod then spun on his heel and strode from the platform. Shouts pierced the air long after Nimrod turned and went into the palace.

Cush strutted around supervising several men while they tore apart the tanniyn's supports in the wagon. He made grand gestures while he explained construction of the stand. It must show the enormous head and feet of the creature perfect from all angles. Cush felt every part of his being swell. This is what he wanted! This is how life should be lived!

By the time they finished, the sun fingered the horizon. The dark man stood akimbo, his back to the monster's head. He surveyed the promenade. Originally he thought the wide straight road ridiculous, the only part of The City that made no sense, a waste of space really. But today proved him wrong. He had to admit, the promenade turned out to be a good idea after all. With this day's events, he didn't mind it at all.

At last he turned to the monster. Most people had gone back to their homes to care for their animals. Only children gathered around to gawk. He and a few other men had a constant battle to keep them off of the display. But Cush knew when the sky turned dark, the adults would be back. He stepped to the side and grabbed his spear. *Better get some of Nimrod's men to guard the kabiyr.* The people would continue to eat and get drunk on wine. Then inebriated men would want to grab a piece of the great head or its claws, something he had already done, for a prize. Yes, the people would soon be back.

Fifteen

Even the dragons (dinosaurs) draw out the breasts, and give suck to their young: but the daughter of my people is become cruel like the ostriches in the wilderness.
Lamentations 4:3 (1599 Geneva Bible)

Shem stood, the reins of Barukh's mount in his large hands warning Jokaan and his small party not to travel south. "On the other side of the Tigris a pride of lions has bothered shepherds for some time. This ancient mare and their owners are fair game to such animals. Besides, I have a good turn to ask. Machlah desires to visit our daughter and I do not wish to ever set foot inside that City again. Would you be kind enough, Jokaan, to escort her there? It will take you a little longer to get home, but it is much safer to take the northern route." He turned to Barukh and Kfir. "Your takhis are strong and fast. You will be fine to journey straight across the southern end of the plain to your home."

Shem let go of the reins and locked eyes with Kfir. "God's provision be with you."

"May we be able to repay your kindness one day." Kfir bowed his head to Shem and Machlah. His ebony hair bound at the nape of his neck by the ends of his headband brushed brawny shoulders. Only the headband kept shorter locks out of his eyes.

Jokaan grasped Shem's forearms. "I will not forget what you have done for us, Shem."

The tall man dipped his head. "Remain in God's ways and all will be well."

Machlah and Nabella rode the brothers' takhis while Jokaan and Tomar led the mare. Kfir and Barukh walked abreast of Nabella's father and Barukh. Nabella glanced at the older woman. A deep sigh that matched the heaviness of her heart escaped. At least with Machlah along, it eased the tension between her and the men.

By the time they reached the Tigris River Barukh had insisted the pain in his elbow was unbearable and would mend better the sooner he arrived home. Kfir ignored his brother and offered to remain with Jokaan and the women. But Barukh complained he couldn't travel in lion country alone with such a badly wounded arm. Jokaan insisted that Kfir stay with his brother. The women dismounted and Kfir climbed on his takhi then turned to the south. Barukh followed, slouched in his saddle.

Though they left at sunrise, twilight had already set in when the small group reached the northern edge of the tents camped around The City walls. Machlah and Nabella had taken turns riding the old mare since little provisions were left. When the small group came abreast of the first tents, Machlah stared at the myriad of dwellings staked in all directions. At last she opted to head toward the river, and the men followed. Nabella swung her leg over the mare's back. Her feet tingled when they hit the ground, and she forced stiff legs to catch up to Machlah. When she reached the woman Nabella felt more than saw the kind smile in the late evening shadows.

A half of a hand-span later the small party still wove their way through the temporary dwellings. In between the tents Nabella fixed her eyes on the northern horizon trying to catch a glimpse of the two distant mountaintops that spewed fire. She had watched the mountains as they crossed the plain but nothing compared to this wonder at night.

"It is a beautiful sight when God shows His power." The older woman continued with a soft laugh. "Until the ashes come this way."

"I've never seen that, but Father says a few ashes are good for the orchard."

"Yes, a few probably are." Machlah touched Nabella's arm and turned toward Jokaan. "My daughter and her husband live near the wall along the river. He fishes while it is still dark and Channah takes his catch to the market each morning. They go to sleep early, so I might have to wake them, but I am sure we can spend the night, if I can just remember where their tent is. Everything looks different at night."

"It'll be good when we finally get there," Jokaan gave a weary chuckle. Nabella's brows rose. Father actually laughed?

At last they paused near a worn tent. No light shown from within. Machlah scratched the flap. "Greetings, my daughter. It is I, mother."

Nabella heard a rustle from within then the flap flew open. A woman large with child waddled through the opening.

"Mother. Ah-he, oh my, oh my." Channah threw her arms around Machlah. The two embraced the best they could around the woman's swollen belly, rocking back and forth. "What good news do you bring?"

Machlah stepped back. "All is well my little one. Your father sends his greetings to you and Eber. Oh, and look at you."

"I'm so glad you're here. I didn't know when I would see you again, especially with all the trouble."

"Trouble?"

Machlah's daughter suddenly noticed Nabella and her family. "Oh, you brought friends. Greetings." Channah turned to the men. "You can high-line your animal at the river. There is plenty of grass. Then please, come in." She wrapped an arm around Machlah's and Nabella's waists. "Come in, you two must be exhausted."

"We are, daughter and thank you. How are you feeling?"

"Oh, swollen feet and hands, tired all the time but you know how that goes."

Machlah gave Channah a squeeze. "You have less than one month to go."

Nabella pulled loose and stepped through the opening behind the other two.

Channah lit an oil lamp. "Eber, my husband wake up. We have company."

An olive-skinned man sat and blinked then ran a hand through disheveled raven hair. The woman's voice lit with excitement. "Mother is here, and this is her friend..."

"Nabella. My father, Jokaan, and my sister's husband, Tomar, are caring for their takhi."

Channah nodded. "Wait." She shuffled to a corner and retrieved blankets.

Machlah clucked. "Let me take those."

Nabella stepped forward and scooped up half of the bedding.

Channah's face fell as she watched the two women lay out the blankets. "I'm so sorry I have no straw to make a soft bed."

"It is fine, motek. Just a place to lay our heads is wonderful." Machlah smiled.

Channah held her hand out when the women were finished. "Come, come sit."

At a scratch on the tent flap Nabella jerked.

"Greetings," her father's tired voice drifted through the tent wall.

"Please come in," Eber called.

The two men greeted Eber then sank onto blankets opposite the women. Channah unwrapped flat bread and smoked fish mixed with barley, handing the platter to Tomar. When it reached Jokaan, he scooped the mixture onto the bread and handed it to Machlah. He gazed at the man before him. "What is this trouble your wife has mentioned?"

"A beast. A great and awful kabiyr tanniyn slain by Nimrod."

"Yes, but there's more," Channah's voice rose.

Eber reached over and patted her leg. "I know motek." Then he leaned forward and kept his voice low. "Nimrod brought it. If you ask me, it's a clever way to let people come to their own conclusion they should live in The City. He is even using it as an excuse to construct more buildings." The man shook his head, "And the people will do it willingly."

"You must go to The City tomorrow and see the tanniyn's head for yourselves. You'll see why it is so easy for the people to want to stay within The City walls," Channah insisted.

Machlah sighed, "I know of this animal. It lived near us and not once did it attack. It knew we were there, and we were always cautious because of it. It hunted large animals and kept well away from the Shinar plain where people live. Nimrod went out of his way to find that creature." Sorrow filled her voice

"It all goes against God's orders." The man clenched a fist. "Machlah, we might just join you and Shem."

Machlah smiled. "You would be welcome." She turned. "Jokaan, heed my husband's words. God is not pleased with disobedience." The sadness deepened across her face and she looked down. "It was like this in the Former World. There will be a time when God no longer waits. When that time comes we will be waiting for you."

Jokaan's brows furrowed, and he set his platter down. "I will remember your generosity, Machlah. But now, and forgive me if this question offends, I have to know. Why haven't Shem and you," he nodded to the man, "and other like-minded people moved far away?"

Machlah looked up. A rueful smile played across her face. "I know it sounds like an excuse. But this is the truth. Long ago when we were finally able to come onto the dried land we built an altar to God. After that Noah told Shem and I that we and our descendants were to stay in this region. Japheth was to go north and Ham to the south. We would have left years ago except for this direct charge from Noah."

"Why haven't the others left?"

Again her face clouded in sorrow. At last she fixed her eyes on Jokaan and said in a voice so soft Nabella strained to hear, "That, you will have to ask them."

***

When Nabella discovered her father actually *wanted* to go into The City and look at the tanniyn she had turned her head in surprise. The thought never occurred to her that Jokaan would want to see the animal. And take his family with him? And Machlah too? Not in a hundred years. Nabella frowned, *if I ever get to live that long.*

When they entered through the northern citadel Nabella stopped, stunned. Though always awed by The City's immensity, her stomach knotted at the sight of the celebration's aftermath. Broken palm fronds and wilted willow branches cluttered the road. She wrinkled her nose at the reek of spilled wine and urine. Nabella dared a glance at her father. Jokaan stepped over broken pottery and half-eaten food then stopped.

Lips pressed tight into his beard, Jokaan shook his head. "Come. The sooner we find this tanniyn the sooner we can leave."

With every step into the center of The City, Nabella clasped and unclasped her tunic a sense of unease washing over her. She did not know much about City life but wouldn't most business owners be at their shops to open for the day? Yet people slept collapsed around the temple steps and empty wine flasks lay scattered about. When they rounded the last corner, Nabella's eyes widened, and she sidled next to Machlah.

Thin columns of smoke spiraled from two huge ash heaps on either side of the tanniyn's platform. A shadow passed over the brick pavement. Nabella tipped her head and pressed closer to Machlah. Vultures, silent sentries of death, circled above. She shivered. One glance at her friend revealed disquiet written all over the woman's face. Nabella linked her arm around Machlah's more for her own comfort than for the sake of the other woman.

A cover lay haphazardly across a portion of the beast's head. Jokaan led the way to the front of the display. Tomar pressed close, his face tight and strained. The monster's head loomed enormous. Its jaw hung loose exposing teeth the size of her father's open hand. Sunken eyes made the brow ridges seem massive. Nabella's hand flew to her mouth.

"It's all jaw and teeth." Tomar shook his head. "And Channa was right, it is a Kabiyr." He and Jokaan hopped onto the platform.

A man with a spear appeared. "That's close enough."

The men halted, eyes fixed on the tanniyn.

"How was it slain?" Jokaan pressed.

"Nimrod slit its throat with his sword," the man boasted.

"It looks more grotesque dead than it did alive," Machlah whispered to Nabella.

"That's hard to imagine." The words squeezed past her hand.

Several boys ran to the stand and threw stones at the display until the enforcer jumped from the platform to chase them away. Nabella looked over her shoulder. A few more people moved about. Women with baskets on their heads began the long trek up the tower steps to the terrace just below the temple.

"God gave us dominion over the animals and charged us to be good stewards of them as well."

Machlah's voice brought Nabella's attention back to the tanniyn. The older woman's sorrow emanated from her. "This is not being a good steward. It is wasteful. God created this animal. Nimrod should not have done this."

Nabella stared at the sunken skull. It smelled of rot and despite the early light flies already gathered on it. She felt sorry for the creature. If it had lived so long in the foothills of the mountains and brought no one harm, why couldn't it be free to roam those canyons now? Nimrod had always protected the people when wild beasts endangered them, but this was different. Nimrod had sought the tanniyn out.

A gentle breeze stirred, loose tendrils drifted around her face and tickled her cheek. Nabella pulled several strands from her mouth. Others wafted across her nose, and she sniffed.

Strange. The aroma of flowers covered the smell of death. Suddenly a man covered in long, white, robes appeared beside them. A pureness radiated from him. Nabella started and stared, realizing the fragrance originated from the figure.

"A tragedy."

When he spoke Nabella felt inexplicably drawn to him. His powerful yet grief torn voice struck deep within her. She tried to make out his face as the man surveyed the tower. Slowly he shook his hood-covered head. Nabella felt compelled to reach out to him, to touch his arm, to somehow comfort him. But at the same time she felt too tainted from her rebellious deeds. Instead she took a step closer and held out her hands palms up. She felt more than saw Machlah's arms rise also. The man's sorrow pierced Nabella and rendered her heart wide open. Tears flowed down her cheeks. If only she could comfort him. There must be *something* she could do. Behind her a sob escaped from Machlah.

Finally the man turned to the women. Nabella strained to see his face, but it remained obscured under his hood. Nothing seemed solid about the man, she saw him as if through a mist or smoke. Suddenly the cloaked arm moved in a great arch, and he spoke. Nabella blinked. His voice seemed to be inside her head and heart, but at the same time she heard him aloud.

"Behold, the people are one, and they all speak the same; and this they begin to do," a hand pointed at the tower, long sleeve trailing. "And now nothing will be restrained from them, which they have imagined to do."

Machlah gasped, fell to her knees dragging Nabella with her. "My Lord," she whispered.

Realization struck Nabella. *God!* This could only be God. Her eyes never left the shrouded being, but He had turned from them and moved in a precise semicircle. When He faced the temple He grew enormous, filling the sky, and his voice magnified around her. "Look at the foolishness of mankind when they turn from Me."

Nabella and Machlah turned their heads where the misty figure pointed. They gazed at the tower where women and men labored up and down the steps and celestial advisors stood so pious at the top.

"How can anyone think they can build a tower to heaven? A change in mankind must come forth. It is the only panacea." God's voice faded and Nabella turned her head back toward Him. Only a minute whirlwind of smoky mist swept upward then dissipated.

Nabella gasped exchanging a glance with Machlah. He was gone!

Machlah whispered, "He speaks an *oth*."

Then the smoke appeared again in the form of a vast misty face shrouded by a hood. His quiet voice reverberated throughout her, "You have a repentant heart, My child, but it is not enough. Sin can only be covered by blood. For Me to forgive your sins a pure and spotless animal must die—for sin is vastly grave." The hooded face turned toward the grotesque head of the tanniyn and the Voice boomed in Nabella's soul. "This animal was spotless before it was wounded and slain by unjust men to further their own froward motives. But what they have meant for evil, I will use for good. I accept the blood of this tanniyn as a covering for your sins. You are forgiven."

"Ohhh." Nabella collapsed. Head in hands she sobbed. *How can He forgive me? How awful that animals have to die!* In the depths of her heart a voice filled her, "To do what is right and just is more acceptable to Me than sacrifice. Trust in Me, child, One is yet to come Who will crush the head of Satan and though Satan will strike His heel, He will take away the sins of the world for those who repent and believe in Him. Then animals will no longer need to be sacrificed. Mankind's sins will be paid once and for all."

Nabella felt Machlah's arms tighten around her. She pressed into the woman weeping relief and wonder, shock and puzzlement. Nabella could feel God's presence as it filled and engulfed her in a sea of loving mercy and forgiveness. Spent at last, she lifted her face.

"Machlah. Did you see Him? Did you hear Him? Did you hear the last thing God said?"

The shine in Machlah's eyes said more than her words, "Yes, my child."

"Oh, Machlah." Nabella flung her arms around the woman. Tears burst forth again then were replaced almost immediately with joyous laughter.

It seemed from a great distance she heard Tomar's voice. "What's wrong? What's going on, Nabella?"

She let go of Machlah and gazed at the sky with a calm soul. Her voice vibrated with reverence and joy, "I'm fine. I am better than I have ever been."

***

Month of Overabundant Rain

Many weeks had passed since Jokaan, Tomar and Nabella had returned from their journey. Nabella's head still reeled, yet her heart ached from the punishment doled out by Jokaan. The day after their return her father had gathered all their immediate relatives together for a meeting.

"You have dishonored the family. You have dishonored me. And you have dishonored Barukh. We will have to see if he still wants your hand in marriage. If he does not, then the people will know of your disobedience only from your mouth for you will no longer live here. For us, it'll be as if you were never born. Your name will never be spoken again by any of us. Nor your act of disobedience."

"No, Father, no!" She had cried.

"Do not argue!" Jokaan roared. Nabella had cowered. Never before had he taken a tone like that with her. "Consider yourself fortunate. Other women have been stoned to death for less disobedience than what you have done." Jokaan's heavy brows knitted together. "You may stay here until word comes from Barukh."

Tears had gushed forth and Nabella groveled at her father's feet. But Jokaan had crossed muscular arms over his broad chest and did not even glance her way when he addressed the rest of the family. "No one is to speak her name or speak to her until we hear from Barukh. Is that understood?" When no one answered he growled, "Good," and stomped from the room. She rarely saw her father after that. But when she did his shoulders drooped lower and lower. He seemed to have lost weight, and his face looked drawn and sallow.

"Father is wasting away," she tried to speak to her older sisters, yet they all obeyed Jokaan's command turning away.

Nabella sighed and leaned her forehead against the wall. The grey skies of the last two weeks matched her grey mood. Even the flowers she had placed in a stone vase drooped wilted heads. She knew how they felt, lifeless and unappreciated. And though her calf had healed, as well as the gouges in her hands, blisters on her feet and the scrapes on her cheek, if only there was something she could do to heal her family.

And how she would have liked to have known what happened with the curse on their groves. But she heard only snatches of conversations.

"Went to take the carcasses down…"

"The Azhdaha got to…"

"Hope that won't…the curse…"

"Creator God is…"

"Build altars and pray every…"

When she drew near, her family turned their backs and became silent. Nabella sighed again. It was one thing that no one spoke to her, quite another when they avoided her altogether. She longed to hear a conversation or just to sit in a room with someone. Nabella tried to ignore the hurt and the hope, instead immersing herself in work. Even today when she announced she would wash everyone's second garments, her sisters drifted one by one from the house until now all worked in the big storage building or in the fields. The rooms shouted with emptiness.

Nabella gazed out a window. A light drizzle had begun again. She strolled outside to take the clothes off the line. One side of her mouth tipped upward while she gathered her father's shirt. Oh they could shun her, but they would still accept her work.

By the time Nabella finished, both the clothes and she were covered in a fine mist. With loving fingers she brushed at the moisture on the tunic Machlah had made. Another sigh slipped out. *Oh Machlah, I could use your kind words right now. And whatever is an oth? I never had a chance to ask you.* Finally Nabella turned, found a ball of twine then strung a line in the small room off the back courtyard.

Nabella clung to the memory of her encounter with God. He must have known what awaited, filling her with His love so she could draw strength from Him.

Lessons Machlah taught her came back bit by bit, and she tried to incorporate them. As the days had worn on she found Machlah's wisdom had a calming effect. Then she began to pray and a realization and acceptance of the situation crept through her. And in this recognition she could finally pray for others. One by one she re-hung the garments and said a small prayer for the owner of each piece. For Jokaan, for her sisters and their husbands. When all the clothes hung in a neat row, Nabella stepped back. At last she prayed for Barukh.

Barukh…*Oh, if only Barukh would come.* Her father had said this shunning would be over when Barukh made his decision. And he would still want her as his wife. Wouldn't he? They had made so many plans together, and their families got along so well. Surely that would count for something.

"Bella?"

Nabella started at the sound of her name, it had been so long since she heard it. She whirled around.

"Shoshana!" Tears welled and she held out her arms. The seven-year-old ran into them.

"I miss you," the child whimpered.

"I know, motek shele, I know. And I miss you too, a lot. How is Father?"

"I don't like him, he's being mean." Shoshana rubbed a wet cheek, and her lower lip puffed out.

Nabella held the child at arm's length and looked her in the eye. "I think he's sick. Every time I see him he looks worse. This is hard on him too. Try to be nice and do everything he says, alright?"

Shoshana's lower lip trembled as she nodded.

"Now listen. You must obey Father and not talk to me. You need to go, motek shele."

"Bu—"

"Shush-shush. It will be alright. It's just until Barukh comes. Then we can talk and play again, alright?"

"So he's still going to marry you, right?"

Nabella stood then stooped kissing the girl on her forehead. "I hope so. Now go." Her voice quivered with nagging doubts.

"Not just yet, Shoshana." A deep voice echoed through the empty house.

"Barukh," the little girl ran to him.

But the man stood stoic in the doorway staring at Nabella. Cold eyes lowered to Shoshana. "Go get your father."

Shoshana backed away and with a glance at Nabella ran out the house. Barukh strode from the room to the far end of the back courtyard. Nabella watched him stand stiff and silent under the arched entranceway.

At the sound of his voice Nabella's heart had caught in her throat but the rush of hope turned to dread. This was not the Barukh she knew; the tolerant man who always flashed a handsome smile at her. She shuffled to the doorway and studied him. Her eyes traveled to his arm still in a sling.

"How, how are you feeling?"

"It hurts."

Nabella nodded. "You were quite brave."

Barukh clenched his jaw and said nothing. Somehow she had to get through to him.

"Barukh, liste—"

"Just wait for your father."

Nabella swallowed. His harsh tone squelched any thoughts of conversation. Her hand clasped her jupe and delicate brows pulled upward as she stared. Every part of her betrothed radiated displeasure. *How can he still be mad at me? I just made a mistake. God has forgiven me, why can't he?*

Barukh scowled and fixed his eyes on the processing building.

"Oh Barukh," she whispered.

Was she mistaken or had he clenched his jaw? *He is making himself angry with me.*

"Barukh, don't do this. Please."

Barukh disappeared into the drizzle. She had her answer. Nabella perched on the stone bench in the family room. When Jokaan and Barukh entered the house, she concentrated on her father. Jokaan took several steps toward her. His face looked yellowed and sunken, and his shoulders seemed thinner than just three days ago. Jokaan stopped in front of her, out of breath. Barukh hung back.

"Nabella…Barukh has…made his decision." Jokaan twisted, shifted his eyes to the young man and gave a slight nod. Barukh shot Jokaan an irritated glance and scowled.

"The marriage is broken. And no one will hold it against me because of your actions."

Nabella felt strangely calm. She nodded then shifted her gaze back to her father.

"It is the only way, Nabella, to preserve our families' names, our families' honor. We will not be trusted if no action is taken to discipline your disobedience. You have until tomorrow to pack." Jokaan's voice choked, and he turned his back to her. He paused then continued, voice hardened. "From tomorrow henceforth, you are no longer my daughter." Jokaan turned to the doorway head down and moved as if his feet slogged through mud.

"Or your son," she whispered.

Jokaan paused and his shoulders sagged farther.

"And you," Jokaan rasped when he paused by Barukh, "are no longer welcome here."

Nabella caught the pain in her father's voice.

"My father and I are moving. We're taking our business to The City. We have a shop right on the main street, so even if this never happened we would see very little of you. But we'll do well there. The shop will be full of many customers. And their daughters." Barukh jutted his chin forward and sniffed.

Jokaan stiffened. "You give in to Ra'anel and Cush and the others? After all these years? What of God? What of His instructions? What does your father say of this?"

"It was his idea." Barukh glanced at his fingernails.

Jokaan's hands balled into fists. He stood trembling. At last he stepped under the lintel of the entrance way.

Suddenly he grunted and put his hand against the wall to steady himself.

"Father," Nabella jumped and ran to him.

"Tomorrow, Nabella," he gasped. Beads of sweat dotted his forehead. "Our…family's…honor."

Barukh stood and watched the man, a look of disdain on his face.

Blood surged to her head, and her temples pounded at his callousness. "Get out," she snapped. Without so much as a glance at her, he strode from the house.

"Father, sit down. I'll get you some water."

He shook his head.

"Let me help you." Nabella shoved her shoulder under his upper arm.

"No."

Abruptly he gasped, clutched his chest and crumbled to the ground.

"Father!" Nabella dropped to her knees and pressed her head against his chest. He breathed. Frantic she dashed to the doorway.

"Help! Someone help!"

She grasped his arm to lift him realizing at once she couldn't. She tried to drag him to his bed. When she moved him less than a cubit, realization struck, she really did need help. Darting across the room she snatched a blanket then stuffed it under his head. Nabella spun around and raced out of the house.

When she neared the processing center Nabella glanced around wild-eyed. "Adara, Adara!"

Nabella knew she broke every protocol Jokaan had laid down, but she didn't care. "Where's Adara!" She screamed at her maternal grandmother. Both grandmothers looked wide-eyed at each other, and Elah raised her hand to her mouth. Tomar paused in his work, a scowl on his face.

"Tomar! Where's Adara?"

When he began to turn his back Nabella clutched his arm. "Stop it, it's Father!" Whether it was the screech in her voice or the fear in her eyes, she didn't know, but he ignored the shunning to seize her shoulders.

"What's wrong?"

"Father's collapsed. Where's Adara?" Wide-eyed, she glanced around again.

"Elah! Go get Adara." Tomar roared then turned back to Nabella and gave her shoulders a shake. "Take me to him."

He let go, and she raced back to the house. Tomar rushed to Jokaan's side and hovered his hand over Jokaan's mouth. "He breathes."

"I tried to move him to the bed, but I wasn't strong enough."

"Grab his legs," Tomar commanded.

She did, and the two carried Jokaan to his bed.

"What's wrong?" Nabella heard her own voice pinched and high-pitched.

Tomar shook his head. Nabella wasn't sure if he had chosen to shun her again or if he just didn't know. She opened her mouth to ask another question when Adara, Elah, and grandmother Nahni crowded into the room. Nabella pressed back against the wall by her father's head and prayed no one would make her leave.

Adara knelt by Jokaan's head and felt his skin. "He's burning with fever. Elah get a basin of cold water and a cloth."

When Elah returned, Adara dampened the cloth in the water and pressed it to Jokaan's face. She repeated the process over and over then felt his forehead. "He's still burning."

"Why does he look so yellow?" Elah leaned over Adara's shoulder.

"I don't know. Nahni, have you ever seen anything like this?"

The older woman shook her head then cleared her throat. "I, ah, have been wondering, he only just started to get this way after he broke the curse over the orchards."

"What are you saying?" Tomar's voice sounded gruff.

"Well, I just don't like what is going on around here."

"Speak clearly, woman! This man is *sick*."

"Like I said, I don't like some of the happenings around here."

Tomar glared at the woman. "You still have said nothing."

"I think what she is trying to say is, where did the curse go after it was broken?" Elah murmured.

"What do you mean, where did it go?"

Adara stood. "What they're both trying to say is, when Father broke the curse in the orchards, did it lodge in him?"

"No. It couldn't have. I was there. We did everything Shem told us, even building an altar to honor God. The Lord would have protected us as well as the orchards."

"Well, the curse had to go somewhere," Elah said.

"Pah! Look, I'm not sick and I had just as much a hand in breaking the curse as Jokaan did. If that were true then I would be sick too."

"Then tell us what's wrong with him," Nahni spoke with tones so soft Nabella had to strain to hear her.

Tomar threw his hands in the air, "I don't know I'm not a healer!"

An idea swirled in Nabella's head. *Could it be?* She shook her head. "No," she whispered.

"What is it, Nabella?" Adara's harsh voice stung. Ignoring the tone Nabella turned wide eyes on her sister. "Could. Could it be possible that someone placed a curse on Father?"

Elah gasped.

"Oh dear." Nahni pressed her hands against her bosom.

Adara pushed herself upright to face Nabella then turned to Tomar. "What do you think?"

Tomar stared at Jokaan. The older man's breathing came in ragged inhales. Sweat beaded across his forehead. Tomar leaned over him.

"Jokaan. Jokaan, can you hear me at all?"

No response. Tomar shook Jokaan by his shoulders. Still, no acknowledgement. Tomar straightened with a shake of his head.

"If someone personally put a curse on him, wouldn't we find some evidence?" Nahni's voice shook.

Everyone stared at each other. Of course. First to move, Nabella ran to the window and looked over the sill. *Nothing. But wait!* "I think there might be footprints here."

"Elah, get Jabari." Tomar's brows pulled together low.

Elah grabbed her jupe and rushed from the room.

Adara dropped to her knees and looked under the bed. "I need a lamp. It's too dark to see under here."

Nahni took the oil lamp from a shelf on Jokaan's wall and left the room. Seven breaths later she scurried back with its bright flame dancing in the wind. Adara took it and leaned over, lamp placed in front.

"No, nothing but a few straws under here."

"A few straws? Why is there straw there?" Nahni asked.

"They're under his head."

"There shouldn't be straw there."

Nabella stared at Tomar. At once they all burst into action. Nahni took the oil lamp from Adara. Tomar gathered Jokaan by the shoulders, and Nabella put her hands under her father's head. She and Tomar lifted Jokaan's upper torso. Nahni leaned close with the lamp, while Adara tore at the wool bedding.

There it was.

A small leather bundle, tightly wound with sinew, lay nestled in straw. Adara's brows pinched together in fright. "Should I open it?"

Sixteen

There they cry, but none giveth answer, because of the pride of evil men.

Job 35:12

A slight breeze wafted across the upper most terrace. Cush groaned quietly to himself and stared out at The City while Ra'anel droned on and on.

"… and that tanniyn is quite odiferous. The stench even reaches the grand heights of this temple. Only the burning of kyphi and myrrh has made it bearable. Surely you can get rid of the carcass by now." The last statement dripped with disdain and self-imposed authority.

Cush ignored Ra'anel's request and glanced at a figure who strode around the corner of the temple. His jaw dropped. Was that Nimrod? The man had shaved his head and beard and wore nothing but a white, full-length wrap. And his arms and chest were shaved too. *Has he gone mad?* Cush looked past Nimrod at his ever present entourage. The youth Terach stood in front of them, Nimrod's sword and spear in his hands. But none of them seemed bothered in the least by the man's presentation. Cush eyeballed Nimrod suppressing a smirk. He would never figure that man out.

Though his physical appearance had changed, Nimrod's stare was unmistakable. The man's eyes bore into Ra'anel, a statement of his displeasure. As if Nimrod's men sensed something, they shifted their weight taking a step closer to their leader.

"It must stay as a reminder of what awaits the people should they choose to go against our City and move away," Nimrod commanded. "The commoners forget all too quickly when there's nothing to remind them."

"We'll bring in some buzzards," Cush interjected. The last thing he needed was Nimrod and Ra'anel at odds. "They'll eat the flesh until there is just bone left. And we can burn incense around the carcass until then. That should help."

"Very well." Ra'anel raised his hand, little finger held high. "Now. There is another pressing task. Other temples are in need of being constructed. Temples that the people can go in themselves to give offerings to the different gods."

Cush pressed his lips together. Would this man ever find an end to the gods? He shook his head. *But then who am I and what do I know about the deities.* "How many?"

"Three for now. Simple shrines, smaller than this, raised on a platform, of ten or twelve steps should do nicely. One temple should be constructed by the western gate for Adad, the great storm god. One for the harvest god, Saturn, by the south gate, and one for Utu, the great sun god who judges. That one is to be constructed right here on the east side across from the temple." Ra'anel pointed to the street below. "You see that bare spot on the other side of the promenade? Right there."

Cush shifted his eyes to Nimrod, but to his surprise the man's attitude had changed. Nimrod nodded then ambled to the edge of the terrace. He surveyed The City, arms crossed over his chest. "And what of Ishtar?"

Ra'anel's lips curled. "Yes, of course you would be familiar with the god of fertility and sexual relations." Ra'anel drummed his fingers on his chin and strolled to Nimrod. "Hmmm, yes. That would be appropriate. I must pray for its location."

"Next to the palace."

Ra'anel turned in that direction and continued to drum his fingers. "Perhaaaps. Like I said, I shall pray about it. In time, the stars will reveal everything. We will study them with this object in mind."

Cush glanced at the temple then let his eyes travel to the roof. It looked dull in the grey mist. Two pinnacles, constructed for celestial measurement and analysis, stood opposite each other. He shook his head. He would never be able to figure out the star patterns and movements. *I guess I should be thankful for the advisors. They spend so much of their time gaining knowledge of such things to benefit us. But, why do I always feel I'm being manipulated?*

"I will wait for your answer before we start building. " Nimrod's deep timbre hardened, "unless you take too long."

"Oh no, you don't have to wait on me. You can get started on the other temples. It may be some time before the stars reveal anything about Ishtar."

Nimrod turned to face Ra'anel and inhaled deep through his nose. "I will prepare bricks and chemar, but a temple to Ishtar will be the first to be constructed." He turned, motioned his men to wait where they stood, and strode into the temple. Terach seemed so young and vulnerable next to them. *Why is he the one holding Nimrod's weapons?*

Cush shook his head again then moved toward the entrance, one brow raised. *Did Nimrod really go in to pray to those deities on the walls? Is that why he shaved and is dressed like that?* Cush had known him since infancy and not once to his knowledge had Nimrod prayed. Did the man actually believe in something other than himself? *How interesting, I think I'll join him.*

Cush stopped mid-stride when he entered. He had not been in the building since the painting and sculptures were completed. Deities, animals, and star assemblages adorned the ceiling, walls, every column, stand, bench, table, and even the floor. Inlays of polished gold, silver and bronze gleamed. Jewels sparkled in the animal depictions' eyes, giving a false sense of reality. Cush turned full circle and the chill washed over him again.

Several celestial advisors worked on clay tablets probably inscribing their observations from the night before. He watched another advisor reach into a number of large clay jars and dump measured handfuls of various herbs into an ornately carved stone vessel. Nimrod stood near the man, arms crossed, peering down at the advisor.

Curious, Cush wandered over. "What are those?"

The advisor glanced up annoyed. "Red wine, tupelo honey, sultana raisins, storax bark, saffron, sandalwood, aloeswood, frankincense, mastic, cardamom seeds, galangal root, lemongrass, and these," the man held several petals and said sardonically, "are rose petals. All carefully measured."

Nimrod snorted, and heat rushed up Cush's neck. The big man stooped seizing the last jar perched on a low shelf. He pulled out a fistful of petals and let them trickle through his fingers. "Be careful, my friend, or you may find yourself going down those steps looking for rose petals at the bottom."

With a click of his tongue the advisor set down his small stone vessel, walked over to Cush, and grabbed two handfuls of petals from the jar. He fixed his eye on Cush, dumped them over the side of the terrace. The advisor glared at him. "Are you ceremonially clean? Have you been in prayer? Is your body scrubbed? Has all your hair been removed?"

Cush's jaw dropped open.

"That's what I thought. No, no, no and no. Then don't touch the offerings to the gods." The man snatched the jar out of Cush's hands, returned to the temple then faced Nimrod. "Follow me."

The advisor shuffled around the central altar, stirred the bucket of ingredients and mumbled something Cush couldn't make out. He doubted any god could understand it either. The anger that had flared an instant before rolled into a quiet chuckle while he watched the advisor circle the altar, chanting with Nimrod, who looked like a giant compared to the diminutive man, following close on his heels.

At last the robed man stopped and eyed Nimrod. "Do you have your incantation bowl?"

Nimrod nodded and pulled a small copper bowl from the folds of his wrap. The Advisor peered into the small basin, twisting it to the right. His lips moved but no sound came forth.

Cush frowned eyes riveted on the basin. *What was that?* He leaned forward and caught sight of an inscription that covered the inside of the bowl spiraling down to the flat bottom. A curse? An invocation? Cush squinted trying to make out the markings. A sharp cough broke his focus. The advisor glared at him, sniffed then flipped the bowl into his robes and turned to the bucket. He dumped the mixture into the shallow copper basin then sprinkled oil over the herbs.

"Go, my child, light your bowl of incense and pray. Stay as long as you want."

The advisor turned shuffling toward Cush. "It would do you good to pray as well."

Cush held up his hands. "I've seen enough." He went out on the terrace taking the first steps of the long trek to the bottom of the tower. He grunted. For the hundredth time Cush wished he had insisted that ramps be built instead of stairs. How much easier the traveling would be.

When Cush reached the bottom he crossed the Processional Way and stood in the proposed space where the temple to Utu was to be built. Fists on his hips he shifted his weight until he completed a full circle. The area seemed too small. In order to go up ten steps, the temple at the top would be tiny. Cush grumped. It didn't seem fitting for the sun god. How could Utu fit into such a small space? Then the temple would be dark and cold. Cush shook his head; he would never understand the world of religion.

"Greetings, Cush." A feminine voice drifted on the damp breeze.

"Well, if it isn't Semiramis." He eyed her and a tiny surge of wariness pinched his temples.

"Tsk, tsk, where are your manners?"

Cush gritted his teeth. "Greetings to you, Semiramis. What good news do you bring?"

A brittle laugh erupted from the pasted beauty before him. "None, none whatsoever." She waved a hand towards the tower. "I saw you come from the temple. Ugh, there's that horrid smell again. Can't you do something about it?"

"I was just speaking to your *husband,* and he said to leave the carcass there. So take it up with him. But I do need to get buzzards to clean the rotting meat. Who of Nimrod's men would be best suited for that task?"

"You spoke to Nimrod? Just now?"

Cush eyeballed her. Her tongue licked her lips like she wanted to devour the man. He knew her well enough to know she was up to something. The sooner he got away from her the better.

"He is at the top of the tower worshipping in the temple. You should worship too, it would do you good." Cush repeated the advisor's words adding an extra dose of sarcasm.

Semiramis poked at the pile of black hair mounded high on her head. A long fingernail scraped against the jeweled bronze clasp holding the twisted mass in place. She pulled herself to her full height then stared up at the powerful black man. "Oh I worship, Cush, don't you worry about that. My spiritual side is quite intact. Unlike you."

"I wish to be as unlike *you* as I can."

"Oh, how quaint," she said sardonically.

Cush snorted. Why did he waste his time with this woman? "Just point out who I can speak to about the buzzards."

Semiramis eyed him then turned to the tower. "Come with me."

Cush watched her move in her finely woven linen as she sauntered across the promenade. The material pulled tight over her torso and swished with every movement. Any other woman and he would be tempted. But not Semiramis. He shuddered at the thought. *Why did I ask her to bring me to Nimrod's men?* He was capable of doing that on his own. Now he would have to be with her longer. He gritted his teeth and followed.

Semiramis skirted far around the rotting carcass, waving a hand in front of her nose until she had moved well past it. When they reached the side of the tower she slowed waiting for him to catch up.

"You look well these days. I heard that boy Terach saved your life."

"News travels fast."

"It does to me."

"Alright then, tell me this. Someone has placed a pagan curse on Jokaan's orchard. Know anything about that?" Accusation rang from his voice.

Semiramis glanced at him from the corner of her eyes. "Why would anyone do that? We all get our oil and olives from him."

"I don't *know* why. Just curious, why and who. And so since news travels so fast for you, why don't you just find out and let me know."

Semiramis paused in front of an arch that covered a back entrance into the tower. She let a finger trail over Cush's hand. "What's in it for me?"

Cush's lips curled, and he withdrew his hand. "What do you want?"

She faced him full taking both of his hands into her pale ones. "Precious stones and metal. I want jewelry, the way we were told it was in the Old World. I want *sabots*. All shiny around my neck and wrists, hanging from my ears and piled high in my hair. Find someone to make me a gold chain to put around my neck. And get those sabots, then you'll have your answer."

Cush stared at her. "You want the world don't you?"

Semiramis's laugh floated through the air. "Oh Cush, you always were witty." She turned and disappeared through the opening. Cush followed and saw her nod towards a room. "You will find two men in there, gambling. Tell them Nimrod sent you." She spun around and swooshed from the building.

Cush ignored the insult watching her go, an uneasy feeling pinched the pit of his stomach. Why did it seem like she got the better end of the deal? He took a deep breath to ward off the tightness and strode into the room. Two men knelt over a shaker and counted sticks.

"Nimrod commands you to come." Cush let the words spew out loud and harsh.

The men jumped and scrambled whatever move they were going to make next.

"Follow me."

The men glanced at each other, then their game. One paused to gather his supplies and stuffed them in a pocket. Cush exited the room, the men close on his heels. Some distance from the carcass he halted. "Nimrod wants you to get buzzards to eat the flesh off that thing. And bring incense to burn around it."

The men looked at each other. Finally one spoke. "Ah, how are we supposed to catch the buzzards?"

"Your problem. Just get a net and throw it over those sitting up there. But if you don't have them by tomorrow, I'm sure Nimrod or Ra'anel will have you on permanent duty by the tanniyn's head."

The men glanced at each other again. "Ah, sir, where are we supposed to get incense?"

"Again, your problem. But I know the celestial advisors have incense. Maybe they have buzzards too."

Cush left the two men and strode through The City to find the fine metal workers.

***

"Do you have it?"

The dark of night made it impossible to identify the small cloaked figure. Even the person's gender remained mysterious, the voice giving no clue.

"Yes."

"Good, good," the voice crooned.

"Tell me what curse you rendered," the man pressed.

A wry chuckle then, "First the gold."

He opened a satchel and shook out a stack of thin, gold sabots, each with a tiny loop fashioned on an end. Even in the dim light of the crescent moon they shined of spectacular beauty and wealth.

The voice pitched low. "You're sure this is from the Old World?"

Could it be a man? "Have you ever seen anything like this anywhere? You know it is from the Old World."

A grimy hand reached for the gold. His fingers were swifter and closed around the gold pieces.

"Ahhh," the voice hissed.

Slowly he pulled open two fingers and extracted a single sabot. "Information." He dangled it in front of the cloaked head.

"The curse is also from the Old World." Quick as lightning the grimy hand snatched the proffered item.

The man clenched his teeth. He had not seen that coming. "That much I already know. How did this curse come to the New World? I cannot imagine Noah, or his sons, even knowing of such a curse." He drew out another piece.

Silence, then, "I have my sources."

He deposited the polished sabot back into his other hand then waited. The cloaked head remained riveted on his clenched hand.

"It is not of this world, either old or new, where I received the information."

"Then where did it come from?"

The figure drew in a deep wheezy breath. "The other world, the one that the gods live in."

He felt the hairs rise on the nape of his neck. "A demon!" Of course. He should have known.

"Depends on who you worship, don't you think? Whether he's a demon or a god."

But the man knew the truth, and his stomach roiled.

"Two," the small, grimy hand extended palm up. *Or is it a woman?*

"One," and he dropped a disk onto the hand.

"Then see if you can figure out the curse," the hand closed into a fist. "And watch your friend die."

He hesitated then drew out another piece. "Which demon told you of the curse?"

A haunted laugh then, "And risk his anger against me? No, I won't give you the name of whom *you* call a demon."

"How long ago did you summon it?"

"You fool!" The low voice hissed. "You know nothing. What do you think? That the demons drowned in the flood?" The wheezy hiss ended in a coughing spasm. The cloaked figure spit then wiped the dribbled drool from their mouth. "Every being from the spirit world was unaffected by the deluge. He came to me! And gives *me* power. You will not break the curse without *my* knowledge." Again the filthy hand extended forward, palm up.

He put another sabot into the hand. "What will break the curse?"

The figure left their hand open. "That will cost you two more."

He knew he had to do it. That would be the last of the disks. Reluctant he stalled then retrieved one and held it in the moonlight. "Was the curse placed upon the man because he refused to move to The City?"

"You only just now figured that out?" The figure reached for the sabot.

He let the coin slip through his fingers. The hand struck like a snake snatching the ancient disk in mid-air.

"How is the curse to be broken?"

"Another coin!"

"You will get the last when I have all the information."

White teeth flashed in the pale light as another hiss escaped.

"Find the potter who makes the idols. Ask him of figurines that are bound. I gave him the knowledge to curse the person through the figure. Tell him I sent you to shatter the spell. Tell him it was only meant to be an omen."

"How will he know I speak the truth; that you sent me?"

The low laugh sent a chill through his bones.

"Tell him Marduk commands it," a deep growl crawled from the throat of the speaker.

Spasms ran through the man's stomach and a chill slithered down his spine. He unclenched his fingers one by one. The dark figure snatched the last disk then held it to the moonlight between thumb and forefinger. The man rubbed his hand against his thigh. The thought of these Old World treasures in the hands of this tainted person felt vile to him. He had to remind himself the trade was for a man's life.

"This will do. Yes. This will do nicely." The owner of the voice pulled the cloak hood farther over their head. He or she stumbled away in perfect imitation of a drunken lurch. He stared as the figure retreated. Whoever they were, they had planned the curse well. And it was worse, much worse than he had thought. He turned to leave when the figure hissed into the darkness. "This will do for now…*Shem.*"

Seventeen

The fool hath said in his heart, There is no God. They are corrupt, they have done abominable works, there is none that doeth good.

Psalm 14:1 (KJV)

"Tomar?"

"No. Don't touch it, not yet anyway." Tomar stared at the bundle, furrowed brows and clenched jaw revealed his tension. Everyone waited, there could be no room for mistakes.

Nabella jerked when the clomp of footsteps sounded through the house. A few breaths later Jabari walked into the room.

"Good. Help me move Jokaan." Tomar jerked his head toward the sick man.

Jabari stared at Jokaan. "Do you think it's wis—"

"Yes, he must be moved immediately." Tomar's voice held no room for argument.

"Tomar, wait." Adara held up her hands. "We have to have a place to lay Father." She tugged at Elah and the women dashed from the room. Nabella looked at Tomar, but he ignored her. Should she go help? Or stay with Father? By the time she made up her mind, Adara and Elah reappeared with a wool-stuffed mattress piled with blankets. Nabella grabbed a corner, and they shoved it against the wall. Carefully the two men hefted Jokaan and laid him on the bedding.

Tomar straightened placing his hand on Jabari's shoulder. "There's footprints outside the window. See what you can do."

Jabari nodded and left without a word. A slow whistle sounded from outside. "These footprints are huge."

Nabella and Elah scurried to the window. "How can you tell? You can hardly make them out, so much has already been washed away."

The sturdy man didn't reply. He stalked the tracks to the pavement stones in the outer courtyard. Then he squatted and peered at the ground from different angles. He pulled himself upright and strode across the courtyard.

"Here's the trail, but now there are two sets of prints. One smaller."

Tomar pushed his broad frame against Elah and Nabella. "Move," he grunted and stared at Jabari. "A child?"

"No, not that small. A woman."

Tomar shook his head and ducked back in. "This isn't right. It's just not right. Why would someone do this? I thought the curse on the fields was bad, but this, this. Who would do such a thing?"

"I thought all such evil things were drowned in The Flood," Nahni whispered.

Adara wrapped an arm around the older woman and turned to her husband. "What do we do now? Should we burn that bundle? Or open it?"

"Open it. We need to see what we are dealing with. And we must pray together to ask God for guidance. Direction from Him is absolutely essential."

Adara backed away when Tomar made his way to Jokaan's bed. He unsheathed his knife and flicked loose straw away from the bundle. One slice cut through the sinew. With the point of the bronze blade he gingerly pushed the tendons aside.

Nabella thought she saw his hands tremble. Tomar balled his free hand. He pushed the knife tip under the folds to open the bundle.

A small blackened figurine lay amongst ashes and the burnt ends of straw. Its clay face had been molded to portray pain and a hole protruded through the chest area. The arms were positioned behind its back as if they were tied. Writing had been carved into the forehead.

"It's been burned." Tomar tipped his head to examine it closer. "The writing. I can almost read it. This says 'be governed by'," Tomar frowned, "I can't make these two words out but the last one is 'die'." He jerked then stared at Adara.

Icy fingers wrapped around Nabella's spine. Tomar stood and brushed his hands together as if to cleanse himself.

"You women stay by Jokaan and take turns watching over him." His tone became harsh with the weight of responsibility. "And we men must fast and pray. No one is to come near this."

"We can't leave that thing in here with Father." Adara's voice trembled.

Tomar hesitated. "I'll move it to the open hearth in the outer courtyard. Do not go near it. Understood? "

A murmur of agreement rippled around the room.

Tomar wiggled his hands deep into the wool below the bundle. He scooped it up and strode through the doorway, figurine held at arm's length. Nabella knew he would end the work for the day and gather the men together to do just what he said.

She stared at Adara. Dare she hope to be included in this? Would Grandmother and her sister shun her still? Adara looked uncertain of what to do.

Nabella's heart went out to her, and she took her sister's hand. "Barukh refuses to come together in a marriage with me. Father said I have until tomorrow. Then I must leave and am never to speak to my family again," she ended in a whisper.

"Oh, Nabella." Adara threw both arms around her sister. Nabella squeezed her eyes shut, but a lone tear trickle down a cheek. A soft sob followed. Suddenly the weight of extra arms engulfed her. Nabella blinked and looked up. Nahni and Elah pressed in, hugging her.

Tears coursed down her grandmother's smooth face. "What are you going to do?"

Nabella straightened and stepped back. "I'm going to stay with Father until tomorrow. Then I'll pack and leave. It's probably better you don't know where I'm going." She drew in a shaky breath and tried to fight the tears. When she failed she flopped next to Jokaan and laid her head against his shoulder. She heard the shuffle of feet then silence. When she looked up only the window covering fluttered in the empty room. Nabella pressed her hand against Jokaan's forehead. The fever raged. She thought of the statue and shuddered. When the figurine had been burned did that cause her father's fever?

"Oh Father." The words had barely left her mouth when Adara and Elah slipped back into the room, arms piled high with blankets. Shoshana followed on their heels with barley stew and a jug of water.

"We'll all sleep here tonight." Adara gave Nabella a wane smile. Nabella closed her eyes, brought arms to her bosom then rocked back and forth. Adara had broken the shunning. At least until tomorrow.

"Thank you."

As the evening wore on Shoshana fell asleep and Adara wrapped her in a wool blanket then laid her near Nabella. Few words were spoken. The three took turns to press a cool, damp cloth to Jokaan's forehead. Nabella fought sleep determined to spend the time with Jokaan. But as the dark gave way to early morning she drifted into a restless slumber.

Nabella blinked. A lone bird chirped outside the window. She glanced around. Somehow she had wound up on the floor with Elah and Shoshana by her side. Adara sat on the floor, her head on Jokaan's bed, eyes closed in weary sleep. Nabella eased herself from between her sisters and stood.

"Adara," she shook her sister. "Wake up, you can go lay down. I'll watch Father."

Adara moaned and rubbed her neck. Jokaan coughed, and Adara scrambled to her feet. He coughed again, and his breathing rasped.

"Maybe if we prop him up?" Nabella glanced at her sister.

Adara snatched her blanket wadding it under their father. But his breathing remained unchanged.

"He needs water," Adara said. "You tilt his head back while I try to get him to drink."

Nabella obeyed, but Jokaan refused to swallow.

"What do we do now?"

"I don't know. Just watch him I guess." Adara's brows knitted together.

"Should I get Tomar?"

"No, he might get mad at you. He's probably sleeping now. I'm sure he prayed all night, I'll get him in a little while."

Suddenly Jokaan gasped, once, twice. He hacked again, breaths coming in jagged puffs.

"Shoshana," Adara cried. "Run, get Tomar. Hurry!"

The young girl woke with a start. She took one look at their father, leapt to her feet and darted from the room. Elah struggled off the floor rushing to Nabella.

Thirty breaths later Tomar skidded into the room, the little girl behind him. Dark circles under his eyes proved Adara right. He had stayed up all night.

Jokaan gasped again and turned his head. "Nabella..." his voice little more than a whisper.

"Father, I'm here. I'm here." She plopped next to him on the mattress grabbing his hand. Jokaan never opened his eyes, but he turned his head toward her as his voice rasped, "Shem...must...get...Shem."

Nabella jumped up. "I will Father. I will!" She leaned over and kissed Jokaan's forehead then ran for the doorway.

"I'll go with you." Tomar caught her arm.

"No," Adara screamed. "No, you can't leave us here with that, that, thing, that curse! I beg you, Tomar."

Tomar opened his mouth to protest, but Nabella jerked her arm away. "I have to go."

The big man turned toward her.

"No! Tomar!" Her oldest sister began to sob and Tomar turned back to Adara. Nabella dashed from the room stopping briefly in the dark storage area to grab a sack and shove the first things her fingers touched into it. She snatched a wineskin and slung both over her shoulder then darted out the door. A pitcher filled with water sat near the well. She poured it into the wineskin and paused. Adara and Tomar's tense voices drifted to her. *I have no time for this.*

She settled into an easy lope toward Barukh's house. When she arrived, her brows raised in surprise. Gideon's place seemed deserted. No one answered her greeting. Then she remembered they had the shop in The City. This could work to her advantage. *I wonder if there is still a takhi in the corrals.* She turned and smacked into Barukh.

"What're you doing here?" Icy blue eyes bore into her.

"It's Father, Barukh. He's dying. I need a takhi to get Shem."

"You're doing no such thing. What kind of fool do you think I am? Go away and don't come back." As he spoke he grabbed her upper arm dragging her across the trampled grass in front of the house. He stopped at the lane leading to the road.

"Let go," she managed to twist her arm free. "I'm telling the truth."

Barukh pointed to the road, "Go."

Nabella's heart sank then beat hard with fury. What kind of monster had Barukh turned into? Or had he always been this way, and she never saw it? She clutched her jupe and ran for the road. Once out of sight of the house she circled around to the stone-walled corral. Yes! Three takhis stood heads down, eyes half-closed.

Nabella ran low along the wall then ducked through the stick gate. "It's all right, I won't hurt you," she murmured. Two takhis snorted and trotted to the other end. The third stood and blinked at her. "Shhh now, it's just me, let me get you."

She glanced around. A blanket and saddle were perched on top of the wall. The halter lay in the dirt. Nabella snatched the halter then sidled to the mare. The takhi gave a soft snort tossing its head, but let Nabella slip the halter on.

"Good girl," Nabella murmured as she led the animal to the wall. She draped the lead rope over her shoulder and tossed the blanket on the takhi's back then hefted the saddle. But when she tried to cinch it the strap came up short. Nabella stood back and looked at the takhi.

"Ah-he, you're fat."

"That's because she's pregnant."

Nabella whirled around, face ashen. "Kfir. Look, I know Barukh told me I can't borrow a takhi, but I have to have one. Father is dying, and I don't care if I have to steal one. I need to get Shem."

Kfir's face clouded with doubt.

"Father asked me to get Shem. Those were his last words before he collapsed."

Kfir pressed his lips firm. "Well, I guess we better get him then. But not on that mare." Kfir strode over yanking the gear off the takhi. In no time he caught the other two and saddled them. Nabella stared at the mounts.

"You're going with me?"

"Well, I'm not letting you travel by yourself. And if we push it we can get there by nightfall. Under the circumstances that should be proper enough."

Nabella closed her eyes trying to still a trembling lip. "Thank you, Kfir." Her knees almost buckled with relief.

"Come on. We need to get going." His voice sounded gruff. "Wait." He shoved both reins in her hand and sprinted to the house. In the span of ten breaths he returned with two javelins, a long dagger and two oil-cloaks. He leaned the javelins against the stone wall and strapped on the long dagger. Then he secured the javelins and oil cloths to his saddle. Kfir pulled his reins free and with a grin gave her a nod.

"Shall we begin?"

Nabella nodded, climbed onto the takhi's back tying her wine flask and sack to the saddle. Kfir waited until she finished then kicked his takhi. Her steed leapt after the first takhi almost tossing her to the ground. She managed to hang on and settled herself into the saddle. When they clattered out of the yard she heard Barukh's angry yell behind them, "Hey, Kfir! What do you think you are doing?"

"Getting Shem," Kfir shouted back then they sped down the road.

When they came to the edge of the vineyard Kfir slowed his mount to a trot, and the animals moved onto the grasslands without hesitation. Soon the takhis lengthened their strides into a ground-eating gait. Nabella craned her neck. A figure atop a takhi broke away from a herd of cattle. Could that be Abel? The herder angled across the plain towards them.

"Greetings, Kfir, Nabella. What good news do you bring?" A grin spread across Abel's face when he reined in next to them. Nabella smiled, but Kfir didn't slow down.

He tipped his head. "Forgive us, Abel, we have to make it to the foothills by tonight. We'll visit when we have more time."

Abel reined his mount in and shouted back, "Soundin' good. May God be with you."

Kfir urged his steed into a slow lope. The sun had not moved more than a hand width when they found the mud hole where Nabella had spent the first night. Her mouth crooked upward, how much faster to travel on takhis. Kfir slowed the animals to a walk and brought them to the water. They waited for their mounts to drink. When Nabella's mount began to splash the water with its foreleg Kfir shouted, "Ha-ya! Get him going or he'll roll in the water."

Nabella's eyes flew wide, and she kicked her mount. The takhi pawed the water a few more times, shook its head then followed Kfir's out of the water.

"Well, you can take a takhi to water, but you can't make it drink," Kfir grinned. "Don't worry, he'll be thirsty enough the next time."

Nabella patted her takhi's neck. *I bet you will, you have no idea how far you have to go today.* Then she moved next to Kfir. "I need to ask you something."

Kfir swung his gaze toward her. A small smile played across his lips, and his dark eyes twinkled. "Well, what is it?"

Nabella took in a deep breath. "Can we swing a little off course? There is a nasty shepherd up there somewhere and…" her voice trailed as a hand searched for the scratches long since healed.

"Did you have a run-in with him?"

Nabella clasped and unclasped the reins then gave a nervous nod.

"Did he hurt you?" Kfir's voice had become thick. She glanced at him and saw his hands balled into fists tight on the reins. He pulled his mount in.

"What did he do?"

Nabella glanced out over the fields. She couldn't lie. In short strained sentences she told what happened. "I didn't want to cut him. Please believe me, Kfir," she finished.

When he didn't answer she feared a tongue-lashing. After a few deep breaths Kfir still remained silent. She chanced a sideways peek. But he stared straight ahead, his tanned sable skin dark in heated crimson. His jaw clenched tight, and the takhi skittered sideways.

Unexpectedly he let out a deep breath and a chuckle escaped. It transformed his face from fierce explorer back to gentle farmer. Nabella stared, confused.

Kfir looked her in the eyes. "You are one amazing woman."

Nabella's mouth dropped open. What? He wasn't mad at her? And what did he mean by amazing?

Kfir looked upward. "Thank You, God, that she had a disguise. And thank you, Jokaan, for giving her the dagger." He turned thoughtful, dark eyes on her once again. The concern and admiration she saw startled her. Even though she felt heat crawl up her neck she couldn't tear her eyes away. She could only nod, mouth still wide open.

Kfir turned his head and muttered, "My brother's a fool."

Nabella blinked and shut her mouth. Now what did *that* mean? She began to tremble and with an impatient swipe of her hand wiped a tear off her cheek. Kfir reached over squeezing her arm. She stiffened and pulled her arm away.

"It's alright, Nabella," he muttered, voice tender. "I'm here, and I will protect you."

She drew in another ragged breath. "Thank you. And thank you for escorting me."

Kfir urged his mount forward, and Nabella followed. She pushed the animal until she could watch Kfir from the corner of her eye. He stared straight ahead. The wide headband ended at the nape of his neck. Its loose ends wrapped neatly around slicked black hair and moved against his back in rhythm to the takhi. His chiseled cheekbones and short cropped beard unexpectedly struck her as handsome. Very handsome.

Nabella rode in silence trying to sort mixed emotions. After a while she ventured, "When you were exploring did you ever have to use your dagger?"

"At times."

She turned wide hopeful eyes on Kfir. "Tonight would you teach me how to use my dagger better?"

Kfir fixed his gaze on her. He sat wordless for some time then sputtered, "Has anyone told you, you have the most soft, beautiful brown eyes, like a doe?"

Nabella blinked several times, and Kfir looked away. He cleared his throat. "You're quite a woman, Nabella. Yes, I will show you how to use your dagger."

"It used to be my mother's."

They rode in silence for awhile.

"The only reason I have it is because my mother's dead." The pain that still gripped Nabella's heart surprised her. She studied her hands. "It was a lone hyena. One of the really big ones. Nobody expected it to be in the olive groves. Tomar found the dagger nearby covered in blood and the tracks were clear. She must have wounded it, but it was too late. She didn't make it."

"I remember." Kfir remained silent for a long while and only the clip clop of the takhis' hooves sounded between them. "I've spotted those animals from a distance. They don't run in packs like the smaller ones. They don't need to. I don't think a lone warrior could even stand up against one of those giants. Your mother fought bravely. That she was able to draw blood is a real testament. Her death would have been quick after that. She did not suffer."

Nabella stared at the grey skies then across the soggy plain. For so long she could barely think of the gruesome death her mother had met. But now, with what Kfir told her, she felt closer to Danya. And full of relief, that her mother had not endured much pain before it was over.

By the time they drew near the tree line that hid the emerald pond, Nabella's heart ache had been replaced with aching muscles. She longed to get down and slip into her woods. But how different it looked from a month ago. Most of the golden leaves had long since dropped and bare branches stretched thin fingers into the overcast sky. What did the pond look like now? She opened her mouth to call Kfir but something stopped her. This was her forest, her secret place. She wasn't ready to share it yet. When they passed it she glanced over her shoulder. *You're safe, I brought no intruder today.* A tiny smile pulled at the corner of her delicate mouth. *Oh, but how I wish I could go there to soothe my legs, and my soul. Thank You, Lord, for the experience I had there.* An inkling of peace tapped her heart, and she knew it had everything to do with God and nothing to do with the emerald pool.

The dull glow behind the clouds had passed its zenith by the time they reached the edge of the tent city dotting the little Euphrates. Nabella drooped with weariness, and her heart beat in gratitude when Kfir dismounted along the edge of the river. With a sigh she swung her leg over the takhi and slid to the ground. Immediately she staggered backward into the kfir's mount. The animal snorted, eyeballed her then stepped forward when Kfir led it into the water. Nabella took a few awkward steps. But try as she might her legs refused to cooperate, and her steps came up short.

Laughter erupted from the bank, and she knew it came from Seth.

"Greetings, Seth, and be quiet. If you rode all morning your legs would bow too." Nabella grinned at the boy.

The boy's laughter ended in a chortle. "Greetings. Do I know you?"

"Yes. I'm, I'm well you know me as Nabel."

"Nabel? Ah-he, you look different! What good news do you bring?" Seth held out his arms, almond-shaped eyes all but disappeared behind a wide smile.

Nabella looked to Kfir, and he held out his hand for the reins. Nabella handed them over then waddled to Seth. She heard stifled chuckles behind her and threw a glance over her shoulder. "You too, Kfir. Be quiet."

She collapsed next to Seth and grasped each forearm in greeting.

"Do you have any more of that meat? It was so good especially the liver."

The meat, her sack! She had forgotten all about it. Was it still tucked in the hollow of the tree? She doubted it. But maybe she could talk Kfir into it. No, maybe she could *ask* Kfir if they could look for it. After all it did have her tunic in it, and she would need that. She drew her knees to her chin. But only if the opportunity presented itself.

"No I don't, but if I did I would give you more." Nabella laid her cheek on her knees and smiled.

When the takhis had watered, Kfir brought Nabella's pack. He plopped next to the two and opened it. "Let's see what you have in here, I'm starving."

Nabella leaned close. She had been in such a rush in the morning she had no idea what was in the sack. Had that only been this morning? Kfir pulled the first stone jar out removing its sealed lid.

"A jar of olive oil." He set it between them and reached for the next item, "Soap." Kfir gave her a sidelong glance, one brow raised, then pulled out another jar. "Another jar of olive oil and," he pulled out a large sack, "unshelled almonds."

"There isn't anything else?" Nabella peered into the pack.

"Well done, my friend, well done." Kfir grinned.

"That's what you brought to eat, Nabel?" Seth looked at her like she lost her mind.

"Well I was in a hurry and, and…"

"Maybe your mother would like to trade?" Kfir waved a jar of olive oil under Seth's nose.

"Motherrr!"

Seth's mother poked her head out of the tent. "What is it?"

"My friends would like to trade olive oil for food."

The woman, her beautiful long hair pulled into a single braid down her back, came out of her tent and took the jar from Kfir. She pulled off the lid smelling the contents. "It's fresh. Wonderful. I'll be right back," and she handed it back to Kfir.

When she returned she carried a platter of dried fruit, flat bread, cheese and nuts.

"Good trade." Kfir smiled. "Here." He handed her the larger of the two jars then stuffed a chunk of bread and cheese into his mouth.

Seth chattered while they ate and brought them up-to-date with the latest news.

"If you're going straight across the plain, the lions attacked not too far from here the day before yesterday so be careful. Oh, and Melek says some foxes have been looking bad, like they're sick, so stay away from them." The boy went on and on.

Before long the platter had been stripped bare, and Kfir and Nabella licked their fingers. Abruptly Kfir stood, "Nabella, we have to go."

"Nabella? That's your real name?"

Nabella grasped Seth's arms and smiled wide. "Yes. And I'll see you later."

"Bye, Nabella. Bye." He stared at Kfir "I can't remember if you are Barukh or Kfir."

"Kfir."

"I like you a lot better than your brother."

Kfir sighed and ruffled the boy's straight black hair. "I know, he can be trying. Good to see you again, Seth."

Kfir tightened the cinch and mounted while Nabella caught her takhi. After she did likewise, they headed across the river the lunged up the opposite bank. Nabella turned waving to Seth. Her heart went out to the boy, maybe someday she could come back just to visit and give him a ride.

She twisted forward urging her takhi into a trot. Thoughts of her father lingered in her mind. How was he doing? Was he even still alive? He had to be.

They jogged along a path through the field of flax as high as their takhis' bellies. When they reached the end of the field Kfir angled his takhi toward a deeply tanned man working with the crop.

"Greetings, Ofur."

"Gre—" the last of the greeting was lost as the reins of Nabella's takhi ripped through her palms, and the animal snatched a mouthful of the tender stalks.

"No," Nabella gasped.

"It's all right." Ofur strolled over, raised the takhi's head and scratched its ears. "He knows something good when he sees it, don't you, boy?"

Nabella smiled at his kindness and gathered the reins.

Kfir glanced at Ofur's waist. "Do you have any other weapon besides your dagger? We heard that a lion attacked two days ago not far from here. You be careful, Ofur."

"Yes, yes. I have a spear by the cart. I'll go get it." But he continued to scratch Nabella's takhi.

"And also it sounds like the foxes around here are sick."

"Yes, yes. I saw a sick one last week." Ofur let Nabella's takhi rub its head against his chest. "It had foam around its mouth, and its fur looked ragged and scruffy. I ran it through with my spear and buried it deep. I didn't want the sickness to spread."

"That's smart you buried it. From what I know if it bites or scratches you, you get sick too. So I imagine if something ate it, ah-he! It would spread fast." Kfir shook his head. "We have to go, Ofur, give my regards to Ashkenazi."

"Yes, yes. I'll go get my spear now. You be careful too." Ofur nodded toward the plain. "Where's *your* spear?"

Kfir pointed to the other side of his takhi where the javelins were strapped.

"Good." Ofur nodded then smiled at Nabella.

"Wait," with deft fingers she loosened her sack and drew out the bottle of olive oil. "Please, if you can do so soon, bring meat to the crippled boy just on the other side of the river. He lives alone with his mother."

As Ofur retrieved the jar, his face softened. "Yes, yes. I will do this. I know Seth."

He let go of her reins, and she gave her takhi a swift kick to keep its head up and away from the flax. She did the right thing, didn't she? Nabella glanced at Kfir when he passed by then wished she hadn't. Heat flamed her face. His eyes radiated a kindness and respect she didn't know how to respond to. At a loss of what to do she leaned forward, patted the takhi and followed Kfir onto the plain.

Eighteen

And Zillah, she also bare Tubalcain, an instructor of every artificer in brass and iron.

Genesis 4:22a (KJV)

The vast grasslands surrounded them on all sides. Nabella eased her takhi next to Kfir. "Don't you think we should be running through here?" She peered over her shoulder, eyes darting about.

"No."

"Why not?" At a slight noise Nabella jerk her head around.

"You're not afraid, are you?"

Nabella swung her gaze back around, brows peaked together. "Nooo. Well, I'm nervous. But remember Shem said it would be fine for takhis to go through here, because we can outrun them."

"Yes, that's true, when a lion is chasing you. But not now. Think about it, Bella, if we ran now what's to keep us from running right *in*to a lion?"

"Well, wouldn't the takhis know?"

"Not until they got right on top of one. Then it would be too late. By walking, we give the takhis a chance to sense something is up. And they'll be fresh to run really, really fast. Without spooking to the side in the middle of a run if the lions attack and dumping either one of us at the lion's feet."

Warmth washed over Nabella. Kfir had included himself in falling off though she couldn't imagine the strong, steady man unhorsed. She knew he had done it for her benefit. The little smile that tugged at the corners of her mouth widened. He had called her Bella. Only Shoshana called her that. And now Kfir. *I wonder if he knew he just called me by my short-name.* Why had she never noticed the kindness of this man before?

Kfir interrupted her thoughts. "See those gazelles over there. If there was a lion between us and them, they would be constantly glancing in this direction. At least the ones on the edge of the herd would."

Nabella studied the gazelles. They grazed in calm beauty, though on occasion one or two lifted its head to check their surroundings. The tension eased from Nabella's shoulders and arms. Kfir was right.

But once they passed the gazelles apprehension returned.

"Now what, Kfir? Who will alert us to danger?"

"Well first and foremost, the takhis. And we need to keep a sharp eye out."

In the distance a flock of birds rose, squawked their protest then landed two hundred cubits from where they first flushed.

"Something like that will alert us too." Kfir stood in his stirrups and looked behind him. "The other thing to watch for is the wind moving through the grass. That is when a predator stalks."

"Why?"

"Because you're much less likely to see their movements. When the tall grass is waving, like it is now in this breeze, then you don't see the movement of the grass when the animals brush against it."

Nabella remembered how she had wiggled through the grass when she snuck up on the wild takhi herd. Had she done just that too? *No, I don't think so.* But a lion, that's different. Nabella glanced over her shoulder again. The whole grassland moved with the breeze. Lions could be anywhere, sneaking up on them. She closed her eyes in a brief prayer of thanks that she hadn't known about the lions the first time out. How fortunate the beasts had been elsewhere or certainly she would have been attacked.

A small herd of aurochs moved in the distance. She didn't want to get close to them either. They were bigger than any large takhi she had seen, with horns the same width across as she was tall.

"Do lions hunt aurochs?"

Kfir studied the animals. "Maybe, if they are desperate. But a lion is not going to want to tackle those horns."

"Kfir? Can I have one of those javelins?"

He gave her a lopsided grin. "Well, I would if you knew how to use one, do you?"

She looked away and shook her head.

"Nabella," Kfir waited until she looked him in the eye. "If the lions do attack, the takhis are going to go wild. All I want you to do is hang on. All right? Stay with your takhi and try to point him east so we don't have to back track. Then fly like a storm."

Nabella clasped and unclasped the reins then nodded. Her mount snorted.

"Leave the killing-the-lions part to me, all right? And try to relax. Your takhi is picking up your tension."

"All right."

They rode in silence. Low wisps of clouds floated under the gray matted skies. The drizzle from the day before returned to cover them in a fine moisture. They paused long enough to put on the oil-cloaks. The dampness muted Nabella's mood and her senses.

Caught off guard Nabella lurched when her takhi's muscles bunched and his head came high. Both animals danced about and broke into a high stepping trot. She felt her takhi's ribcage expand as he drew in a heavy breath then blew a loud warning snort. Nabella stood in her stirrups, eyes darting about. She saw Kfir pull a javelin loose. *My dagger. I should get my dagger.* Nabella let go of the saddle to reach for the small weapon.

In that instant a roar burst all around that shook every fiber of her being. Nabella froze. Her takhi bound sideways then forward in one giant leap. She careened off to the side grabbing at the saddle. Her fingertips snagged the edge and somehow one leg managed to stay draped over the top. The takhi spun, and she clung with all her might. The air split again with a lion's mighty roar. The takhi bound once more then bucked. Nabella's fingers tore from the saddle, and she watched the world turn sideways. She landed with a heavy thump on her side then rolled to her stomach as pain exploded in her hip, breath squeezing from her chest. She turned her head just in time to see the lioness bound over her. Stretched out to full length, it became a furry tan blur against misty gray skies then was gone. Nabella lay stunned. *My dagger,* she thought again. But she couldn't even get her breath let alone move. In the distance she heard fierce snarls and a takhi squeal. Then shouts.

Kfir, I'm so sorry. I didn't do what you asked.

Panic swelled when a gruesome picture of the lioness in full attack against Kfir swirled through her mind. She tried to move her legs then her arms, but her body reeled with pain. *Get up, Nabella!* She pushed herself over. Pain shot through her hip. She forced herself to control her breathing. *Be quiet, be quiet.* A lion roared again then more shouts. *Kfir! Oh God—save him, please save him.* Little by little she forced herself upright. Her head spun, but at last she managed to sit.

Brutal snarls ended in a roar. It sounded like more than one lion now. *Oh God, I have to help him.* Legs wobbled as she tried to gather them under her. Stars shot in front of her eyes and the pain dragged an unintended gasp from her lips. Nabella felt her body go limp and she flopped to her back. Black dots floated before her eyes. Strange, she didn't hear any more snarls or roars. Or Kfir.

Oh no, Kfir! Did the lions get him? This time she forced herself to sit despite the pain and blackness that threatened. Knees drawn against her chest she pulled the dagger from its sheath. *I have to get up. I have to help Kfir.* A wave of black specks spun about her. She lowered her chin to the top of her knees. Arms wrapped around her legs and both hands gripped the dagger pointing it skyward. Nabella took a deep breath willing the dizziness to leave.

"Now that was smart. You did just what I would have told you to do if you fell off." Kfir's head then his body appeared as he strode through the tall grass.

Nabella felt her muscles go weak. "Kfir." The whisper tore from her mouth as tears pooled. She unwrapped one hand from the dagger and leaned back.

"Hey there, little doe. It's all right, papa buck took care of those lions just like I said I would. Those two won't be bothering us anymore." Kfir squatted facing her. Nabella had never in all her twenty years ever been so happy to see anyone. Her breath came out in a small laugh, and she lowered her dagger. "Kfir, I have a confession. I was trying to get to you, bu—"

Before she knew what happened Kfir stood, reached over and scooped Nabella to her feet. She gasped at the sudden movement and throb that shot through her hip.

"You're hurt!"

"No, well, just a little. Let me stand here awhile." She clung to his shoulder. Gradually Nabella tested her weight on the injured leg.

"Where're you hurt?"

"It's my hip." Nabella expected an explosion of pain any time. At last her full weight rested on the leg and to her surprise only felt sore. But when she pressed her hand on her hip another gasp escaped.

"What is it?" Kfir's grip tightened around her elbow.

"It hurts to press on it but only a little when I stand," Nabella gave a soft apologetic laugh.

"Well, let's see if you can walk. The rest of the pride will be coming soon."

"Will they be mad at us for killing those other two?" Nabella leaned against Kfir and placed one foot in front of the other. It hurt a little, but she gritted her teeth trying not to limp.

"Lean on me more," Kfir said, "and no, I don't think the rest of the lions will be mad at us or know we're the ones that killed those two females, or anything like that. But they will be hungry."

Kfir's takhi stood close by, its reins drooped to the ground.

"It's a wonder he stopped."

"I've trained him to stop when his reins touch the ground. And to come to my whistle." The man pursed his lips and let out a shrill blast. The takhi pricked its ears, shifted its head to the side to avoid stepping in the reins then trotted toward them.

Nabella gave him a pat. "That's amazing."

Kfir shrugged, "Can you ride?"

"I think so." Before she could say anymore Kfir lifted her onto the saddle. He gathered the reins and began to walk the takhi. Nabella pressed her lips together at the movement but relaxed a little when she realized it was endurable.

"Where's my takhi?"

Kfir jutted his chin. "See him there halfway to the aurochs?"

Nabella's heart sank. "Oh no, now how are we going to get Shem's help in time?"

"Don't worry. That takhi will come running as soon as he sees we aren't going his way."

Nabella's shoulders sagged with relief. *What a great horseman he is.* They made their way across the grassland, Kfir in front as he led the takhi. The drizzle had stopped, but the tips of the wet grass soaked her feet. Nabella clutched the saddle, grateful that Kfir let her ride. He would be wet from the waist down.

The gentle rock of the takhi swayed her hips. After awhile the pain turned to a sharp throb. At last she spoke.

"Kfir, I need to walk for awhile." Kfir halted and lent a hand. Nabella's hands lingered on Kfir's shoulders for just an instant. With a grin he tapped her on top of her head.

She clasped her hands and looked down. "I know, I'm too tall."

Kfir chuckled. "Says who?"

"Well, I'm only a half head shorter than you."

He put a finger under her chin and tilted her head until their eyes met. "You're fine just the way you are, Nabella."

His contagious grin lifted her spirits.

Once again they trudged forward. She hung onto a stirrup and let the takhi support some of her weight. Kfir hiked in front and glanced at her every now and then.

"I have been through some really beautiful lands in my travels." Kfir almost seemed to talk to himself.

"How far did you go?"

"This last time, far to the east."

"Is that where it's so beautiful?"

"There and other places too."

"What did it look like?"

"Hills covered in dark green forests with golden valleys and sparkling rivers running in between. Bright orange sunsets and rosy sunrises that bathed the land in a glow." Kfir's voice had a wistful tone to it. He glanced back, a shine in his eyes.

"And you should have seen some of the animals. Strange creatures, unlike anything we have here. Beautiful birds and large flying creatures with heads like crocodiles and bodies like enormous bats. And the sounds they made," he threw her a grin, "would make the hair on the back of your neck stand straight up. Sometimes they dove through the air so fast they sounded like thunder."

"Was it like that everywhere?"

"No, to the north it's *really* cold. Sometimes so cold in the early mornings it was hard to breathe. It snowed almost continually too, even when it was supposed to be summer. And when we went south we came to a body of water that was so big you couldn't see the end of it."

He paused, and they walked in silence.

"There were other animal calls too. Some eerie and some almost like a flute. There is a kind of small hyena that even sounds like it's laughing when it's about to make a kill. And once I saw a flock of huge birds with really long legs and a long neck but it couldn't fly! They ran so fast, it was incredible. I think," he paused, "I think you would really like it, Nabella."

"As long as I don't fall off my takhi," she said with a grin. A hearty laugh from Kfir rewarded her.

Nabella's eyes scanned over the vast plain. "Have you ever seen any other people out there?"

"No. Not on any of the explorations I've gone on."

"Do you think any people live out there? Where you haven't been?"

Kfir stared at the cliffs for quite a while. "No. I really don't think so. I have never seen any sign, any tracks, or things that people normally leave behind. Ever. Anywhere."

"Well then, are we in disobedience to God for staying so close to The City?"

A chuckled escaped from Kfir as he shook his head. "That's a big question."

"Well, are we?"

Kfir pulled the headband lower on his forehead. "Probably. I think that's why I like to go exploring so much. I believe that sooner or later people will move away from the City. Whether they have to or by their own choice, I don't know. There are other places just as wonderful as Shinar to live. People will need to know where to go."

"What do you mean they might have to move?"

"Well, the people who run The City might force things upon us we don't want."

"Like trying to make Father move to The City."

"Or making things so bad people will be forced to eventually move away all together."

When a distant whinny drifted across the tall grass Kfir twisted his head to look behind. Nabella started when Kfir's takhi answered with a loud neigh. Kfir grinned but kept up his pace. They continued east and her takhi, after several protesting whinnies galloped to them. He fell in behind Kfir's mount, plodding steadily along.

"Take the reins, I'm going to drift back and grab his."

A dozen breaths later Kfir called, "Alright, Nabella, I have him."

She stopped, and Kfir swooped her onto her takhi. "Let me know if it gets to be too much again." He mounted and led them in a fast walk. Nabella glanced at the sky. A light spot in the clouds gave away the sun. Soon dark-time would be upon them, in less than three hand-spans. Nabella shook her head. It always set so early in these late autumn days, and the clouds made it worse.

"Can we go faster?"

"Yes."

Kfir set his mount into a slow jog. Gritting her teeth Nabella put most of her weight on her good leg. It hurt but thankfulness enveloped her as the ground skimmed by. She just wanted this day to end. Then she would be able to give the burden of the curse to Shem and Machlah, to get a cure.

After awhile Nabella noticed Kfir had pointed his takhi to the south of East Lake and would miss the temporary outpost all together. She wanted to ask why but guessed he did it so there would be no more delays. Soon they reached the Tigris River and Kfir motioned her to come abreast.

"When the takhis get to deep water, stretch out on this side," he jabbed a hand in between them. "I'll do the same. That way if you're having a hard time I'll be right there to help you."

Nabella nodded. She didn't look forward to a soaking this late in the cool day but obeyed without complaint. On the far side Kfir helped her up the bank and onto her takhi. He set the pace at a slow lope. Nabella gripped the saddle and put as much weight as she could on her hands and good leg. Finally she found a position that eased some of the pressure on her hip.

By the time they reached the foothills the grey sky began to darken. Kfir slowed to a walk glancing at her. She could feel the strain and knew it marked her face. She must look a sight.

Kfir's brows wrinkled up under his headband. "We're pretty close, Bella. Hang in there," and he gave her a wink.

His kind words gave her the strength she needed. Nabella sat a little straighter and sucked in a deep breath. She could do this.

By the time they reached Shem's cave the grey had deepened. Dark crimson shot out from under the clouds and painted their fluffy bellies a dull red.

"I'll wait while you check if they're still here." Nabella's voice sounded weak even to her own ears.

"What do you mean—if they're still here."

"Please, just check."

Almost immediately Kfir returned from the mouth of the cave. "You knew. You knew they wouldn't be here."

Nabella shook her head. "No, I only had a feeling. Machlah told me where they would move if Shem decided to leave this cave."

"So you know where they are?"

"Machlah mentioned a place. She gave me some landmarks."

"Which direction?"

"North."

Kfir mounted, and they started out. "What are we looking for?"

"We have to go down to the edge of the foothills. She said seven canyons north is a very deep and long one with a waterfall at the end. There's a cave next to it. She said the tanniyn used to live there before it was killed. Shem always liked that cave."

"And what if he decided to move someplace else?"

"Machlah said she would leave a marking on the cave wall so I would know where to find her."

"I wonder why he wanted to move."

"She said he didn't want Cush to find them."

The takhis picked their way through boulders and rocks in the shadows of the foothills. The only sounds were the occasional clack of hoof against rock or a muffled snort.

At last the man let out a deep sigh. "I sure hope they'll be there. I'm done for the day."

Nabella noticed for the first time exhaustion in his voice. No wonder. They had ridden a little over a two-day's journey in one day, and he had fought and triumphed over two lions. All on a little bread, cheese, some nuts and berries. Nabella clutched her jupe. And she never bothered to ask if he had been wounded from the lions.

Kfir stopped his takhi. "This one is the seventh canyon. It's hard to tell how long it is, it's getting so dark."

"I think we should give it a try. Kfir?"

"Yes?"

"Did the lions hurt you?"

"Cut me wide open and left me bleeding back on the plain," he said then chuckled.

"Oh, you." But despite her fatigue she smiled.

They rode side by side in silence until the walls closed in too tight. The shadows within the canyon walls brought on an early darkness, and Nabella could hardly make out Kfir's takhi. The canyon curved and in the deep twilight they finally had their answer.

At the end of the cul-de-sac a soft glow came from a cave halfway up the cliff. Next to it, Nabella could hear the sound of cascading water. They had made it. Kfir pushed his takhi through the brush until they stood by the pool beneath the waterfall.

"This is as far as we can go on the takhis." He dismounted coming to her side. "Grab my shoulders." He held out his arms and put strong hands on her waist when she leaned forward. Her hip hurt worse dismounting the takhi than it had all the time she had been riding. Nabella tried but failed to stifle a small cry.

"Did I hurt you?"

"No. It's just my hip."

"Can you make it up to the cave?"

Nabella let go of his shoulders and limped to get a clear view. The cave entrance looked so far away.

"Yes, but I'll need your help."

A crescent moon climbed above the rim of the canyon, and its pale light glinted onto the pool of water. Kfir swiftly unsaddled the takhis and unbridled Nabella's. Her mount pushed past him splashing into the pond. Kfir followed with his takhi. First one then the other takhi's head dipped and soft slurping carried across the water. Nabella gathered her jupe heedfully sinking to her knees. She splashed her face and arms then cupped her hands. How good it tasted, so cold. Kfir tied his mount, knelt by her, and did the same. When he finished he stood then lifted her upright.

"I'll go first, and you hang onto me."

Nabella nodded. More than once she would have tumbled to the bottom had she not clung to Kfir. *I can do this.* Suddenly a rock rolled past them from above. Nabella peered into the darkness. Only a little farther. Another rock launched past them then a scrape sounded above their heads.

"Who goes there?" Machlah's voice shot into the darkness, hard and uninviting.

"It's me, Nabella and Kfir."

"Nabella?" Wonder replaced coldness. Then, "Is something wrong? What has happened?"

Kfir topped onto the flat area in front of the cave dragging Nabella with him. Machlah stood with a spear in one hand, a club in the other and a bow and several arrows at her feet.

"Greetings, I'm so glad to see you're well, Machlah." Kfir laid his hand over hers and lowered the spear. Then he placed his hands on the woman's shoulders and gave her a kiss on each cheek. When he let go, Nabella fell into her friend's arms. Machlah dropped her weapons embracing the exhausted girl.

"You are shaking, child. Come inside, both of you." Machlah put an arm around Nabella's shoulders guiding her into the cave. "If you would please, get my weapons, Kfir?"

Machlah guided the wounded girl to her own bed. Nabella sank onto the soft blanket and immediately leaned onto her good hip. She stretched her leg to ease the pain.

"What happened?"

While Nabella told of the afternoon's events, Machlah hurried to her jars and baskets, tongue clucking.

"You two must be famished." She pulled a clay pot from the ambers. "Please sit, Kfir. Let me just make this tea for Nabella then I will fix you something to eat."

Kfir sank to the ground opposite the fire from Nabella and leaned against the wall, elbows on his knees. When Machlah brought the food he held the plate and gave thanks to God for their safe arrival and health for Jokaan.

"So this is why you are here? Jokaan has taken ill?"

Hands clenched tight Nabella shook her head. "He has been cursed."

"Cursed?" Kfir almost choked on his mouthful. "You didn't tell me that, Nabella."

She blinked. "I guess I didn't. Please forgive—"

Kfir held up his hand. "Stop, it was an innocent oversight. Tell us now."

"Adara found a wrapped bundle inside his mattress. We opened it and there was a tortured figure with strange writings." Her voice trembled. "Father got worse after that. I just know it was placed on him because he refuses to move to The City. And Jabari found a set of huge footprints under Father's window and another smaller set on the other side of the courtyard."

"Did he track down who they belonged to?" Kfir's voice turned hard.

"I don't know. I left right away. I, we came here."

"Semiramis and Nimrod. I am sure of it. They have given themselves over to the Serpent. Does your father know you came?" Though Machlah's voice sounded gentle the question rang sharp.

"He asked me to come. His last words before he lay unmoving were 'Nabella, find Shem.' Kfir came with me and protected me. And I'm not disguised like a boy. Did I do right, Machlah? I didn't make the curse worse?"

"It is not possible for you to make the curse worse. You have done well, motek."

Nabella closed her eyes shoulders sagging. It was so good to be with Machlah again. Memories of her previous visit came flooding back. "Machlah? What is an oth?"

"It is a sign revealed by God that is directed at the future. It is often brought about through some form of aid or understanding, a benefit, or even a warning. An oth has eternal value, bearing witness of God's promise to act in our future and often calls us to personally be ready."

"So when God said mankind must change, that was the oth?"

"Yes."

"But change how?"

"I know not, child. That is why we have to be personally ready."

Kfir blew out a long breath, "Ready for what?"

"To do whatever He asks of us."

A long silence followed. At last Kfir pushed himself upright with a groan. "Thank you for your hospitality. I'll stay with the takhis tonight." He stretched and looked around. "Where's Shem? I'd like to speak with him."

Machlah looked up, brows drawn together. "He is not here."

"Not here?" Tears brimmed on Nabella's lashes.

"Where is he?" Kfir demanded.

Machlah's voice rang with fear. "He went," she glanced at the cave entrance. "To The City."

Nineteen

But the Lord came down to see the city and the tower the people were building. The Lord said, "If as one people speaking the same language they have begun to do this, then nothing they plan to do will be impossible for them."

Genesis 11:5-6

Ra'anel stepped out of the palace, ran a hand through his scraggly beard and glanced at the sundial in the courtyard. The shadow pointed to one hand-span past the sun's zenith. *Hmm, I got up early today.* He blinked squinting at the sundial again. Then it hit him. The sun was shining. He sighed, such a pleasant change from the overcast drizzle they'd experienced for the past three weeks. Fingers trickled through his beard again, and he turned in the direction of the shops. It was time to pay Gideon a visit. Ra'anel had waited long enough, the man had been in The City for over a month now. After all, he needed to know how the bargaining had been going so he could set the tariff.

The head celestial advisor stepped through the courtyard onto the busy street peering at the sky again. Not a cloud. *Good, the sky will be clear tonight.* His thoughts jumped to the business he needed to attend that night. *I must check the position of the tanniyn and woman star assemblages against the great hunter. Nimrod's request for the temple of Ishtar will be revealed there. I must have everything ready tonight. With winter so close the rains could come back any time.* Ra'anel sniffed studying the crowds while he made his way to the main street.

Most people looked away. Some even crossed to the other side when he approached.

Such easy, prey. A corner of his mouth tilted at the thought. *I could get most anything out of any one of these commoners. Look, they don't even want to get near me. They recognize power when they see it.* Supremacy surged through him and disgust. *Peons. They were so, uneducated.* Ra'anel squared his shoulders. The motion lasted fleetingly. The hump on his back forced him to hunch over again. It didn't matter those plodders still moved out of his way. At least they'd better, or they'd be in Nimrod's mud pits making bricks. Ra'anel smirked. Yes, how excellent to know the stars better than anyone else and know the power they held. After all, his name meant high, lofty god. And the celestial objects certainly knew that. He glanced at a couple that cowered as he passed and snorted. *The people see it too.*

Ra'anel rounded a corner and headed down the main street. He squinted against the sunlight that bounced off the sandstone buildings. Several scribes stood on the steps of the Hall of Records. A few spoke with potential clients, others amongst themselves.

"You there," Ra'anel beckoned a long finger at a man who stood by himself. "Come with me."

"Yes, sir."

Ra'anel eyed the scribe as he jogged down the wide steps. Yes, he would do. The man's dark hair and beard were neatly trimmed and no offensive odor clung to him. He shouldered a heavy satchel that bounced with each step. Ra'anel turned quickening his stride deliberately. *Let's see how long it takes for him to catch up.* The man trotted to catch up then fell in step with Ra'anel.

"I see you're prepared," Ra'anel noted grudgingly.

"I am. Even a flask full of water to moisten the tablets and make changes."

Ra'anel snorted. "What's your name?"

"Datan."

"Well Datan, once we finish, make another copy to file in the Hall of Records."

"And the first copy goes to whom?"

Ra'anel eyeballed the man. He wanted a copy for himself. This was uncustomary therefore Datan wouldn't know, but did he suspect? Clever man, he would have to make sure that Datan didn't find out he kept copies for himself to alter and exchange with the original later. Ra'anel sighed and waved a hand. "The merchant, of course."

A small line of people stood outside Gideon's shop. Ra'anel surveyed the variety of items tucked under arms or that lay at their feet. Not too bad. The items for trade actually had value. Barukh's voice drifted through the open doorway. Ra'anel hid a grin as he pushed his way through the entrance.

"No. For that amount you get either, one of these, or two of those. And that's final."

"I want to speak with your father. He gave me two flasks of the good wine for this same amount." Ra'anel stepped through the entrance in time to see the man flashed three fingers in front of Barukh's face, "three laying hens."

"That's the point. Isn't it? You just traded with my father yesterday. How many chickens do you think we need?"

Ra'anel pressed a bony finger into the client's shoulder. The man turned with a scowl and a raised fist until he saw who pushed him. The celestial advisor almost laughed outright at the plethora of emotions that crossed the man's face.

"I suggest you take the two flasks of, hmmm, the less quality wine. It is the last bargain Barukh will do until later." Ra'anel turned his head and nodded to Barukh. The man grabbed the two jugs glaring at Ra'anel. The advisor ignored him and held his arms high in front of the small crowd, the robe's flowing sleeves dangled past his waist.

"This shop is temporarily closed. Come back in a half a hand-span to get more wine."

When the people grumbled Ra'anel clapped his hands. "Come, come. You don't want to displease a servant of the gods, or the gods themselves, do you? Now go."

Drifting from the premises, people protested.

"Now," Ra'anel fixed his attention on Barukh. "I see business is going quite well."

"Yes. Father made a wise choice. We've tripled our dealings just this last month."

"Good, good. And how much would that be?"

"Normally we trade out four hundred flasks of the good stuff in one month and three times that of the, lesser quality. But last month, well, we traded twelve hundred flasks of the good wine." Barukh rubbed his hands together. "Can you believe that? I'm in the process of planting my own vineyard. Those vines will grow none too soon to meet this demand."

Ra'anel jutted his chin toward Datan. "Record that. Gideon's winery traded three times as much quality wine and how much of the lesser?"

Ra'anel had to glance away at the look on Barukh's face or he would have burst out laughing. It became all too apparent that Barukh just realized what had taken place, Ra'anel had come for tariffs.

"Ah," the young man glanced over his shoulder.

"I imagine it was three, if not four times as much?" Ra'anel flicked his thumbnail under the nail of his forefinger.

"Ahhh…"

"Datan, go to the back and record how much is there." Ra'anel leaned an elbow against the tall table and studied the tips of his fingers.

"Yes, sir." The scribe strode past the two men.

Ra'anel leaned forward fixing his gaze on Barukh. "Where is your father?"

"He should be back soon."

"It is not necessary. It would behoove you to always speak the truth with me. I *will* find out sooner or later. Oh, and there is a penalty for holding back. Right now, the tariff for the shop is five percent. You don't want that to increase, do you? What would your father think? And have you been putting five percent of your trade goods aside?"

Barukh's face turned ashen.

"No need to worry. You can settle the debt in wine. Quality wine. Let's just say hmmm, one hundred twenty flasks."

Barukh's mouth dropped open.

"That is five percent. I'll send someone tomorrow to collect." Ra'anel called into the back room. "Are you done, Datan?"

The scribe stepped from the storage room before Ra'anel had finished.

"Good, there you are. Now record that Gideon's winery will pay the sum of one hundred twenty flasks of quality wine for the month of Autumn Harvest."

Datan's hand flew as Ra'anel spoke. But when he heard the amount he paused, glanced at Ra'anel with a raised brow then continued.

"I expect you to come back tomorrow with the tablet and record the actual obligation being fulfilled. When it's completed, find me in the tower, I will take care of it from there and give you your due."

Ra'anel turned with a grand flounce of his arm sweeping out of the shop. He would not wait for questions or arguments. The line had quadrupled extending around the corner of the street. With a flick of his wrist he waved them in. "The shop is now open."

A smirk sidled across his face. How long did that take? He brought his hand to shade his eyes and glanced at the sun. A little over a half hand-span. When Ra'anel brought his hand down he started at thick storm clouds boiling along the western horizon. How could they have come up so quickly? The head advisor frowned. *I'll go to the temple. There's a much better view from there.*

***

Darkness still shrouded the early morning when Machlah reached up to hand Nabella two wine skins of medicinal tea and a journey sack of food. With a smile she helped Nabella strap the flasks to the saddle. "You can sip on this one during the day. I know it is bitter, but it will make the ride tolerable without rendering you drowsy. And the other is for tonight. It is already brewed for I know you will be too exhausted to do so when you stop. It will be a very long day for you, first to The City then home." She shook her head. "And this," she held up another sack, "is to make a tea for your father. Just a pinch two times a day. It will help him to become stronger while he recovers." Machlah pressed her hand against Nabella's. "You must hurry."

Despite the pain Nabella reached down from the saddle and embraced her. "Thank you again for all your help."

Machlah nodded, "I understand. And from what you revealed last night child, I know this. You *must* trust in God no matter what."

Kfir nudged his takhi next to Machlah. "I don't like leaving you here alone. Please, come with us to The City."

"I thank you, but I cannot. If I leave, the wild things will raid everything here. Eber and Channah should be coming soon. Unless she had her baby."

"I don't like it. It doesn't sit right to leave you by yourself."

Machlah placed a hand on Kfir's knee. "I have lived now for over two hundred years. One hundred of them in the Former World where life was much, much more treacherous. Please rest assured, I will be well."

Kfir shook his head then nodded and headed out of the canyon. Nabella followed looking over her shoulder until the thick brush obscured her view of Machlah. She straightened squinting through the darkness to study Kfir. He sat in the saddle with such ease. Muscular and straight, handsome. Nabella caught her lip between her teeth. What was she thinking?

With a rueful shake of her head she forced her thoughts to Shem. Today they would find him. They had to. If the sun came out from the cloudy retreat it had been in these last weeks that surely would be a good sign.

At a hand-span past noon, with the sun smiling on them since it had tipped over the canyon rim, Nabella and Kfir rode by the first tents surrounding the eastern edge of The City. She shaded her eyes gazing at the tall citadel with its formidable walls near the northern City gates. Would they actually be able to keep out tanniyns the size of the one Nimrod had brought back? Her eyes ran westward along the length of the wall. *Yes, but...what was that?* "Kfir? Look at those clouds. Where did they come from?"

"I don't know. The sky was clear when we were riding through the tents."

"They look, odd."

Dark forbidding thunderheads raced across the sky. Kfir paused and they both watched the clouds churn and boil.

"Those are no ordinary storm clouds." He gave his takhi a kick. "We need to find Shem now!"

Nabella trotted her takhi behind Kfir's through The City gates. She swung her eyes back and forth from both sides of the street. No Shem. The turbulent clouds grew pressing in overhead. Nabella gasped when the thick black layers parted around the sun. A tangible ominous heaviness surrounded her. She shivered despite the heat then glanced at Kfir. He had moved several paces ahead.

"Slow down, Kfir. We could pass him up going this fast."

Kfir slowed to a walk but at once they were stalled by crowds of people that bunched in front of them. Most stared at the odd clouds that swirled and piled onto the already thick mass. At times Kfir had to forcefully rein his takhi into people to get them to move. He peered along each street. No sign of Shem. They continued down the main street.

"There." Kfir turned his takhi down a side street then an alleyway. Nabella saw a tall, sinewy man, but when he turned she could see it wasn't Shem. Kfir stopped short.

"You would think we could spot him right away." Nabella reined her takhi next to Kfir as she grasped and ungrasped the reins with one hand. Both takhis snorted and tossed, their heads eyes wide and round.

"Easy boy, easy." Kfir placed a firm hand on his takhi's neck. "Yes, that's if he's outside. What if he's in a building somewhere?"

"Oh, Kfir. I didn't even think of that. What are we going to do?"

Nabella caught Kfir's eye. He studied her. "Well, what would Shem do?"

"What do you mean?"

"What would we do if we were him?"

"I don't know, maybe pray?"

"Exactly. Let's go over there by that courtyard wall."

At the stone partition Kfir jumped down then grabbed the reins of Nabella's takhi. Sliding out of the saddle a groan escaped. Kfir looped the reins around the thick branch of a willow tree that hung over the wall. The takhis snorted and stomped, but Kfir laid a quiet, steady hand on each animal. They settled and Kfir took Nabella by the elbow, moving between them. He leaned close then bowed his head.

"God, we are in great need of Your leading hand. Jokaan hangs between life and death by the hands of evil. Shem knows what to do. He has been in Your presence in both the Old World and this new one. He has seen wickedness in both. Please, we beseech You, bring us to Shem. Show us where he is. And please let Jokaan live." Kfir lifted his head, dark eyes full of compassionate concern. Suddenly he seized her shoulders, "I know where he's at."

Nabella's eyes flew wide. "Where?"

"We haven't checked by the ziggurat yet."

"Of course."

"Remember he said that the temple at the top of the tower was something God would abhor the most. If he's here, he's probably trying to do something about that."

Kfir didn't bother to mount. He grabbed the reins and Nabella's arm pulling her next to him then strode down the street, high stepping takhis in tow.

***

Cush stood next to Nimrod, hands on his hips. "You're going to do it anyway, aren't you?"

Nimrod paused in front of a cart half filled with bricks. "When Ra'anel sees this he'll give me his answer."

"Listen, at least go find Ra'anel and tell him you want to start building the temple for Ishtar. Don't let him find out about this through someone else."

Nimrod reached into the wagon pulling out another stack of bricks so big no other man could have lifted it. Deeply browned skin stretched taut over bulging arms. The mighty hunter stopped, muscles rippling, fixing his eyes on him.

What is he thinking? Cush wondered as he stared into the unblinking man's eyes. Unexpectedly, Nimrod swiveled his head and looked toward the tower. Cush followed his gaze.

Startled, Cush blew a soft whistle. "Where did that storm come from?"

"The gods are not pleased." Nimrod set the bricks on the ground.

"What? What do you mean?"

"There is disorder somewhere."

"I have known you all your life and you just keep getting stranger and stranger."

Nimrod ignored him continuing to stare at the sky. "Strange that the gods did not blot out the sun."

Sweat beaded on Cush's forehead. "Are you sure it's the gods doing this? If they are angry, why is there a tunnel of light through those clouds allowing the sun's rays to shine on us?"

Nimrod turned unreadable eyes on him then without a word strode in the direction of the temple.

Cush cursed, rubbed his brow then trotted to catch up. "So you think it's a good idea to speak with Ra'anel after all."

"It won't hurt."

As they approached the long tower steps they could see a large number of people gathered near the bottom. Cush shook his head. *I bet they all want to go to the top to see the storm coming.* But when he looked again he realized they didn't face west nor were they interested in the turmoil that was building above them. They were congregated around someone on the steps.

Cush grabbed Nimrod's arm. "Let's go the back way. It'll take forever to get through them."

Nimrod yanked his arm free and marched past the long set of protruding steps toward the base of the tower then looked up. "Ra'anel! Show yourself," he bellowed.

"What are you doing?" Cush shoved Nimrod's shoulder so the man faced him in the gathering darkness.

Nimrod jerked his shoulder turning back to the tower. "Ra'anel!"

Blasts of winds roared around the structure randomly changing directions in short bursts. In an instant, the ominous clouds from the western horizon stretched above their heads.

"You fool," Cush shouted. "You are the one who angers the gods."

"Ra'anel, answer me!" Nimrod's deep timbre carried strong upon the winds. People on the terraces stared over the edges. Others scurried toward them.

"Look what you have done," Cush yelled at Nimrod pointing to the sky.

Nimrod, eyes fixed on the top of the tower, reached over and grabbed the front of Cush's shirt.

"Ra'anel, do you see how you have angered the gods? Answer me!"

The head advisor peered over the edge of the upper terrace. His pale beard and hair whipped in the wind. The folds of his elegant robe wrapped then unfurled around his hunched frame only to cling tight from another direction. He shook his scepter. "It is you, Nimrod, who has brought the wrath of the spirit world upon us all. Beware, beware of what they'll do!" Then he straightened, raising his hands to the sky.

The charcoal gray thunderheads roiled and rolled faster and faster then turned black.

***

Kfir and Nabella rounded a corner onto the Processional Way near the tower into a full blast of wind. Nabella squinted through the dust swirling around them. A crowd had gathered on the steps. She glanced at Kfir.

"Shem," Kfir and Nabella mouthed in unison.

Kfir nodded towards a large sycamore tree. "Tie the takhis there."

They could hear Shem even while they tethered their mounts.

"God is displeased. Listen to Him, people. What is the command He gave that you all have ignored?" There was no mistaking Shem's voice.

They pushed their way through the mass of people. A man bumped Nabella as he raised a fist in the air. "Ah, what are you talking about, look at the tower, how could God not be pleased with that?"

"Who is this giant anyway?" Another yelled.

The man next to Kfir shook his head. "He's been talking that same message for two weeks now to anyone who will listen."

"God has spoken and given His command. We are to fill the earth! We cannot do so if we all live in one city. We must spread out, explore this land, we mus—"

"Who are you to accuse us?" Another shout carried on the wind.

The gale slammed them from all sides. Kfir pulled Nabella close then shouted through cupped hands. "Shem speaks with authority of the Creator God!"

"Shem," someone gasped.

"Shem from the Old World?"

Shem bellowed. "Move away from The City, make your own villages governed by yourselves and depend on God! Do so or God will scatter you Himself."

"I didn't know God wanted us to move," a woman next to Nabella wrapped a shawl tight around her. "Where does God want us to move to?"

"God knows your heart. Do not this evil thing in the sight of the Lord."

"Evil, what do you mean evil?"

Suddenly thunderheads swirled around the sun. They blotted it out then immediately were swept away to show the sun again. The afternoon changed between sunlight and deep shadow again and again with dazzling speed that created an odd flickering light. Nabella gasped. Fiery darts of tingling fear trembled through her. She pressed into Kfir. A strong arm wrapped around her shoulders. From the corner of her eye she saw his free hand grip his dagger.

People cried out. Others stood staring at the sky, mouths open. Still others ran away, some screamed and shouted at each other. Nabella heard a great bellow and looked toward the base of the tower. She blinked then blinked again. The flashing light made it hard to see.

Nabella drew in a sharp breath clutching Kfir's arm. "It's Nimrod and Cush."

Somewhere in the back of her mind she became acutely aware of the sweet smell of distant rains. All at once the temperature plummeted, sending shivers through her. The winds grew stronger pushing first in one direction then the other. Dust and debris swirled stinging as it pummeled against their skin. Nabella's hair whipped around her face. If it wasn't for Kfir she knew she would have been flung to the ground. Clouds shifted back and forth in front of the sun quicker than the blink of an eye. The sun sputtered like a candle in a dark room. Hairs rose on the back of her neck.

"Shem!" Kfir shifted dragging her toward the tall man.

The ominous thunderheads suddenly engulfed the entire sky plunging all into instant deep twilight. The two froze staring. Nabella's knees quivered as she cast wild eyes about. The eastern portion of the sky had been blue a step ago; now the entire sky was filled with these giant thunderheads. How had that happened? How was it even possible? The man spread his feet leaning into the gusts. She stumbled when Kfir pushed forward.

"Shem!"

This time the giant heard and strode over. Nabella clasped his forearm with one hand, the other gripped Kfir with all her strength. Strands of hair whipped across her face stinging her cheeks and eyes.

"What's happening?"

Before Shem could answer a light flashed to her right. Nabella snapped her head around. It flashed again, and she gasped. A translucent being in white robes hovered several cubits above the ground. Then twilight closed in again, and it disappeared.

"Did you see that? Did you see?" Nabella squeezed and rocked both of the arms she gripped.

A flash and the being appeared again. This time closer. It loomed larger and larger. Arms raised and spread away from its body, long sleeves fluttering behind. Then darkness engulfed it once more.

Another light flashed in the distance and another bright translucent figure hovered above the ground. It too turned and spread its arm wide before darkness closed around it. Then another and another, and another—all appearing in the flashes. Each one in a different area. All majestic. And Nabella sensed all were beings that could only have come from heaven. Holy beings.

Shem dragged them to the ground then lay prone, arms spread in front of his head. Kfir and Nabella at once stretched out. Nabella still clutched both men's arms. With her face pressed onto the cobblestones suddenly she knew. This was fulfillment of the oth, the warning God had spoken of. God's words rushed to her *"A change in mankind must come forth."* And Machlah's answer, *He speaks an oth."*

Her whole body shook as fear shot through her.

"Shem! It's the fulfillment of an oth God spoke to Machlah and I." She could feel the great man from the Old World tremble. The giant turned his head toward her. "Yes. Machlah shared this with me." Then his voice boomed, "The Lord has judged and found us unworthy. Oh Great King, Mighty Creator God. God of first father Adam and first mother Eve. Forgive us our trespasses, have mercy upon us! Mercy upon us," Shem shouted over and over as tears poured down his cheeks.

Nabella raised her head, eyes darting from flash to flash. The beings looked like robed people but different. Some had great wings and some had halos. Some she could distinguish every wave of their robe and feature of their faces. Others were like a bright glow with portions of figures outlined in it.

Abruptly a being appeared right in front of them. It spread its arms wide then looked directly at her. One arm dropped and its hand opened. A myriad of brilliant, minuscule stars shot straight at them. An explosion of dazzling light blinded her. She gave a soft cry, tucked her head under her shoulder and lay, quivering heart in her throat. The gale continued to buffet them. Was it ever going to stop? Then as quickly as it had started the wind died.

At last Shem stopped his interceding cries and pushed himself to his knees. Kfir followed pulling Nabella to him. She blinked and touched her eyes. They didn't hurt, and she could see. She sighed with relief. She was fine. And the world looked fine. The dark clouds had vanished as if they'd never been. The sun stood exactly where it had been before the whole event took place.

Stunned and still on her knees, she tried to figure out what had just happened. Somewhere someone screeched. Another distant bellow reached her ears. More and more screams. Eerie shrieks of terror. From all directions came yells and shouts, their echoes bouncing off brick walls. Her breath came in shallow draws, wide eyes flitting around. Her gaze landed on Shem, and she leaned into Kfir.

Now what?

Twenty

Come, let us go down and confuse their language so they will not understand each other.

Genesis 11:7

Barukh surveyed the crowded shop. A sour taste lingered in his mouth. He had disclosed too much to Ra'anel. Ah -he! He'd make sure that would never happen again. Suddenly the daylight flickered then everything plunged into darkness. A few customers raced to the entrance spilling onto the street. Others fell to the ground covering their heads with their hands. Barukh crouched against the back wall too frightened to move. Screams and shouts erupted outside. A large flash lit the room then once again blackness engulfed it. Distant lights flashed outside. A cold sweat broke out across his forehead. A howling wind raced passed the open doorway then into the shop encircling him, tearing at his garments and lashing his face with his hair. It seemed to go on forever. Barukh screamed then whimpered as the scourging continued.

Abruptly a complete silence, as loud as the howling wind, engulfed him. With a trembling hand he swiped the hair from his eyes. Outside the sky cleared, rays of sunlight streamed into the shop. The rest of the customers stumbled from the shop. At last Barukh pushed himself onto shaky legs and stared around the empty room. A scream just outside the shop made the hairs prickled on his back. He rushed out just as Cush ran past uttering strange noises.

"Hey, what's going on?" Barukh yelled.

The man stopped eyes rimmed with fear, he glared then bolted away. Barukh took a step after him and nearly tripped over a woman hunched in the street, babbling.

"What are you saying, woman?"

She looked up, tears on her cheeks pressing hands over her ears. "შეჩერება, შეჩერება, ვერ ვხვდები!"

Barukh gasped stumbling back. Was the woman mad? And what was wrong with Cush? He had never heard such nonsensical noises in his life. And they didn't seem to understand him either. He turned and saw the owner next door dash out of his pottery shop, entrance left wide open. Barukh yanked the door of his shop closed, his eyes catching the rows of effigies just inside the doorway of the potter's shop. His mind swirled, what had just happened? But no answer came. He peeked left then right. Once more he stared at the idols.

Another scream. Barukh jerked. He glanced over his shoulder and slipped into the shop. With a trembling hand he slid a small idol into the fold of his tunic. His gaze landed on a different idol. Short breaths rattled in his chest. Well, he would need all the help he could get. Fingers darted forward then wrapped around the figurine. With a sharp twist of his wrist he shoved it on top of the first effigy. A quick peek outside then Barukh dashed to the corral. He caught his takhi, threw the saddle on then turned it onto the pave-stoned street. Barukh whipped the reins against its neck leaning into the saddle. The figurines lay heavy in his tunic as the takhi leapt forward.

***

Shem visibly shook as they knelt in the street. The man from the Former World glanced around then whispered, "The Creator has given His verdict."

Another scream. Nabella twisted her head in the direction of the shriek. A shudder spread from the pit of her stomach through her body. Then her hands and feet began to tingle.

"What is His ruling?" Kfir leaned toward Shem.

"I know not." Shem looked around again, then toward the sky. "The Most High God gave us His promise he would not destroy the world again with water." He swept an arm toward the heavens, his voice full of awe. "And He has not. Praise be to God."

A loud argument broke out on the steps between two men. Nabella glanced in their direction, and her eyes grew wide as she listened. They obviously understood each other, but *she* could not understand *them*.

"Kfir, listen to those two men over there. What are they saying?"

The man turned an ear toward them. He shook his head, forehead creases disappeared under his headband. "Shem?"

Shem shoved himself upright striding toward the two. Kfir leapt up and in one scoop placed Nabella on her feet. Grabbing her hand they hurried after Shem.

When the giant came abreast of the men in full argument, he halted. The shorter of the two took a step toward Shem.

"ఏమిటి?" The man gave Shem a strained look, "ఏమి చెబుతున్నారు? "

The three exchanged a glance and Shem said, "I know not what you say."

The man backed up, motioned to Shem and jabbered to the one he had just argued with.

Shem shook his head. "I understand you not."

A woman dashed past, a small child on her hip. Nabella turned watching her run across the pavement stones, panic in her voice. Words that made no sense, words different than the men who spoke to Shem. Nabella's head spun. Less than a hand-span ago The City had hummed with one tongue. Now there was nothing but noise, a babble that grated against her ears and filled her heart with dread. The bright sunlight seemed to mock her fear, yet she could not shake the quiver in her stomach or the violent trembling. She pressed close to Kfir and a strong, warm arm wrapped around her.

"What happened?" The words squeaked from Nabella.

Shem looked her in the eyes. "Two weeks ago the Lord impressed upon me that a vileness had been conjured against a friend, and this led me to The City. The task to identify the invocation began immediately. Once completed, I wished to return to Machlah to try and find who had been stricken, but I had a sense that God desired me to stay. He reminded me of how my father preached righteousness for many years. My father understood God wanted to save His people from the great Flood. And so too the Lord extended His hand touching my lips.

"I knew God would discipline our current disobedience, and I could do no less than my father. I believe God wanted one last effort made to reveal to the people their rebellious hearts so they could change before His judgment. So I stayed and preached to the people."

Kfir and Nabella stared at Shem. Somehow Nabella knew Shem must be right. She looked up at Kfir but no words came. Though he shook his head, Kfir's eyes radiated warmth and concern. For her. Nabella felt a rush of heat creep up her face and turned to hide the confusion that exploded in her heart and mind.

Suddenly Shem's words echoed through her, *a vileness had been conjured against a friend.*

"Father," Nabella gasped shaking Kfir's arm then turned to Shem. "It's Father! A curse has been conjured against him."

Kfir touched Shem's shoulder. "We came to you for help. Jokaan is," he hesitated then glanced at Nabella. "He's dying." Kfir looked around. "I don't know if any of this has anything to do with the curse, but please, can you help?"

Shem's shaggy brows pulled together. "Jokaan must be the one I sought the cure for." He glanced once more at the two men and stepped away with a shake of his head. "I cannot help them, but I may be able to help Jokaan. Tell me what you know of the curse."

Nabella's voice trembled. "It's a clay figurine. The arms are pulled behind its back and there's a hole through its chest. There's something inscribed on it too, something about dying and being governed. And it was burnt. The ashes are still there. All tightly bound in a bundle. Do you think someone cursed Father, because he refused to move into The City?"

Shem nodded. "Yes. And I know this curse. It is from the Former World. One that came here into the New World through a demon."

Nabella and Kfir stared at each other. Her eyes grew wide and shallow breaths shot in and out. A *demon*? What chance did her father have against a demon? Tears pooled and threatened to spill. Coldness splashed Nabella's stomach as she clasped and unclasped her jupe. As if Kfir could read her mind, he spoke gently. But Nabella caught the strain in his voice.

"Shem too is from the Old World. He *will* break this curse, Nabella."

Shem stood tall and drew in a deep breath. "Do you see it is all in God's plan? The Possessor of Heaven and Earth, He who has created everything knows what has taken place and what is about to happen. Once I received the means to break the curse, I still did not know whom it had been conjured against. Then God impressed upon me to urge the people to change. Because I obeyed, He has brought you to me," Shem glanced around. "And we are of the same tongue. It has come full circle."

Nabella gripped the huge man's arm. "Thank you. Thank you for listening to the Creator and caring so much about my father, your friend." Her hands slide from his arm then she whispered, "And thank You, God."

Shrieks echoed from a side street. The cries sounded different than the two men that argued and the woman who had run past. The three strode down the steps when a voice from far above reached them. Nabella craned to see the top of the tower.

"Is that Ra'anel?" Kfir shaded his eyes.

Shem nodded, but before he could say a word a man not far from them bellowed an answer.

Nabella's jaw dropped. "Its Nimrod and Cush."

Cush stared at Nimrod. Then the mighty hunter raised his fist and shouted at Ra'anel. Cush took a step back, then another, spinning on his heel he raced toward them. He slowed as he came alongside, fear rimming his eyes white.

"Gaaloraacyo jy hom? Waxa socda ?" Cush pointed at Nimrod. Shem, Kfir, and Nabella exchanged a glance.

Deep red flushed Cush's dark face. Eyes narrowed, he struck Shem's shoulder then yelled, "La hadal!"

Shem whacked Cush's outstretched arm away. "I understand you not! God has judged mankind, and we have failed."

Cush sucked in a sharp breath stepping back. His broad nostrils flared as dark eyes flew wide. With a jerk he turned and ran down the Processional Way.

***

Cush ran until his sides heaved, and he couldn't take another step. What just happened? Demons must have possessed Ra'anel. And Nimrod too. Or the gods had cursed them. He drew in a shuddering breath. His questions were not difficult to understand. How hard could it be to answer "Do you hear him? What's going on?"

Even Uncle Shem had spoken gibberish, though different sounding than Ra'anel and Nimrod. Shem had stared at him but then, "םיהולא .ךתוא ןיבמ אל ינא רצק ןאכ ונל, תושונאה הזחש," had come from his mouth. Gibberish! Babblings!

Cush straightened and paced. He grabbed the first man that ran past. "Speak! Let me hear you speak."

The man struggled to get away and spouted nonsense. Cush shoved him and ran on.

"You, you there," he bellowed to a man darting across the street. "Can you understand me?"

The man stared wild-eyed, and Cush knew the answer. He sprinted onto a cross street. A boy of ten or twelve ran in the same direction.

"Hey you, can you understand meee?"

The boy skidded to a stop. "You understand meee?"

Cush closed his eyes and shoulders sagged. Someone in the distance shouted something unidentifiable, and his eyes flew open. The boy stood twisting a short length of rope, eyes darting about.

"Take me to your father."

The boy bound away, Cush close on his heels. Loosing count of the twists and turns he became disoriented. The boy finally stopped in front of a small dwelling and held his hand open toward the entrance.

Cush ducked through the doorway. A dark-skinned man and woman huddled together.

"Can you understand me?" Cush demanded.

"Cush!" The man brushed the woman's hands off and pushed himself to his feet.

"Oh," she gasped as the boy sunk into her arms.

"What's happened, do you know?"

Cush shook his head. "No, but I'm going to find out." He strode to the doorway then paused. "Go around and find out if there are others who speak like us. Meet me with them, at the tower steps."

"When?"

"A hand-span before sunset."

Cush found his way back to the main streets. Everywhere he went, people milled about, frustrated and frightened. Some recognized him clutching at his tunic. He shoved them off trying to focus. The tower, he had to get back to the tower. Ra'anel would be at the temple and the other advisors too. He needed to know. Were the others in position of power like him? Or did they all speak like Nimrod and Ra'anel? The thought made his stomach roil, and he clenched his hands into fists.

By the time he reached the top terrace Cush's heart raced, and he panted for breath. Ra'anel must have heard him. He charged out of the temple.

"Cush!"

The big man stopped and blinked. Hadn't he heard Ra'anel babble just a short while ago? Maybe he had misunderstood the shouts from so far above. *Oh please, please let it be so.*

"మాట్లాడు! మీరు ఇడియట్?"

Cush began to shake. The exertion of racing up the steps and the events of the afternoon overwhelmed him. He stumbled to a temple column, placed his back against it and slid to the floor, forearms on his knees. He let his head droop to his chest.

"Cush, თქვენი ა. არ ჭურჭლის არის რეს შეამოწმეთ. კომპეტენტურ მაკიაჟი."

Cush started at the sound of his name then stared into space.

"კომპეტენტურ მაკიაჟი." There could be no mistake the babbles were a demand. But what?

Suddenly his temper flared. Cush bound to his feet and marched through the temple entrance, hands balled into fists. "Who can understand me?"

Two advisors stared at each other then at him. One spoke, "we can."

Cush leaned against the wall, head tilted back, eyes closed. *Now maybe I'll get some answers.*

***

"Father," Nabella pleaded again.

Shem nodded.

Kfir thrust his chin in the direction of the sycamore tree. "We have two takhis. If they're still there, Nabella can ride behind me."

Shem shook his head. "It is too far for both of you to ride one takhi and get there quickly. We will go to Channah. Eber has several."

Kfir widened his pace. "Machlah said Eber and Channah were going to your place any time now."

"We must hurry then."

The takhis rolled wide eyes, but Kfir eased near. "Easy now, easy," he murmured pressing a hand to their necks. He handed Shem the reins of Nabella's takhi then leapt onto his mount. "Until then, Nabella, you can ride behind me. Shem, she injured her hip. Can you put her up?"

Before Nabella could protest Shem slung her behind Kfir then mounted her takhi.

"Ha-yah!" Shem slapped the reins, and the animal bound forward.

"Hang on," Kfir yelled as Nabella threw her arms around his waist. The takhis wove through the crowd. She sucked in her breath when her hip jarred, then shifted her weight between bounds until the sharpness evened to a steady ache. Only then did she realize they were headed down the Processional Way. She glanced over Kfir's shoulder as they rode down the Processional Way. When they trotted under the great arches of the gate people scattered in front of them.

As they entered the tent city Shem slowed to a walk. There were no real streets here, just paths between structures that were often rearranged. The babble of strange tongues rose around them. Nabella looked down from her perch. The anxiety and fear written on people's faces made her heart ache. She clung to Kfir. His strong body reassured her. Pressing her cheek against his back she closed her eyes. *I'm so glad Kfir and Shem aren't speaking that crazy talk. I don't know what I'd do if they did.*

Shem reined his takhi in a slow circle. "Eber, Eber! Do you hear me? Do you understand?"

"Here! Is that you, Shem?"

"It is I."

Eber rounded a tent, "I can understand you, what has happened? Do you hear everyone? People I've known for years I can no longer understand. And did you see how day turned into night and back again? Then the thunderclouds disappeared altogether?"

"Yes. It is the hand of God. He has passed judgment."

"Like The Flood?"

"I believe so. But I have yet to see the full extent of His righteous decision."

Eber studied Shem. "Channah had her baby. A boy."

"When?"

"Just this morning. She rests in a neighbor's tent upriver." Eber jutted his long bearded chin in that direction. "Come, stay with us until tomorrow and we'll go back to the cave together." He glanced at Nabella. "She'll be thankful for another woman to travel with."

"No. You will have to take Channah to Machlah alone. I must go with Kfir and Nabella, a man's life is in danger. When I am finished I shall join you." Shem's face fell, and he added, "My apologies we cannot stay. We have come to borrow a takhi."

"Ahhh, that I have. Come, come." Eber waved his hand for them to follow. He worked his way to the river bank. "Here, father of my wife, take this one. She is a good sturdy animal even if she is short." Eber untied a mare that grazed near an ox and several other takhis.

"Nabella can ride her," Kfir offered to Shem while he eased her to the ground.

A wide grin spread across Eber's face. He nodded at Kfir, arms open wide. "I can understand you. Greetings and what wonderful news!" Then he glanced at Shem. "At first I thought I had gone mad when no one understood me." The man grabbed a saddle that leaned against a tree.

Nabella smiled. "And you can understand me too."

A tear rolled down the man's cheek. "God has provided once again."

Kfir jumped off his takhi. "Wait Eber please, keep your saddle. Channah will need it with the new baby." He turned to Nabella with a wink. "I'll put mine on the mare for you, and I'll ride bareback."

Nabella blew out a sigh. Once Kfir finished saddling the mare, she climbed aboard and looked down at Eber. "What will you name the baby?"

Eber let go of the mare's bridle and stepped back. He shook his head and fixed his eyes on Shem. "Peleg. His name will be Peleg, for in his days was the earth divided."

Shem nodded his approval. "Well done. And so it shall be known."

Once again Shem, Kfir and Nabella raced along the Processional Way. When they reached the southern citadel they were forced to rein the takhis in. They could push through the southern portion of the tent city no faster than Grandfather's old mare. Men, women and children wandered—some dazed, others frustrated or in a panic, most bewildered. Others took advantage of the chaos. They grabbed items and ran, while owners shouted and chased after them. Nabella's heart wrenched again. What had happened? It seemed the community had lost their minds. People reached out and touched her, Kfir, and Shem eyes full of questions, but their words made no sense. She could only offer a wane smile and gestures of solace.

Shem reined in and when Kfir and Nabella came abreast he surveyed the people. "So far I have noticed those who are husband and wife and their young children are able to understand each other. I have picked up certain patterns in some of the talk. Listen. Try to differentiate one set of speaking from another as we go along."

Kfir nodded, and they pushed on single file. Nabella strained to distinguish some type of word pattern. Shem *was* right, families seemed to be intact. She watched mothers soothe their children, and the young ones respond. Husbands commanded their sons and spoke with their wives. Most arguments seemed to take place between grown men and women of different families.

They passed a group of adults that appeared to be siblings. One man waved his arms and pounded his fist. The others stood and stared. Two of the women clung to each other and wept. Nabella's brows knit together. Just when she thought she had a grasp of the situation it changed. By the time they wove their way through the last tents the initial panic had submitted and people, though fear still rimmed their eyes, seemed to be trying to get their lives back together.

Once again she prayed, *Thank You, Lord, that I was with people whose speech didn't change when You came down. I don't know what I would have done otherwise. Thank You for Your mercy.*

When the tent city began to thin Shem reined in his mount. Nabella urged the mare on one side of Shem's takhi, and Kfir moved to the other side.

"I counted fifteen distinct speeches and ours makes sixteen."

"So far." Kfir looked out over the plain of Shinar. "I wonder what Abel speaks now."

"And Seth." Nabella thought of the crippled boy.

Shem let out a weary sigh. "We have much work to do. Kfir, lead the way."

Kfir waited until Nabella took a long swig of the pain-killing tea Machlah had prepared then urged his animal into a jog. Of the few people they passed, none waved them down or called out. A quarter hand-span after sunset Kfir veered down the path to his father's house. When they neared the building Kfir slowed his mount to a walk.

Nabella clasped and unclasped the reins. Oh, how she wished this could be avoided, but she knew all along Kfir would swing by, just long enough to hear Barukh utter some words.

She didn't have to wait long. Barukh stood in the dusk by the corral and waved his arms at a few field hands. He glanced up, did a double take then strode toward them.

"How do you speak, brother?" Kfir called out.

Barukh stopped dead in his tracks. "Apa? Lupakan saja. Waktunya kau kembali, Kfir. Aku butuh bantuan Anda, orang-orang ini bertindak seperti idoot."

Kfir shook his head and turned his takhi. Nabella and Shem followed.

"Nabella," Barukh barked.

She pointed toward her home. "My father, we have to go to my father."

Barukh shook his head, lips pressed together in a thin line. "Shem?"

Shem jutted his chin toward Nabella's home and spoke one word. "Jokaan."

***

Ra'anel paced back and forth on the top terrace. He stopped each time he passed the steps at the end of the terrace to peer at Nimrod. The man moved with a steady, ground-eating pace. Earlier Cush had left with the two advisors who understood him. Now he alone had to deal with Nimrod. What had happened? Nothing in the stars forecasted this, this plague, this gibberish people were speaking.

He paused at the west entrance to the temple and gazed in. Of the advisors still here with him, only two spoke intelligently. The rest babbled amongst themselves and arguments broke out. They were still at it now.

Look at them. They're like a bunch of idiots, waving their arms and talking louder and louder, as if that's going to help. Fools! Ahhh, I can't stand this!

Abruptly he strode into the temple. "Get out all of you, except you two who can understand me."

Silence fell over the group, the advisors staring at him blank looks across their faces.

"Out! Get out," Ra'anel screeched. When no one moved, heat rushed up his face, and he knew his pasty white skin had turned beet red. He rushed at the nearest advisor, seized the man's robe and yanked him toward the door. A long jagged tear ripped through the fabric. He went for the next advisor and shoved him out the arched entrance with a foot to his rear. The others caught on and raced out the entrances closest to them.

Ra'anel knew people would want answers, and he had to tell them something they would believe. Could it be the gods were dissatisfied because Nimrod started construction of the Ishtar temple? Or maybe some of the other gods were angry because he hadn't constructed a temple in their honor first.

He had seen nothing in the stars that indicated something could be wrong. Ra'anel paced. How long would this nonsense last? Nimrod would want answers and right now he dreaded Nimrod more than the gods. Ra'anel raced to the edge of the Terrace at the thought of the man. Where was he? Almost to the top. Ra'anel rushed back inside.

He must come up with some explanation. It was imperative that Nimrod think he had a connection with the other world and therefore be superior to him. Ra'anel raised his hands toward a pinnacle.

"Oh, Utu, Ishtar, Bul, and Adad. Supreme gods of the other world. I worship you. Only you are so mighty. Only you have the greatest powers. I call upon you now. Oh great deities, what has happened? Only you have the answers. I ask in all humbleness to reveal the answers of this riddle to m—"

Abruptly the temple interior dimmed, and Ra'anel spun around. Nimrod's huge frame blocked an entrance. How had he reached the top so fast? Nimrod marched to Ra'anel, seized the front of his robe then lifted him with one hand, black eyes seething and dark olive skin livid. A vein bulged on his thick neck disappearing under the dark stubble of his newly growing beard. Ra'anel tried to hide the quiver that shot through him.

"Tell me what is going on, and you better make it clear."

"Put me down and I will."

Nimrod opened his fist and let the head advisor plop to the ground. He brushed Ra'anel's robe smooth and patted his chest. "And it better be good."

Ra'anel cleared his throat then strode across the room. His eyes landed on the two advisors. Suddenly he knew what to do.

"You two and you," he looked at Nimrod, "tell me exactly what you saw."

Nimrod stared at the two advisors until they squirmed.

One worked his jaw, his long beard bobbing up and down. "Ah, the clouds, they came out of nowhere."

"And the sun blinked off and on," the other added.

"Then it got dark and stayed that way."

"And there were flashes of light."

The first advisor thrust his chin at an entrance. "Then the thunderheads disappeared and that was it."

"Except, almost everyone now speaks strangely," number two murmured and smoothed his beard.

Ra'anel nodded and eyed Nimrod. "And you?"

Nimrod crossed his arms over his chest then splayed his feet. "The same."

Ra'anel held his hand open and swept it deliberately across the front of all three. "None of you saw anything in the flashes of light?"

Nimrod stared, and the other two shook their heads. Ra'anel pressed his lips together, perplexed. He thought he had seen, well, a being, a person of sorts, during the last flash here in the temple.

"Did any of you see a flash happen right here inside this temple, hmmm?"

Again the two advisors and Nimrod shook their heads. Ra'anel's brows creased together, and his heart thudded heavy against his chest. Surely he had observed something in that last flash. Someone, that is. And it did not look pleased. Ra'anel could still see the accusing finger pointed at him. He shook his head cringing. But the image lingered. He should be thrilled, he tried to tell himself, this was proof he *did* have power into the principalities of the other world. A power that others didn't possess. That's what he wanted. But the disapproving eyes of the spirit bore into him. Everything in Ra'anel told him the being was a messenger from the Creator God, but the head celestial advisor choked on the thought and began to pace. He refused to believe the Creator God of Adam and Eve had that kind of power. Or did He? Sweat beaded across his forehead despite the breeze that blew through the temple. And didn't he hear that spirit say something? What was it? Ra'anel tried to smother a gasp, eyes widening. *"You lead the people astray against the Lord's command to fill the earth."* The celestial advisor reeled. Could the Creator God really know he had been trying to influence the people to stay in one place? No! That God couldn't possibly know anyone that well. No god could.

"Well?" The sarcasm in Nimrod's voice pulled Ra'anel back to the present.

Ra'anel drew in a deep breath and in pseudo calmness strolled to the northern temple entrance and waved an arm. "The whole incident was a message from the heavens." He stared out over The City to stall, desperate to find the right words. Fingers drummed against his chin. "The gods are not pleas—"

"Obviously," Nimrod snorted. "Tell me something I don't know."

Suddenly Ra'anel knew. "The confusion of tongues is a curse." A jolt ran through him. He *did* have mystical powers into the other world. How else would he have realized this whole mess was a curse? A malevolent laugh bubbled from his lips. *Ahhh, the gods did answer me. The words just poured out of my mouth without any thought. I* am *supreme.* He turned toward the three men, eyes filled with abhorrence for Creator God.

"It is a curse from the God of Adam and Eve. He wishes to make mankind suffer. Forever." Ra'anel's snarling hiss turned into an insane laugh. Then his mind became clear, focused, and he narrowed his eyes. "We must remove all knowledge and worship of Him from our City. Build the temple to Ishtar, Nimrod, and we will place an altar here for her as well."

Nimrod's dark eyes stared back at Ra'anel. Then he strode past the head advisor halting at the edge of the terrace. A deep chuckle turned venomous. "Yesss. I like it." He jammed fists onto his hips inhaling deeply. "Very good. The City without that contemptuous God." Nimrod shifted to face Ra'anel in full. "And those who don't understand our wishes *will be removed.*"

***

Cush stood on the bottom stair of the grand steps to the tower. He surveyed the small group below him. To his surprise he saw his two youngest sons, three youngest daughters, all unmarried, and five of his adult grandchildren push their way forward with their families. His eyes roved over their children, fourteen in all. Though he recognized only several of the oldest, Cush realized he didn't know even one of the great grandchildren's names. He barely remembered some of his grandchildren's names. Besides his immediate family, only the two advisors and the boy with his parents he had spoken with earlier were familiar. No one else he knew or associated with had come to this meeting. Almost eighty in all were present. They all stared at him with fear in their eyes. The corner of his broad lips pulled downward. *We just haven't found everyone yet.* But he struggled to keep the queasiness in his stomach from grinding into full blown fear.

"Cush, what happened?" A man called out.

"Why are the gods punishing us?" A woman yelled.

"Cush. I, we, are so thankful you speak like us." The father of the boy pushed his way to Cush. "Tell us what to do."

"Yes, Cush, lead us."

The big man held up a hand. He liked being in charge, being a part of the government. But that was the problem. He had always been a part of government. Always had others to go to for advice, and to blame. He studied the crowd and knew he had no stomach for leading alone.

"Raamah, Sabteca, come here," he barked at his sons. "Stand beside me."

Then another realization struck him. All these people who gathered here were dark-skinned like himself. Various shades of ebony but none had the light skin of

Ra'anel or even the brown skin of Shem or Nimrod. What did that mean? And what should he do?

"Can anyone here scribe?" Cush raised his voice so all could hear. No one came forward.

He turned to Raamah. "You were taught some scribing."

"Very little, Father. And that was a long time ago, I don't remember much."

Cush laid a hand on his shoulder. "I need your help."

At last his son nodded.

"Draw pictures if you must but record what every family does for a trade. I will get you clay tablets." Then Cush raised his voice again, "Listen! For the rest of today go around and try to find more who speak like us. Tomorrow morning, the head of each family is to meet here with Raamah. Give him your trade and where you live. Once we know where each of us dwells and what trades we are in, we'll know more of what we'll be able to do."

"But what if none who speak like us have what we need?"

Cush ground his teeth. "We'll just have to try to make the others understand."

"But what if they don't want us here?" A woman's voice quivered, riddled with fear.

"Yes, what if Nimrod sends his men after us?" A man from the back shouted. Others joined in.

Cush swallowed and glanced at his sons. They seemed as uneasy about Nimrod as the rest. He remembered how Nimrod acted at the tower. It was entirely possible the man would become intolerant. He could feel the fear rise even within himself. Then like a bolt of lightning, it came to him. A conversation his father had with Noah a long time ago.

"*Why should* we *move? Just because you think God told you?" Ham had argued. "The land here is fertile and there is plenty of it. Go south you say but we know nothing of the land there or the animals in it. No, Father. My family are few. I will not take them away to perish. We stay here.*"

And Ham had stayed training Cush in leadership, to manage people, and governments.

He surveyed the crowd. They all looked like lost sheep, frightened and confused. A sense of pity, then responsibility swept through him. They didn't know what he knew. None of them had the benefit of sitting at Noah's knee. Only his first sons were taught by their grandfather. And other than the two advisors no one had even worked with Ra'anel. He surprised himself at how his heart went out to them. Cush rubbed his chin. *I must find my brothers. If Ham had been told to go south then they might speak the same as me.* Cush raised his hands once more to settle the people.

"Then we, as a people will move." Cush swept his arm along the crowd.

"Move?"

"I don't want to go."

"Move where?"

"What about the great tanniyns, one of whose head is right over there."

Cush could feel anger and panic once again sweep through the crowd and motioned for them to calm down. Then he looked as many men in the eye as he could. "You men, you know how to wield a spear and atlatl, and a blade. For those who don't, we'll train you. I was with Nimrod when the tanniyn was slain. It took only eight of us and a boy. There are many more than eight fighters here."

The shouts had calmed to mumbles, and people listened intently.

"We will make our own way and take care of one another." Cush drew himself to his full height. "We will not fall under Nimrod's blade."

He drew in a deep breath through his nostrils and gazed southward. "If we have to, we will move south. South, to a whole new land."

Twenty One

So the Lord scattered them from there over all the earth, and they stopped building the city. That is why it was called Babel—because there the Lord confused the language of the whole world. From there the Lord scattered them over the face of the whole earth.

Genesis 11:8-9

Nabella didn't even bother to tether the mare. Exhausted, she let the reins drop and stumbled through the black into the house. "Adara, Tomar."

Lamplight flickered from Jokaan's room. She plodded into the room and jerked at the sight of the torn mattress. Then she swung her gaze to the crumpled figure on the blankets. Adara stared at her from the floor near the makeshift pallet. Three oil lamps placed around the room cast deep shadows.

"How's Father?"

Adara, face red and puffy from tears, spoke softly. "He's so weak. Were you able to find Shem?"

"Yes." A spurt of energy surged through Nabella. She dashed to the doorway, all thoughts of different speech gone. "In here, bring Shem in here, Kfir," then she darted back to Adara's side.

"He looks worse."

Every breath Jokaan took rattled his chest. He looked so thin. How could just a few days change him so much?

"Father," she whispered, "Shem is here."

Nabella glanced up spotting Elah. Back pressed against a corner of the room, she looked from Adara to Nabella and back. Nabella strode to her and held out the small satchel that contained the healing herbs Machlah had prepared. "Elah, please make a tea of this for Father."

Elah stared at Nabella then the satchel then back at Adara. Her brows furrowed as she trembled. Nabella heard a soft sob escape Adara's lips. "Elah doesn't understand. She only babbles. It's almost as if she's been struck dumb."

Nabella grabbed Elah wrapping her arms around her sister. With a sob Elah laid her head on Nabella's shoulder.

"No. She's not dumb. She just doesn't understand what we speak. I saw lots of that on the way here."

Nabella gripped Elah by the shoulders and gently moved her at arm's length. Nabella made motions while she spoke. "Elah, get hot water and pour it in a cup to make tea with this. Add this amount."

Elah's face brightened. She snatched the satchel, rushed from the room nearly bumping into Shem.

"You mean there are others like Elah?"

"Yes," Shem answered for Nabella and knelt next to Jokaan. "We've counted sixteen different speeches so far."

Adara gasped and shook her head. "Did, ahhh, the day turn to night with flashes of strange floating peop—"

"Angels of the Lord most High. Yes. It all happened. But I must tend to Jokaan now."

Adara slid to the head of the mattress. Shem brushed Jokaan's hair back then took the sick man's hands in his own.

"Bring me a small bowl of water."

Nabella dashed from the room. By the time she came back Jabari and Tomar stood next to Adara. Eyes wide, Shoshana knelt next to her eldest sister. Nabella slipped into the room just in time to see Shem close his eyes and bow. Nabella could not hear him, but she knew he prayed. She stood to the side, praying her own prayers. From the corner of her eye she saw Elah step into the room and press herself against the wall. Shem beckoned Nabella then took the bowl of water from her praying over it.

Then to her surprise Shem stood, dipped his palm into the water and poured a handful on Jokaan. He walked about the room, sprinkled water about all the while praying.

"Everyone remain here." Shem eyed the family. "Kfir, Nabella, where is the cursed figure?"

Nabella grabbed an oil lamp then led Shem to the courtyard. She hesitated in the entryway, held the lamp high and nodded towards the open hearth. Shem and Kfir moved past. Again Shem prayed sprinkling water around the courtyard. He stopped to sprinkle Nabella and Kfir and himself as well. Nabella clasped her tunic. Then he extended the bowl for Kfir to hold. Only a little water remained.

Shem motioned for Nabella to bring the light closer then lifted the opened bundle from the hearth, set it on the ground and knelt next to it.

"We know what it says except for this word." Kfir ran his finger under the unfamiliar imprint careful not to touch it.

"It is the demon Marduk." Shem said.

"Ah-he! It tells us to be govern-"

"Do not speak the curse out loud!" Shem commanded. "Demons can understand our words but not our thoughts. Some of the lettering is slightly different because it is from the ancient times of the Former World. That is why you did not recognize it. But it is still spoken the same." Resuming his prayer, he pushed himself upright then without pause retrieved the water from Kfir. He moved to the head of the effigy sprinkling water in tighter and tighter circles around the figure.

"Almighty God, Creator of heaven and earth, You are our shield and our great reward. Before there was anything, You were! You alone nourish and provide for us, You alone are strong enough to meet every need. With all the power behind Your Great Being—from creation of the universe to the miracle of the life in a mother's womb—Lord, we ask You to vanquish this curse of the evil one who crawls on his belly and eats dust."

Shem poured the last drops of water on the figure. A small wisp of smoke rose vanishing an instant before Shem's foot crashed down on the figurine. Nabella gasped and jerked back. The man from the Former World stooped, gathered the scattered pieces of broken clay onto a piece of bark without touching them then placed them back in the wrap.

"It is finished." Shem let out a weary sigh then turned to Kfir. "Burn all of this. Keep the fire going for seven days."

Kfir accepted the bundle. "I'll start the fire and let Tomar know."

Shem motioned to Nabella and strode from the courtyard toward Jokaan's room. Adara had Jokaan's head and shoulders propped. She brushed the persistent strand of dark hair gently from her father's forehead. Nabella's heart leapt when Jokaan opened his eyes.

"Father," tears blurred her vision. She stumbled to his side, knelt, and placed her hand on his arm. Jokaan closed his eyes leaning his head against Adara with a sigh. But not before Nabella glimpsed into his eyes. She saw a grand smile then profound sadness.

She had forgotten. She was shunned. A tear slid down her cheek. Exhausted she leaned to Jokaan and kissed his forehead. Her voice caught in a whisper, "Father, with your permission, may I stay until morning?"

***

Dawn's early light shone dimly through her open window. Nabella groaned and pulled the wool blanket tight around her shoulders. *Must be overcast outside. I hope Kfir went home last night. I don't want him to see my family this way.* She curled into a ball listening to the little noises throughout the house. Laughter, soft voices, a log in the fire crackled, someone's footsteps. A great heaviness filled her. Never again would she hear the stirrings of her family in the morning. She squeezed her eyes shut then blinked. With a resolute sigh she forced herself from the warm pallet.

Nabella brushed her hair, splashed water on her face then tiptoed from the sleeping area, afraid if she made a noise everyone would scatter. She padded through the living area. The crackling fire in the open hearth had just been started and dampness still clung stubbornly to the room. But no one was here now. So far, so good. She slipped through the inner courtyard. Lamplight flickered in the room reserved for eating. Well, she needed to eat before she left. When she slunk around the corner into the room, she heard a deep voice. Kfir. His back was to her maybe she could…

"Bella!" Shoshana dashed across the room and wrapped her arms around Nabella's waist. "Can we talk to you now?"

Nabella cringed and glanced at her relatives. One by one Adara, Tomar, and Nahni turned away. All except Kfir. She clenched her teeth and looked down. *And he will too, eventually.*

Nabella sighed and untwined Shoshana's thin arms. She stooped to the young girl's eye level and forced a smile. "I have to go today, little one."

"No, don't go." Shoshana flung her arms around Nabella's neck.

"Tsk, tsk. Come with me, Shoshana." Grandmother held out her hand.

"No." Shoshana clung unyielding, voice tight with tears.

"I have to leave, motek. Someday you'll understand." Nabella stroked the girl's hair, trying to control the tremble in her own voice.

"It's 'cause Barukh doesn't want you to be his bride, isn't it?"

"Well…"

"It is, don't lie to me, Bella." The girl stepped back and wiped her cheek with the back of her hand. "Why doesn't he want to marry you?"

"I, I don't know."

"Because he's a fool." Kfir shoved himself to his feet. "Look, Nabella. Get something to eat then pack. I'll go with you and Shem to see you safely to his place."

"I want to go too." Shoshana took Nabella's hand.

"You can't. Now come with me, Shoshana." Nahni looked at Nabella. Her eyes shimmered. Nabella saw a great chasm of unspoken pain immersed in the tears that threatened to spill. Then the older woman gripped the little girl's hand and led her away. Shoshana twisted as she walked, one side of her tunic slipping off a shoulder. Her lower lip jammed between her teeth and large green eyes lingered on Nabella.

"I will come to say good-bye," Nabella called as she fought her own tears. "And stop biting your lip…" Her voice trailed off.

Kfir moved to her side. "Come here and sit." He nodded to the stone wall-bench he just vacated. "I'll get you something to eat."

"Kfir," Tomar's voice sounded rough. "I wish to speak with you."

Kfir squared his shoulders and Nabella could see the muscle in his jaw bunch.

"Tomar, I understand the customs, and I do not wish to interfere with your family's affairs. I'll be happy to speak with you about anything you want, when this is over. But right now I am taking care of Nabella. She has done everything asked of her, and she's done it graciously. She gave of herself without thought to spare others discomfort and to save her father's life. So I am going to make this forced move as painless as possible. We will be gone by the end of a hand-span. I ask for your leniency until then."

Tomar stared at Kfir for a long time then gave him an almost unperceivable nod. Nabella caught a look of deep sadness as it pierced his face before he trudged from the room. Kfir turned to her and his face softened. He took her arm and led her to the bench. "Look at it this way little doe, by moving away you'll be the first of your family to obey God's command." A crooked smile hung on his face.

Nabella blinked clutching her jupe. Emotions and thoughts swirled together into a jumbled mess. She ought to say something, anything, but no words came. At last she gave up staring into space and let numbness seep in.

Kfir returned with a platter of eggs, smoked quail, bread and watered wine. Nabella stared at the food and blinked back tears. No one had ever brought her a morning meal, ever. Let alone one so luscious.

"Eat. We have a long journey ahead of us." Kfir's voice sounded thick.

Nabella reached for the plate, and their fingers touched. Warmth shot through her. Warmth and gratefulness for this man. Why had she never noticed his gallantry before? She had always thought of Kfir as an adult. As Barukh's older brother. Someone who had teased her relentlessly since she was a small child. Someone she enjoyed being teased by. She shook her head sucking in a shaky breath.

"Thank you."

"Now graze away, little doe."

Nabella let out a soft laugh. Maybe everything would be alright after all. And she *would* need her strength. Suddenly ravenous, she dug into the food.

When Nabella finished, she padded to Jokaan's room. Adara held a cup to Father's lips. From the scrunched look on Jokaan's face she guessed it to be Machlah's medicine. But at least he seemed better.

Nabella laid her hand on Adara's arm. Her sister stared at the wall then without a word, left the room.

"Father, I know the shunning is in effect. But I also know you can hear me and right now you are a captive listener. And I don't mean that with any disrespect." Nabella knelt by her father's side placing her hand over his. Her voice became a whisper. "I just want to tell you how much I love you. And that I'm so sorry I put you in such an awful position. Thank you for sparing my life." She drew in a soft sob and stroked his hand. Then she rose, "I'll leave you now. And thank you. For everything."

Nabella shuffled to the entrance and paused. Looking back she studied her father. She wanted to always remember him, to etch his features in her mind. Light streamed in the window, flowing across the blankets that covered him. His dark hair had been brushed and hung to his shoulders except for the one wayward strand. Nabella cocked her head. Did she imagine it or was the healthy brown color coming back to his face? Even so, he still looked weak with sunken eyes and cheekbones. As she watched, a single tear trailed down his cheek.

Nabella's throat squeezed tight. "I love you, Father." And she fled the room.

Nabella huddled in the storage room amongst the chickpeas and bags of barley until she could cry no more. Finally she stood, wiping her tears then slipped through the courtyard to draw water from the well.

I have to get a hold of myself. I can't let Shoshana or Kfir see me this way. Nabella splashed a handful of cold water on her face. It dripped from her chin where just a little while ago there had been tears. Nabella gripped the edge of the well and leaned against its frame, face pressed onto the stone until she drew her emotions under control.

Footsteps strode into the courtyard and she looked up. Kfir stood opposite the well.

"There you are. I packed food for the trip and saddled the animals. Go get your belongings and say good-bye to Shoshana then we can leave."

Nabella nodded. She drew a deep breath, clenched her hands into fists and marched back into the house. When she approached her father's room, she heard Shem deep voice and paused.

"I have just walked around your grounds and tried to communicate with your workers. As far as I can tell you have four different tongues here, each unable to understand one another's speech."

"But there are at least some people that speak each, ah, how did you put it? Tongue?" Jokaan's voice sounded wheezy but stronger.

"Yes. And we counted sixteen different tongues on the way here. Two of the tongues your workers speak are part of the sixteen, but two are new."

"What does that mean?"

"I believe there may be many more different tongues out there."

"Maybe we should try to call a meeting with all the people that speak like we do."

"I had that thought also. I will try to organize it on my way home. Jokaan, may we meet here in two weeks, on the full moon?"

"You don't want to meet in The City? It's far for some to come out here."

"No. The City is in such disarray, full of chaos and misunderstandings and arguments. Fights are breaking out from all the people's babblings and grievances. It would be frightening for those who do not live there to come into that mess, and I want to avoid the government. But more than that, I want to discuss settling away from The City, to come into obedience with God and follow His command."

"That's what that City is, and was so even before this happened. Babblings. That's what we should call it. The great city of Babel." Her father's quiet laughter brought a smile to Nabella's face. "You don't think two weeks is too long?" Jokaan continued. "The people may have scattered by then."

Nabella heard Shem snort then sigh. "That's what God's judgment is, Jokaan. You figured it out. He told us a long time ago to replenish the whole earth. We rebelled and all stayed in one spot. It really is a very mild judgment. The wickedness has been growing yet God kept His promise. He did not strike us with a flood as He did in the Former World. He simply changed our speech, so we would scatter abroad, moving all over the face of the earth just like He intended. Yes, Jokaan, Babel is an appropriate name for The City, because the

Lord did there confound the one tongue of all the earth." Shem's voice became quite and reverent, "His will be done."

A long pause followed and Nabella moved on to gather her belongings. She placed her spare jupe, the one Machlah had given her, in the middle of her blanket then grabbed her comb and brush, a pair of foot coverings, her warm cloak and oilskin and a few other small possessions. Her hand hovered over the small jars of eye and rouge makeup Adara had given her. Gently she picked each one up and held them to her bosom, eyes closed against the dull ache that radiated from her heart. Then she wrapped them in the spare jupe setting it with great care in the center of her bundle. At last Nabella gathered the corners of the blanket securing it with a length of twine.

She met Kfir by the takhis and handed him her bundle. "I need to find Shoshana."

"If she's anything like Barukh was at her age, she's off pouting somewhere."

"I'll check her favorite places."

A cursory look around the grounds brought Nabella back to the courtyard with no Shoshana in sight. Nabella tapped her foot. Now that everything was packed, she wanted to leave. But where had Shoshana gone? She marched toward the processing building to ask Tomar for help then changed her mind. Instead she went to Kfir.

"I can't find Shoshana. Can you ask my family for their help?"

Kfir nodded.

Before long it became clear, Shoshana had run off.

***

Nabella stood between Kfir and Shem while Elah and Jabari spoke. It was obvious they understood each other but each time Jabari turned to Tomar, Kfir, or one of the others he became agitated when communication faltered. Finally he broke etiquette, pointed to each of the men to pair up then signaled for them to go in different directions to look for the missing child. He pointed to Kfir and Shem, but Shem shook his head and motioned to the house.

"Jokaan."

Jabari scowled, looking at Shem with both arms raised, palms up. "Shoshana."

Shaking his head again Shem placed a hand on Kfir's shoulder. "I dare not leave Jokaan alone with all this mischief going on." Then he turned and went into the house. Jabari's gaze followed the man then he shook his head. He fixed his eyes on Nabella. Finally he spoke.

"Nabella," he pointed to her head, then, "Shoshana," with a sweep of his arm toward the groves.

"He says you know Shoshana," Kfir interpreted, "and you do, probably better than anyone."

Nabella nodded.

"So where do you think she would go?"

"Well, many times she goes to the swing behind the processing building, but we've already checked there. Did anyone look in the chambers below ground, or behind the well, or the storage room?"

Kfir nodded, "more than once."

"Oh." Nabella's shoulders sagged, her mind blank. Where else could Shoshana be?

"Do you think she would go to my house?"

"Your house?"

"Yes. To try to talk my brother into marrying you."

"Oh, oh no." Nabella seized Kfir's arm. "She wouldn't. But I bet you're right. Yes, now that you say it I'm sure that's where she went."

Nabella turned to Jabari and pointed north. "Shoshana went to Barukh's. Barukh's." She could tell by Jabari's response he understood.

Kfir and Jabari jogged down the path towards Gideon's place. Nabella ran to keep up with their pace. Though the sun had climbed well above the horizon, the canopy of evergreen olive leaves and the developing rain clouds kept the orchard in a perpetual early dusk. They slowed to a walk peering at the ground. The light pitter patter of raindrops sounded above but the thick canopy kept them dry. After five hundred cubits, Jabari came to a stop holding up his hand. Kfir and Nabella halted next to him.

"Περιμένουμε εδώ. Πρέπει να ελέγξετε για κομμάτια."

Jabari scrubbed his face at their blank looks. A drop of rain landed on his brow then another at his feet. His face turned thoughtful. He gestured to the ground, jabbed a finger at his chest then his eyes and once again motioned to the ground.

"He wants to look for tracks." Nabella said. Jabari held up a hand for them to wait then proceeded step by step stooping close to the ground.

"Εδώ. Εδώ είναι το κομμάτια," Jabari threw a hand up gesturing at the ground.

"He found something."

The man knelt and flicked a few leaves to the side. Kfir and Nabella peered over his shoulder. When Jabari moved his hand, Nabella could see the indent from Shoshana's small sandal.

"Shoshana," Nabella scolded.

Jabari chuckled then nodded his head. "Θα βρούμε της."

As they turned to the north Kfir tapped Nabella's arm. "We'll find her now that we know where she's going."

Nabella nodded thankful for Kfir's encouragement.

"Shoshana," Nabella called. Jabari and Kfir moved off to either side and joined in. Their voices sounded singsong to Nabella. If it hadn't been for the circumstances, she would have enjoyed the camaraderie. The brush thickened when they approached the north end of the groves. Soon she couldn't see Kfir or Jabari. Nabella paused cocking her head. *Well, at least I can hear them.*

Leaves rustled to her right and a branch snapped. What was that? Her heart thudded as her eye flicked over the growth. Then a faint little voice called her name.

"Stop!" Nabella scanned the brush.

"Where are you?" Kfir's voice carried through the trees. "Keep talking, we're coming."

"I'm here, I heard her call me."

Jabari and Kfir stepped through the brush. She put a finger to her lips. There, she heard it again. Faint but clear.

Jabari and Nabella exchanged a glance. "Shoshana."

"Shoshana, where are you?" The three pushed toward the sound.

"Bella! Come here." Shoshana's voice became louder.

"I'm coming, Shoshana. Just keep talking so I can find you."

Silence.

"Shoshana? You have to yell, so we can hear you."

"All right. But hurry. I found something."

"We're coming, motek, we're coming."

Jabari held up an arm and thrust his chin to the right. Beyond the brush stood a meadow a bit larger than their processing area. Light rain continued to fall, reaching the tall grass stalks of the meadow. The small girl crouched low to the ground at the far end.

Nabella's knees wobbled. Relief showered over her. "I'll get her." She held up a hand for the men to stop then skirted a clump of tamarisk, leaves yellow orange from the cooler weather, and started across the field.

"Bella, come look." The girl glanced over her shoulder at Nabella, pulling dark locks out of her eyes. She sat crouched and pointed with a branch. "Look at this fox, he's so sad."

Nabella's eyes trailed to a hole behind her sister. A fox lay on its belly near its den. It covered both eyes with its front paws and gave a slow wobbled shake of its head.

"Wait. Something doesn't look right about that animal." Kfir sounded uneasy.

Jabari grabbed his arm. "Λύσσα, έχει λύσσα."

Nabella froze at the intensity in the man's voice then glanced to see Jabari shake Kfir, fear in his eyes.

"Can we take it home?" The girl stared at the fox.

Kfir stepped forward. "Shoshana, come away from there."

Shoshana reached to pet it.

"No!" From the corner of her eye, Nabella saw Kfir's hand dart forward though he could do nothing from where he stood.

Nabella's voice rang sharp. "Shoshana, do as Kfir says. Now!"

"Aaaw-right." The girl dropped the branch and trudged toward them, head down.

Suddenly the fox lurched from under the thicket. Its ragged fur unkempt and matted, the rain making it look all the more pathetic. When its mouth twisted into a snarl Nabella could see foam gathered at the corners. She gasped. Shoshana stopped, and the animal stopped.

"What's wrong, Bella?"

"Come slowly," Kfir called in a low voice.

Shoshana took a step, and the fox bounded two staggering leaps in her direction.

"Stop," Nabella hissed. Shoshana halted, large eyes fixed on Nabella's face.

The fox stopped.

"What's wrong?" Shoshana whispered.

Nabella's heart lurched. One side of her sister's tunic had again slipped off a shoulder, and she stood balanced with a small sandaled foot poised in midair. The delicate pink in her cheeks reminded Nabella of rose petals, a rose—Shoshana, her name. The little girl's wide eyes locked on hers'.

"Don't move, motek, the fox is very sick. He's following you."

From the corner of her eye Nabella saw Kfir slide a hand to his long dagger. Without moving her head she snapped her eyes to Jabari. He had drawn his knife.

"Bella?"

Shoshana twisted her head and looked behind her. A screech squeaked from her throat. The little girl raced toward her sister. With a twitching snarl the fox lunged forward.

Nabella didn't stop to think. She bolted toward Shoshana, leapt through the air and landed on top of the girl, stifling her shrieks. She grabbed her and rolled. After what seemed like a hundred spins they stopped, bunched together in a heap. She ignored the stab of pain in her hip pushing Shoshana under her. Nabella's eyes swept the meadow. Where was the fox? Three cubits away it lunged at them. A dagger swished by and sunk into the fox's throat. The animal skidded into a heap off to one side. In the same instant a guttural roar rose behind Nabella. She jerked her head toward the noise.

The Azhdaha!

Only the softly falling rain stood between them. Nabella tried to scream but nothing came out. She rolled to her side, her back jamming against a tree stump. Instinctively she pulled Shoshana tight to her stomach curling around the girl. She twisted her head in time to see the Azhdaha burst from the brush. Its injured foot no longer inhibited the animal. Nabella watched in horror as the tanniyn charged in her direction, each stride moving it forward ten cubits. Her wide eyes darted for the nearest tree. She would never make it, even if she didn't have Shoshana. A puny shriek dribbled from her throat.

Move Nabella, move! But she could only stare as the animal closed the distance. Sixty cubits, fifty cubits, nine more leaps and it would have her. And Shoshana. She had to do something! It felt as though she sloshed through a vat of crushed olives as she shoved Shoshana to the ground. Her muscles seemed to work against each other when she gathered her feet and pushed upright, fighting to rise. Shoshana shrieked. Nabella gritted her teeth forcing her leg to stomp the girl back down.

"Don't move," she croaked.

If she acted like she had been wounded, maybe the beast would come after her. Nabella took a step to the side and fluttered her arms. Shoshana screamed again.

"Quite!."

Nabella fluttered her arms again. It was the best she could do.

But would it be enough?

The Azhdaha shifted. Bounding for her, the sharp-clawed front legs tucked together in its final leap. Nabella's eyes fixated on the open mouth. Long pointed teeth lined thick jaws. Fascinated, Nabella watched drool slide from the tip of a jagged tooth. It glistened in the air for an instant then disappeared. The tanniyn tilted its head, the angle unmistakably aiming for her chest. Nabella caught the intense gleam of a sure kill in the predator's eyes.

Calmness washed over her. It worked. Shoshana would be safe.

Suddenly an immense spear soared past plunging into the animal's chest. Almost the same instant a long dagger followed, its length running through the side of the creature. A great roar escaped the animal's throat. It jerked in midair and went limp. Nabella's eyes flew wide. The great head flopped down careening the body through the air right at them.

She dove for Shoshana the dead Azhdaha crumpling over her. She tightened her muscles to keep from crushing Shoshana. A yelp of pain and fear broke loose. Shoshana shrieked. Both sounds closed in on Nabella under the weight of the tanniyn. Her arms buckled, and she dropped to her elbows. Her chin smacked Shoshana, and the child whimpered. Nabella's chest heaved as she sucked in played out air. Muscles trembled as Nabella fought to keep from collapsing onto her sister. Sweat trickled down a cheek. The strong odor of Azhdaha filled her nostrils. Muffled voices sounded above. She closed her eyes.

Lord? Nabella felt a powerful sense of calm. *You have been so very good to me.* The carcass began to move. *Help us to survive this.* The weight eased, and one of the men gave a huge grunt. *Help me to obey, Lord.* Sounds became clearer. *Thank You, Creator God, You have done so much for me.* The pressing force slid off and at last fresh air rushed around her. Nabella gasped deeply and sat upright dragging Shoshana with her.

"Are you all right?" She soothed the girl's walnut colored hair out of her eyes. Shoshana nodded, bottom lip stuck between her teeth. Nabella smiled at her sister. Large, green eyes bore into hers and Nabella hugged Shoshana to her chest.

"Oh, motek shelek, it'll be alright. And stop biting your lip." Somewhere behind them she heard twigs and leaves snap as Jabari and Kfir hauled the Azhdaha to the side.

Nabella rocked the girl back and forth, brushing back her sister's damp hair. She glanced up, realizing the rain had stopped and as she lowered her eyes she froze. At the edge of the clearing, astride the old mare, sat her father. Everything that had made her feel secure and loved in her life had come from this man. Now he looked weak and thin. Why was he here? He should still be in bed. He slid off the mare and struggled toward her. Nabella's heart went out to him. She was torn between her great love for her father and irritation that he left the house risking a relapse.

Kfir slid on his knees next to her. "Nabella, are you alright?"

When she didn't answer, he followed her gaze. "Jokaan."

Her father paused in front of Nabella as tears streamed down his cheeks. He straightened his stooped frame and placed a hand on her head.

"Nabella, you have shown extraordinary courage. The courage of a son. You have given your life freely three times to aid others. First to bring Shem here you risked everything. And twice just now, you covered your sister's life with your own. There can be nothing greater than that. Your debt has been fulfilled." Jokaan let his hand slide off Nabella's head. "Jabari, Kfir, Shem. You are my witnesses. Nabella is no longer shunned."

"Oh, Bella." Shoshana hugged Nabella's neck then bound to her father and threw her arms around Jokaan's waist. "Oh thank you, thank you, Abba."

"Shem?" Nabella skimmed the meadow until her eyes landed on the great man. "When did you get here?"

Shem knelt, his voice vibrant. "I was with Jokaan at the house when I heard the Lord. His urging became very strong. I grabbed my spear and atlatl racing here as fast as I could. He guided me to the other side of this clearing just in time to see the Azhdaha leap. I hurled the spear. Before it even left my hand I knew the weapon would find its mark for God's hand guided it. Then I came into the clearing and God's plan was revealed unto me. For you, Nabella, are safe and Shoshana also."

Shem stood, a smiled creased his bronzed face. "And now you have been restored to your family. I am a joyful witness to that."

Suddenly Kfir leapt to his feet and clasped Jokaan's forearm, eyes intense. "Jokaan, I have a question to ask, if you feel strong enough to listen. It burns within me."

Jokaan eyed Kfir then gave him a nod.

"Your daughter is an extraordinary woman. I have watched her all these years and hoped against hope that somehow we would be brought together. I cannot let her go." He glanced at Nabella, sable skin turning a deep hue of red.

Her eyes grew wide.

"May I, marry your daughter, Nabella? I would gladly give twice the dowry you and Barukh agreed upon."

Nabella's mouth hung open. Kfir? Wanted to marry her? This kind, strong and brave man desired to spend the rest of his life with her? Nabella's head swirled. Yet somehow the thought seemed right. It felt true, as if life would then be complete. Warmth spread through her, and her fingers began to tingle.

Jokaan gazed down at her. "Stand my daughter."

Nabella stared at Kfir's proffered hand. For an instant she squeezed her eyes together then gave one shake her head, could he be the one for her? Her fingers slid across his calloused hand. Strong fingers wrapped around hers and a bolt of heat shot through her body. She couldn't take her eyes off him. Kfir helped her to her feet then stepped to the side. Nabella studied her father.

Jokaan took both her hands. "Is this something you desire?" His features looked ragged, but his eyes were strong. They scrutinized the depths of hers.

And then she knew. At last the answer became clear. Kfir, with his deep eyes that always seemed to pierce her. Black hair and tanned face that captured her thoughts, replacing Barukh until he was no more. Mighty warrior who had always treated her with kindness and respect. A man who would allow her to be herself. Nabella turned her gaze on Kfir and the tingling in her fingers spread through her arms and legs. "It's been you all along," she whispered. Her delicate brows drew together then arched with amazement. "You are who my heart has always longed to be with." She blinked and gave a soft laugh of wonder.

"Then so be it. Shem, Jabari, you are my witnesses. Let it be known that Kfir and Nabella are betrothed."

Jokaan placed her hands in Kfir's. Nabella felt the weakness in her father's grip, and her heart swelled when Shem took Jokaan's hand and placed it on his own shoulder. The two great men turned and headed for the mare.

Kfir pivoted to face Nabella and placed his strong hands on her shoulders, his voice thick and warm. "And now my little doe, you will always have a meadow to come home to."

Nabella felt moisture gather along her bottom lashes and a smile tip the corners of her lips. Kfir grinned wide, a twinkle in his eye. He grabbed her around the waist and swung her in circles. A tiny squeal escaped despite her efforts to squelch it. She heard Jokaan call Shoshana, and out of the corner of her eye saw Jabari follow the men.

Oh, thank You, God. Nabella tucked her head onto Kfir's neck. Astonishment changed into laughter. *You do care about us; You just want us to obey. Thank You for sparing us from a worse judgment than confusing our speech, and for restoring me to my family and, most of all, thank You for Kfir.*

She felt Kfir set her light as a thin mist onto her own two feet. Steady, courageous eyes searched hers.

"God wants mankind to fill the earth, Nabella. What do you think of going east with me? To a place far from here where birds sound like flutes and animals laugh when they hunt?"

Nabella blinked. Move from here? Away from her father and sisters? Yet she could not deny the tug in her heart. Everything would be different from now on. Surely there would be no more threats or curses placed on them to move to The City.

"We could see if anyone wants to come with us." Kfir leaned forward, "Including your family, and we can bring olive and grape seeds and even seedlings, so when we settle we can start a farm. Then you would have olive trees like here."

How wonderful it would be if her family came along. Nabella gazed at Kfir, and her heart swelled. He had thought of everything. Even to include her family. No wonder he had stolen her heart.

She brushed fingers along his jaw line. A strong desire to obey this man and God filled her. She knew she could trust them both more than herself. "Yes, I'll go with you to the land where birds sing like flutes! I love you and will follow you wherever you go."

A slow smiled creased his face. "And I have loved you for a very long time."

Nabella's brows raised and her jaw dropped. It *was* true. Now that her heart had been opened she remembered all the times he had been there for her. Just like now, wanting her family to go with them. Slowly she shook her head in awe, a small laugh escaped.

"You are amazing." She placed her hands on his shoulders. "Thank you for always being there for me. And for thinking of my family." Nabella paused, thoughts on the future, their future. "And don't you think, surely some of the people who speak like us are bound to come too?"

Kfir beamed, "Yes, I believe others must have come to the same conclusion. That Creator God had caused the split of our one tongue. I think they'll be just as eager to obey Him and move too. I'll start asking around tomorrow."

"It'll be worth it because it's God's will." Then she suddenly knew. Kfir would be their leader. Wide-eyed, she stared at him. The twinkle in Kfir's eyes deepened. Nabella inhaled sharply and bit her lower lip, grateful that for the rest of her life she would be under his wing of safety and love. Kfir tilted his head and slowly leaned forward. Tingling shot through her body, heat rising from deep within. Nabella tipped her head. Her eyes closed halfway as she watched his lips draw near.

Suddenly Shoshana's voice broke through. "Bellaaa! Stop biting your lip! How else are you going to kiss Kfir?"

The Story Doesn't End Here...

25 years later

***

The Golden Strand
Chapter One
2216 BC

"Ouch!"

Shoshana rolled her eyes tugging at her plaited tresses caught on a chipped stone edge of the sill. This happened every time she leaned out the second story window. Why didn't she have her husband fix it? Better yet, use a different opening. Or maybe not lean out at all—she could just stick her arm out to dump the scrap pot.

Shoshana eyed the string that held the ends of her braid together. Dark walnut strands stuck out at awkward angles. She sucked in her lower lip and flicked the braid to her back. *Why don't I ever think of that until my hair rips?*

With a quick shake of her head, Shoshana bustled to their sleeping quarters. She glanced toward the framed pallet in the corner and saw her youngest son scramble behind a wadded blanket. A small foot that protruded from under the wooden frame gave away her middle son. She smiled when six-year-old Seva popped up from the foot of the four-poster pallet to tease his younger brother, Simon.

"Boys, I hate to break up your fun but I need to tidy up. And when Sibi gets back we're going downstairs to your father."

Shoshana wondered if her oldest son had stopped for a pastry. He had recently discovered the shop owner relinquished day-old sweets in exchange for work done around her bakery. Even so...he should have been back by now. Willowy fingers fluttered like the small winged creatures that flew at dusk. She plucked two wooden toys and a rag off the floor. At the sound of a small noise she paused, then unable to resist, scurried to the doorway to peer down the steep staircase. But of course, no one appeared.

Sibi's recent habit to straggle behind in his errands disrupted her routine. Shoshana's brows furrowed. *I will just have to add Sibi to my worry list.* With a hand on her hip, the young mother wondered when she had become such a creature of habit. When things were in their place her world remained secure—and that's the way she always wanted it.

Shoshana sighed gathering her husband's one spare shirt off the wall peg. She pressed it to her face and inhaled his scent. Her worries slipped away, everything would be fine. Adam always made sure of that, didn't he? He had reassured her that the move to Akkad, a Babylonian city, would be beneficial. Despite her reservations to leave her large Shemite family over a fifteen days'-journey to the south, Adam had made a good decision. Shoshana had been surprised at the warm welcome Adam's younger sister and new husband gave her. She felt if the rest of her husband's family lived in Akkad they would have been just as hospitable.

Once they arrived in Akkad Adam's name as a skilled bone healer spread quickly and soon he had several proposals. But he had declined these lucrative positions across the city. Instead he offered his bone healing services in the Shemite section where they rented a two story abode with living quarters above and room for his practice below so he could remain close to her and the children.

Suddenly the floor felt like it rolled beneath Shoshana. She staggered toward a wall and smacked a hand on it to steady herself. Shoshana clamped her eyes shut but still felt dizzy. The room seemed to sway. In the adjacent room her pottery and wooden dishes hummed, then clattered like the locust swarm that had stripped the farmer's crops three summers ago. Shoshana's eyes flew open. Next to her an unlit clay lamp crashed to the floor. Its oil pooled on the wooden slats.

"Mamma!" The scream ripped from Seva.

A ground quake. Her hands and feet tingled in alarm. *The children!* But before she could move Shoshana pitched forward and slammed onto the bucking floor. Helpless she watched her middle son tossed to the ground like a small sack of grain.

"Seva I'm h—" she thrust her hand toward him. The boy rolled arms flailing across the floorboards and crashed into the wall with a thud. His little body jerked then lay motionless. Shoshana's mouth opened but no sound came out.

At a loud crack the young mother's eyes snapped to Simon. Tentacles of fear slithered through her as the head of the framed pallet tipped down broken planks. Pieces of floorboard fell through a gaping hole the same instant a crash resounded below. Simon's scream pierced the air.

Bit by bit he slid across the pallet toward the yawning gap.

"Mamma!" Terrified eyes locked on hers.

Icy fingers stole Shoshana's breath. She shoved herself upright. *Move!* The floor heaved. With heavy steps she staggered back and forth then lunged toward Simon. Her shoulder struck the corner of the frame. A stab of pain shot down her arm. She ignored the throbs and clawed toward the four-year-old.

The planks groaned again.

Shoshana dragged herself forward and watched in horror when the head of the four-poster pallet dropped through the cavity with a thump. The force tossed Simon toward the hole. The boy twisted and clung to the mattress. Tears streamed down his face.

"Ma-ma-a!"

Shoshana panted, mouth dry, as she struggled to reach her son. She could almost grab him—*just a palm's width away*. But he drifted faster then she could reach him—the gaping hole below him.

Then for a brief instant Simon's slide halted. His right foot, pressed against the corner post, stalled the inevitable plummet. He wailed and groped for his mother's hand. Shoshana drew muscles tight for another lunge. Instinct screamed it would be her last chance.

Suddenly a small form rammed into her side. Seva flung his arms around her and his weight shoved Shoshana to the floor. She landed with a grunt, the wind knocked out of her.

"Mamma, Mamma, what's going on?" His grip tightened around her waist.

"Seva…" she gasped, "let go."

But it was too late.

Horrified, Shoshana watched Simon's foot slide off the post. A pillow dropped through the opening behind him and the boy sank out of reach.

Oh, God, no!

***

Don't miss the exciting story of Shoshana in the book "The Golden Strand" next in the trilogy "Sign of the Oth."

Glossary

Aurochs (ou′rŏks′) an extinct type of large wild cattle that possessed enormous horns. They are thought to be the ancestor of domestic cattle.

Azhdaha (Ăz-dă-hă)—a *Tetanuran* dinosaur, *Baryonyx* meaning heavy claw. This dinosaur (or dragon as all dinosaurs were known in ancient times) is a very strange looking animal. The design of its hips and pelvis allow it to be bipedal. It had a long curved claw on the thumb of each forehand, about 31 cm (12 in). However, for a bipedal its forelimbs were unusually large (large enough to support its weight) but smaller than the hind legs. The bone structure suggests a huge muscle ran down the sides of each front leg and its probable these muscles were designed for the thumb claw. This type of structure also grants it the ability to spend a great deal of time on all fours. This predator dinosaur ate fish and other animals. Bones of an *Ornithopod* dinosaur, *Iguanodon*, were found along with fish remains in a *Baryonyx* skeleton. Its skull is similar to a crocodile's therefore devouring other animals besides fish would be no different than what crocodiles do today (see appendix two).

Caracal (Kār-ă-kĕl)—a wild feline similar to a bobcat except with a solid color coat.

Cuneiform (kyoo-nee-*uh*-faurm) (see appendix) a form of ancient writing where small wedge-shaped characters have been pressed with a stylus into hand sized clay tablets and larger cones. This type of writing was used by ancient Babylonians, Sumerians, Akkadians, Eblahites and others (see appendix eight).

Day's journey—twenty miles.

Froward (froh-werd) perverse, vulgar, stubbornly disobedient.

Half-day's journey—ten miles.

Half a Hand-span—equivalent to a half an hour.

Hand-span—equivalent to one hour of time.

Jupe (joo-p)—an ankle length skirt.

Kabiyr (kah-bee-er)—enormous. Used in this book as the reference to the tanniyn (dragon/dinosaur) Nimrod hunted (see appendix two).

Marduk (mahr-dook)—an Old World demon worshipped as a deity.

Mastic (mas-tik)—a plant resin obtained from *Pistacia lentiscus*; a shrub native to the Mediterranean region.

Motek (moo-tek)—an endearing term such as sweetie or dear.

Motek-sheleh (moo-tek shā-lăh)—a more personal endearing term such as sweetheart.

Month of Autumn Harvest—October.

Month of First Harvest—June
Month of Overabundant Rain—November.
Month of Second Beginnings—September.
Myrrh (mur)—a spice often used to prepare the deceased.
Nahni (năh-nē)—endearing term for grandmother (see appendix three).
Oth (ooth)—an ancient Hebrew word revealing a sign as an expression of the reign of God, aimed at a (temporary) future reality and brought about through some form of pleasure, aid, relief, understanding, benefit, or warning. An *oth* contains five elements: practicality, temporality, eternal value, a call to personal readiness, and the bearing witness of God's promise to act in our future.
Panacea (pan-uh-see-uh)—a universal cure or remedy.
Pay—to settle (a debt, obligation, etc.), by the transfer of goods, or by doing something in exchange.
Pre-cuneiform—(prē-kyoo-nee-*uh*-fowrm) see appendix) inscriptions similar to cuneiform but pre-dating cuneiforms and undecipherable. Found only in the Ahoru Gorge on the north side of Mount Ararat, and thought to be of the pre-flood language carved by Noah, his three sons, or their immediate descendants (see appendix eight).
Ryphi (rī-fī)—a spice used for ceremonial purposes.
Sabot (să-bōh)—a thin, solid disk-like shaped object made from metal or glass, often used for jewelry (see appendix one).
Tanniyn (tă-ńeen)—the dinosaur kind, also known as dragons which is what people referred to as these large beasts before the word dinosaur was coined in 1841 by English scientist Sir Richard Owen (see appendix two).
Tanninim. (tă-ńeen-um)—plural of tanniyn (see appendix two).
Tannur oven (tăn-ūr)—Cylindrical-shaped clay ovens that are heated to a high temperature by a firebox at the bottom. Unleavened dough is slapped against the inside wall and bake within a minute or two. Meats are roasted on long vertical spits over the top opening.
Ziggurat (zig-oo-rat)— (see appendix) massive structures built in the ancient Mesopotamian valley and western Iranian plateau, (and later around the world), having the form of a terraced step pyramid often with a religious temple placed at the top (see appendix four).
Zenith (zee-nith)—highest point.

Appendix One

Advanced Knowledge

"And the Lord said, Behold the people is one, and they have all one language; and this they begin to do: and now nothing will be restrained from them, which they have imagined to do." (Genesis 11:6, emphasis mine).The implication is that the people at Babel possessed tremendous knowledge. "I dare say that the ziggurats and cities at Babylon and Ur in lower Mesopotamia reflect nothing of what these people were capable of. Even the pyramids of Egypt, which are still today a great engineering feat, probably can't compare to whatever was begun at Babel '...nothing will be restrained from them, which they have imagined to do.'"[1] What could this mean? What were they capable of doing? No one knows. But there is evidence that man both before and after The Flood possessed tremendous advanced knowledge. I suspect had the people remained united and of one language with the Pre-Flood knowledge they retained, a level of technological advancement would have been reached in just a few years equal to or beyond what we now possess. To the puzzlement of modern archeologists and scholars, evidence abounds in the Mount Ararat region that the earliest people possessed very advanced technical knowledge.

metallurgical furnace with traces of copper

"One of the oldest, if not the oldest, metallurgical factory archaeological sites in the world is located in the foothills of Mount Ararat. Analyses of copper found

---

[1] Gray, Jonathan. *What Happened at the Towel of Babel?* http://www.scribd.com/doc/229287161/Jonathan-Gray-Books#scribd

there showed 14 different alloys, including tin, lead, antimony and zinc. The centre was sophisticated. Clay pipes were found inserted into the furnaces, as well as phosphorus briquettes, used in the smelting of cassiterite to obtain tin. Here vases and objects made of all the common metals have been found. Fourteen varieties of bronze were smelted for different purposes. Medzamor also produced metallic paints, ceramics, and glass. And the Medzamor craftsmen wore mouth-filters and gloves, as do modern craftsmen. The factory is believed to have had more than 200 furnaces. Medzamor was the industrial centre of this early post-Flood period."[2]

The main reason that metal is rarely found in archeological sites is implements made out of any kind of metal were precious to the owners (and those who conquered the owners). Anything made out of clay, wood, woven material, hides, etc., could easily be replaced, but not metal. It would have been handed down from generation to generation, or smelted and reformed into another use. If this seems farfetched, Ezekiel 28:13-15 mentions that in "Eden, the garden of God" there was "every precious stone... sardius, topaz, and diamond, beryl, onyx, and jasper, sapphire, turquoise, and emerald with gold." That would mean Adam and Eve had knowledge of mining, metal work, and the wheel. All would have been brought from the Former World by Noah and his sons. It is reasonable to think this knowledge would have been put to immediate use and is evident in ancient archeological sites (i.e. the pyramids).

Another area where sophisticated construction commenced shortly after the dispersal of mankind from the language split is the Indus region, northwest of modern India. "Some of the houses are so well preserved that they could be occupied today, and use made of the bathroom as well as the irrigation and drainage services. The city lacked neither grandeur nor comfort. It contained a most ingenious and complete drainage system...The brick conduits, arranged under the streets, received the efflux from pipes placed in each house, and were linked to stone sewers. At intervals these sewers were supplied with cesspools which were easy to clean, while it was only necessary to move a few bricks to clean out the small drains in the streets if they became blocked up...They constructed a whole system of water mains which collected the water from the rain falling outside the city and distributed it via ingenious brick conduits which conducted it to wells in each house (see photo). These water mains fed the

[2] Gray, Jonathan. *What Happened at the Towel of Babel?* www.scribd.com/doc/229287161/Jonathan-Gray-Books#scribd

bathrooms. Each house possessed its own—and they were much the same as those still in use in India today."[3]

Such advanced technology includes the ability for production of crops and the processing of their products. Such manufacturing would not be nearly so enormous compared to today's production, but for that time it would have been large enough. "Mankind is fascinated with the world and in a constant state of search and discovery. In ancient times, with such long lives and intelligent minds, the people could have made discoveries and advancements that present-day man does not yet understand. Yet this knowledge they may have had has been mysteriously forgotten in most cases."[4]

---

3 Brion, Marcel. *The World of Archaeology*, vol. 1 (New York: Macmillan Co., 1959), pp. 97-98.

4 Landis, Don. *The Genius Of Ancient Man Evolution's Nightmare*, (Green Forest, AR: Master Books, 2013)

Appendix Two

Dragons: Legend or Dinosaurs?

"What is a dragon? From monstrous, serpentine creatures of the sea to the fire- breathing beasts and others that made the ground tremble when they came near, it is evident the word 'dragon' isn't referring to one creature but several types of creatures.

"Clearly, these animals—some even able to breathe fire—were terrifying to behold and real. They live and died like other creatures. They were witnessed by men who spoke and wrote extensively of their encounters in cultures around the world..."[1] Other documentation of these creatures survives even to today in ancient historical books and records, legends and myths from many civilizations.

It wasn't until 1842 that the word "dinosaur" was coined by Sir Richard Owen, an anatomical researcher from England. He had an interest in fossils and after some years of uncovering huge bones, understood that at one time animals roamed around that no longer exist today. He proposed to the scientific community to place them in a whole new category: Dinosauria.

But what did people call these animals before 1842? Dragons! As a matter of fact, the Bible mentions dragons (dinosaurs) in the Old Testament twenty-two times: Deuteronomy 32:33; Nehemiah 2:13; Job 30:29; Psalm 44:19; 74:13; 91:13; 148:7; Isaiah 13:22; 51:9; 14:29; 7:1; 30:6; 34:13; 35:7; 43:20; Ezekiel 29:3; Jeremiah 9:11; 10:22; 14:6; 49:33; 51:34; 51:37; Malachi 1:3; Micah 1:8.

In addition, the Bible calls two dinosaurs by name: the behemoth (Job 40:15-34) and leviathan (Job 41:1-34), giving physical descriptions and behaviors. For example, the behemoth "eats grass like an ox," has "his strength in his hips," "his power is in his stomach muscles," and "he moves his tail like a cedar tree." Some Bible commentaries compare this animal to an elephant or hippopotamus. However, both of these creatures have small tails and certainly don't have their power in their abdomen, nor strength in their hips. In actuality, this description matches quite nicely with a Tyrannosaurus rex or sauropod dinosaur.

The description of leviathan, in the same regard, is a creature very much like Kronosaurus or other ancient marine reptile (not a crocodile or whale like some commentaries claim).

In the Geneva Bible, there are two more references to dragons: Lamentations 4:3 and Ezekiel 32:2. And the book of Daniel 14:23-28 in the Apocrypha

---

[1] Miller, Russ, www.creationministries.org , photo of hadrosaur petroglyph

describes how the prophet Daniel killed a dragon by feeding it a ball made of a mixture of pitch, fat, and hair. This is not a fairy tale or poem. It was a real life event.

There are so many mentions of dragons (dinosaurs) in the Bible because dragons/dinosaurs were created on day five (marine and avian) and day six (terrestrial) and existed alongside man. The Bible gives us an accurate account of what the physical evidence is.

All around the world we find paintings and carvings on pottery, cave walls, and rocks that confirm this. We also find sculptures in the far corners of our planet that depict dinosaur/dragon like creatures. And since a picture says a thousand words, here are just a few:

Figure 1

Figure 2

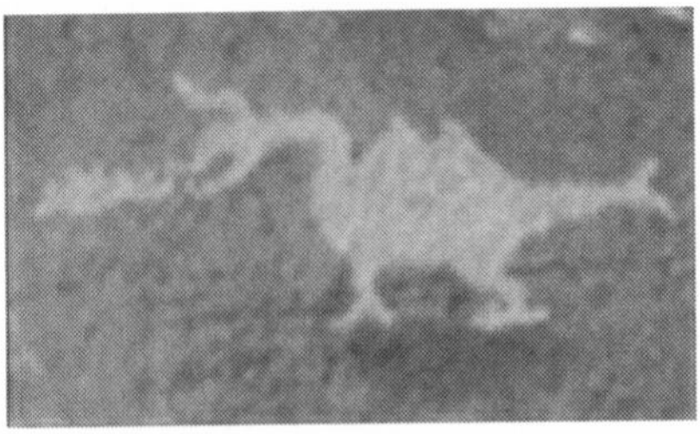

Figure 3

Figure 4

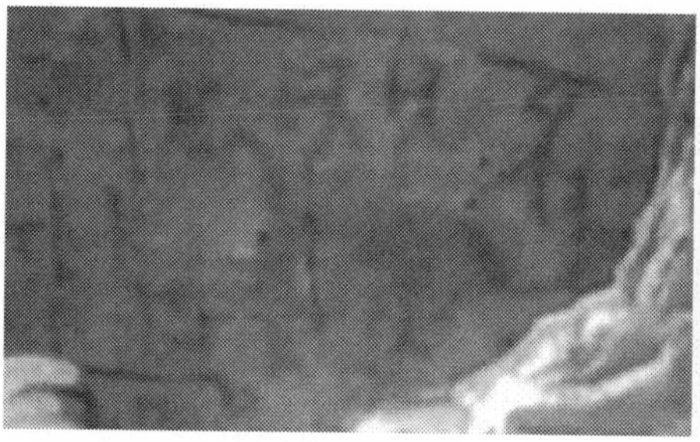

Figure 5

Figure 6

Figure 1) This carving is from the walls of an ancient temple in Cambodia. The lower circle depicts a stegosaurus. And why would they have it right under an accurate carving of a water buffalo if it in itself is not accurate? How could the ancient people of Cambodia know what a stegosaurus looked like unless they saw the animal alive roaming about?

Figure 2) This is one of many Ica burial stone carvings (from Ica, Peru) found alongside skeletons and other artifacts. They are believed to be several hundred years old. These accurately carved depictions of dinosaurs/dragons alongside of fish and birds could only have been etched if the artist knew what these animals looked like.

Figure 3) In Australia the aboriginal people that live near Lake Galilee and tribes farther to the north tell of a long-necked animal with a large body and flippers. "Elders of the Kuku Yalanji aboriginal tribe of Far North Queensland, Australia, tell stories of Yarru (or Yarrba), a creature which used to inhabit rainforest water holes. The aboriginal painting to the lower left depicts a creature with features remarkably similar to a plesiosaur. It even shows an outline of the gastro-intestinal tract, indicating that these animals had been hunted and butchered."[2]

Figure 4) This is a portion of a large mosaic created in the late 1400s that depicts African animals being hunted by native tribesmen. In this segment the men are pursuing what could only be a dinosaur. "The Greek Letters above the reptilian animal in question are: KROKODILOPARDALIS which is literally translated Crocodile-Leopard. The picture shown here is only a small portion of the massive mosaic. It also contains clear depictions of known animals, including Egyptian crocodiles and hippos."[3]

---

[2] Hodge, Bodie. *Answers in Genesis. Dragons, Legends and Lore of Dinosaurs* (Green Forest, AR: Master Books, 2011), p. 1.

[3] Woetzel, Dave. *Chronicles of Dinosauria, The History & Mystery of Dinosaurs and Man* (Green Forest, AR: Master Books, 2013), p 55. www.genesispark.com/essays/fiery-serpentiv

Figure 5) In May of 2012 researcher Vance Nelson discovered a panel of pictographs found at the edge of the Amazon rainforest basin in northern Peru. It is located on a rock ledge under an overhang. This artwork is said by secular archaeologists to be thousands of years old.

Figure 6) The slaying of a ferocious dragon by St. George is an extremely common motif in medieval art. Various European artists interpreted the dragon differently, depending on local knowledge and lore. A wonderful medieval depiction is seen at the Palau de La Generalitat in Barcelona Spain. St. George's Chapel contains an altar cloth illustrating St. George's slaying of a dragon. The depiction bears an amazing likeness to the Nothosaurus, a semi-aquatic reptile (see fossil below). Notice the correct-size, the crocodilian body style, and the fascinating long, curved teeth at the front of the jaw that gives way to finer dentition towards the back.

And there are many, many more historical writings and pictures of dinosaurs/ dragons—some with people and some in their natural habitat.

Other evidence of dinosaur/dragon interactions with humans can be found in dinosaur track ways. The most famous is the Taylor Trail. Again a picture is worth a thousand words (maybe ten thousand in this case!).

---

www.bible.ca/tracks/taylor-trial.htm
www.fossilera.com/pages/about-hadrosaurs

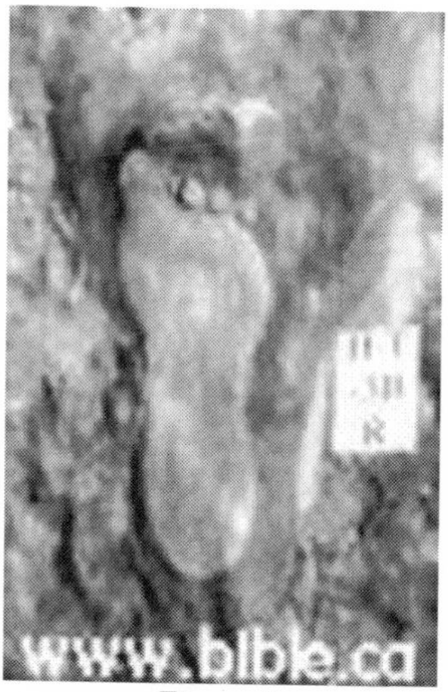

Figure 1

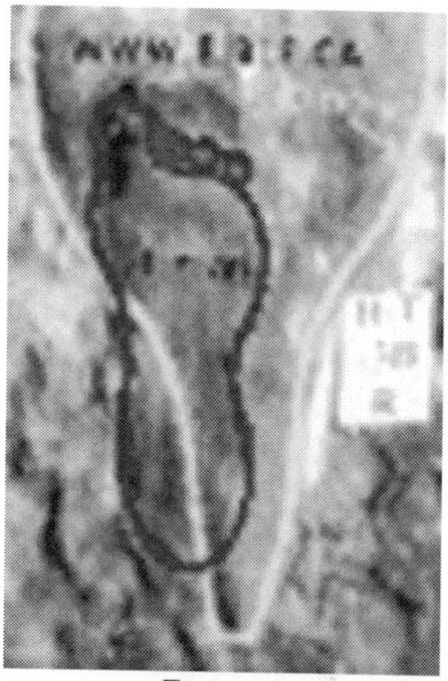

Figure 2

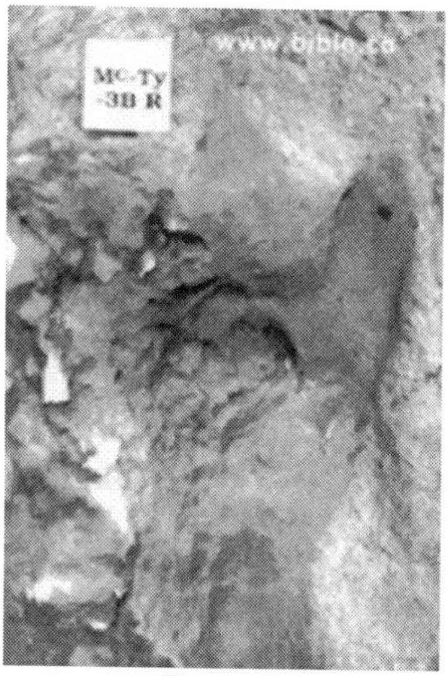

Figure 3

Figure 4

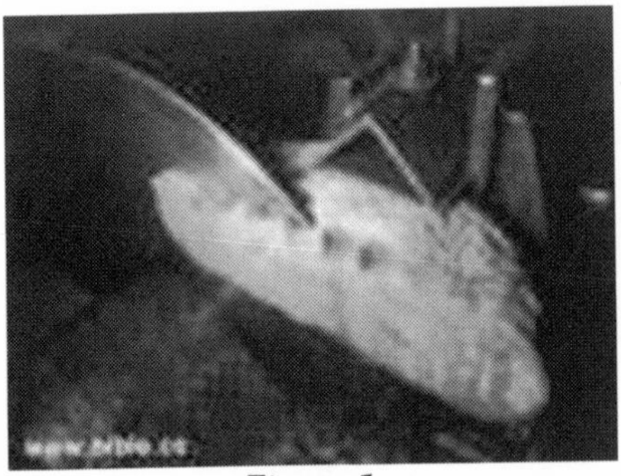
Figure 5

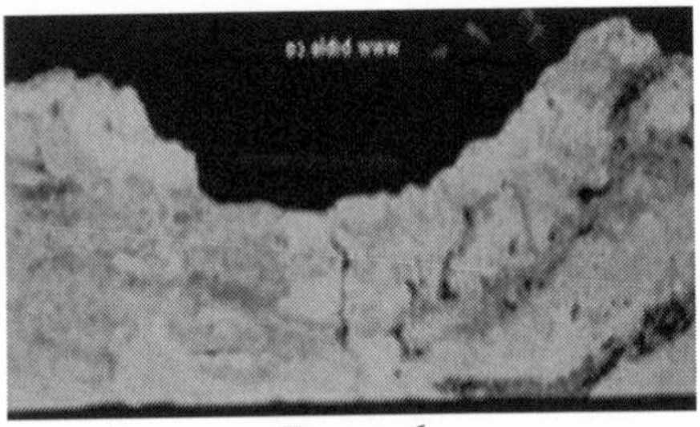
Figure 6

Figure 1) Famous human track in the Taylor Trail where the human steps into the dinosaur/dragon track. Here the human impression is filled with sand to give a better outline.

Figure 2) The human track (blue) inside and on top of a dragon/dinosaur track (yellow).

Figure 3) After evolutionists attended a creation science conference where they learned about the Taylor Trail, they were observed the following day leaving the Taylor Trail with a rock bar. Later that day when others from the conference came to view the track, they found it had been sabotaged; pieces of the human print in the rock had been bashed.

Figure 4) The famous Taylor Trail in Glen Rose, Texas. The dinosaur/dragon tracks veer off to the right while the human tracks are going straight, intersecting the dragon tracks.

Figure 5) A cross-section being cut from human toe imprints in rock (the Murdock print, also of Glen Rose, Texas). This was done to repudiate the evolutionist claim that the human footprints were carved into the stone.

Figure 6) It is obvious by the close up of the cross section of the toe imprints that they were not carved. Note the curved strata under the imprint which denotes downward pressure. Had the prints been carved, the strata would have been straight and the layers cut into. (All photos are courtesy of www.bible.ca).

I have given you just a few in-depth facts into the fascinating subject of dragons/dinosaurs. Hopefully you will go away with a better understanding of how our ancient history really happened; dinosaurs/dragons lived at the same time as man—sometimes even with humans as work animals. See the Resource page if you would like more information on this topic.

Perhaps now you, the reader, understand these beasts were real and lived with people, instead of putting the book down to never pick up again because you had the misconception I mixed history and fantasy. It is my hope that from this novel the reader will gain a much better comprehension of the unaltered history recorded in the Bible.

Appendix Three

Longevity of Early Mankind

The Bible records long life-spans of mankind in the Pre-Flood world and even for a time after The Flood. The longest record of a person's life documented in scripture is Methuselah who died at nine hundred sixty-nine years old. Noah was five hundred years old when he began construction on the ark, which took one hundred years to build, then lived another "…three hundred and fifty years. And all the days of Noah were nine hundred and fifty years: and he died." (Genesis 9:28-29). Adam lived a long life as well, "And all the days that Adam lived were nine hundred and thirty years: and he died." (Genesis 5:5). "And all the days of Seth were nine hundred and twelve years: and he died." (Genesis 5:8). Enos lived nine hundred and five years; Cainan lived nine hundred and ten years. Many more people's ages are recorded in Genesis.

How can this be? There are, actually, two major factors involved in prolonged life spans of the people who lived in the Former World: environment and genetics.

First, let's look at the environment. How much did the earth differ in the Pre- Flood world from the way it is today? The Bible tells us it was quite different. The topography was much less pronounced since all present mountain ranges are made up of sedimentary rocks or volcanoes attributable to the Flood. Since it didn't rain before the Flood (Genesis 2:5), yet rivers flowed (v. 10), there must have been great subterranean reservoirs of water. "And God made the firmament, and divided the waters which were under the firmament from the waters which were above the firmament: and it was so' (Genesis 1:7)."[8] What does that have to do with long life spans? Well, one of water's properties is that it gives protection against the sun's ultra violet rays. For example, people who work outside in hot arid environment where there is little moisture in the air tend to wrinkle faster than those who have the same amount of outdoor exposure in foggy, rainy areas such as the far northwest. Wrinkles are a sign of the breakdown of epidermal (skin) cells and it is a well-known fact that ultra violet rays from the sun contribute to this (thus the invention of sunscreen).

It is quite probable that thin layers of clouds over the Former World continents were a constant, thus protecting the Pre-Flood people from the sun's harmful rays, which in turn would promote longer life spans. In addition, it is

---

[8] Morris, H. M. 2006. *The New Defender's Study Bible.* Nashville, TN: World Publishing, Inc. www.godandscience.org/apologetics/longlife

believed that the Pre-Flood world had an ideal, temperate climate, similar to the Mediterranean of today minus the intense rays of sun. Also it is believed that the oxygen content was greater in the former world than it is now. All would contribute to cellular health and longer life spans.

The second thing to take into consideration in regards to longevity of life is genetics. After the global flood the Bible records human ages decreasing but not immediate drastic differences. For example Noah's son Shem lived to six hundred and two years. But then we see their descendants' life spans decreasing. First Post- Flood generation Arphaxad lived four hundred and thirty eight years, Peleg two hundred and nine years, Nahor lived a hundred forty eight years, and Terah father of Abram, two hundred and five years. (There are several generations between some of these people). By the time Abram (Abraham) passed, he was considered old at one hundred and seventy five years: "Then Abraham gave up the ghost, and died in a good old age, an old man, and full of years; and was gathered to his people" (Genesis 25:8).

The environment certainly had something to do with the reduction of longevity and could very well be reflected in the somewhat shorter life spans of Noah's immediate descendants (the first, second and third Post-Flood generations). The Bible states they did not live six or nine hundred years like the Former World residents did. But it wasn't until after Peleg (fourth Post-Flood generation) that years drastically dropped off of human lives.

The cause? A bottle neck of genetics at the tower of Babel. Peleg is mentioned in the Bible ("in the days of Peleg the world was divided") in reference to the splitting of the original language. When God proclaimed His judgment on mankind, confusing the language at Babel, people split into different groups with others who spoke the same language. Genetics became very limited because of intermarriage which was not considered taboo at that time. However by the time Moses came along, the genetic limitations had grown so detrimental to humans, God instructed the people they could not marry immediate family members anymore.

Environmental factors such as reactive oxygen, caloric restriction, and a vela supernova, and genetic factors including telomere and genome loss affected human longevity during that time. Creation scientists still don't have all the details worked out on exactly how human lives shortened, "However, recent discoveries in the biochemistry of aging continue to build the case for the reliability of Scripture [scientifically speaking]—even of Genesis 5 and 6."[9]

---

[9] Morris, H. M. 2006. *The New Defender's Study Bible.* Nashville, TN: World Publishing, Inc. www.godandscience.org/apologetics/longlife

Appendix Four

The Tower of Babel

Many if not most archeologists, scholars, historians, and teachers dismiss the account of the language change recorded in the Bible. They believe it is a legend or etiology (a mythical story made up to explain something important).

However, they either do not know or do not want to acknowledge the solid historical fact that two ancient clay tablets record Mesopotamian versions of the event. "Briefly, the first tablet (pictured at left), now in the British Museum and very fragmentary, tells of the destruction of a building on a mound in bābel, by a god who 'confused or mixed' (bālal, as in Genesis 11:7, 11:9) the speech of the builders.

Photo courtesy of Answers in Genesis

"The second tablet, now in the Ashmolean Museum in Oxford, England, contains an intact account of the incident. This version, embedded in a much longer composition called 'Enmerkar and the Lord of Aratta,' helps us pinpoint where the event might have occurred.

It says, 'In those days . . . (in) the (whole) compass of heaven and earth the people entrusted (to him) could address [the god] Enlil [lord of the air], verily, in but a single tongue. In those days . . . did Enki, . . . leader of the gods, . . . lord of Eridu estrange the tongues in their mouths as many as were put there. The tongues of men which were one.'

"We know from archaeological evidence that a mass migration referred to as the 'Uruk Expansion' took place from this area in the prehistoric Late Uruk Period. The spread of southern Mesopotamian culture from this region is consistent with the biblical description of what happened following the confusion of tongues: 'From there the Lord scattered them abroad over the face of all the earth (Genesis 11:8).'"[10]

Most people think of the Tower of Babel as a conical shaped building with arched entrances and a ramp coiling around the structure. This is so because of the famous Renaissance paintings of the Babel Tower. However, it is unlikely that the artists ever traveled to the Middle East and thus would have no knowledge of ziggurats. Ziggurats are found world wide with the highest concentration found in the Middle East. More evidence that is where the origin of this type of building came from.

Renaissance artist depiction of theTower of Babel

[10] www.answersingenesis.org/archaeology/digging-past-doubts/#one

Appendix Five

Astrology

Knowledge of the stars and planetary movements, astronomy, would have also come to the new world with Noah and his sons. The perversion of this knowledge, astrology, would have come from something entirely different. Some scholars believe that astrological knowledge came to the new world from demons, since astrology is identified with demonism/satanism in the sense that Satan and his hosts were actually being worshipped in the guise of the signs or planets. This is the reason for the Bible's denunciation of these practices. I believe it is entirely possible this knowledge was imparted after The Flood by supernatural principalities.

Astrology was devised primarily as a tool to calculate planetary positions in the past and future as an aid for prognostications. It is possible that astrology was actually a satanic attempt to direct worship of the human race to the serpent and those former angels who, having rebelled against God, are now demons.

Dr. Henry Morris suggests, "This project (the tower) was originally presented to people in the guise of true spirit. The tower in its lofty grandeur symbolizes the might and majesty of the true God of heaven. A great temple at its apex would provide a center and an altar where men could offer their sacrifices and worship God. The signs of the zodiac would be emblazoned on the ornate ceiling and walls of the temple, signifying the great account of creation and redemption, as told by the antediluvian patriarchs."[11] But God was not in this worship. Satan was.

Thus, astrology became increasingly debased; the worship of the devil and demons became more noticeable. "Satan is a great corrupter, so it is even possible that this system of religion (astrology) was a version of an earlier, true revelation of the heavens. God's plan of redemption has been suggested seriously and considerable evidence that the formations of stars were originally named by God (or the godly patriarchs) as a reminder of godly things, perhaps to the point of forecasting the coming of the great Deliverer who would crush the head of Satan." (Dr. Henry Morris).

The rebellion against the Creator God very likely involved astrology. With the passage of time ungodly men perverted the original account of creation and redemption displayed in the stars. They mingled it with pagan mythology and

---

11 www.answersingenesis.org

ultimately turned it into the religion of astrology. Witchcraft and astrology are among the earliest false religions that have moved in the minds of men. Astrology is the belief that stars and other heavenly bodies can reveal the future. The Bible exposes that demons may invade and seek to control humans (Luke 22:3-4). The Greek word for "demon possession" denotes "demon-caused passivity." It is used for an internal control that manifests in either physical or psychological problems.

"...astrology was the work of deceiving spirits, which accounted for the astrologers' ability to occasionally make accurate predictions. After all, demons are extremely intelligent, have lived for a long time, and have learned some things from the holy angels. So they are capable of making well-educated guesses about the future, and sometimes have the ability to bring these things to pass" (Augustine 2002b, II.37).[12]

---

[12] Morris, H.M. *Institute for Creation Research. The New Defender's Bible, Understanding the Critical Issues of the Faith from a Literal Creationist Viewpoint* (Nashville, TN: World Publishing, Inc., 2006).

Appendix Six

Horses

The horse family includes Przewalski's and modern horses, zebras, donkeys and several extinct species such as the three-toed horse. These animals are descendants of the original horse kind, though evolutionists take it a step beyond that—still using an outdated 1841 "horse evolution tree" that claims unrelated extinct animals are the true horse ancestor. Both evolutionists and creationists recognize that multiple modern "species" can arise from the same ancestral group. For evolutionists, this is the idea of evolution from a single common ancestor. For creationists, this is the idea of variation within a single created kind.

Even evolutionists agree this chart is not accurate

Life coming from creation is a much more logical explanation for the existence of all life. For example, coexisting anatomical diversity within the horse kind, both in fossil layers and the modern world, is an example of original DNA diversity, not evolutionary gain from new genetic information obtained through mutations (the definition of mutation is the loss or rearrangement of genetic information). The variations that developed within the horse kind are a result of environmental pressures developed since the global Flood (and perhaps even before The Flood). Physical evidence supports this reasonable line of thinking.

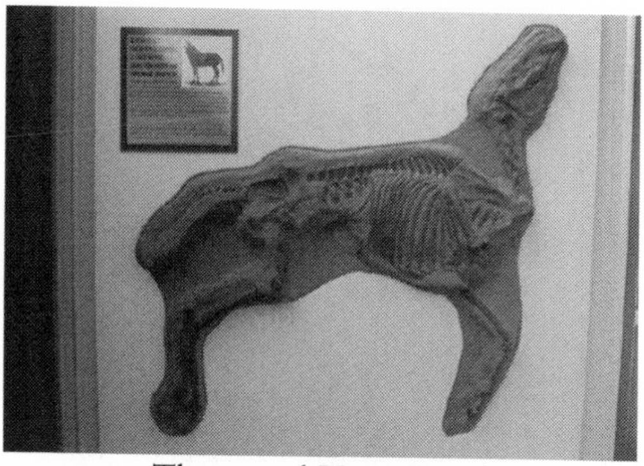

Three-toed Horse Fossil

For example, in Nebraska, North America the Ashfall Fossil Beds, three-toed and one-toed horses have been uncovered side by side. If the three-toed horse truly is the ancestral creature of our modern horses, why are they found side by side? "Clearly, the one fact that is 'verified' is that three-toed and one-toed horses both existed at the same time. Both specimens were trapped in the same volcanic eruption, in the same locality, 'frozen in time'. This hardly supports the idea that one type was the ancestor of the other! Creationists, on the other hand, see in-kind differences as just that: morphological, genetic, and behavioral differences explained by adaptation to environments and selective forces. Offspring end up with less genetic information than their ancestors, not more. Their differences reflect selective forces at work since the Flood. As members of the horse kind have diversified, no new kind of genetic information has been produced. Existing genetic information has simply—or not so simply!—been shuffled, rearranged, and re-sorted."[13]

[13] www.answersingenesis.org/evidence-against-evolution/horse-find-defies-evolution/

www.shannafern.com/2012/09/ashfall-fossil-beds-state-historical.html (picture of three-toes horse fossil)

www.answersingenesis.org/creation-science/baraminology/a-horse-is-a-horse-of-course-of-course/

Przewalski's Horse

More physical evidence that supports creation rather than evolution comes from the DNA of an ancient horse's foot, excavated in 2013. It was discovered preserved in the permafrost of the Canadian Yukon. Scientists have compared its DNA with various modern and ancient equine genomes. The findings sugges that horses, in all their remarkable variety, have been horses for a very long time.

Mule

In addition Przewalski's and modern horses, zebras, and donkeys are al considered members of the "horse kind" by creation scientists because they ar able to hybridize extensively producing viable offspring a lot more than give credit for. However, evolutionists list horses, donkeys and zebras as separat species. One of the definitions of a species is that it cannot produce viabl offspring if bred outside of its own species. Zonkeys (zebras bred with donkeys) zorses (zebras bred with horses) and mules (donkeys bred with horses) confirm these seemingly incompatible animals are varieties of the same created kind.

Zonkey

Zorse

So what did the ancient horses look like? Well, here are some clues...donkeys, zebras, and Przewalski's horse all have stiff Mohawk like manes. All three have some kind of striping or banding marks on their bodies. In addition our ancient ancestors drew pictures of horses on cave walls that look very much like the Przewalski's horse. And the first recorded history of donkeys is in Egyptian hieroglyphics and ancient art about 900 years after The Flood. These are pictures of men hunting wild donkeys. This fits well with the unaltered time line recorded in scripture.

Donkeys are well adapted to hot, dry environments which didn't come about until around 700 to 800 years after The Flood. This was due to dramatic climax changes that begun during deglaciation of The Ice Age causing a global drought. This was recorded in scripture when Joseph interpreted Pharaoh's dream of seven years of worldwide famine (Genesis 41:54).

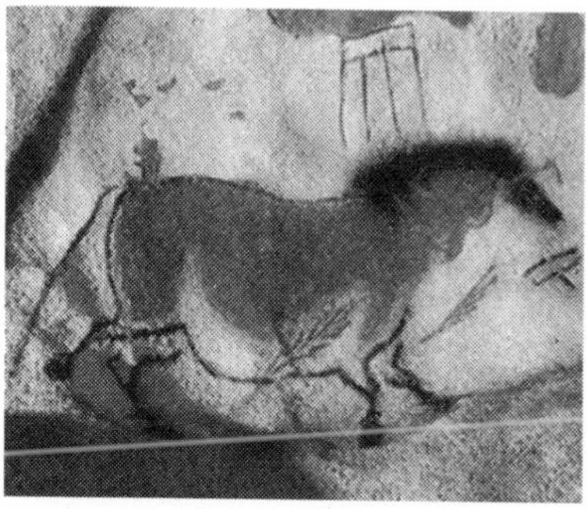

In this novel glaciation and The Ice Age had just begun. Thus the land was lush and fertile and the horse kind had not yet been exposed to the environmental conditions (harsher dryer deserts) that started adaptations to develop. These variations we know today as donkeys, zebras and several extinct species.

Appendix Seven

Climate/Early Environment

The time period this novel takes place in is one hundred thirty-six years after the great Noachian flood. The global climate would have been vastly different from today and continued to change rapidly. For approximately the first thirty to fifty years after The Flood the newly formed land masses would have been warm and moist, providing perfect conditions for plants and animals to spread and colonize the earth. We know this is true by the tropical plant and animal fossils found in both polar regions. But by the second Post-Flood generation, the southern polar cap due to its location, smaller size, and isolation from other continents, would have begun to glaciate. By the time the novel takes place the Ice Age would have begun in the northern polar cap as well. Animals such as aurochs, giant fallow deer (see picture), mammoths, giant ground sloths and many more roamed the earth at that time along with the dinosaurs (dragons).

Also at that time only about thirty percent of the world was covered in ice and snow, mostly in Canada, the northern parts of North America, northern Europe, Asia, and Siberia. Because of these conditions the animals responded by diversifying utilizing the vast variations within their DNA. Many animals survived by being huge in size including the Fallow deer and the arouchs mentioned in this novel.

So how did the Ice Age climate come about?

Conditions for an ice age must include: 1) cooler summers; 2) as odd as it seems, in very frigid winter areas, winters would be warmer. In warmer winter areas, winters would be cooler; 3) massive precipitation—snow in polar regions and rain in warmer latitudes; 4) and it all must persist for many years.

Volcanic dusts and aerosols cause cooler summers over land. These volcanoes would have had to be big enough for particles to reach the stratosphere because dusts and aerosols tend to dissipate in one to three years. Many volcanoes (due to the earth's settling after The Flood) would have been active over a several hundred- year period (thus our characters are able to experience the active volcanoes over a long period of time).

The opening of the great fountains of the deep and underwater volcanism would have caused warm homogenized oceans (warmer oceans means greater evaporation), and these conditions would have persisted for several hundred years. But with cold land masses in the northern and southern poles, the warm air over the oceans met the cold air over the land, turning the moisture in the air to snow in colder areas and rain in warmer regions, creating The Ice Age.[14] This condition would continue until the ocean waters began to cool at glacial maximum (the peak of the Ice Age), about five hundred years after The Flood. The Bible even tells us of the Ice Age in the book of Job: Job 6:15-16, "...as a brook, and as the stream of brooks they pass away. Which are blackish by reason of the ice, and wherein the snow is hid"; Job 37:9-10, "Out of the south cometh the whirlwind; and cold out of the north. By the breath of God frost is given: and the breadth of the waters is straitened." And again in Job 38:22-23, "Hast thou entered into the treasures of the snow? Or hast thou seen the treasures of the hail..."

But since only thirty percent of the world was under ice, what did the rest of the world look like? It would have flourished under almost perfect climate conditions with several exceptions: frequent violent storms and earthquakes, and enormous (super) volcanic eruptions, all due to the settling of the earth's crust. After the fountains of the deep opened up during the global flood, it resulted in the plate tectonic movements with the earth's outer shell dividing into several plates that glided over the mantle. This would have continued for about seven hundred years; five hundred to glacial maximum and two hundred in deglaciation, causing mountains to rise, islands to form and large bodies of water dammed inland to breach.

It is in such an environment our ancient ancestors (and the characters of this book) survived and lived out their lives, exploring, learning trades, developing different cultures, fighting and helping each other.

---

[14] Oard, Michael. http://www.youtube.com/watch?v-jhzbl-jbL0Y&feature-relmfu

Appendix Eight

Writing

Scripture indicates that the very first humans were able to read and write. "Since only Adam could have personal knowledge of all the events in Genesis 2, 3 and 4, it is reasonable to conclude that this section was originally written by him."

"Adam may have even signed his own name at the end of his written portion of Genesis (Genesis 5:1a), recorded as 'This is the book of the generations of Adam.'"[15] This is typical of ancient Hebrew writing when the author signs off.

And Adam wasn't the only one. "Later Noah added his record of the antediluvian patriarchs, signing it: 'These are the generations of Noah' (Genesis 6:9). The account of the Ark, the Flood, and the Noachian prophecy on his sons was written by 'the sons of Noah' (Genesis 10:1). The post-Flood records were kept by Shem, Terah, Isaac, Jacob, and probably Joseph, each normally terminating his record by the standard closing phrase: 'These are the generations of ..."[16] (Genesis 11:10,27; 25:19; 37:2; Exodus 1:1). It is reasonable to understand all these records were eventually collected and edited by Moses into the book of Genesis."[17]

Also there are archeological findings of ancient pre-Flood writings (see above photo). On a trip to Mount Ararat, Dr. John Morris (Institute for Creation Research) took several pictures of rocks that contain pre-cuneiform inscriptions (Cuneiform is the first known writing. It was pressed into clay with a stylus. See round picture to the right). One is even on a rock near an ancient altar in the Ahora Gorge, located on the north side of Mount Ararat. There are several places where undecipherable inscriptions on rocks were found within the Ahora Gorge. Could these have been engraved by Noah or his sons? It is a reasonable thought, since the cuneiform writing is thought to be the earliest form of inscription (some of the Elba tablets, once thought to be the most ancient writings, translate an ancient form of Hebrew [paleo-Canaanite] to Sumerian indicting this was after the confusion of languages at the tower of Babel [see photo top of next page]).

---

15 Morris, H.M. Institute for Creation Research. Notes for Genesis 5:1, *The New Defender's Study Bible* (Nashville, TN: World Publishing, Inc., 2006).

16 Thomas, Brian, M.S. Institute for Creation Research. http://www.icr.org/article/stone-age-art-holds-hints-language. April 13, 2013.

17 Morris. H.M., Notes for Genesis 5:1

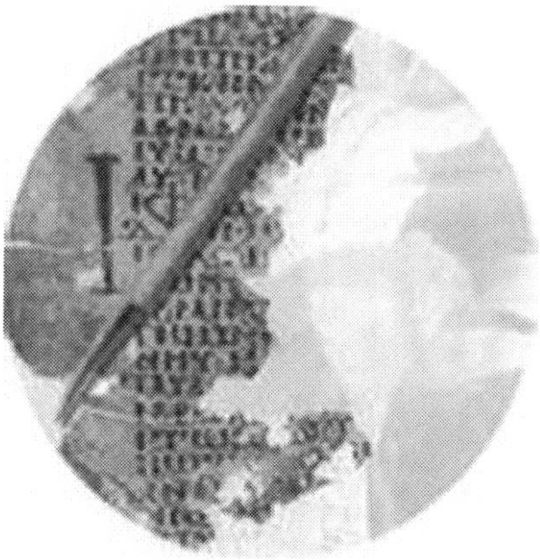

It is very likely the inscriptions engraved on the rocks in the Ahora Gorge being, 1) undecipherable, 2) in the location near the resting place of the ark, and 3) of ancient origin, may very well be of the pre-Flood language (see previous page and below photos). And we know that God has books in heaven (i.e. the book of life), so we know there are written records there. It is only logical to think the Lord would have passed the knowledge of book making and writing on to Adam and Eve who would have then passed it on to their descendants, including Noah.

Appendix Nine

Early Dispersion Of Mankind

The dispersion of man after the confusion of the language at the tower of Babel can still be found in names of cities and regions around the world.

Japheth's (whose name means light or fair) descendants in a general sense migrated to the European and Russian regions. For example, the names of Japheth's sons, Meshech and Javan, are still in use today: Mechera (derived from Meshech) is the ancient name for Russia. And in Russia there is still to this day a Mechera lowland and a Mechera park. Javan, on the other hand, is the Hebrew translation for Greece. Japheth's first son was named Gomer. This name is reflected in Galatia, Gaul, Galla, and Galiecia. Gomer's son, Ashkenanzi, is the lineage of the Europeans. To this day, the Jewish people still call Germany Ashkenaz. Tubal is the fifth son of Japheth. He and his descendants migrated to Siberia as reflected by the name of the city of Tubil (Iberia is the Greek translation of Tubil), Siberia, and near it is a river called Tobol. The seventh son of Japheth is Tiras. From him, amongst others, we have the cities of Thrace and Troy. And there is a river in Europe still called the Tiras River.

Ham's descendants settled in the great African continent and in the Middle East. Ham had named his third son Phut. The Northwest region of Africa has been referred to as Phut. Ham's fourth son is Canaan. Remember...the land of Canaan is the promised land God gave to the Israelites. Out of Canaan came the Sinites, some of who migrated to the Orient (this name is still reflected in places and even in the Sino/Japanese war). Ham had another son whom he named Cush (one of our historical people in this novel). Cush is another name for Ethiopia (proof that Cush did head south!). As a matter of fact the Ethiopians today still call themselves Cushites. Another of Ham's sons is Mizraim. Mizraim is the Hebrew name for Egypt and is still used in ancient versions of the Old Testament.

From Shem's second son, Asshur, comes the land of Assyria. From his fifth son, the Arameans (Syria) and the Aramaic language. Shem's fourth son, Lud (Laud), settled in the southern Turkey region as reflected in the names of the Lycian, Lydia, and Lud.

Around the globe today, there are approximately 6,900 spoken languages (not all of these came about at the tower of Babel). Creation scientists can trace languages back to a minimum of seventy-eight language families that came as a result of the rebellion at the tower of Babel. Evolution scientists claim every language developed from one primal half-ape, half-human gruntal language. Interestingly enough, linguist experts (Ethnologue and Vistawide World Languages) estimate ninety-four original language families. Hmmm, who matches up better with the linguists…the biblical or the worldly viewpoint?

An important thought to keep in mind is that before the language split according to their families, people of all skin color, facial features, and body types lived together, built together, and traded with each other. No one would have thought it odd or be prejudiced against another because of the way a person looked. Everyone would have survived together.

After the split in language, not only would certain family groups take their language and specific knowledge with them, but they would also take, in their genes, certain physical features as well. All to be passed down from generation to generation, until we now think of ourselves as "ethnic" and having "nationalities/ races."[18] We shouldn't think this way for we, as a people, are all one race.

---

18 Hodge, Bodie. *Tower Of Babel The Cultural History Of Our Ancestors,* (Green Forest, AR: Master Books, 2013) pp. 122-179.

References/Resources

Answers In Genesis—www.answersingenesis.org
P.O. Box 510, Hebron, KY 41048. 800-778-3390
This ministry has a wonderful Creation Museum in Kentucky and has a constructed a life-sized ark that is a museum/zoo, has speakers available for talks and conferences, and also has a wonderful book store and website.

Arizona Origin Science Association, Inc. (AZOSA) - www.azosa.org
This ministry provides creation speakers for churches, schools, camps and conferences and organizes creation seminars around Arizona. It also promotes creation thru a free annual trip to the Grand Canyon for Christian leaders.

Babylonian Words:
trumpetsound.faithweb.com/History-LunarSabbathDays_Part1.html
www.ancient.eu/article/701

Creation, Evolution & Science Ministries - www.creationministries.org
Rus Miller, Phoenix, AZ
This ministry provides faith-building messages, creation based Grand Canyon tours, books, DVDs, and speakers available for churches/ conferences/camps and has a great website.

Creation Ministries International—www.creation.com
Australia, Canada, New Zealand, South Africa, Singapore, United Kingdom, United States of America, and other countries.
This ministry has both a family friendly magazine and professional science journal. They have an informative website, speakers available for conferences, scheduled speaking events, multimedia specials, DVDs, Videos, study guides, books, radio spots and Q&A topics.

Creation Research Society—www.creationresearch.org
Chino Valley, AZ 86323. 877-277-8665. 928-636-1153
This ministry provides short term living quarters for scientists doing research in the Grand Canyon area and has a wonderful bookstore.

Creation—the Written Truth, Willow Dressel
www.creation-thewrittentruth.blogspot.com
This is the author's blog where all issues of creation science are addressed in short, concise writings backed up with photos.

Cuozzo, Jack. ***Buried Alive The Startling, Untold Story about Neanderthal Man***. Green Forest, AR: Master Books, Inc. 2008. Print.

Dolphin, Lambert. ***The Tower Of Babel And The Confusion Of Languages.*** N.P., n.p. Web; 28, Aug. 2012. www.ldolphin.org/babel.html

Colantoni, C., and Jason Ur, 73:21-69. ***The Architecture And Pottery of a Late 3rd Millennium BC Residential Quarter at Tel Hamoukar***, Northeastern Syria. Iraq. The British Institute for the Study of Iraq, 2011.Web. 28 Aug. 2012.
www.fas.harvard.edu/~anthro/ur/field_hamoukar.html.

Gray, Jonathan. ***What Happened at the Tower of Babel?*** Scribd. Copyright 2004, n.d.Web. 28 Aug. 2012.
www.beforeus.com.
www.scribd.com/doc/40230066/Babel.

Ham, Ken. ***"Kids Feedback: When Were the Angels Created?"*** Answers in Genesis, 09 Sept. 2010. Web. 28 Aug. 2012.
www.answersingenesis.org/articles/kw/feedback-angels.

Hodge, Bodie. ***Dragons: Legends and Lore of Dinosaurs.*** Green Forest, AR: Master Books, 2011. Print.

Hodge, Bodie. ***Tower of Babel, The Cultural History of Our Ancestors.*** Green Forest, AR: Master Books, 2013. Print.

Institute For Creation Research—www.icr.org P.O. Box 59029, Dallas, TX 75229. 800-337-0375
This ministry has a wonderful creation college available for those who are interested in the technical aspect of creation science. They also have a great web site and have speakers available for events.

Landis, Don. ***The Genius of Ancient Man Evolution's Nightmare.*** Green Forest, AR: Master Books, 2013. Print.

Morris, Henry M. *"Notes for Genesis 5:1." The New Defender's Study Bible: King James Version*. Nashville, TN: World Pub., 2006. 29. Print.

Morris, Henry M., PhD. *The Genesis Record: A Scientific and Devotional Commentary on the Book of Beginnings*. Grand Rapids, Mich.: Baker Book House, 1976. 231-286. Print.

Morris, Henry, Ph.D. *"God's Library."* Institute for Creation Research Articles, n.d. www.icr.org/article/gods-library/.

Morris, John, Ph. D. *"More Archaeological Discoveries and Views from Mount Ararat."* Answers in Genesis; 29 Mar. 2007. Web. 28 Aug. 2012. www.answersingenesis.org/articles/am/v2/n2/ararat- photos.

Nelson, C. W. *"Genetics and Biblical Demographic Events."* Answers in Genesis, 01 Apr. 2003. Web. 28 Aug. 2012. www.answersingenesis.org.

"OOPARTS (Out Of Place Artifacts) & Ancient High Technology-Evidence of Noah's Flood?" www.s8int.com, n.d.

Osterholm, Tim. *"The Table of Nations."*. N.p., July 2012. Web. 28 Aug. 2012. www.soundchristian.com/man. Print

Pettinato, Giovanni. *The Archives of Ebla: An Empire Inscribed in Clay*. Garden City, NY: Doubleday, 1981. Print.

Phillips, Doug. *"One Nation Over God."* AM Articlemanager. Answers in Genesis, 06 Feb. 2008. Web. 28 Aug. 2012. www.answersingenesis.org/articles/am/v3/n2/one-nation-over- god.

Potts, Daniel T. *Mesopotamian Civilization: The Material Foundations*. Ithaca, NY: Cornell UP, 1997. Print.

The Tower of Babel, Can the 'Story' Be Trusted Today. Dir. Bodie Hodge. Answers in Genesis-US, 2011. DVD. www.answersingenesis.org.

Thomas, Brian, M.S. ***Stone Age Art Holds Hints of Language, "Stone Age Art Holds Hints of Language."*** Institute for Creation Research, 13 Apr. 2012. Web. 28 Aug. 2012.
www.icr.org/article/stone-age-art-holds-hints-language.

Wikipedia, ***Antikythera Mechanism/Analogue Computer***
www.en.wikipedia.org/wiki/Antikythera_mechanism#Description

Woetzel, Dave, ***Chronicles of Dinosauria, The History & Mystery of Dinosaurs and Man.***, Green Forest, AR.: Master Books 2013. Print.
www.genesispark.com

About the Author

Willow Dressel is married to her wonderful husband, Greg, and is a mother of four adult children. She has three wonderful grandsons and one beautiful granddaughter, and lives in the country with two dogs, chickens, fish, and a horse. Willow and her husband attend a First Southern Baptist Church where they both serve on the worship team. She also teaches mid-high/high school students and substitutes for fifth and sixth grade. Though faithful to writing, she is also has her own animal/botanical line of work and is the secretary of her husband's construction business.

Willow was born in Cleveland, Ohio in 1960, and grew up with her parents and older sister in a small suburban home. Her fascination with nature drew her to study God's creation at a very young age. Even though she lived in a town setting, at every chance she headed for the countryside. Horses, hiking, and exploring the wilds became her favorite pastimes. When she discovered studying nature could be turned into a career she attended the University of New Mexico and holds a Bachelor of Science degree in wildlife biology.

In 1994 Willow gave her life to our Lord Jesus Christ and learned about creation science a year later. At last questions and problems concerning evolution began to be addressed. She researched and studied this area extensively and realized the physical world supports Scripture and that the Bible describes this physical evidence. By 1998 she became a creation scientist. Since then she has written lessons and taught many classes on creation science, often incorporating live animals.

For over eight years Willow has been writing a blog; creation-thewrittentruth.blogspot.com that are viewed weekly by a national and international audience of over 700. She also has been a featured guest on other blog-sites and radio programs that reach thousands of people. She attends writers' workshops and webinars to keep up with current subjects. She is a member of Root Writers Professional Writers, Arizona Origins Society Association, the Creation Research Society, and a lifetime member at Answers in Genesis.

God's Plan of Salvation

1. We have all sinned at one time or another in our lives. God acknowledges this in the Bible; "For all have sinned, and come short of the glory of God." (Romans 3:23)

2. There is a penalty for sins. It is eternal death—separation from God and existence in hell. For God tells us about this in the Bible; "For the wages of sin is death; but the gift of God is eternal life through Jesus Christ our Lord." (Romans 6:23)

3. We cannot pay for our sin—it is too much and too serious. But Jesus paid our sins by dying on the cross and paying our penalties; "But God demonstrates His own love toward us, in that while we were still sinners, Christ died for us." (Romans 5:8)

4. You can call upon the Lord to save you any time and repent from your sins. God promises that when you do that and have a repentant heart He will give you eternal life in heaven as a free gift. "For whosoever shall call upon the name of the Lord shall be saved." (Romans 10:13)

Please consider turning your life to Jesus today. I would love to hear from you if you do or if you have any question about Jesus, Christianity, creation science or anything else. You can get in touch with me through my blog creation-thewrittentruth.blogspot.com

Don't miss the exciting story of Shoshana!
Available now at Amazon
And the thrilling video trailer at
https://www.youtube.com/watch?v=YigrMvxTKIs
Or simply type in Willow Dressel and click on the image of
the boy on a horse (a 2.16 minute trailer)

How you can help

If you have enjoyed reading this novel and would like to recommend it to others, please do! Write a review on Amazon simply by going to the book and scroll to "review" by the yellow stars. Click on it, than scroll to "write a review" by the bar-graph.If you didn't know, reviews tremendously help out authors to get a book from invisible to visible. You don't have to buy the book from Amazon to write the review. Anyone can do it! I personally thank you for this little bit of extra effort in my passion to make the Truth available to all who are searching for it (and even those who aren't or don't realize that they are). Many purchase books solely on good reviews. May God bless you all!

Newsletter

Want to keep up on the latest happenings with the *Sign of the Oth* series? Sign up for our free monthly newsletter! You can see the progress of the next book in the making and get the hottest information (including the release date) in the letter!

Sign up by sending us your email address and a note saying you'd like to receive one at:

willowdresselauthor.gmail.com

Thank you for your support!
Willow Dressel

Made in the USA
Columbia, SC
13 September 2022

67179293R00171